Praise for

Jina Bacarr's

the Blonde Geisha

Jina Bacarr

The Blonde Samurai

Spice

Recycling programs
for this product may
not exist in your area.

Spice

THE BLONDE SAMURAI

ISBN-13: 978-0-373-60540-8

Copyright © 2010 by Jina Bacarr.

All rights reserved. Except for use in any review, the reproduction or
utilization of this work in whole or in part in any form by any electronic,
mechanical or other means, now known or hereafter invented, including
xerography, photography and recording, or in any information storage
or retrieval system, is forbidden without the written permission of the
publisher, Spice Books, 225 Duncan Mill Road, Don Mills, Ontario,
Canada M3B 3K9.

This is a work of fiction. Names, characters, places and incidents are
either the product of the author's imagination or are used fictitiously,
and any resemblance to actual persons, living or dead, business
establishments, events or locales is entirely coincidental.

Spice and the Colophon are trademarks used under license and
registered in Australia, New Zealand, Philippines, United States Patent
and Trademark Office and in other countries.

www.Spice-Books.com

Printed in U.S.A.

To my husband, Len LaBrae, whose steadfast loyalty and belief in me makes him my perfect samurai.

THE BLONDE SAMURAI

San Francisco
15 September, 1876

'Tis not an easy task I have, dear lady reader, to respond to the vicious gossip spread about me through Mayfair drawing rooms since I returned to England. Whispers of euphoric nights with not one but *two* men pleasuring me; mysterious items to soothe a woman's burning need for clitoral touch and fill her with orgasmic bliss; the erotic game of domination with girls strapped down and flogged upon their bare buttocks. Did I take part in these wild imaginings? Or are they merely tales fabricated by a besotted male scribbler to sell his stories and make his fortune?

You be the judge as you continue to read, and I hope you will, for pages and pages of erotic delights await you. What *is* undisputed is that I ran away from my husband and disappeared. Some say I went mad and was confined to an asylum. Others insist I entered a convent. Neither is true, but the scandal I provoked shook the standards of bland respectability and sobriety that govern the upper class and started non-stop discussions about what they deemed to be my outrageous behavior and what should be done about it.

Done about it? As if they alone exist on a lofty plane and rule all those below. I subscribed to no such rules and they shunned me for it. I will shock you further, for I shall begin my story with a confession, one that will titillate you and give you another reason to speculate whether what you've heard whispered about me is true. 'Tis a fact that I, a spirited daughter of Erin by way of America, came to London in the summer of 1872 seeking a titled match. Be it known my looks were plain and my opinions brash, sending my marital prospects into discord among my suitors, though for reasons I shall make clear in these pages, I married well. Yet the first man I took to my bed after my wedding night was not my husband—or yours—but one of the most mysterious, elusive and enigmatic men in all Japan. A samurai.

His name was Shintaro.

I shall never forget the moment the tall, muscular samurai swept into the room, his heavy walk making the wooden floor tremble, his presence commanding, electrifying, his melodic, deep voice speaking to me in his native tongue about waterfalls and flowers and the gods as if he was a poet and could produce an alchemy of words to create harmony between us. I burned with such desire I could not catch my breath. All I wanted was him. Bold, handsome he was, and as persuasive as the wind nudging a morning glory up the vine with his heated breath, exposing her to the sun, then seducing her to open up to him and live her vivid, unspoken dreams in his arms.

I knew Shintaro as a man with a deep passion for everything artistic and refined, including the grace and repose of the erotic "spring drawings." He took great joy in demonstrating to me the sexual acts depicted upon these woodblock prints, down to the most exquisite, savory detail. Yet as a member of the warrior class, he harbored an intensity for warfare and honor and adhered to their strict sense of personal loyalty with a readiness to fight and die without hesitation; he also possessed a readiness to make love to me with the same vigor, his need for me burned indelibly into his soul. When I was with him, my spirit was as light as a cherry blossom floating slowly to earth, its pure fragrance scenting the passion of our union with a fresh innocence, yet hiding no thorns under its petals like the English rose.

Then a great tragedy came upon us and I was forced to leave Japan and return to London. Not an easy venture for me, dear lady reader. I harbored a profound uncertainty that I had assimilated so deeply into my life there that coming back to England would be unsettling and difficult. Had I known what scorn and ridicule faced me, I would have changed nothing, for I am destined to write this memoir and be faithful to the tale as I have lived it. I admit I have crafted my story in an enchanted world owing much to feminine perception and fancy, but 'tis my belief my memoir will evoke a response in you that will have far-reaching consequences beyond the telling of this tale. My hope is you will discover another side of your intimate self as I have, a side which will tempt you to deviate from the prevailing standards and expectations in your romantic life and allow you to enjoy the sexual act with his lordship to its fullest—or with any gentlemen you take to your bed.

To allow you to do so, I have chosen to write the story of my adventure as an *Erotic Tome for Young Ladies*. I came upon this idea because of a certain incident known to many readers of this book that occurred on the twenty-fifth of April 1876 at the London town house of the Viscount Aubrey. An evening of fun and gaiety was in play until I entered the room and all heads turned. Curious, questioning, some envious, for arousing tales about my powerful and masterful samurai lover had preceded me. Word passed quickly among the sanctimonious ladies of Mayfair. *"That Carlton woman has arrived,"* they whispered. They couldn't take their eyes off me, scrutinizing my gown, my figure, my jewels, for I had dared to leave my husband and seek my own life among the samurai. In the eyes of the British aristocracy there was no greater sin.

I shall not spoil the story if you are unfamiliar with the newspaper accounts of the scandal, but suffice it to say I've left unnamed those of you living in London who are innocent of any wrongdoing. And though the exclusive upper class is well represented in my story, be advised their names have been changed. 'Tis a spicy tale, dear lady reader, replete with the words and phrases known to and used by the male sex. Before we begin, you may wish to open your reticule and remove your smelling powders. You will need them. I warn you, you may be shocked by my story, but never bored.

Tomorrow I sail for Yokohama from the port of San Francisco aboard the SS *Oceanic.* By the time you read this, I will be home, for that is what Japan is to me now. Hearth and home. There I have known the joy of a passionate love, the pain of suffering a great loss and the importance of duty if one is to survive. I count the heartbeats until I arrive back in Japan, but first I shall send off these final pages by post to my solicitor in London, Mr. Robert A. Brown, to give to my publisher. I wish to thank him for his unending support during these long months of writing and deliberating over whether or not I should pen this memoir. He has given me the courage to do so and made it possible for me to secure a contract with the best publishing house in London. In many months hence, this book will be in your hands. Then it will be up to you, dear lady reader, to decide its fate. I realize your fascination with reading my memoir lies in making your heart beat faster by recalling with me my romantic interludes with my handsome samurai. Fear not, in due course, I shall set into motion the frightening incident in Japan, which thrust me into his arms. But first I shall sketch the previous acts of the drama that make up the fabric of my story, beginning with my wedding night and what followed so you shall understand *all* the events that transpired, be they sensual, provocative or tragic.

If when you come to the end of my story you accept my words as truth, then I have succeeded. Shintaro will live not only in these pages, but in your heart, as he does in mine.

Lady Carlton née Katie O'Roarke

1

Mayfair, London
26 August, 1872

My extraordinary journey to embrace the way of the warrior began in a posh town house in Mayfair.

On my wedding night.

It was a London society affair replete with the trappings of engraved wedding invitations, cascades of floral abundance adorning the church pews and lavish gifts whose glitter dared not be anything but gold. And me with a diamond tiara atop my head ornamented with so many pear-shaped stones I creaked my neck trying to sit like a swan, though I was more the Yankee ugly duckling. Did I mention we had a bishop among the clergy presiding?

I can hear you groaning at my description, ready to toss the book aside before we land upon the silken earth of the Orient, fearing you have chanced upon the prim meanderings of a young matron lost in romantic illusions before she takes to her bed while her husband visits his mistress. I assure you this is no such missive. 'Tis fire and passion I reaped when I dared to abandon a life of privilege and taste for the way of the warrior. Riding the wind to meet the gods, slashing through the rain, my arms bending from the weight of the heavy steel sword in my grasp, a dirk nestled between my breasts near my heart. But I'm allowing my passion for this life to raise a fever in me and deliver me from the memory of what happened on my wedding night. It was a different instrument of pain that made me twitch and moan. An item worn and smooth and without the sharp point of the sword but just as accurate to reach its mark.

A black riding crop.

I shall never forget what should have been a night woven with satin threads and romance, wanton kisses and honeyed sighs. Instead, I was shocked to see my new husband racing up the stairs after a saucy redhead and whipping her plump backside. I ran and hid in a teak garderobe that smelled of whiskey and snuff and mold. A strange desire awakened in me, making me want to know more about this suggestive, mysterious world that disturbed me, stimulated me.

Are you shocked? Insulted? *You're a young woman of good breeding,* I hear you say, *modest, shy.* I'm Irish-American and proud of it, though too often my fiery race is dismissed with a cutting glance meant to be a public snubbing by stony-faced termagants suffering from the social disease of snobbery. I ignore them. I don't care about their political citadel with its perfunctory restrictions and bloodless debutantes in their swinging crinolines keeping their suitors at arm's length. I grew up riding bareback, my hands and face often gritty from digging into the wet, soggy bowels of the earth to feed our empty bellies before my father made his fortune.

I come from a hardworking, God-fearing family and never had it in my mind that I'd live in a posh house. But here I am, Thomas O'Roarke's daughter, Katie, hiding and holding her breath as she watches the intoxicating scene played out before her in this Mayfair town house. Not what I expected married life to be when I attended Miss Brown's School for Young Ladies, where I was bred to become a grand lady by the headmistress herself, Miss Herminone Tuttle. I wanted to please my mother (who so desperately wanted *one* of her daughters to make a successful marriage), so I dabbled in the folly of silks and corsets, gossip and scented notes, singing and drawing lessons, all necessities coveted by a girl of my nouveau riche status to furnish her female arsenal. Day after day Miss Tuttle lamented about my chatty nature, spurred on by my insatiable curiosity to question everything. Not wise, I discovered, for a girl born in a white frame house in the Pennsylvania woods, a plain girl with more brain than bosom who linked her dreams with her emotions and sensibilities. No wonder I was rejected by every eligible bachelor approved by the Knickerbocker Society matrons.

But it was my mother, dear soul that she is, who established my power base of teachers and dressmakers and embarked with me to London with one goal in mind: husband hunting. She emphasized to my suitors I had money and plenty of it. (My father is a railroad tycoon, a self-made man with more guts than schooling. He's a grand da, always encouraging me to be the inquisitive lass that I am. "Katie, me girl—" my father is fond of saying when we spar over a political issue "—you have more fighting spirit in you than any man I've met." How I love him.) But I had no real path, no realm laid out to pursue my dreams. I often asked myself, *What is to become of me?* We

Irish often find ourselves taking up the more unsavory professions, such as following the life of an actor, or worse yet, a writer. 'Tis the gift of words bestowed upon us by the rulers of the heavens, and I be no exception. I find myself more oft than not in trouble because of it, but I can't keep my thoughts to myself. I speak before thinking, making my observations with a keen, dry wit and at times without tact, which is why I kept neither beau nor my mother's faith I'd ever make a match. No amount of primping and lavender water could take the smell of horses and hay out of this girl who crossed the Atlantic to find a husband among the British aristocracy.

To my mother's dismay, more than one London suitor complained I was too quick with the sassy remarks and too eager to express my opinion. She chided me for my boldness, emphasizing that eligible males were more interested in the sway of a girl's body than the wit of her words. Here again, I failed the test. I was taller than the fragile English girls paraded around the circuit for three months out of the year. Thin as paper doilies they were and each one cut from the same curlicue pattern. I was fair-haired and blue-eyed and cut a good figure with a small waist, though I had boyish hips.

Then the forces of nature took it upon themselves to present a delicate rearrangement of destiny (also known as the exchange of a great deal of money), and I received a proposal of marriage. As was more the custom than not in these hasty marriages, I went to the altar knowing little about my husband, save he had a title and a manner of looking at me that made my pussy burn with longing.

My hunger for romance proved to be my undoing when I allowed myself to be wooed by this deviant aristocrat with wild black hair and a slight limp. His chest and shoulders were broad and strong, his head held high as was his ego. I noticed the wide dimple in his chin deepened when he set his mouth in a grim line. Lord James Carlton was as handsome as a prince of the realm and he knew it. He exuded charm, though I would later discover this show of assuredness and sybaritic demeanor concealed a different side of him that when challenged erupted into a dark, decaying soul.

I knew none of this when I accepted his hasty proposal of marriage. Trying to hide my surprise as well as my girlish pleasure, I fancied myself in love with him and could not admit that what I felt was mere infatuation. What did I know about love? Nothing. What I didn't know I concocted into stories, romantic tales too often centering around an idealized heroine created out of an alchemist's bottle.

And now this display of bare skin and beautiful breasts and round buttocks askew before my eyes, what God himself had designed to covet the devil's lust, made my mouth drop. How can I explain to you the emotions racing through me? I was a young girl, barely nineteen, and though I rarely admitted it, I was rather naive about the ways of the world save for what enticing books I'd read in this house, their salacious descriptions never matching the rise of anticipation playing out before me. I couldn't take my eyes off the girl's buttocks. Red streaks crisscrossing her cheeks. Long, straight marks. A wild craving hungered deep within me, something I never expected, as if my dark alter ego was *enjoying* the pleasurable lashing. I never dreamed so innocent an item could induce such a look of pleasure on a young woman's face. Eyes closed, plum lips parted, jaw slackened, head back, glorious red hair tossed to and fro over her pale nude shoulders, her expression could only be described as saintly, as if the blows from the crop erased her sins from her soul and she floated toward the heavens in a state of spiritual ecstasy.

Hail Mary, full of grace…

I envied the freedom she possessed to accept the shadow of her other side, something I dared not do. Though I prided myself on my independence and my modern view of a woman's place in society I was, through no accomplishment of my own, Lady Carlton, wife of Lord James Carlton, his lordship born to Braystone House, a fifteenth-century limestone goliath situated somewhere in the Midlands and unknown to me.

As was this side of my husband.

A mischievous giggle escaped my lips. *Who ever dreamed his lordship fancied a taste of the whip for his pleasure?*

Settling in, I'd had little time to accustom myself to his persona since I was a stranger to this new reality, but this display of flesh and depravity took my breath away and evoked a different feeling within me. A feeling that both puzzled and delighted me. Sniffing the sweet, odorous scent between my legs off my fingers, I smiled and accepted it as a sign of my readiness to abandon my virginity for pleasures promised. I pulled the thin wrapper closer around me and in doing so, awakened a family of dustballs from their slumber. I couldn't deny my ego was as fragile as the ball of dust I crushed beneath my bare foot. It was obvious my husband took no interest in the fact that his bride yearned for his embrace and had performed a succulent toilette for his benefit. Hours ago I had wiggled into a cocoon of peach silk and fancy ribbons, insisting the maid loosen the lacings on my night corset, then peeled down my white stockings and attempted to do the same with the constrictions of my staid upbringing. I was determined to enjoy this night, asking him to *"Touch me here, milord, and there. Yes, I like it. Do it again."*

I was at this moment *without* words. Dry lips parched, I could only stare at the scene being played out in the dimly lit room in the five-story house in London's Mayfair district near

Berkeley Square. Flanked on either side by equally elegant facades, I had been impressed by the crest of arms upon the gate piers nearly obscured from view by the rich foliage surrounding the mansion. No doubt so was the ribald behavior of its occupants.

Cramped, I continued to watch my new husband wield a riding crop with a dexterity that not only slapped the pink rump of the willing girl with inviting sounds, but clearly indicated his familiarity with both the pretty subject *and* the leather instrument. *Calculated, solid blows.* Each perfectly aligned and making the girl cry out. Breathy whimpers at first, then rising sounds both shrill and anxious, accompanied by the fast, constant cracking of what I perceived to be a very ordinary-looking riding crop.

Ordinary? I shook my head. *Nothing* here was ordinary, I protested inwardly, knowing far more than skin and flesh was revealed here. I saw a man who craved power, who must conquer, dominate. Such a man intrigued me, but I was too innocent to see the treachery inside him that would eject me from my ordinary world and into a place where temple bells sounded to announce the changing of the winds, monks uttered incantations to keep demons away and the echo of a man's voice reverberating in a hidden valley urged me homeward. As you can see, I find it difficult to pull myself away from what has become so familiar to me in Japan, but I must because it is important you understand the unique happenings on *this* night that sent me upon that journey. Curious thoughts pricking at my mind. Odd murmurings nudging me not to turn away, but watch, listen. *Sigh.*

I couldn't look away.

Strange stirrings awakened deep within me, the same sensual, wiggly feelings I'd experienced only when I rode through the woods on my mare, my pubic mound pounding hard into her flanks. I didn't resist the stream of pleasure overtaking me. I imagined should anyone gaze upon my shocked face, they'd see me wide-eyed and incredulous, then a slight smile, my lower lip quivering, turning into a look of amazement then awe that such a thing could make me wet.

Very wet. Yes, I detected a stickiness between my legs similar to what I'd noticed on more than one occasion when I was near Lord Carlton. *James,* he insisted I call him. When we first met, my mother doted on him when she discovered his father was a duke, then shooed him away when he revealed he was a second son. It wasn't until his lordship made his business connections known to her that she convinced my da he was a proper match and our marriage banns announced. I had no idea then the marriage would set the course for a great adventure that tugged at the transparency of my youth and made me realize the life I led was as fruitless as rich, fertile earth without a plow to penetrate her, nurture her.

But at that moment, hiding in a closet like a rag doll teetering on a shelf, I could think only of what my new husband was doing to the redhead and how much she enjoyed it.

'Tis not a sight for a girl of your station, I could hear my mother saying. *Look away, Katie, before the devil himself claims your soul.*

But he already had. And what games he played in what I perceived to be a *spanking room* by the looks of the nefarious items I saw tossed about on the floor, strewn on the table, thrown across padded chairs. Wooden paddles, thorny evergreen brushes, a cat-o'-nine-tails, leather straps and restraints, manacles attached to wooden beams, a black hood, a high-back wing chair, even birch canes standing in a china vase filled with water to keep them pliant and green. I had read about such items, but I had never been privy to seeing them.

I perceived here a woman desirous of a spanking, whipping, birching, scourging or prickly brushing could get her bellyful. The thought was scandalous to me. My eyes, wide with curiosity, stared and stared. I tried to swallow, but my struggle against what I was seeing and what thoughts it provoked in me tightened my throat muscles, nearly choking me. The idea of my new husband as master of such items altered my perception of married life and changed it from a light romantic flight of fancy and awkward physical coupling to a sensual, highly erotic, naughty union of flesh.

Would he lay the crop upon my bare backside?

No, he wouldn't *dare* take such a liberty. I was his bride, not a woman of the streets or a spritely maid with a taste for domination, a pawn in the game known as the English vice.

Flagellation.

Was this what the two maids chirped about whenever I hovered near this room, this den of decadence? Dressed in shiny black polished cotton and white lace collars, cuffs and caps, the younger miss, Lucie, and Campbell, her older counterpart, made no secret of their curiosity of me. My American ways, my wardrobe from Paris, my light-colored hair bleached a pale gold from sun-drenched days astride my mare. They stared and stared, their sturdy low-heeled boots banging on the wooden floors as they scurried back and forth all day to make our rooms ready for this night....

Though I wasn't involved in the daily ministrations of this London town house, earlier I had overheard the two maids chattering about a night dark and decadent where his lordship might "fancy a lick or two with the belt on a mott's pretty haunches before he found the keyhole to her ladyship's door."

When I confronted them and asked what a *mott* was, Lucie

blurted out that such a person was a prostitute from a low-class neighborhood. She was quickly rebuked by the older woman, a portly soul who wore her white lace cap on her head as straight as a ruler, and sent away, leaving the rest to my imagination. Campbell apologized for the girl's insolence and insisted she was fresh from the country and knew nothing about what she spoke, then attended to my toilette, offering me no further explanation. I pretended to dismiss the incident, since I was certain the maid believed I had aligned my expectations about marriage with the puritan ideal that the wedding night was a dreamlike state consisting of whispers and rustlings in the dark. Nothing more. I dared not change that in her eyes lest she discover *my* secret.

What I had found in the town house library.

While Mother spent her time fretting about my white satin wedding gown from the House of Worth, the arrangements for my marriage at St. Peter's Eaton Square, and the newspaper coverage following my every move, I yearned for something else to read besides the *English Lady* fashion magazines or domestic guides she deigned I should acquaint myself with before my marriage. I was hungry for heartier literature, though I had no reason to suspect what I'd find in the library would be of a salacious nature.

Upon entering the room, I was pleased to observe that the top-floor study had a clublike atmosphere: wood paneling, oil paintings, leather armchairs and chandeliers made from Venetian glass. Its sensual energy overwhelmed me when, and to my delight, I discovered the owner of the town house entertained a most interesting collection of rare books. *Very* rare. And quite scandalous.

Hiding several slim tomes under my skirts, I secreted them to my rooms, where I devoured the reprint of *The Decameron of Pleasure,* along with *Lascivious Gems* and *A Night in St. John's Wood.* Dog-eared copies showered with brandy stains and cigar burns. A gentleman's retreat that I have no doubt had never seen the delicate step of a lady's fine leather boot. Until mine. And stamp my footprints upon its polished floor I did. Many times. I inhaled the erotic literature as if it were an overpowering perfume that opened the door to the secret life of this British nobleman.

Lord Penmore.

It was his house where we resided and *his* library.

After our engagement was announced, James had insisted Mother and I enjoy the privacy and comfort of the elegant West End residence owned by his friend and associate away on business in Japan. Poking about the library, I also discovered a cache of letters of a most dubious nature written by Lord Penmore to my husband. Accounts of his visits to a disreputable quarter in Tokio known as Yoshiwara with brilliantly lit streets, people eating and laughing, bony fingers plucking a tune with no beginning, no end, the discord of life forgotten in the dark corners where young girls beckoned him with sweet smiles and slender bodies wrapped in white silk kimonos. He also wrote of turmoil and dissent among the military men he called samurai. Burly, hard-drinking soldiers who, according to Lord Penmore, wielded their swords at whoever insulted them. I shall neither confirm nor deny his reports, for I fear revealing too much will raise such disbelief in you that you will return this book to the shop where you purchased it and demand your funds returned.

I retreated back to my books, lost in the lurid details of French courtesans and lords engaged in a pleasing act known as *soixante-neuf.* I had hoped to engage in this robust position with my new husband, head to tail, his cock within reach of my lips, his tongue busy at my pussy, licking and sucking, exploring the sweet juices oozing from my folds. As I read, each word dripped from the pages and into my psyche as easily as the morning dew settled onto a thirsty flower petal. I failed to acknowledge that I had not yet blossomed under a man's touch. Such hopes I had, since this elegant town house was also where I was to spend my first week of married life before embarking on a honeymoon to Paris.

So you can understand why I smiled when, after the lavish wedding reception, my mother kissed me on both cheeks and whispered in my ear I could loosen my night corset but *not* remove it. And if I lay very still, she assured me in an even voice, it would all be over quickly.

My father glanced toward me but said nothing, though I saw a grim look on his face that troubled me, as if he hadn't accepted the idea his daughter was a married woman and subject to the erotic whims of her new husband. What would he say, I wondered, if he knew Lord Carlton had a penchant for riding crops and plump bottoms?

I turned my attention back to the scene playing out before me, knowing I was trapped inside the garderobe, dust up my nose, the scent of snuff adding to the precarious teetering of my psyche. A bride living out her fantasies and creating a world where she was merely a voyeur instead of a player. A little voice reminding me *we're trapped by our deeds only if we choose to be.* I couldn't deny I was curious to see what happened next, as I believe you are, too. You wouldn't be reading this far if you weren't. I assure you, by the time you arrive in the land of the samurai with its scattered pine woods, crimson foliage and the floorboard that sings when the head of the samurai clan approaches, you will be perspiring (yes, ladies *do* perspire), your chemise unbuttoned, the lacings on your corset loosened. So pray, do not lecture me, telling me I should have leaned back in the closet, fallen asleep and waited for them to leave, since curiosity has been known to skin the pubic hairs of even the most careful pussy. I *should* have. But I didn't. And I would pay the price for my folly.

"Please, my lord, more, *more…*" the girl yelped.

"I shan't disappoint you, wench, though I can't wait much longer to fuck you."

To my horror, though jealousy was a more descriptive *mot* for what I was feeling, I could see James kissing her buttocks; then he drew the riding crop through his fingers, caressing it and making it shine with the sweat of his palms.

"I'm ready for you, milord," the girl said, cooing.

An unseen female voice laughed, then said, "His lordship won't have enough energy to fuck his new bride if he takes us *both*."

Who else watched the intrigue being played out here?

"Mind your mouth, Sally," the other girl said, her voice breathless. "Lord Carlton has enough rod to please both of us *and* his new bride."

"Who said I intended to bed the American?" said Lord Carlton, rubbing the back of the girl's bare thighs. "I dare say I imagine the twit is asleep, though I should wake her. Observing a good whipping might open her eyes to what's expected of my wife, eh, Bridget?"

How dare he speak about me in such a manner!

"Begging your lordship's pardon, but who needs *her?*" Bridget laughed. "You can whip me arse for as long as you like." She wiggled her buttocks, then parted her fleshy cheeks with her small hands, exposing the puckered hole for his lordship's visual delight. "*And* make use of me back stairs for your pleasure."

I couldn't close my mouth. Did James intend to do the same to me?

"Not before you slide into *me,* milord," said the girl called Sally when she moved into my view. I could see a tall brunette wearing a scarlet corset with white laces, her pubic hair blacker than jet and glistening with her juices as she expertly drew a rubber phallus from inside her. (Such an item was known to me by way of a novel I found in the library about a young Parisian's foray into self-gratification with what she labeled a "dildo." I don't recall the name of the story.) I drew in my breath, excited by its length as well as its breadth.

Could his lordship compete with such a wonder?

I couldn't wait to find out.

I gasped when I saw my new husband put his arms around both girls and squeeze their breasts, twisting their nipples between his thumbs and forefingers and making them moan. He said, "Lord Penmore was correct in his assessment of the talents of you two charmers—"

Lord Penmore. The mention of his name startled me. I should have known by the tone of his letters he was behind this gala interlude. Yet he was also a shrewd businessman. I remember him detailing to my husband a nefarious commercial enterprise surrounding the expansion of the empire into Japan, *whispered about then hushed up,* he said. I dismissed the item then, though I detail it here to note its significance in my journey, a marker on the game board that lingers under your eye but has not yet been put into play, yet is important to the outcome of the ad-venture.

Then I was more interested in watching Lord Carlton wiggle his fingers into the brunette, probing and making her sigh with anticipation. I also emitted a sigh, wistful, needy, heat making me want to contract my pubic muscles in a de-lightful series of spasms. I forced myself to hold back. I didn't wish to miss a moment of their prelude. For that's what I told myself it was, a prelude to the moment when my husband would come to my rooms, his body still bathed in sweat, his cock primed for a night of passion with his bride. Naive, yes, as I'm certain you were on your wedding night, but I shaded my view of what I was seeing as if I looked at it through the ornate, opaque lace of my bridal veil. Not to do so would have evoked not only anger in me but disappointment, a far stronger emotion for a young girl to absorb and one I was not ready to deal with on my wedding night, cramped and brooding in a closet.

His lordship finished with, "—though I prefer a virgin to satisfy my needs."

"I've played a virgin on the boards, milord," said the redhead, turning over and caressing her lower lips, then opening them wide, inserting a finger inside her and wiggling it back and forth and pleasuring herself in a secret spot familiar to her. A myriad of tiny tremors worked their way up and down my spine. I'd never seen such boldness, though I dare say I had found my way to the same spot between my legs on numerous occasions. Don't gasp and mutter, then pretend you don't know what I'm talking about. You do and that's that. Let's continue.

"I prefer spending my wedding night here with you, my pretty pink maids," Lord Carlton was saying, his eyes remaining on the girl's lower pubic region while he cupped her pussy and held her, pushing his fingers into her while unbuttoning his breeches with the other hand.

To my amazement, out popped his prominent erection, the head shiny and large. I had seen anatomical drawings of the male organ in the books in Lord Penmore's library, but none like this. Thick, bobbing up and down, he grabbed his cock and pulled on it once, then again, pointing the eye directly at the girl's pulsating pussy. I was so enamored of the size of him, I leaned forward, failing to illuminate in my mind the dropping of a large dustball onto the tip of my nose. It tickled, but I didn't brush it away. I couldn't stop watching them as the girl lay down on a wooden table, then raised her head and shoulders to look at him. *Smiling, waiting.* He lifted her legs, running his hands up and down the backs of her black stockings as if he were paying homage to her slender calves before pulling them apart to expose her, forcing her pussy to open wider than the expanse of her dainty fingers had dared reveal to him.

Before I could catch my breath, Lord Carlton plunged his swollen cock into her, sliding it up easily against her velvet walls, finding his rhythm, even and smooth, making me sit up and shift my weight off my legs, numb as they were. I dared to inch forward, opening the closet door a little wider, my nose peeking through, my body squirming, the seat of my pleasure full and throbbing as I watched the girl wrap her legs around his hips, pulling him to her and embracing him with an urgency *I* had dreamed of knowing. Her thighs tightened around him, thumping his buttocks with her heels and sending my husband into a tirade of passionate words, his voice demanding, shouting, his body pounding deep, thrusting into her again and again—

I sneezed.

Loud.

And out I tumbled from the closet, landing at my new husband's feet.

Staring straight up at his nude buttocks.

2

Chaos followed. Cursing, Lord Carlton stopped pumping the redhead, she screamed, he pulled out of her and the brunette dropped the dildo. No one paid attention to the hard rubber object landing on the plush carpeting at his lordship's feet. They were too busy staring down at me.

Steadying myself, I brushed the dust and mold off my silk wrapper and stood in front of the unholy trio, all three completely baffled by my sudden appearance. I imagined they believed me to be an apparition. *I* couldn't believe the power of a sneeze had unmasked me. I wiped my nose with a delicate swipe of my fingers, and a whiff of my own sweet scent reminded me I was just as guilty as they in my pursuit of delights. Still, I refused to be humiliated by my new husband in front of these two *motts*. I was determined to act as the lady of the manor and not a female libertine pursuing her own pleasures.

I got to my feet, careful to avert his lordship's cock slick with juices and dangling close to my lips. He made no attempt to push it away. The sod. My confidence shaken, I quaked inside with an insecurity at assuming my new role as Lady Carlton under such circumstances. But, being the girl I am with the sassy mouth, I blurted out the first thing that came to mind without weighing the consequences.

"I've no doubt you possess the stamina to pleasure two women in the due course of an evening, my dear husband," I began, wrapping the silk tighter around me. "But I doubt if your capabilities include *three,* so I shall leave you to play out your sordid games."

I don't know why I dared to speak to him in such a manner, except to say I'm an O'Roarke, a proud breed more oft than not given to brandishing a fierce will that puts us in a strange state of persistence. We don't give up, no matter what. What I *didn't* know was that James had a game of his own in mind. A game that included bedding his new wife in a very public manner.

"So my bride has fire in her veins after all," Lord Carlton said with a note of pride as he stepped in front of me, blocking my exit, his tall, nude muscular body leaning slightly to one side, his raw masculinity holding me hostage with a power I vowed to resist.

"Let me pass," I demanded, chin up. I ignored a trickle of sweat making a slow journey down the length of my neck and into the valley between my breasts. My husband *did* notice and traced its path with his finger. His touch mesmerized me. I couldn't move.

"No," he said coldly. "You shall stay."

Panic washed over me, telling me to flee, but his voice stirred a magic within me that yet resided in my romantic soul. When his hand moved down to cup my breast, in spite of my resolve not to let him pleasure me, I moaned. Loudly. His touch sparked a reaction in me that made my knees buckle. Damn, I *hated* showing weakness in front of him.

Knowing he'd made his point, he said, "I shall prove you wrong, milady, about my capabilities. This is my wedding night and I intend to make the most of it."

"I won't allow you to touch me again in front of these women," I cried out, regaining my courage. "Debasing what should be pure and godly between us." I grabbed a flogger off the wooden table and threw it against the padded wall with the force of an avenging angel. It barely made a sound.

"Would milady prefer to be on the *receiving* end of the whip?" he ventured, a curiosity creeping into his voice that unnerved me.

"How *dare* you speak to me in such a manner," I shouted, a strange fever gripping me. "I'm not a cheap girl off the streets—"

"If I may be so rude as to interrupt your ladyship," the redhead said, indignant. "Me and Sally don't come cheap. We was recommended by the best gentleman's house on York Street."

"That's right, milady," chimed in the brunette. "We can take the crop all night long without smudging our lip rouge. Ain't that the truth, milord?"

"I'm more interested in seeing what Lady Carlton will do when *she* tastes the sting of the whip." Lord Carlton narrowed his eyes. "Will she scream and beg for more?"

I inhaled deeply when my husband picked up the flogger and swept its smooth leather tails across my breasts swathed in silk, tantalizing me with its sweet promise and making me squirm.

"You'll never find out!" I said, aware of an offensive scent as he waved the flogger under my nose. Black shoe polish came to mind.

"Won't I?" he asked, tossing the flogger aside and grabbing me around the waist, then pushing me down on the rough wooden table, startling me. My backside hurt, bruised by his rough treatment, and the soles of my bare feet stung when I scrapped them on the chipped wood.

Determined as I was to fight like hell, I was outnumbered when he ordered the two girls, squealing and giggling, to shackle me. 'Tis a pitiful plight for any bride on her wedding night to find herself shivering in the midst of confusion and disarray, waiting to consummate her marriage with her eager husband, but not like *this*. Two prostitutes pulling on my arms and holding me tight in their grip, fastening leather restraints around my wrists and drawing them through the iron rings embedded in the wood, making them so taut I could hear the leather crunch in my ears.

"You can't do this, James," I cried out, tossing my head back and forth, pulling on the restraints, chaffing my skin until it was raw, but I couldn't free myself. "I'm your wife, dammit. *Stop!*"

"All the more reason to explore your lovely body," he said, my actions inflaming his desire. I looked down and knew why. My arms were pulled up, forcing my shoulders back and inducing my breasts to stand up in a most provocative manner.

Taking advantage of the opportunity, James ran his hand up and down my neck, my face, then slid his hands down over my breasts, my midriff, setting off a slithering wave of anticipation within me and a sensual warmth that swept over me, making me ashamed that although I detested his deviant games, I couldn't stop the white heat pulsating in my lower region.

Before I dared to take another breath, he ripped my wrapper down the front, exposing me to his view. I gasped.

Loudly. Round and bouncy, my breasts spilled out over my corset. I gritted my teeth when he squeezed them, pulling on them, rubbing them against each other, then pinching my nipples and flicking them back and forth between his thumbs and forefingers. I protested his assault upon my person, but he merely laughed then picked up the crop and drew the instrument of pleasure across my bare breasts, flicking it over my taut nipples, stinging them with a sensation that both aroused and frightened me.

I shudder as I write this passage, remembering that night. I was in the most awkward and alarming predicament. Imagine yourself in my position, dear lady reader. I was about to be whipped by my new husband and I couldn't do anything about it. I ask you, what would you do? I've no doubt several of you ladies are licking your lips and wiggling about in your chairs, thinking, wondering, anticipating this delicious treat about to be rendered upon your bare bottom. I, too, would have found such an idea interesting and provocative, not to mention naughty, had I been with a man I trusted.

Lord Carlton inspired no such emotions within me with his brusque manner and sharp orders.

Why not induce a fainting spell? you ask. *It worked for me when that old lecher, Lord —— leaned over and put his nose down my cleavage last week.*

That wouldn't stop James, though I was grateful I wasn't wearing my new *cuirasse* corset, the silk ribbons laced up so tightly you can barely breathe. I surely would have succumbed to unconsciousness, then his lordship could have done whatever he wished with me and—

Enough about the damn corset, you insist, fretting about, twisting the fringe border on your overskirt until you pull it off. *Get on with the scene.*

I shall, but first I must explain to you that should I have not come up with a grand scheme to extradite myself from his lordship's domination game, I never would have gone to Japan and you would have no story to titillate you, so please allow me this moment to catch my breath. Putting words down on the page is not easy, decidedly so when the memory is not a pleasant one.

It didn't help my thinking process when he rubbed my nipples back and forth, then took them between his teeth and bit them, not hard, just enough to make me cry out with more pleasure than pain.

Was his hand wielding the whip just as provocative? Enticing me to take pleasure in such a deed instead of being repulsed? What other roguish certitudes would he undertake to engage my emotions?

I had no intention of finding out. No matter how my body betrayed me with delicious sensations slithering up and down my spine, a flogging was *not* my idea of romantic love. Many of you would have no doubt fainted, then opted for the cathartic effect of Seidlitz powders to purge his evil deed from your body and purify your soul. I searched my mind for another alternative.

Divorce?

I mention it here should the curious idea have crossed your mind, albeit 'twas not a practical one for a girl in my situation. British law dictated that I could only obtain a divorce from James by proving he performed some bestial act such as cruelty upon my person (calling the two prostitutes as witnesses was not an option since their livelihood would shrink considerably if they testified against his lordship in an open court). *He,* on the other hand, could divorce *me* simply for the act of adultery. I had to think of something else, but what?

"I *demand* you stop this display of power, James," I said,

stalling him with a steady but weakening voice that threatened to betray me. God, now he was teasing me with gentle stroking between my thighs. *When would he stop?* "Or I shall scream for help."

"And who do you think will come to your assistance, milady?" he said in a mocking tone. He leaned closer, the smell of a fragrant liqueur on his breath scenting his words with a menace I dared not ignore. "The room is soundproof and the servants are used to such goings-on."

I ignored his remark. "I imagine that is Lord Penmore's best cognac I smell on your breath."

He laughed at my impudence. "And *this* is his favorite crop." He raised his arm in a long arc, his handsome face gleaming with sweat, his dark hair matted and wet and sticking to his forehead and cheekbones. "The moment is at hand, my dear wife. Before I take you to my bed, I shall tantalize you with a most erotic stimulant upon your beautiful breasts—"

"Release me, James—" I demanded. No matter how aroused I was by the crop, I refused to allow him to dominate me in a situation where I had no say in the matter.

"And end our little game?" he taunted me. "I intend to enjoy myself as I watch you squirm—"

The hiss of the flogger cutting through the air chilled me as the implement struck the wooden table with such force splinters of wood bounced upward and landed on my breasts, stinging my bare flesh and making me jump. Seeing my reaction, he threw his head back and laughed, then raised his arm again, taking aim at my nipples, hard and taut and quivering.

"I won't miss this time," he vowed.

"You wouldn't dare," I yelled, my breath becoming erratic. He wouldn't stripe my nude flesh pink then rip my maiden-

head from me with such cold audacity, would he? "If you do, I swear I shall faint—"

Yes, I said it. After all my preaching about the silly, inane things aristocratic ladies do to keep their noses out of undesirable, odorous places, I had succumbed to the same devices and uttered a weak, feigned excuse. What choice did I have? I'd married a man devoid of any sense of propriety.

"You give me cause to think, milady," he said, smirking. "You *should* be primed with a whipping to stimulate your sexual juices, but I wouldn't wish my bride to have a case of the vapors before I can pleasure her with my cock."

"It's about time you came to your senses," I muttered, relieved. "And stopped playing this deviant game."

"Who said the game was over?" He put down the flogger, allowing me to slow down my breathing for a precious few seconds before he slid his hand down my belly, covering my pubic region with a protective caress, then rubbing me with a sensual touch. I groaned. I couldn't stop myself. "You will find I am a man who covets his bridegroom privileges with great ardor," he continued, then he grabbed the soft flesh of my pubic mound and squeezed it, ripping the buttons off my pantaloons and finding his way inside me, his fingers probing me, looking for what I imagined was proof of my *virgo intacta,* that fold of mucus membrane yet unbroken by a man's cock. Or had my robust riding upon a steed already done the job?

I've no doubt there are those among you who have sworn to your husband that vigorous exercise was the culprit when he thrust into you on your wedding night and found no obstacle on his path to marital joy. Was it the handsome young lord with no yearly stipend? Or your groom with the strong, muscular body, or the foreign gentleman with the charming accent? I make no judgment upon you. Whoever he was, I've no doubt you were young and in love. I have since learned the uncontrollable power of such a physical love, the driving need for touch, smell, taste and penetration with a beloved, how impossible it is to stop it, thinking about how much you crave it, the gnawing inside you that hurts so much you can't control yourself when his fingertips touch your cheek or brush your lips.

But I was, at this moment, still a virgin and untouched by any man. I have nothing to gain here by delivering an untruth to you. Still, I prayed my virginity was intact, for a wild idea was forming in my brain, a way to save my virtue *and* my pride. But without proof of my purity, I had nothing to bargain with, for his lordship had made a contract for a virgin and I feared more wrath from him if he didn't believe me untouched.

"Release me, James, now," I said with more insistence than before. "Or there shall be hell to pay." I struggled to force apart the leather restraints that fastened me to the table, turning my body from side to side while each prostitute held an ankle, spewing lewd expletives at me and keeping my legs spread apart.

"Keep still," he ordered, paying no attention to my plea and pushing deeper inside me with his two fingers, exploring me, making me gasp, then he smiled. "So you *are* a virgin." *Was he playing a game or did he really know?* He withdrew his fingers and sniffed the honeyed smell off the fleshy pads, then waved his fingers under my nose. The strong scent of my desire hit my nostrils, making me gasp. "But not for long," he finished.

I have no doubt my cheeks flushed as red as the girl's corset, creeping down the side of my face to my jaw then down my neck, not with embarrassment but shame. My husband intended to rape me and he believed me helpless to stop him.

Damn if I'd allow him to perform such an odious act upon me. I must put forth my proposition *now.*

"If you violate me, James," I said quickly, "I shall go to my father and tell him everything."

He laughed. "What ridiculous plan is hatching in that small female brain of yours?" he said, the curiosity in his voice pressing me to speak further.

"I shall tell him about the prostitutes," I said, ignoring his insult. He would pay for that dearly. "As well as the whippings and floggers and other instruments of domination, *everything* that takes place in this room. I've no doubt my father will break our marriage contract and withdraw any funds he's already given you then cut off your line of credit at the banks." I spoke in a rapid pace without taking a breath, my flippant remarks a way for me to cover up my embarrassment and bruised ego. Even as I said the words, I harbored a deep hope that my husband retained feelings for me, feelings that he would show me in a time of duress. I was hungry for his affection. A tender stroke on the cheek, a lingering look into my eyes, a brush of his lips with mine. Simple things, but so important to me.

I saw nothing but a cold look in his clear blue eyes. I shivered.

"You'll get nothing from me," I said, attempting to keep up my act without my voice cracking, "do you hear, *nothing.*"

Lord Carlton pulled back, thinking about what I'd said, then motioned for the two prostitutes to exit the room and leave us alone. Snickering and complaining, the two girls did as they were told, giving me a moment to contemplate where the situation would lead. Hard to believe that before tonight I had made the mistake of imagining my life with him down to the last detail, describing him to my female self in the most glowing terms, giving him attributes no man could possibly attain. In doing so, my fabricated lover overshadowed the man, swallowing him up in my subconscious. Signs of his infidelity were always there—his wayward glances at other women (perhaps even you, dear lady reader), his lips brushing the skin of my soft gloves but not the heated skin of my palm, never asking my father if he could be alone with me. I didn't see him as he was until now.

I prayed his love of women and drink and the life of a bon vivant were more important to him than fucking his bride. Yes, I said f— Wait, don't close the book, then pout because I spoke so freely. It's women like you who perpetrate the whole idea of sex as something indecent. Open your eyes and understand that I use the vulgar word with no excuse, for that's what his lordship had in mind. *Fucking.* Any girlhood illusion I had about the debonair lord I had married vanished. The man I had perceived to have a great wit had proven he had no honor, was debauched but so charming he could tempt a sister of the cloth to denounce her savior. All my romantic ideas were gone. Shattered like a beveled-glass mirror and broken into so many pieces no illusion remained. I was a fool to believe our marriage was different, that I could change the behavior of a man from the upper class, a class that thrived on infidelity in an aristocratic society. I had been warned that in my new position it was expected that I would ignore James's indiscretions, as I'm certain you do those of your husband. I couldn't. I was in a state of excitement on my wedding night and believed I could *make* him become the man I thought I'd married by threatening to leave him. Foolish on my part, but that's how it was. I threw myself into a panic, knowing this was my moment to bargain with his lordship regarding the intimate details of our marriage contract, a contract that allowed no pleasure for a wife. I hadn't wanted to believe my life would follow such due course. I became aware that I would proceed at my own peril.

"If I permit you to return to your rooms without being pleasured by my cock," Lord Carlton said finally, his voice even, "I shall have your *word* we will continue to live as man and wife?"

"Yes, milord. In all matters *except* in the bedroom." I hated making a pact with him, a dirty, vile agreement based on his lust and my temerity, but I had no choice. The scandal of an annulment would cause my mother such grief I couldn't bear it. My marriage to Lord Carlton and entrée into British society meant everything to her. Though I didn't approve of my mother's brashness, I understood her hunger for the finer things in life. Reared in poverty, Ida O'Roarke didn't have a pair of shoes to wear on her scarred feet until she was seven. Now she owned a hundred pairs made of the finest Italian leather.

No wonder my mother put an end to the heated whispers and snickers when she took her seat in the bridal pew at my wedding. Head held high, she stared them down until they turned away, shamed by her strength and fortitude. No doubt the rumors of an O'Roarke indiscretion had followed us across the Atlantic after my younger sister, Elva, found herself with child after lessons of another sort from her French fencing master. I knew it bothered my mother even if she didn't show it. She couldn't bear up under more aspersions cast upon us.

Such a scandal *célèbre* would also have far-reaching repercussions on my father. He had such great hopes for his business ventures in the Orient with the opening up of Japan to the West. It was no secret that companies from the United

States hadn't been able to catch up to the British in forging their part of the Yokohama trade. Many nights I'd listen to Da lamenting to his cronies about how American merchants eked out a tenth of the Japanese imports compared to the British. My marriage to a titled Englishman had assured him of the entrée he needed to compete in this exciting new commercial venture.

A surge of hope raced through me. His lordship had also done *me* a great service. I was now Lady Carlton and as such, I was included in the dalliances and nuances of British society. I sensed a new arena would open up to me as an intimate member of the royal set, where I could speak my mind without being rebuffed, where I could meet famed personages and learn from them, where I could delve into politics and the arts and explore them without fear of reprisal. Something I couldn't do in New York because we were considered nouveau riche and were not invited to society soirees.

Tense, I prayed my line of reasoning would keep my husband from violating me. Whatever his choice, I must remain strong. It wouldn't be easy to recover from such a sexual betrayal of my innocence, but I must if I were to survive. If I couldn't give completely of myself to a man, my heart, my soul, I wanted *no* man—

Until I met Shintaro. Then I couldn't get enough of his masculine sexual energy, him stroking me, licking me, touching the back of my neck with his strong hands, coddling my breasts, rubbing my nipples, nuzzling my belly, slapping my buttocks, thrusting into me…his heavy breathing, his sensual grunting expressing his pleasure, though it took many months for him to reveal his spirit to me, his hopes, his dreams. For the way of the warrior demanded he keep those feelings hidden, though at times I'd see them flicker in his brooding black eyes when he looked at me, like an elusive wind blowing restlessly in the dark recesses of his samurai soul.

I couldn't stop breathing hard, panting. But that part of my story must wait until that enchanted time when the samurai and a maiden chanced to find each other in a hidden valley in the land of the shoguns. First, being a part of *this* world was something I wanted, wanted it dearly, and it all hung on the next few words tripping off the tongue of my husband, Lord Carlton.

I shivered, though the heat from our bodies dripping with sweat from arousal and need warmed the room with intensity. He raised his eyebrows and snorted, as if spewing fire from his nose announced he was in control of my fate. Finally he loosened the bindings holding me down.

"You've won, my dear wife," he said coldly. "For now."

Then he left me to revel in my triumph. Alone.

I lay back as the leather restraints fell from my wrists, the sudden relief coursing through me and making me lose control of my pubic muscles and bringing me the pleasure I had fought so hard to repress. I didn't try to stop it when the tension in my lower body reached a crescendo, experiencing spasmodic contortions. I thrust out my belly, rocking my hips and buttocks as I writhed from the probing of phantom fingers pleasuring me...

Arms aching, chills making me shiver, I pulled myself to my feet, fighting back nausea and the light-headedness that seemed to overwhelm me as I dragged myself back to my rooms. I opened the door and was nearly inside when I heard my husband's voice beckoning the two prostitutes to rejoin him. Giggling, squealing and the sound of the flogger hitting its fleshy mark echoed in the hallway. I turned and to my relief, no one followed me.

My emotions spent, I collapsed atop the pure white eider-down and sank into its virginal folds, then wiped the sweat from between my breasts with the torn silk of my wrapper, the fine threads unraveling between my fingers. I had seen a new side of my husband tonight, one that disturbed me. James was impetuous, disquieting, illusive, and I sensed a desperate need within him to assert himself upon women.

Yes, I had won, but how long would he keep his end of the bargain?

I didn't trust him, but one thing I knew for certain: I wouldn't allow him to dominate me, mentally or physically. From this moment on, whatever unpleasantness I might experience with my husband, whatever actions he might take to rouse my emotions or disturb my sense of reasoning, I would fight back.

I would endure.

3

Mayfair, London
Six months later…

Since assuming my role as Lady Carlton, I have developed an intense dislike of the smell of freshly polished leather, the tangy odor rutting up my nostrils like tiny maggots eating away at my brain with their sorriest secrets.

His secrets. Women. Floggings. Tempestuous howls. As if the cheeky maid who caught his lordship's eye relished the sensation of being skinned alive, *a practice best served by a skilled master,* according to a slim tome I found in the library called *The Misadventures of Molly Pearlbottom.*

Quite a bawdy read and one I recommend highly, a story that will instruct you in the delights of spankings and whippings, where Molly uses her role as a submissive to dominate her master to pleasure *her.* Confused? Read it and you'll see what I mean. *I can't bring a book of that nature into my home,* you insist. You bought my book, didn't you? *But that's different,* you say, *you're a member of the peerage, albeit tarnished around the edges with the venial sin of being Irish.* I understand your concerns, dear lady reader, so I shall exercise my writing skills in hopes of re-creating a scene for you from the novel that will please you *and* make you swoon. *You're not a novelist,* you sputter, smirking. What is a novel but a memoir with the names changed? I believe I've reached the point in my writing where you toss the rules out the window and follow your instinct (*and* your nose, if you're writing a sex scene) and let it happen. So, in accordance with the memory of what I read on that stormy afternoon in Lord Penmore's library with the steady sound of rain beating on the roof and moisture seeping between my thighs, *and* what I've since learned about the delicate art of bondage from a true master, I will re-create a chapter in the life of Molly Pearlbottom.

The licentious goings-on still make me sigh…

Molly Pearlbottom, daughter of the town vicar, had one aspiration in her young life: to be flogged by the dashing Lord of Malworth Hall. He was taller than any man she'd ever seen, and his world was one of aristocrats and power, strappings and aggression, strength and domination. Every time she walked by the great manor house, she daydreamed about being bound and nude before his approving eye, then wrote about it in her curly handwriting in her copybook. All the other girls in the village had received their share of whippings and spankings by the roguish lord, who dutifully followed the family tradition of all the lairds before him. Every third Wednesday of the month, precisely at noon, he chose a willing recipient of his silver-handled, blue riding crop from all the girls who lined up under the great oak tree on top of the hill. Dropping their drawers and turning their bare backsides toward him, they all wondered, Who would be the lucky lass today? *Her ivory-smooth bottom smarting from delicate pink welts rising up on her skin like fresh blossoms, her flesh quivering with delight, her squeals and whimpers signaling a secret code of pleasure?*

Not Molly. *Her father kept her so busy on Wednesday afternoons washing down the rectory with soap, a brush and a pail of water, she never had the chance to find out. Fervent, irrational, her father allowed her no leeway, overwhelming her with chores. She had no opportunity to assuage her hunger for whippings and the pursuit of her secret pleasure.*

Until today.

The Honorable Horace Pearlbottom had been called away from his vicarage to London in light of a fiscal emergency (funds liberated from the church bank account for a new organ that never materialized had not struck the right chord with the church elders) and he had not yet returned, sending Molly into a gleeful tizzy. Today was the third Wednesday of the month…

…and so it was this innocent found herself bound and tied to iron rings embedded in the hard belly of the towering oak, nude except for her Sunday blue bonnet, white stockings and garters, the Lord of Malworth Hall about to take a crop to her virginal arse.

Molly shivered, the riding crop making a sharp sound when it cut through the air, tantalizing her with its whispered promise of pleasure, her nervous expectation heightening the experience. She stood waiting, waiting, hot juices flowing from her sex and down her thighs and dribbling onto her best stockings. She gave it no further thought, for a girl couldn't wear anything but her best to be pleasured by his lordship. She licked her lips, dry and cracked, her mouth parched and tasting like rotting peaches, sweet and sour at the same time. Her wrists hurt from the tight bindings and she was losing sensation in her arms pulled straight above her head, as if the nerves in her armpits were so taut they experienced a numbing effect.

Closing her eyes, shuddering with an emotion she could only describe as blissful anticipation, her sensual need blurring with a taste of fear, she heard the crop find its mark, strike with full force it did, the sound filling her ears, but where? When she wiggled her arse, she experienced no pleasure, no excitement, no dubious badge of honor stamped upon her buttocks. Nothing.

"Here, girl, stick out your arse more so I can reach you," his lordship bellowed, his tremulous voice exciting her. "Without delay!"

"Y-y-yes, milord." Molly poked her backside outward in a most ungainly manner, releasing gas as she did so, her embarrassment at letting go like that in an unladylike pose replaced by her pent-up need for deviant pleasure. What was he waiting for? She'd longed for this moment, dreamed of it, the heat of her excitement filling her neck and face when she doodled in her book, drawing a female stick figure bent over and receiving the ultimate kiss of fire over and over again...

She couldn't stop a sudden shiver announcing her imminent expectation of the crop finding its mark this time.

His next stroke landed before she could swallow, making her choke on her saliva. But it was a sublime pleasure, she had to admit, panting, her need building to a higher peak. Her loud, guttural sounds inflamed the lord's passion for his work. A rawness in her produced a flow of sweat on her body that made her naked buttocks shine with an illumination as if a regal white halo circled her arse. She heard his lordship uttering with amazement the number of strokes falling on her behind with an even regularity.

"...eight, nine, ten, eleven..." he counted as she settled into the rhythm of the whipping, the white heat emitting from the crop branding her pearl-white bottom with the pleasure she craved.

It was no wonder she let go with a loud, frustrated groan when he stopped before her twitching pussy had found its release, the wildly burning sensations making her belly full and heavy and bringing her back to the edge. She clenched her teeth, trying to hold on to the pleasurable sensations, begging him for more. Silence. What was hap-

pening? It was as quiet as an empty pew on a church holiday. She opened her eyes and turned her head, praying he hadn't deserted her, when the next stroke found her hungry arse and sent her back up the spiral, laughing and gushing with joy.

"Yes, yes," she groaned without shame. "More…more."

Dear, sweet Molly, the vicar's daughter, got her wish. His lordship laid one, two, three *quick strokes upon her red-streaked buttocks, hot and fiery, the tip of his crop striking the crack between her cheeks and sending her into wild abandon, her sweet juices oozing down her stockinged legs. She never heard the sweat-soaked lord pause for a breath as he continued his strokes, her cries of want turning into a crashing cacophony of wails and screams as she reached the height of an orgasm that never seemed to dissipate.* And why should it? *she asked herself as the laird's strokes continued until he pulled every quiver, every spasm from her hungry pussy. No matter what happened, she* must *find a way to take her place under the old oak tree as often as possible. But how?*

"I've never seen a lass take to the crop with so much enthusiasm," his lordship said, soothing her red bottom with soft caresses after he'd released her, then he surprised her by taking off her bonnet and stroking her hair as if it were soft velvet, running his fingers through it with a careful and loving touch. "Why have you not come to me before?"

"My father, the vicar, keeps me busy on Wednesday afternoons." She mewled softly, snuggling her body closer to him. She wanted to hold on to this moment and never let it go.

"A pity, my fair Molly, for I'd like to see you quiver again under the stroke of my crop." He sighed. "But I cannot go against the vicar's wishes."

"If I may be so bold, milord," she began, thinking.

"What is on your mind, Molly?" he asked, turning her face to his and studying her eyes beaming with excitement.

"*Since you're the laird of the land, why not start a new tradition?*" *she asked, giving him but a moment to think it over before she pressed onward. "Shall we say, every Thursday at three in the afternoon?" She twisted her body to show him her lovely bottom crisscrossed with red welts, then wiggled, making him take in his breath. "I'm finished with my chores then."*

He smiled. "Thursday it is, Molly, just for you, and don't be late, for I'll be bringing a surprise for you. Now, spread your buttock cheeks, girl, and show me your arse hole." He unbuttoned his silk breeches the color of a ripe plum and out popped the biggest cock she'd ever seen, not that she'd seen many, but she was sure his was the biggest. "I've got something here I know you'll like."

Molly did as he asked, a smile on her lips and a new feeling of independence surging in her soul as he mixed her juices with a rose-scented oil, his fingers gently massaging her puckered entrance before he slid his cock into her, stretching her anal hole with a deliberate slowness. She groaned, but she didn't complain. How could she? She, Molly Pearlbottom, the vicar's daughter, was as happy as a nectar-filled flower being sipped by a hummingbird, her bottom dewy and tinted pink, her eyes glowing and a naughty, curious voice inside her wondering what that surprise could be…

I can't reveal the rest of the tale without spoiling it for you, but I assure you I found books like this and others in Lord Penmore's library. I admit I embellished the scene with a new ending, giving Molly the upper hand with his lordship. I predict that someday you, yes, *you*, dear lady reader, will have the opportunity to read such stories about empowered females.

Until then, you shall have to make do with your imagination as I did, evoking speculation as to what went on in that padded room in the London town house. A girl tied to a cross, struggling with feigned distress and teasing his lordship with her tongue circling her lips. Or James strutting around the room cracking a single-tail whip, his willing victim bent over, her arse quivering with anticipation. Not to mention my husband orchestrating the regal decadence of a hot wax scene, the gummy residue trailing an elaborate pattern around the girl's nude breasts and hardening on her taut brown nipples. I prayed it was not the melted wax of votive candles, such unholy thoughts grabbing me and not letting go.

Were these scenes conjured up by my starved libido? Or demon nightmares of flesh and blood? That is for you to decide, dear lady reader. I spin these tales not merely to tantalize you, but to give you heed as to what may be going on under the confines of your own roof. I beg you to confront your husband if you believe 'tis so. Then again, you may wish to participate…

Though I was not acquainted with what other depravities went on in the upstairs back room, his lordship devised a clever method to let me know when his private hell was in session. The smell of turpentine, beeswax and charcoal powder, along with other smells I couldn't identify, permeated the air. I couldn't help but inhale the arousing odor when I went searching for a new book to read in the library, the fancy of my imagination overpowering my need for literature when I rustled my silk skirt and pearl-embroidered petticoats up the stairs. I would grab a book without more than a glance at its title then pretend to look through it, while inside I discarded the idea of reading as a way to soothe my hunger and focused instead on the illuminating power of smell to satisfy my lust. I would inhale the pungent odor and imagine a bundle of twigs tied together with crisp blue ribbons taken from my hair and wielded by a tall man with shoulders the breadth of an ancient Spartan and dressed in black from head to toe. In my daydream, I lifted up my skirts and turned my bare backside to him, my white stockings held up by blue garters, my quivering flesh covered in quick succession with crimson stripes from the striking of the rods, blow following blow, and groaning gave in to more groans.

I grew so accustomed to the scent of fresh black polish, quite distinct it was, that my capacity to ignore it barely diminished. On the contrary, the vitriolic odor awakened a dark side of my personality I had previously left hovering in that limbo part of my mind that existed between dreaming and doing.

Would I enjoy the reality of a whipping as much as the fantasy? I often wondered. I couldn't answer. I was either going mad or I was a fool to deny my husband access to my bed. *Or* my bottom.

Much to my surprise, Lord Carlton kept to his promise to keep his hands off me, but he fancied tormenting me with a constant fluctuation of upstairs maids with more than a willing backside to please him. Chaste with their speech *and* their manners when I was within earshot, giggling and flirty, they skirted past me, keeping their eyes down, reminding me of aberrant schoolgirls begging the headmaster for a strapping.

Distraught as I was by this uncomfortable situation, I was also curious. To relieve the itch in my mind as well as on my behind, I sought the confidence of the maid, Lucie, inquiring as to why the household help changed so frequently. I wondered if she would open up to me, but I needn't have worried. The young woman was eager to expound at length on the indiscretions in this house, including the wicked games played by its inhabitants (such as Blind Man in the Buff and French Licking), and making me promise not to say anything to Campbell, the housekeeper.

I assured her I wouldn't, and oh what tales she told me! About canings alternating with whippings, nipples pierced with gold rings, pony games astride nude girls. And masked evenings when the master of the house, Lord Penmore, drizzled his most expensive cognac over the bare buttocks of a girl tied to a post, then dipped his fingers in the liqueur and lit them on fire. The alcohol on his skin burned off quickly, she told me, when he ran his fingers over the girl's naked backside, the flames skimming over her skin and disappearing faster than a maiden's sigh.

Take a moment, dear lady reader, to compose yourself as I must do.

Feel better now? Did you...? Of course you didn't. *Ladies don't do such things,* you've been taught, but if you dare to question your physician about a common thread woven into the fabric of our femininity, I daresay he'll tell you it's not uncommon for him to find milady's hairpin stuck in her vulva. Yes, I'm talking about masturbation. Will you continue reading if I tell you I discovered my own vices to seek pleasure? I am aware 'tis a sin by the holy sisters, but the church and I have been on shaky ground since the night I denied my husband his connubial rights. So you can imagine how delighted I was to find illicit tomes in the library that alluded to mysterious items known as *olisbos* depicted on vase paintings in ancient Greece. These drawings of dildos left nothing to a woman's imagination. Further investigation revealed these charming toys came from the magic of a shoemaker's hand, his skill molding the wood then covering it with finely stitched padded leather.

Since I knew of no shoemaker in London who possessed such talent, I relied upon my own culinary skills with the vegetable variety. Unfortunately I found them messy, ill fitting and difficult to procure out of season (unless I was able to locate a greenhouse that cultivated various Mesopotamian delights). I must admit, that with the help of a natural implement, I reached orgasm in less time than it took to brew a proper cup of tea, something I've learned to appreciate on cold English mornings. It was the cold English nights that left me fretting about on my bedsheets, a rising heat making me perspire despite the chill, a need to capture intimacy in my life even if it wasn't with a man (taking a female lover wasn't practical since I could trust no one in my social circle. Not even you, dear lady reader).

I amused myself by adapting the principles of a children's game and devising a word square with the various Latin words for clitoris: *virga* (twig), *mania* (madness), *dulcedo amoris* (sweetness of love), *tentigo* (lust) and more. When I ran out of Latin words, I went in search of another dictionary and, to my delight, I found a discarded dildo in the spanking room. (I admit, the door was open and I peeked inside.) After making sure the snoopy housekeeper wasn't watching me, I hid it under my skirts and took it back to my rooms. I was tempted to make use of it in the privacy of my boudoir, burying my loneliness under layers of silken sheets while allowing my unabated curiosity free rein to insert it inside me and feel its heat radiating through me. I'm sorry to say that after inspecting the dildo at a closer range, I returned it. It became apparent to me no amount of washing or scrubbing could purify away the lingering scent of its previous owner.

I didn't let that stop me from continuing my search for self-gratification and from imagining what delights such an implement could bring to me. A pleasure so exquisite that a secret longing deep in my belly made me shiver with anticipation. That indefinable hunger drove me to explore other means to find satisfaction, though I hesitate to share it with you if you've turned pale and are experiencing indigestion because of the indelicate subject matter. Skip over these next few pages if you must, but I'll not deny these enticing thoughts ran through my mind on many a lonely day.

Such as today. Desiring not to be disturbed, I closed the curtains and locked the door to my rooms before I opened the polished wooden box lined with red velvet. Sitting next to my china ring stand shaped like a tiny tree with willowy branches, the dark walnut box held the jewels James had given me on our wedding day, as propriety dictated. Family heirlooms including a garnet necklace surrounded by stars, a diamond brooch with a large ruby in the center and a turquoise bracelet set off with diamonds. Cold stones given with a cold heart.

The box contained another jewel. One I enjoyed wearing above all others. Sleek, round and bulbous. The energy oozing from it when I slipped it inside me awakened my soul with a gentle vibration I could only describe as magic.

My dildo.

Tempering my need for physical release with practicality, a fortnight ago I decided to forgo my embarrassment regarding my predicament and embarked on a secret shopping trip. Armed with an address I found scribbled in the back of a gentleman's magazine I removed from the town house library, I sought out a certain shop on Holywell Street not far from Waterloo Bridge. A seedy establishment selling pornographic pamphlets as well as male enhancements and sexual aids. There I found the perfect item to assuage my hunger.

A dildo made of rubber with the wistful moniker the Widow's Comforter.

Taking it home wrapped in plain brown paper, I made quick use of it, its shape and size becoming as familiar to me as a lover's touch. So it was no surprise I found need of its heated comfort on this cold February morning. I caressed its tip nestled among the jewels, warming it with my fingertips. Then I sucked in my breath, begging my body not to betray me with a sudden rush of heat to my pubic region. Tightly laced and sweating, I couldn't hold back my need any longer. I gave in to temptation, seeking the solace of the secret shadowy space behind the pearl-inlayed dressing screen in my bedroom. Hiking up my skirts, the rustling whispers of silk filling my ears with enchantment, I found the slit in my pantaloons and slid the love instrument inside me, my body closing around its rubbery thickness. With familiar dexterity, I guided the shaft in and out of me in time to a silent rhythm in my head. I groaned, pressing the dildo against the walls of my throbbing flesh hot with my juices again and again. Moving my hips, my musings became so strong I couldn't stop myself. My breath quickened, my muscles deep inside me contracted, holding tight around the illusion of a hard penis inside me, *begging* for that delicious instant of release. If you've indulged in such an activity then you were rewarded as I was with powerful, gut-wrenching orgasms. Lingering for what seemed like hours, days, my pubic muscles experiencing the most delicious spasms…

But the satisfaction I found was not to last. After two weeks of errant use, the lack of an emotional connection became so unappealing to me I considered taking a lover. I immediately tossed the idea into the rubbish. No doubt such an affair would be discovered, since the household staff here and at Braystone House amuse themselves by spying at us through holes bored through the wainscoting on walls and solid mahogany doors. (If you don't believe me, check your walls and doors before you indulge in a tryst when your husband is out of town.) I've heard many servants line their pockets with guineas by becoming "witnesses" in adultery trials, acting out what they've seen for the judge, complete with moans and compromising positions. Within days, the whole sordid mess is published in scandal sheets and licentious gentleman's magazines.

I shivered at the thought. I relished my privacy, not to mention how distasteful the idea was of shaming my family with so thoroughly a bourgeois faux pas. Social mores notwithstanding, I harbored a deep-seated resentment that while my husband indulged in appeasing *his* salacious sexual appetite, I remained sensually starved. It was disconcerting at best to believe I would spend the rest of my life writhing under the probing of my own fingers and nothing more. Sometimes my craving for the connection of flesh on flesh was so daunting, I pulled up my chemise and cupped the firmness of my breasts in my hands, rubbed my nipples and stroked the tender skin on the insides of my thighs. I wanted so to be touched, caressed, anything over the cold deadness of the rubber phallus.

I sought an outlet for my loneliness and found it in the world of society, where I exuded a flaunting of ego I found so satisfying. At home, I was the girl with the empty dance card, my views scoffed at, my mind ignored. Here in London I was Lady Carlton, a member of the peerage, albeit through marriage, who could trace their lineage back to the first duke of Braystone. He was a brave ancestor of my husband who distinguished himself in battle with King Charles II, then fought alongside his sovereign on an expedition to Scotland, where he sacrificed his own life so Charles could escape.

Unfortunately, my husband, James, possessed none of the valor of his forebear nor the nihilistic intolerance for the wrongs done to humankind. He had no principles I was aware of and swayed so far from the model of moral rectitude, I dared not challenge him for fear of reprisal of a salacious nature. Yet in spite of or because of his failings—I'm not sure which—he entertained a lively and fashionable existence in London drawing rooms and clubs.

Which meant I was also included in the invitations.

What can I say? I reveled in the glitter and elegance, the youthful splendor, the gaiety, the daring subterfuge, the arts and the opera. I forged my path with aristocratic arrogance and made a place for myself in British society. And that included fashion. I've always loved color and developed a sense of how to use its pure, uncomplicated beauty to enhance what I saw as my shortcomings: my tall body and long face. I used simple diagonal lines in the clothes I wore to create an illusion of prettiness, draping myself in hues of rose, apricot and blue to create the illusion of a creature beautiful and mysterious.

I nurtured my instinctual attraction to lace and silk with frequent trips to the House of Worth in Paris, as well as art galleries and museums, to achieve a new level of refined smartness. My unique sense of taste and fashion matured like a ripening fruit, my raw talent at the core sweetening my outer skin with a prettiness I'd never felt before, whether I was tipping my ivory lace parasol at a cocky angle while flirting with Lord —— at a garden party or slipping on my third pair of lamb-white kid gloves since morning before sitting down to afternoon tea at Brown's with the duchess of ——.

This new courage I found meant I could assert myself,

flaunt my skill at repartee, show off my knowledge of world politics and play the game as the men did. I was a notable player in this milieu of the high-society hostess.

And I had no intention of giving it up.

4

I replaced the dildo among the red velvet folds hungry to hug its hardness, then wiped the stickiness off my fingers with a cotton handkerchief monogrammed with my initials. The perfume of my folly lingered to tempt me, but I snapped the box shut. I had no time to linger. Tonight I would entertain visitors.

Important visitors.

At James's request, I had invited the Viscount and Lady Aubrey to join us for a light supper along with my parents (my mother was eager to make the acquaintance of Lady Aubrey, a lady-in-waiting to the queen). The viscount was a family friend of his lordship and quite an interesting gentleman. No doubt you will have guessed his identity before you turn the page. He has the ear of the queen on foreign affairs and reputedly has been invited to Windsor Castle by Her Majesty to see her personal collection of miniatures. I was impressed with his keen sense of politics and I was certain he had no idea James was a scoundrel. His lordship was very adept at keeping his father's friends unaware of the dark side of his personality.

I planned a simple menu starting with a clear soup and two entrées instead of the usual four, followed by a dish of duck and ending with creamy pudding and light airy confections smothered with cream. Nothing to tax the digestion, since I knew the viscount suffered with gout.

Dissention set in when my husband informed me he wished to speak to my father alone after dinner about something important. I should have known James never did anything without wanting something in return. *What was it this time?* I wanted to know. He ignored my outburst and disappeared upstairs "to polish his leather toys." I wasn't fooled by his diversionary tactics to take my mind off the situation. I had no doubt the entire visit was a thinly disguised plot for James to elicit more funds from my father for his costly lifestyle.

What I couldn't have foreseen was a chance remark from the Viscount Aubrey that enchanted me and planted a seed in my mind that grew so quickly I couldn't stop it, as surely as I couldn't stop the shadows of night from descending upon us.

"I don't know what's gotten into the British government, James," I overheard my father saying after dinner when I entered the room filled with smoke, "opening the railway in Japan before fixing the damn roads."

James agreed, his easy compliance making me certain my suspicions about his motives were correct. He added that the roads were muddy and unruly and nearly impossible to travel in wet weather. Neither he nor my father noticed my entrance, so involved were they in their conversation, but the Viscount Aubrey stole a glance in my direction, his bushy eyebrows moving up and down in a curious twist. I imagined he wasn't accustomed to a lady joining the gentlemen in their frog-trimmed, padded smoking jackets after dinner in the gun room, but I insisted upon it. I had no desire to accompany my mother and Lady Aubrey upstairs with their fluttering fans, bottles of scent, filmy scarves and innocuous talk about croquet, archery and the latest divorce gossip. Nothing that would raise an eyebrow or illicit a nervous cough.

"There was little the British government could do, sir," James insisted, offering my father a cigar, "since the Japanese government demanded the railroad between Tokio and Yokohama open on time."

"That project was started more than two and a half years ago," my father said, leaning back in the padded wingback chair, enjoying its comfort as well as its girth. It did my heart good to see my da enjoy himself, knowing how much turmoil he'd faced these past few years. "Since then, the funds to build more railway lines in Japan have either dried up or been withdrawn."

"It's no secret, Mr. O'Roarke, that the situation is at an impasse," added the viscount, his smoking cap slightly askew on his head. He reminded me of an overgrown elf. "The cost to build more railways in Japan is prohibitive, especially with the financial state of European banks."

"With all due respect, Viscount Aubrey," said my father, sticking his thumbs under his plaid suspenders as he always did when he was certain he was right, "I'd bet a barnful of hay the cost could be kept down if you Brits paid more attention to your suppliers. I hear these fellows use twisted rails and build weak bridges."

"What you say is true," James added, his manner somewhat condescending, which made me even more suspicious, "but the biggest mistake was that the European director of the railway didn't know how to handle the Japanese."

"And I suppose you *do,* milord?" my father inquired, biting down on his cigar.

"To put it bluntly, sir, yes," James said with a confidence that surprised me. "I've become acquainted with their way of thinking, how they move together as one unit, not individuals. How they use a subtle form of communication when dealing with westerners and never answer a question in a direct manner."

My father laughed. "Back home we call that hedging."

"The Japanese call it business as usual," James answered in a glib manner. He smiled like a little boy trying to fool his governess. I looked away, refusing to be drawn into his game.

"Then you've been to Japan?" my father asked, surprised.

"No," James said, "but I've been escorting the Japanese emissary around London. He's a likable chap with a solid knowledge of English and a good head on his shoulders."

Escorting him to the brothels on York Street and the newly fashionable Bayswater district, I imagined, easing myself down on a plush divan after pouring an after-dinner drink from the row of decanters of claret, port and sherry sitting on the sideboard.

I leaned forward, eager to jump into the conversation. I thrived on lively discussion, from a rousing round of politics, discussing the iniquities of the parties—whether they were Tory or Whig or Labor—to current books and plays. This evening I was eager to discuss the latest filibustering in the House of Commons. I had no desire to listen to their mindless prattle about Japan, a barbaric country where, according to what I'd read in Lord Penmore's letters, packhorses were the choice of transportation, carrying items for trade from city to city by means of narrow footpaths cut into fields of farmland.

"The Japanese will beat us at our own game if we don't beat them first," my father bellowed, his stiff celluloid collar choking him and turning his face red. I had to smile. I knew he'd rather be lifting a pint with his cronies in a pub. He hated the formalities required of an English drawing room, while my mother reveled in it.

"What are you saying, Mr. O'Roarke?" the viscount asked, his eyes stealing a glance at me when he thought I wasn't looking. I tipped my glass to him and smiled. His features softened and he returned the smile.

"The Great Western Railway from here to Swindon barely tops fifty-three miles an hour and it took you British *years* to build it." He looked at my husband and grinned. "I'm certain we can build a railway from Ōzaka to Kobé in *half* the time. And my son-in-law has convinced me he's the man to handle the deal."

So that was the reason James invited my father for this get-together.

Angry with my husband's subterfuge, I fiddled with my fan, bending it until it cracked. James had convinced my father there was a fortune to be made by working with the mikado's government to finance a string of railways across Japan with Thomas O'Roarke investing in the rails, tank engines, wood for bridges and carriages needed. All financial arrangements, his lordship added, would be handled through the Oriental Bank of London.

He didn't count on his frustrated young wife playing a game of her own. Bored, restless and sex starved, I remained defiant in my approach to this marriage. I refused to be treated like an aftereffect of his greed and often baited him with subtle, sexual innuendos regarding his secret life.

As in this instance, when Viscount Aubrey dropped a casual remark that the British government held fast to its goal in bringing Occidental values to Japan. Curious, I asked him how they proposed to change a pagan country cut off from civilization for nearly two hundred fifty years (Lord Penmore's letters contained material of an informational nature as well as salacious). He answered in his wry manner that the British Legation had already engaged a governess and a seamstress to teach the female gentry of Japan about English household customs.

"I imagine visiting the mysterious Orient tempts the adventurer in all of us," I said, envisioning myself floating in a world of silk, flowers and fans. And bare breasted with numerous combs and needles decorating my hair, as I had seen in the tinted photographs of the geisha included in Lord Penmore's letters. "Including me."

"I had no idea you were so interested in Japan, my dear wife," James said, laying his hand on the back of my neck and rubbing it, making me stiffen. "I see I was mistaken."

He kissed my hand, expecting me to quiver. I didn't withdraw it, signaling to him that I alone controlled my emotions. Instead, I said, "There are many things you don't know about me, my dear husband."

"That's my Katie," my father said, smiling at me. "A girl with spirit. I see no reason why you couldn't accompany your husband to Japan."

"Splendid idea, Mr. O'Roarke," the viscount added, as if the thought were his own. "Your daughter would be a most excellent addition to the British delegation at the mikado's court."

"That's impossible, milord," James blurted out, startling me. *And* making me angry. How dare he speak for me?

He continued, "My wife has no intention of leaving London during the Season."

Ignoring his outburst, I replied, "You flatter me, Viscount Aubrey, but tell me, how could I be of assistance to the legation? I know nothing about the Japanese, though I admit I've been reading about their fascinating country in Lord Penmore's letters to my husband."

The look of fury on James's face was instant. Cold, fierce. I swear if he could have, he would have taken the whip to me at that moment so intense was his anger toward me.

I pretended not to notice and continued discussing the British alliance with the Japanese with the viscount, though I was more interested in contrasting the volatile state of my relationship with my husband with my seemingly innocent remark about the romance of travel.

"I'm certain the mikado's court would be honored to receive you and be graced by your wit, Lady Carlton," said the viscount, ignorant of the drama being played out between my husband and me, "as well as your charm and intelligence."

I smiled. I was beginning to enjoy the game. I curled my fingers around my broken fan and tapped it against my cheek in a coy manner. "In that case, how can I resist such a delightful invitation?"

"What *are* you saying, my dear wife?" My husband's voice held an edge only I recognized.

I lowered my lashes to veil my naughty thoughts from him. "Isn't it a wife's duty to accompany her husband to his new post?"

"Not if he wishes her to stay home," he countered. "A wife must obey her husband's wishes in all matters."

"*All* matters, James?" I flipped open my cracked fan and

fluttered it about me wildly. "This wouldn't be the first time I've gotten my way, would it, my dear husband?"

I could see his eyes flashing with contempt, knowing I had baited him and he couldn't bow out gracefully in front of Viscount Aubrey.

I laid my fan down on the divan, fingering the broken spine. I wouldn't break as easily. I'd made my point, shown him he couldn't make me surrender to his will. I'd let him simmer for a few days, feed his sexual temperament with provocative thoughts of me watching his every move in the Orient, then I'd invoke a woman's prerogative.

I'd change my mind.

You see, dear lady reader, I had no intention of going to Japan. The idea disturbed me, images of intense strangeness and violence making an indelible mark upon my mind. Besides, I'd made my place here in London and occupied it with a surety and confidence I'd never experienced at home. The viscount would understand my position when I explained my trepidation and withdraw his offer gracefully. After all, what sane woman would wish to travel halfway around the world to such a barbaric country?

"Katie, me girl, you saved the old man a heap of anguish tonight."

"What *are* you talking about, Da?" I asked, curious. I poured myself another glass of claret, still gloating over how I had perturbed my husband about accompanying him to Japan. I also knew the power of an eloquent silence and didn't protest when James excused himself and left the gun room in haste with a feeble excuse about finding his manservant to bring more liquor. Most likely he ventured off in search of a plump bottom to vent his frustration upon with his favorite crop. The viscount finished his port then rang for his driver, citing his gout as the reason for his early departure.

Leaving my father and I alone.

"I don't know how to say this, Katie, but I'm worried."

"About what, Da? Is Mother overdrawn on her account at Fortnum & Mason again?" I was well aware of my mother's appetite for fine pickle relishes and peach preserves.

He smiled. He never denied his adored Ida anything, but it wasn't my mother's spending habits that made him peel off the wrapper of another cigar and hold it tightly in his palm before crushing it. "I overheard something about that husband of yours that set the old man's ears atwittering."

"You did?" I asked, trying to keep my voice steady. Did he know about James's sexual indiscretions? This upset me more than I would admit. After all the times I spoke with my father in blunt terms about the world of politics and life's frailties, I felt embarrassment at the thought of my da knowing about my husband's sordid liaisons with prostitutes. Rare to blush, I put my hand to my cheek and the burn meeting my finger-tips surprised me.

"Yes," he continued. "Some braggart from Parliament mentioned a stock deal James got himself involved with that had shady overtones." He paused, tossing down the cigar, then said, "Though he couldn't prove it when I challenged him."

"I never heard anything about it, Da." I bit my lip the second I said the words. Why was I defending my husband?

"I hope you're right, Katie. I was leery about sending that husband of yours off to Japan with a letter of credit worth thousands of pounds sterling honored by my bank here in London," my father said, laying his hand on my shoulder, "but with you going with him—"

"*Me?* Go to Japan?" I turned around so quickly I spilled

the wine, the deep burgundy staining my fingers red. I grabbed a cloth from the table and wiped up the mess, my victory over James dissolving as quickly as the cloth soaking up the liquid. "I—I can't go, Da."

"But you seemed so eager—"

"I was. I mean…it sounded so romantic…." I shuddered, my breath ragged. *What had I done?*

I couldn't tell my father about the dangerous game I played with my husband, the sexual innuendos, unfulfilled lust, his blatant adultery. Thomas O'Roarke already harbored a prejudice against the Englishman because of James's high financial demands for our marriage settlement. My father had paid the exorbitant amount to make my mother happy and to secure my future. Or so he believed.

"A sea voyage will do wonders for you both," my father answered in that glib manner of his I knew so well when he wanted something. "Think of it as a holiday."

I tried to smile, but couldn't. It didn't matter what I said or did. My father would see only what he wanted to see, the range of his vision clouded by his personal motives.

"A trip to Japan *would* be most illuminating," I lied, "but Mother needs me here in London to help her, especially since Elva and the baby are coming to visit."

Though we had our differences, I was looking forward to my younger sister's visit. Elva was the pretty one, dark and dainty, the daughter my mother groomed to marry a duke or a prince. Instead she'd gotten pregnant at seventeen and had her baby in a Paris hospital. I was eager to see her.

I continued, making excuses. "I spoke without thinking, Da."

"I'm mighty glad you did." He lowered his voice. The glibness was gone. That surprised me, made me uneasy. So unlike the rogue Irishman who could talk a gang of rail busters into working extra hours for no pay. "I *need* this deal with the Japanese, Katie. Need it bad."

No fragmentation of thought, just straightforward talk. I stared at him, something about the edge in his voice frightening me. "What are you saying?"

"We're heading for bad times with the railroad boom in the States coming to an end. Banks are overextending themselves and President Grant invoked the gold standard for the money supply." He paused, chewed on his cigar. "I'm dead certain we're going into an economic crisis before the end of the year." He thought about what was on his mind, then finished with, "I fear I could lose everything if I don't diversify my holdings."

"I had no idea it was that serious."

"It's worse, Katie." Thomas O'Roarke shook his head, his jowls drooped, the toll of many years of track walking for the railroad in his younger days showing on his face. Success had its price, I knew, though my father would never admit it. He'd come up the hard way, working with his hands till they bled, but it was his quick, mathematical mind and keen business sense that had put him at the top of the railroad game.

"If what you're saying is true, Da, wouldn't it make more sense if *you* went to Japan with James?"

I rattled my brain for an excuse, *any* excuse not to go on a long, tiresome journey halfway around the world with a man I feared and hated. No warmth existed between us, any attraction I may have felt toward him disfigured by his deviant games of domination, and if I stripped away the pretense we had forged with each other, it revealed only emptiness.

"I wish I could, Katie, but I can't." He spoke harshly. "You *must* go to Japan and keep an eye on my business interests."

"But Japan is a pagan country," I reminded him, "run by barbarians and samurai."

My father ignored my plea. "You're a strong girl, Katie, not letting anyone get the best of you and speaking your mind." He smiled, pleased. "You remind me of meself when I was starting out, all fired up with ambition, a wild temper and always breaking rules."

I grinned, remembering the photo I'd seen of my father back in his youth, a tall, thin young man with pants too short for him, a lantern in his hand and a whistle between his lips. I saw that young man come alive again when he said, "There's nothing more beautiful in the world than miles of railroad track, all straight and shiny, calling to you." He laughed. "Except your mother, of course."

I poked him in the ribs. "You always did know how to turn a phrase, Da."

He didn't give up his cajoling, now that he had my attention. "Railroading is in your blood, Katie. When you were a wee girl, I'd take you along with me down to the tracks and we'd watch the big trains roaring into the station. Side by side they came, the crew heaving coal into the engines, the iron horses puffing, straining every bit of steel and muscle, passengers hanging out the windows and waving handkerchiefs, the rolling black smoke turning the sky dark overhead, the great iron steeds rounding the sharp curve and arriving at their destination, brakes screeching, tracks sparking." He let go with a heavy sigh. "'Tis a sight to behold, but railroading is a young man's game and the old man is running out of steam." He patted his belly protruding over his trousers.

"Not you, Da. You can do anything." I remembered those days with my small hand clasped in his, hanging on to my soft blue bonnet whipped by the wind. I hugged him with warmth in my heart, but I couldn't stop a cold fear growing in my bones.

"Not this time, Katie. Your husband may be what we call an upstart back home, but he's shrewd and can get the job done." He leaned forward and looked me square in the eye. "I'm counting on you to see that he does."

I found the courage to return my father's hard stare, though turmoil raged inside me, a smooth sheen of sweat moistening my upper lip. I remained silent for several minutes, my insides churning with something I didn't understand, an anticipation of the unknown knocking my inner compass off course. I'd been so sure of myself, filled with self-direction, capable of making my way unaided, asserting my freedom as Lady Carlton, but all that ended if I followed my father's wishes and journeyed to Japan.

I looked away, guilt flooding me. How could I explain to him my husband was a madman who reveled in floggings, whippings and spankings? My father believed I was a happily married woman, though sexually I moved in the shadows, darkness cloaking my secret, my cries of ecstasy mingling with silence, my solitary game bringing me release but little joy.

How I longed to crush my nude breasts against the muscular bare chest of an imaginary lover, rubbing my hard nipples against him, the heat of my need stirring his desire. Moving his body on mine, then thrusting his cock into me until the loneliness I lived with day after day ceased and my body hummed with a comforting rhythm I had yet to experience.

When we *did* meet, my samurai relit my soul with acts so profound and passionate, so brilliantly intense I existed in a floating world. Every gesture, nuance and caress teasing me with the finest blue silk pulled taut over my breasts so my nipples peaked through the sheer fabric, inviting my samurai to linger at the task before stripping it off me and exploring me further, capturing my spirit and giving me pleasure with consummate skill. My nude body glimmering with such translucence it was as if I were bathed in mica dust.

Yet at that moment I believed that would never happen with this new set of circumstances entering my life. Strange, I had gotten myself into this situation because I wished to strike back at my husband, make him see me as an equal, not as a sexually repressed woman. Agonizing, meandering thoughts consumed me. Questions haunted me, but the answer didn't change. I had no choice but to embark on this journey.

Reluctantly, over the next few weeks I assisted James with making the necessary arrangements regarding our identity papers, letters of credit from the bank along with a signature book and visiting cards, as well as securing passage to America, then Japan. I owed my father that much, but I couldn't shake the uneasiness overtaking me as his lordship and I undertook our long journey to the Orient, a land of myth, pagan rituals and strange customs. I prayed I would survive nameless dangers I had yet to contemplate.

What I *didn't* know, dear lady reader, was that I would face a clear-cut danger the night we were to board the steamer to Yokohama from San Francisco.

I shiver still, remembering the frightening incident that nearly cost me my life. Read on, if you have the courage. You won't be disappointed. I have worked hard to re-create that night with witty dialogue and pertinent details as I remember them; but I must warn you to keep your smelling powders close at hand since I have also included a most explicit scene with my samurai that will—

No, I will let you see for yourself, but I beg you to read the chapter in its entirety so as not to lose sight of the story line.

That *is* why you're reading this book, isn't it?

5

Cliff House, San Francisco, California
Six weeks later…

We made the journey from London to New York, then across the continent by railway, and I must say I was flattered by the endearing personal service afforded to me as Lady Carlton. It mattered not that I was Thomas O'Roarke's daughter, more that I commandeered the title of aristocrat with a handsome husband at my side. James cajoled the wives of business associates we met along the way, impressing their husbands with my father's money, paying for lavish parties and handing out Cuban cigars. He was on his best behavior.

Until tonight.

We were dining in a private room at Cliff House, marveling at its lofty view overlooking the coast and the bellowing seals romping about on the rocks below, when James made an off-putting remark about the fashionably low décolleté of my gown. In a not-too-subtle manner, he insinuated I was intent on seducing every man I came in contact with, including our sober-faced waiter.

Me? A seductress? The idea amused me since the art was unknown to me, though I had travailed in my reading about infamous mistresses, their style, repartee, even the popularity of their scent. (The next time you smell a musky odor upon his lordship's handkerchief, be advised it *could* be the natural perfume of a certain courtesan residing on Lupus Street known for imparting her body aroma on a gentleman's handkerchief.)

I knew the daring gown was stunning, too dazzling for an early dinner, but I ventured to wear it anyway. Shoulders straight, bosom high, hips buoying the twenty or more flounces on my overskirt, I walked with a sensual flair to make every man dream about what was underneath. (I learned to affect a certain disinterest in what I wore from watching ladies of the British aristocracy, as if the nature of wearing garments was a plebian aptitude one merely adopted on a divine whim.)

Aside, I must tell you I loved the feel of the satin swishing between my legs, the velvet caressing my breasts, the lace pricking my nipples and making them taut. I wore such frilly, pretty clothes to evoke a mood and create a world of my own, a world where I played the role of a woman beautiful and mythical, a woman desirous to men, a woman so legendary no man could resist her. I cared not if that world collapsed when I stood nude before a full-length oval mirror and examined my features, plain as they were. When I swathed myself in glittering finery, I embarked on a deep and satisfying adventure that allowed me to indulge in my romantic wanderings, to race forward into the mirage I had created and walk through the fire of criticism unscathed.

Which was why I chose the color red. A defiant color, bold and perfect. I relished how the velvet gown in crushed strawberry hugged my body, the small cap sleeves sliding down my bare shoulders while the tiered soft bustle swayed behind me, the long train sweeping over the muted Oriental carpets. A long row of pearl buttons gave off an opaline luster, racing down my back like a game of dominoes.

I also enjoyed the effect this gown had on the ladies who gossiped about me at the Viscount Aubrey's soiree when I returned to London. (You remember what I wore that night, of course you do.) I also relished the attention of the gentlemen who couldn't take their eyes off me. Especially my husband. He hated the idea of another man looking at me, even a servant, when *he* couldn't bed me.

"What do *you* think about my husband's remark?" I asked the black-tailed server as he poured me another glass of claret. My fourth. I needed no excuse to indulge in spirits. My nerves were frayed from fatigue, my mind listless. I admit the wine as well as his comment brought up my Irish dander, knowing as I do my susceptibility to lose my tongue when imbibing spirits, so I tossed aside any reserve I held in abeyance.

"I beg your pardon, your ladyship?" the server answered quickly.

"*Am* I trying to seduce you?" I drank the wine quickly lest I spill it on my gown and sour the rich red color with a dark stain. The wine teased my tongue with its tartness as I swallowed it, the choker of diamonds around my neck bouncing up and down when I tightened my throat muscles. I held my glass up and the waiter poured me another with hesitation.

"Whatever your ladyship wishes," he answered automatically, without moving a muscle in his drawn face, then realized too late the consequences of maintaining his cool exterior.

I smiled at my husband, showing my teeth as I answered him. "You see, my dear husband, you're not the only man I've charmed with my…wit."

James threw his head back and laughed. "I may have agreed to your terms, my dear wife, but the game between us isn't finished." He glared at my cleavage, smacked his lips, then took another bite of his half-eaten salmon, pink and moist. He rolled his tongue over his lips, teasing me. "Seeing how I've yet to taste your American…*wit*."

I ignored his sexual innuendo, preferring instead to stir up naughty mischief of my own, something, *anything* to assuage the emptiness in my soul. I refused to allow his remarks to hurt me, though I suffered from an illness of the mind brought on by the infusion of indulgence when a loving touch would have meant so much.

"Then I shall order dessert to tempt your palate." I waved at the waiter who hadn't moved a muscle, though I detected a persistent twitch under his right eye. "Bring us a tart."

He cleared his throat. "What kind, milady?"

"It doesn't matter," I said. "Blond or brunette will do."

"*Your ladyship,* what you ask for is…indecent," the waiter sputtered. "We are a *reputable* establishment."

I pushed my empty plate away from me. "The man refuses to serve me, James. What are you going to do about it?"

"Shall I shoot him?" he asked, the intent in his voice not serious, but the waiter didn't know that. The poor man's shoulders slumped and his eyebrows flew upward. He bowed and excused himself without delay, leaving us alone to play out our depraved game in private.

"I'm surprised you didn't flog him," I mocked, picking up my napkin and twisting it around my fingers. "Isn't that more your style?"

James leaned forward, resting his elbows on the table in a laissez-faire attitude. "I prefer a plump, feminine bottom to satisfy my need."

"*Any* female, James?" I probed, pricking his mind with my verbal needle. "Or must they be young and saucy?"

"I prefer virgins." He pulled the cork from the wine bottle the server had left on the tray and stuck his forefinger inside. "They're tight and *so* willing."

I ignored his blatant exhibition of erotic double entendre and drove home my point. "Like the poor girl you ruined in London?"

"Which one?" he dared to ask, making a popping sound as he withdrew his finger from the bottle. He licked his finger clean, his eyes never leaving mine. I couldn't suppress a shiver at the thought of him probing inside me with his fingers, then licking my juices. I preferred my dildo.

"The girl's name was Lucie," I said. "I stopped her from jumping out of the library window on the top floor."

I remember that afternoon before tea, scrambling as I was to procure a new story to titillate me, when I heard sobbing coming from the library. I opened the door to see the young maid teetering on the window ledge, her cap missing, her apron and shoes tossed onto the floor, her body poised and ready to jump. Only by the grace of God and a quick Hail Mary—and with my promise to find her another position in a Mayfair residence was I able to talk her out of jumping.

"The poor girl was desperate," I continued, "when Lord Penmore's housekeeper found out she fell victim to your charms and sacked her."

"Lucie fancied herself in love with me." James ran his finger up and down my cheek in an intimate manner, making me squirm. I *hated* him for it. "It happens with women, you know. I'm powerless to stop it."

"You can't have every woman you wish, James."

"Can't I?"

"No."

"You won't admit it, my dear wife, but you *want* me to flog you. Yet you're afraid of what you'll feel when I do."

"I don't know what you're talking about," I insisted.

He leaned in closer to me, his voice heavy with anticipation as he whispered, "The ecstasy, the thrill, the joy when my whip finds the curve of your lovely arse, that curious romantic dichotomy of pain and pleasure, the inescapable emotional confusion racing through you that seems at once both wicked and frightening. I guarantee, you'll *beg* me for more."

I tried to turn away but he grabbed my wrist and squeezed it hard, hurting me. "Let me go, James."

"No, I want to see your legs spread, your buttocks up in the air," he continued, "your lower lips opening and closing, aching for my cock while I strike your arse with my flogger—"

"You'll never touch me," I said, pulling away from him and bolting from the table to rid myself of his reckless threat. Throwing on my wrap, I raced out of the restaurant, not looking, not seeing, my emotions overtaking my reason until I heard the barking of the seals on the rocks below. I stood on the edge of the cliff, my blinding anger making me oblivious to the wet, violent winds tearing at my marron-colored satin cloak, the deep red silk lining becoming soaked and making it difficult for me to walk along the soggy earth on the edge.

As I put one foot in front of the other, I became aware of a simmering fear of this man. It was a revelation that came from my deepest inner self, a cry from my unconscious not to be seduced by his words and threats, to retreat, though I wondered if there was any possibility of escape from my husband's arrogance and hunger for debauchery.

Fearing he'd find me, I searched the shadows for his distinctive figure, his body sloped to one side, but I saw nothing. Instead, a cold, callous wind slapped me in the face, making its presence known to me. I shivered then turned back toward the sea, dragging the train of my opulent gown in the soggy dirt behind me. Where had the sudden storm come from? The carriage ride along the Point Lomas toll road had been pleasant enough, followed by an early dinner at Cliff House. No clouds in sight. I pulled my cloak around me. The oncoming storm didn't bode well for our journey to Yokohama. What would happen to me when we arrived? I had been briefed by the Viscount Aubrey and the Foreign Office to be prepared for a society where no one said what they meant, to do anything required of me by the mikado's government, to keep my opinions to myself (in Japan, James was quick to tell me, a wife could be divorced for talking too much) and *not* to ask about geisha.

I had to smile at that last request. I already knew about these sensuous women from Lord Penmore's letters and the floating world of sexual arts where they plied their trade. No, it was more than apprehension about my trip to Japan causing me discomfort. I rubbed my forehead, but to no avail. I couldn't explain it, but a feeling of anxiety took hold of me and wouldn't let go. My good humor and impish sense of play had dissipated, something I'd noticed happening more often. My mother would say it was because I was growing up and taking my place in society. I suppose that meant I would turn into a gossipy, sour-faced matron tugging at her corset garters and trying to hide her protruding stomach. *Where was the excitement, the thrills, the adventure?* Though I was barely twenty years, I had been bestowed the prestige and power of someone far older in experience, someone able to flow with the expansion of their world, knowing they were powerless to stop it but accepting it. I, on the other hand, was sorely lacking in confidence about representing western womanhood in the mikado's court when I was yet a virgin.

I remained standing along the edge of the cliff, the incessant noise of the seals adding to my throbbing headache, the hinges holding my psyche together lopsided, threatening to come loose and reveal a different reality beneath the surface of my carefully costumed self. I took deep breaths as waves dashed against the rocks below, while howling seals rushed about in a maddening frenzy to escape the wild breakers covering them in spray and foam. I reveled in the rush and excitement, wanting to stay here, live only for this moment with the wind whipping my cloak around me. So intent was I in relishing the solitude, I didn't hear the sound of familiar footsteps behind me.

"You can never escape me, my dear wife." *James.*

"Can't I?" I refused to turn around and face him, though I'd no doubt my dismissal of him fueled his passion.

"No. You denied me my spousal rights on our wedding night, but I promise you it shan't happen again. *You're mine.*" He enunciated each word, tightly controlling his voice so I could hear him against the pounding surf, his hot breath on my neck, burning my skin with his intent.

"We made a bargain, James, in case you've forgotten."

"I can make you change your mind," he said.

"You can't bend me to do your bidding."

He laughed. "Your defiance amuses me since I alone can

tame you, pleasure you," he said, his voice low and hypnotic, believing it would have a charismatic effect on me.

It did not. In a firm voice, I said, "I wish to be left alone. *Please.*"

He shook his head. "What husband would leave his wife on the edge of a cliff with a storm coming?" He grabbed my arms, pinning them to the sides of my body.

"You're hurting me." I shuddered, his possessive grip setting off unwelcome sparks inside me. He hadn't touched me since our wedding night.

He said, "I'm here to protect you."

"I don't need your protection," I said, trying to keep the fear out of my voice. The wind ceased and all I could hear was the rapidly beating pulse in my ears. "Take your hands off me. I'm your wife and I wish to be treated with respect."

"Respect?" he mocked. "I'm only taking what's mine." His lips brushed my cheek, then he slid his hands up and down my wet cloak, rubbing my shoulders, my arms, as if he engaged in the pleasant task of peeling off my clothes, intensifying his emotional contact with me to get what he wanted.

"I shall never belong to you or *any* man," I dared to speak. Brave words. I meant them, but then I had no idea I would fall under the spell of a master with a mystical flair, a sword-wielding samurai who introduced me to the art of lovemaking with an unbearable expectation of pleasure at the sight of his sharp blade. It was I who impaled myself upon his cock, yet *it* possessed me, sending me into a deep thrusting ecstasy, losing myself in wild, burning sensations, my body closing tight around him, holding him inside me, squeezing him until his hot semen burst into me and he was spent. Then I closed my eyes and curled my nude body at his feet, satiated.

My husband, James, was not a man to bring me to such

heights. He focused on sex as an obsession, on reducing a woman to a physical receptacle for his lust. Yet he surprised me on that night with a perception I didn't see coming, though my state of mind was such I don't recall his entire speech.

"You interest me, my dear wife, though your plain looks repelled me at first." He continued his exploration of me, his words as well as his actions no doubt designed to make me uneasy. "I've since discovered your face reflects a distinct exterior which contradicts the passion and excitement raging inside you."

"James, please—"

I tried to push him away, but he possessed a strength I never imagined, keeping me tight in his grip while he lifted my wet cloak and ran his hands up and down my midriff, then, with a boldness that surprised me, he cupped my breasts, lingering on the twin mounds outlined in red velvet. I cried out when he squeezed them before circling his hands around my small waist, setting off a rather unsettling contraction in my pubic region.

"And your figure is magnificent," he said.

"Why waste your time trying to seduce me?" I asked, finding my courage. "I'm immune to your charms. Or lack of them."

My words angered him. He pulled up my overskirt and pushed his hand into my crotch, squeezing it. Hard. I fought back a scream and tried to pull away from him. I couldn't. "You had best watch your step, my dear wife," he said, "or I shall bed what is mine without delay."

"You have nothing to gain by such a foolish move," I said, composing myself, the realization that the more he taunted me to feel the kiss of fire from his whip, the more compelling my disdain for him became. Which made him desire me more. "You need my fortune to maintain the habits of your bachelorhood."

"You leave me no choice but to seek other women since you see fit to deny me my marital rights."

"Why should I allow you into my bed when you resort to debauched games to stimulate and tease poor defenseless girls and paid whores?" I challenged him with a directness he'd never faced before, though a chill of fear made my shoulders shake, my fingers stiff, my limbs waver.

"Man is a hunter," he said casually, "and I find the pursuit of my prey most enjoyable, whether it be a pretty maid bending over and pulling down her drawers for a caning or the saucy young wife of Sir —— exposing her breasts for my pleasure." (I leave it to you to speculate the identity of the gentlewoman I've left unnamed. It will make a delightful afternoon parlor game before tea.)

"You can't fool me, James. You fuel your physical needs by unholy acts because you see yourself as only half a man," I shouted back at him, so angry I was I abandoned the sensitivity I was careful to maintain around him, creating drama where I shouldn't have, the question of his manhood never before uttered under my breath.

"Don't you ever say that to me again. *Ever.*" His mocking tone was gone, his anger fueled by my rash statement.

Before I could stop him, he grabbed me by the throat, choking me so I could do nothing but sputter guttural sounds. I panicked, flailing my arms about, light-headedness taking over my power of reasoning. I had touched on something peculiarly vulnerable in him that made him even more dangerous, as if I'd wakened something hostile and vicious in him and intent on hurting me.

"How I've longed to put my hands on you, my dear wife,"

he continued, his eyes glowing with a purpose I didn't understand, "Stroke you, touch you, tease you with maddening caresses until you begged me to strip you naked, then lay the whip upon your quivering buttocks before I fucked you." He paused, his breathing hard and fast. "Yet I never dreamed how much more I would enjoy holding your life in my hands—

He made the statement with an undeniable confidence aligning itself with his malignant behavior. I realized then I was experiencing an intimate moment with my husband, more intimate than the coupling of our nude flesh, his cock probing me, thrusting into me, filling me. He had put away his mask and transformed into a madman in front of me. A frightening, dangerous, pathological man obsessed with controlling me.

Why, *why?*

Would I ever know?

"You're…a…fool, James," I sputtered, knowing I had to make him stop. I choked, spit up phlegm, my chest heaving. To my surprise, he released the pressure on my throat enough for me to gasp a breath.

"I, a fool?" he said.

"Yes. If you kill me, you'll lose *everything.*"

"Who said anything about killing you?" he scoffed, his tone arrogant and manipulative. "The night is dark, the winds fierce. My distraught young wife drinks too much wine, loses her footing on the crumbling cliff, crashes below on the jagged rocks." I looked hard into the night, trying to see his face, but the blackness of his words hid it from me. "Who will dispute the word of Lord Carlton?"

"You wouldn't dare…"

He didn't answer me, but instead grabbed me again around the neck, his fingers tightening around my throat, then he laughed, a cruel, echoing laugh. Before I could resist, he swept me up into his strong arms, his footing steady, firm. I pummeled his chest with my fists, fearful and scared but not giving in to him.

"Put me down, James. *Now.*"

"Why should I?"

"You can't fulfill your lust if I'm dead."

He hesitated, then to my relief he set me down, but he continued to hold me tightly around the waist, crushing my face, my breasts against his hard chest. I could smell the sea spray wetting the fine wool of his lapels and hear the beating of his heart. I couldn't stop a perverse rush of fear taking hold of me when I heard him say, "Our bargain holds, but I promise you this, my dear wife, before this journey concludes, I *will* bed you."

On the carriage ride back to San Francisco, James prattled on about the upcoming sea voyage and how he resolved to ease the boredom by gambling and drinking with his fellow passengers, no doubt losing a goodly sum since he was a poor cardplayer. This time I made no wry comment about his remissness with my father's money and remained silent, my Irish wit abandoning me as fear gripped me as surely as if I faced the devil himself, so absorbed was I in assimilating his threat into my psyche. I had never been so frightened as when he threatened to throw me over the cliff and onto the rocks below.

Get ahold of yourself, Katie, me girl, I need you, I could hear Da saying to me as surely as if he rode next to me in the grand carriage, giving me renewed confidence in myself. I vowed I would protect my family's interests in a strange Oriental culture, but I would never let my guard down around James again. *Never.* My life depended on it.

I had no premonition then this was the first of many tests I would face to empower my spirit with the strength I needed to become samurai. I wish I could have seen into the future, seen how this shaken young girl would defy the gods to forge her own path, but I couldn't. I remained convinced I would never feel the strength of a man's arms around me except to frighten me, control me.

With a heavy heart, I boarded the Pacific Mail steamer with my husband at my side. We sailed for Japan at midnight aboard the SS *Colorado,* a single-smokestack steamship with the American flag at the stern. We left port shrouded in a deep fog on choppy seas that mirrored the state of my soul. Salty, bitter. But the sea was also good and strong, I discovered, as gentle as a whisper when the wind was down or rising up during a storm to take your breath away. Like Shintaro. I had but to open my eyes to uncover this truth.

When will I glimpse this samurai, this warrior who creates such a stirring in you? you ask, *making you take leave of your senses and crave a man as madly as you do.*

Soon, I promise you, though I imagine you've already formed a picture of me in your mind succumbing to my samurai, this barbarian as you think of him, a picture taken from the morose description of a classic painting of a maiden about to be devoured by a monstrous creature, her slender form bent over and cowering in front of this giant of a man, her manacled hands and wrists straining at the long chain he holds in his hand, while her golden-blond hair flies wildly over her white shoulders and across her beautiful, horror-stricken face.

Such a tableau makes me smile. Nights when my samurai made love to me, the soft fragrance of orange blossoms comes to mind, tempered with the rushing stream of a tiny brook and grass so green that when I lay upon it, my nude body shimmered with an emerald glow as he took me in his arms in his noble boudoir *en plein air.* Tracing the line of my neck with his tongue, he moved downward to my belly then lower to the patch of springy blond hair between my legs, pausing to marvel at its ripe color before thrusting his tongue into me, tasting the sweetness of my excitement, lapping up my juices and pressing the tip of his tongue into such places I never knew existed, then sucking on the hard ridge of my clitoris, making me burn so I didn't protest when he pushed his hands under my buttocks and lifted my hips to his mouth. I hung between the walls of time itself, praying he wouldn't stop, concentrating on every movement of his tongue so as not to miss out on his loving strokes until I could stand it no more and I cried out when he made me burst apart inside like the rising of the winds, his secret art making me shiver with pleasure…

I don't believe you, you insist. *No man would show a proclivity to pleasure a woman in such a manner unless she was the type to haunt street corners, bareheaded, raising her skirts of cheap blue silk to tempt him with a display of her dirty white muslin petticoats underneath. Surely everything you've written is a curious though provocative web of dreams and whimsies that you've woven to entertain us. Or do you seek revenge for how we treated you at the Viscount Aubrey's soiree in London?*

Your petty thoughts amuse me, dear lady reader. I seek but to tell my story, nothing more. If you could see me as I write this, you'd see the truth etched upon my face. Be patient with me. The sea voyage will pass quickly, I promise you. No long speeches from me about the uncomfortable wooden benches in the dining saloon or the lack of running water in my cabin, or the incessant rain flooding the decks or the unexpected sunny winter weather that lasted but a day. A boring, monotonous trip without seeing another ship, some days so cold I couldn't sit on deck, others so blustery and windy I kept to my room altogether.

I will also promise you this, dear lady reader. If you're of a prudish nature and find my discussion regarding my samurai off-putting, I give you fair warning: he is a man who wields two swords and always keeps his weapons at hand, a man whose desire to see me nude is so overpowering he will slice through the silk of my finest kimono so it falls to my ankles as I stand before him, my nipples hard and pointy, my skin glistening with sweat, my breathing fast. If you are yet undecided, I will wait until you feel comfortable with reading my story before I continue. I suggest you go shopping, buy a new corset or have your dressmaker add a fashionable new bustle to last year's gown. Then relax with a cup of mint tea and mull over what I've said. When you're ready to accept the idea of my coupling with such a man, this samurai, pick up my book and turn the page and you will be in Japan.

Until then I shall sit upon my heels and indulge in pleasuring myself with a most interesting item I brought back with me from Tokio, a charming leather dildo attached to my ankle by red silk ribbons. As I rock back and forth, it moves in and out of me…

6

Gulf of Yedo, Japan

A breeze sprang up when we steamed into the Gulf of Yedo, parting the gray mist with a subtle hint of blue showing itself for the briefest of seconds then vanishing, like the kimono sleeve of a geisha girl disappearing behind a sliding door. Disappointment came over me since I had left my breakfast untouched in the dining saloon and raced out on deck to catch my first glimpse of Japan after more than three weeks at sea. But it was as if the steamer sailed through a milky gauze, an open portal if you will, to a land stilled by time, a land washed in grays and charcoals to keep it so, as if the divine Painter Himself decreed it.

I, who love vibrant color, felt drained and listless when I scanned the rugged coast for the beauty of this land, the miles of inland forests, hidden green valleys and mountains capped by eternal snows. I could see nothing but hundreds, no, thousands of fishing boats and smaller craft called sampans with white square sails rushing out to meet us as we slowly headed toward the harbor. The gulf narrowed as we took an inshore passage to find a favorable current, passing a chain of tiny islands misted with fog, hiding from view what I would later learn was a sandy beach and low hills populated with sparse trees. I caught a glimpse of a lighthouse when we rounded the cape, its familiar summit hidden in the clouds, but little else to delight my eye, so I returned to the dining saloon to finish my breakfast. I would later discover I was wrong about the endless grayness that dulled my first impression. As with the last cherry blossom on the branch to open, I would see the beauty of this land unfurl the more intimate I became with these mysterious islands, its resplendence alive and unchanged for centuries, full of promise, danger and—

Passion.

I would know all three, as will you, dear lady reader. Unloosen your lacings. The journey you have breathlessly waited for is about to begin, a journey where you can let yourself go, the fragrance of tea and orange blossoms bewitching you, allowing you to slip beyond what at first frightened you, then intrigued you. Tempted you. Do as I did and let it take on the quality of a dream and never look back.

As soon as the ship dropped anchor outside the harbor and the harbormaster came on board, a blend of humanity ranging from the copper-skinned native in scant attire to the pigtailed coolie to the white-suited Englishman alighted from the motley assortment of boats surrounding the steamer and swarmed on deck.

I rushed to my cabin to grab my reticule and black cloth traveling bag (my luggage was, I presumed, aboard a steam launch). Before the passengers were allowed to disembark, there was the matter of examination by the quarantine officer. A British physician had come aboard ship to check the passengers for symptoms of disease and ordered the female passengers into the dining saloon.

Seated upon a cold wooden bench, I wasn't the only woman wondering what sort of examination we'd be forced to undergo. Chattering Chinese matrons from steerage and their offspring received the most scrutiny, while the quiet missionary woman I'd spoken to during the voyage disappeared back to her stateroom in a flurry of gray linen, since she was headed for Hong Kong. I would miss her presence and the smell of fresh lavender rising from her plain cotton handkerchief when she wiped the sea spray off her nose or waved it at the steward to gain his attention. I couldn't imagine when I'd see another Englishwoman again.

I, alone, remained. I expected no special treatment. This wasn't England and the deference I received strolling along Regent Street in London was of no import here. I sensed a hurriedness about the physician and the desire to move on to the next task in an orderly manner. His wandering eyes did little to ease the tension racing through me when he asked me several questions, including if I was with child.

Dropping my eyes, I faltered, hesitant to answer him. *What if he wished to examine me?*

I'd refuse. 'Tis worry enough I had about keeping my husband to his own bed without allowing any doubt about the consummation of my marriage by a stranger. Yet I was aware that by keeping separate quarters from my husband, I had doomed myself to a life left unfulfilled. The reality of what they meant raked across my heart, grabbing me, my faith shaken, my mood saddened. *Would I ever know the joy, the soft smells, the magic of motherhood?* A dull ache settled in my empty womb, disheartened as I was by the thought of a life of barrenness.

Taking my quiet manner for shyness, the physician assured me he made the same inquiry of all married women then told me that once I'd answered him, I was free to go ashore. I tried to smile, then I whispered a quiet no, at the same time wondering what he would say if he knew I remained a virgin bride?

Which brought to mind his lordship, the perpetrator of the current state of my melancholy mood. Cooing and acting the perfect spouse aboard ship, my pandering husband had disappeared down the plank and into the first hotel steam launch to arrive on mooring. *Rushing to meet his business partner,* he assured me before leaving me to fend for myself. I didn't have to be a clear-sighted muse to know he wished to be rid of me.

We shall see about that, I vowed, grabbing my travel bag and racing out of the dining saloon to join the other first-class passengers aboard a steam launch to take us ashore. With the crested waves hitting the sides of the launch and foamy spray wetting my nose, my cheeks, I looked out over the gray-misted ocean toward the harbor as we approached what was known as the *hatoba,* or pier. A most extraordinary sight piqued my curiosity when my breath caught on a wisp of late morning fog. Fuji-yama. The highest mountain in Japan towered over the islands with a presence that was indeed godly. A gentleman behind me clapped his hands in glee, explaining this was his third trip to Japan and the first time the icy-capped mountain had shown itself when the ship approached land. He was quick to add that a few years ago he was with the party to reach the summit with the first woman to climb the mountain in tow. An Englishwoman, he said. Hearing that an Occidental woman had conquered an ancient taboo in this land of tradition and obligations gave me courage and helped me believe that I, too, could defy tradition and succeed.

When we reached the pier and I walked down the wooden landing steps built of heavy planks, I saw a soft pink tint hanging over the scene, heard the babble of many languages playing upon my ears and breathed in the strong, salty smells of the sea mixed with the sweat of labor. It was a cyclorama come to life. Without warning, the loud blast of a signal gun fired. *The noon signal,* the man walking next to me said. A tall, handsome young man I recognized as the ship's clerk. Mr. Edward Mallory. I remembered his kindness and efficiency aboard ship. He had made certain my communications to my father weren't lost among the flurry of "BV" (bon voyage) messages, as they were called, flooding the ship's mail room. I nodded, acknowledging him with a smile, though it was bold of me to do so. He smiled back and I admit I flirted with him, believing I'd never see him again. I squinted, trying to get a clearer look at the westerners, native jinriki-men and Chinese coolies racing up and down the quay. The large crates bulging with slimy, scaly fish. Cargo freight discharged onto the landing pier by means of long planks. Angry shouts. Running bare feet. Pounding boots. It was maddening, exciting, the atmosphere overwhelming and heavy with exotic sights and sounds, as if I viewed a postal card of Yoko-hama harbor come to life before my eyes with all its frenetic energy and bustling disorder.

A cold shudder claimed me, the stark realization I had left behind a world I could recognize and entered a world I would find strange, indifferent, even hostile toward me. I couldn't put it into words, but I believe I had thoughts then of writing a memoir, though the soul of my story had not yet presented itself to me and wouldn't do so until I had my feet firmly planted on this rich earth blessed by the gods. At that moment the only literary thought running through my mind was I found it a pity my life wasn't a novel where the character of Lord Carlton was revealed to me in fragments and enticing pieces instead of *knowing* him to be the worthless cad that he was. Unfortunately for me this was reinforced by what happened next in this drama.

When the harbormaster informed me my luggage was nowhere to be found, I fought hard to retain my regal carriage under the patterned shade of my ivory-braided umbrella, my demeanor calm and fluid as if I swam through cool currents. Inside, I fumed. *James.* He wished to send me back to England, so why not have my trunks mysteriously disappear? His lordship knew I needed my wardrobe to define my social position. A lady without the proper clothes would not only be at a disadvantage among the circle of foreigners residing here (mostly British), but must spend her days in an opaque existence. I couldn't go anywhere, receive anyone. I'd be confined to an inner world and left to my own imaginings, much like an unhappy turtle residing in her cold, empty shell.

Damn his lordship and his games. What was I going to do?

The harbormaster ushered me inside the customhouse on the landing pier, a place where I was to experience more delays and frustration when he excused himself, and the local native official in a blue uniform and black leather boots took his place. Bowing repeatedly, he kept asking me in broken English, *Where is your luggage?*

I had no intention of explaining to him that most likely

my silk petticoats had been doomed to an afterlife among the fishes. Like you, dear lady reader, I wasn't used to being questioned by strange men, but I didn't need a male protector by my side to tell me what to do about the situation.

I left the official babbling and waving his arms about and walked outside along the long stretch of seafront, looking for my husband so I could inform him that his plan to rid himself of my presence didn't work.

Katie O'Roarke didn't run away from a fight, and it was about time he accepted that.

Muttering under my breath about the foolishness of leaving my field glasses in my luggage, I shaded my eyes with my hand, looking for James. All I saw was a boatman from a sampan sculling in and out with crooked, wobbling oars and bumping into other craft with indifference. Ignoring the waves crashing against the seawall and splattering foamy brine upon the hem of my forest-green and gray traveling outfit, surprise took hold of me when I saw my husband approaching, his attention occupied by a close conversation with another man. Lord Penmore, I presumed, but it was James I watched. His gestures were wild and excited, those of a rogue, devilish and calculating. His body sloped to one side, his tall frame imposing just the same with those broad shoulders and slim hips, like a stone god come to life, a master who, by the sheer power of his presence, would impose his will to suit his own purposes as only a man with his vain confidence could. Even from this distance, I could see his eyes alone contained the fever of a man obsessed.

He saw me. Waited for me to do something. Try as I might, I couldn't stop my body speaking to him in a language of emotion. My pace became rapid, my eyes riveted to him. Tugging on my tight-fitting velvet jacket, I told myself he no longer held a deep fascination for me. I forced myself to look away from his stare, though since that night in San Francisco I feared him more than I could have foreseen when I agreed to embark upon this adventure.

For I knew now that madness drove him.

"Looking for me, my dear wife?" I could hear James saying behind my back before I felt the brush of his gloved hand against my neck. I shivered, though not from the coolness invading the jetty in Yokohama harbor. I didn't understand why our lives were entangled in such an uncanny way, but I was certain it would lead to my death if I didn't play his unholy game. We had never spoken of his violent actions toward me, but the threat was always there. I have to admit the pressure was taking its toll on my psyche, fraying my nerves. I was tempted to ask him to arrange return passage for me to London, but I couldn't forget the worried look on my father's face, his plea for me to help him. I saw a man far older than his years, gnarled hands and sloping shoulders from working the tracks. I couldn't let him down. Or my mother, who pined for the acceptance she never knew as a girl. And Elva and the baby. I couldn't let my sweet sister suffer in a society that condemned her because she fell in love. I laid my hand upon my belly. The emptiness in my own womb ached for want of filling it with life, but I must push aside my selfishness and go forward.

I would remain in Japan.

I pulled away from my husband and turned around. He glared at me, his cruel smile challenging me.

"Where have you been, James?" I asked. "I'd like to go to my hotel to freshen up."

"The harbormaster told me your luggage was lost," he said,

ignoring me. "Surely you can't be serious about staying here. You're not the sort to survive under such dismal circumstances."

"Then you don't know me, my dear husband, because I'm not leaving," I vowed, shielding my face with the brim of my yellow straw hat, the purple mist nipping at my ankles, the silk rustling of my petticoats a strange accompaniment to the prattle of clipped accents I heard all around me.

"Then I look forward to your undoing," he said, smirking. "For I feel certain you'll not last more than a few days in this pagan country, as you aptly stated back in London."

I was taken aback by his harsh words. Was my husband correct in his assessment of my moral platitudes? Did he think I was that weak? No doubt strange smells, uncomfortable transportation, fear and more humiliation from James waited in my future. I didn't care. I refused to allow him to beat me at my own game.

"And leave you to ruin my father?" I said, planting my hands firmly on my hips. I was pushed by a force over which I had no control to make my stand, whatever the consequences. "You'll not get rid of me *that* easily, James."

With that terse statement, I set into motion a drama I couldn't have foreseen with an alarming alacrity that pushed me headfirst into this exotic, alluring world. Beguiling, yes, dazzling, more than I could have imagined.

My husband was joined by a rotund gentleman pushing snuff up his nose with a short fat finger while he observed me from under heavy-lidded eyes, their puffy hoods reminding me of a greedy serpent ready to bite its prey. I could only describe the wild look in those eyes as filled with an earthly passion no proper gentleman would extend toward a lady. (Should you guess his real identity, dear lady reader, I forewarn you: any close contact with him could result in you getting caught flagrante delicto, your drawers down to your knees, the tail of your filmy chemise tucked out of the way so as to give his lordship full view of your magnificent arse.)

Breaking his gaze, I spun around, swishing my long skirts in his direction, my quick movement startling the babbling Chinamen and local natives hovering nearby, lifting crates and hoisting sacks onto their bare shoulders. The gentleman I presumed to be Lord Penmore informed me their smiling and snickering came in response to my exaggerated bustle bouncing as I turned around (a new Paris fashion I had embraced before leaving London). Their fascination, he added, with his eyes riveted to my posterior, led to speculations that my bustle was indeed a coiled-down tail.

Embarrassment pumped through me, not because of Lord Penmore's absurd observation (James was laughing so hard he could barely get through the introductions), I imagined he also found great amusement in forming a mental picture of my naked buttocks spread out and quivering before he laid a shiny riding crop upon my flesh. I burned inside, the lascivious thought sending a different fear through me and making me shiver despite the vapid humidity and misty air. No one would come to my aid should James or his cohort wish to take advantage of me.

Still, I refused to cower like a caged animal.

I gave no indication I was under duress, laughing and chatting with Lord Penmore and commenting on the sea voyage. My ability to hide my emotions was a trait I'd learned growing up, seeing how my plainness made me the subject of teasing. Allow me to explain how this trait would serve me well. Here in Japan no one showed their true feelings, especially distress or any emotion that would upset those around them. The natives communicated their thoughts differently than we do, conveying intent with the slightest movement or a simple word. It was a way of life and adhered to in the strictest sense.

It was also a place where a tradesman in a shop turned his palms out to beckon you inside or a servant swept the stairs outside the house from the bottom up because more dirt gathered there. Stranger yet was the role of women in their society. The female sex resided in a place that reminded me of a great railway balanced on smooth tracks that ran side by side: the woman at home and the *other* woman. These feminine Medusas with their numerous combs, high clogs nearly a foot high, the childlike attendants who hovered over them with an oil-slicked paper umbrella, women who wore their elaborate sashes tied in front.

Geisha.

No doubt in my mind which woman Lord Penmore preferred.

"You will be a welcome addition to the legation here in Yokohama," Lord Penmore said, kissing my hand, his lips lingering on my kid-leather glove soiled by my sweat. I smiled, determined not to show my discomfort. In London, I often changed gloves three times a day. A silly habit and one I would discard in due time.

"Thank you, milord," I said, swaying my shoulders with a delightful dip as I'd learned to do at Miss Brown's School for Young Ladies, but not too sassy. I had every intention of playing the game, but I expected to be treated like a lady. I wanted to make certain Lord Penmore understood that. "I shall look forward to—"

"Lady Carlton has changed her mind and is not staying in Japan," James interrupted, leading me by the elbow along the seawall and back to the customhouse. Lord Penmore needed no invitation to accompany us, sniffing me like a hound about to take a bite out of a hare caught in a trap with her bottom up.

"Why not, James?" the older Englishman asked, sounding disappointed. "She has a magnificent—"

"Her ladyship's luggage is lost," James added, his change in temperament amusing to watch. Was he jealous? "I'll make arrangements for her to return to the ship where she'll be comfortable until the steamer sets sail."

"You'll do no such thing, my dear husband," I said, resentful at being discussed by the two gentlemen as if I were a piece of barter to be traded back and forth. "I intend to stay in Yokohama and replenish my wardrobe."

"I *forbid* you to remain here," James said in a harsh whisper, his grip on my arm tightening.

"I don't believe you're in a position to *forbid* me to do anything," I retorted, pulling away from him. "We have an agreement, in case you've forgotten. Things are no different here than they were in London."

"Don't be so sure, milady." He curled his upper lip in a nasty snarl, marring the usual attractiveness of his full and sensual mouth. "You can't escape me *wherever* you go, remember that."

I ignored his threat. "The Viscount Aubrey is expecting me to represent him at the British Legation in Tokio and I intend to complete my mission even if I have to dress like a geisha girl with needles sticking out of my hair and clogs on my feet."

Lord Penmore threw his head back and laughed. "Egad, James, you picked yourself a spirited wench."

His big, hearty guffaw drew stares from the bustling natives and few westerners meandering along the stretch of the seawall on foot or riding in what I recognized from the postal cards in his lordship's letters as jinrikishas. That gave me an idea. I spied an empty vehicle and headed toward it.

"She may have spirit," James said, his absorbing glance drinking in my obstinance but not releasing me from his power. "But her ladyship's talents won't save her if she loses her way again in the dark."

"I don't expect I shall be caught unaware the next time," I said with bravado. Holding my parasol over my head, I climbed into the waiting conveyance. *I refused to yield to him.* I motioned for the young fellow manning the jinrikisha to take off before James could stop me. I had no idea *where* I would find western clothing, but it didn't take a seasoned globe-trotter to figure out the nearly naked native pulling the big, two-wheeled baby carriage could take me somewhere, *anywhere* where I'd be out of his lordship's reach. That old fear from that night in San Francisco revisited me, making me shiver. Or had it never gone away?

"Lady Carlton, *Lady Carlton!*"

I set my lips in a grim line, determined not to be deterred from leaving, though instinct and good hearing alerted me it wasn't James or his pompous business associate calling me.

"Yes, I'm Lady Carlton. Who are you?" I asked, turning around to see a gentleman jabbering with the jinriki-man in Japanese, the native bowing over and over and putting down the shafts. The newcomer was a portly man with a stout face, his brown tweed suit cut with a flair one would find on Bond Street, the wide-brimmed white hat pushed back on his head, his hair and scraggly sideburns the color of dried spice. Who was he? And how did he know my name?

"Seymour Fawkes here, milady," he said, tipping his hat and

presenting his card to me. "The British Legation sent me to meet you. Sorry I'm late, but I had pressing business."

"What could be more important than attending to her ladyship?" James dared to inquire, his sarcasm not lost on Mr. Fawkes nor me.

Ignoring my husband, a slight which endeared him to me immediately, Mr. Fawkes said in his clipped British accent, "You'll be pleased to know, Lady Carlton, I've found your missing luggage."

I'd like to take a moment, dear lady reader, to reflect upon that day and meeting Mr. Fawkes. He was a sly and learned gentleman, a speaker of many languages and a man who enjoyed his rum. On this misty February morning he was also a sleuth. He had come on board the steamer when I was with the quarantine officer and, when he couldn't locate me, he inquired about my luggage. He informed me it was his duty to make certain my trunks and portmanteau were loaded onto a hotel steam launch and deposited at my accommodations in Yokohama. After questioning several natives, he discovered a gentleman had paid them to hide my luggage in the cargo hold until the ship left port.

An *English* gentleman.

My dear husband, no doubt.

And now you know the tale of my missing luggage, a footnote at best, but important to my story not because I considered it part and parcel of my femininity, but because it granted me a valuable ally in Mr. Fawkes against my husband, something I would need in the months to come.

On a personal note, I found Mr. Fawkes to be entertaining and intelligent and I miss his funny habit of checking his gold pocket watch for the correct time whenever he mulled over a problem. He preferred the native system of telling time with hours of varying length. *Imagine what one could accomplish with more time as needed?* he often lamented.

Mr. Fawkes was what was known in Japan as a broker, an English gentleman who earned his sustenance by concluding a business transaction for two parties in need of a go-between. He earned a commission for his services and no proper native official would conduct business with a foreigner without one. The Viscount Aubrey had arranged for him to be a bridge between the mikado's government and me.

On the personal side, Mr. Fawkes claimed to be a man of letters, a great reader of the classics and travel lore, which led him to the Orient years ago in search of cultural endeavors. His sharp hazel eyes noticed every detail, whether it was a loose thread on a kimono sleeve or a nervous hand clutching a sword, but he retained a simplicity about his observations that allowed him to go beyond what was on the surface. That trait was what induced him to accept this Irish lass with my tall, lean frame and mess of blond hair, not to mention my stalwart insistence to turn a phrase even at the most inopportune time, though he was quick to point out to me I would have to work hard to understand the natives.

He could also laugh at his own foibles, such as the spot on his head as bald as an infant's bottom and his abundant paunch, which he carried with pride as a sign of a man well paid for his talents. His callused hands and ruddy complexion reminded me more of a man who worked in the fields, though I never questioned him about it. He was a true gentleman, so unlike my husband and his cronies with their righteous countenance, men who hid their perverse desires under a genteel persona. Mr. Fawkes was a right-minded, common man who didn't subscribe to the idea that the aristocracy was beyond reproach. He was also a dear friend and a man I shall never forget.

"Why did the legation send *you*, Mr. Fawkes? And not a native official?" I asked, holding on to my yellow straw hat (I noted the jinriki-man wore a similar straw hat, though his was flat and shaped like the head of a mushroom) as the runner hoisted up the shafts of the jinrikisha, I mean, *kuruma* (the local European residents preferred the native word to the Chinese phrase) onto his broad shoulders and took off in a fast trot. I couldn't stop smiling, turning and seeing James and his business associate mumbling interrupted phrases of a non-delicate nature. Mr. Fawkes's appearance had riled my husband's anger (to my intense delight) and ruined his plans to rid himself of my presence.

"Besides my charming personality," Mr. Fawkes answered without a trace of ego, "the natives are a rather shy people when it comes to expressing themselves, especially with *gaijin*—"

"*Gaijin?*" I repeated the strange sounding word.

"Foreigners. The natives fear making mistakes and embarrassing themselves," he said as I listened intently, trying to understand. "To counter that, they have this bourgeois habit of thinking over everything before answering you, and when they do they speak in short syllables."

How well I remembered his words when I met my samurai, grunting but making his meaning clear regarding his interest in me. At that moment, I had another thought on my mind. "Where are we off to, Mr. Fawkes?"

"Arrangements have been made for you to stay in a house built for foreign guests on the Bluff," Mr. Fawkes said casually, "since private inns often refuse admission to *gaijin* because they fear and distrust us."

I decided against asking why this was so, since it took no stretch of my imagination to surmise James wasn't the only profiteer who had come to Japan in search of launching a quick business venture for monetary gain.

"Is Lord Carlton aware of our living accommodations?" I asked, curious.

Mr. Fawkes took out his gold-plated watch, looked at the time, then closed it again. In a dry voice he said, "His lordship has made *other* arrangements."

I feigned disappointment, but I was secretly relieved to be residing on the Bluff and not in what Mr. Fawkes called the settlement. He told me James had elected to take rooms at the International Hotel on the Bund, the street facing the bay. The Englishman assured me his lordship would be more comfortable in town with billiard tables to amuse him as well as the nearby United Club, where the gentlemen gathered to discuss business. He was too discreet to mention what *other* entertainment was available in Yokohama, though he hinted that *he* frequented the rum mills. Knowing my husband, I was certain his lordship would pursue the lurid delights of the geisha. I imagine he was relieved to have Mr. Fawkes tend to my needs, leaving him at liberty to pursue his affairs without an inquisitive wife checking his every move. I dare say his thinking was premature. I had no intention of allowing his lordship complete freedom. I had promised my father I would keep an eye on his business interests, which meant checking with the bank manager to make certain James delivered the funds for the railway into the proper hands and not squander them on heavy gambling losses.

"Why wasn't I also given hotel accommodations?" I asked

Mr. Fawkes, sinking into the cozy vehicle and running my fingers over the decorative shells adorning the padded door. I couldn't keep the inquisitive tone out of my voice. I wondered what other games James had planned to make sure I was out of his way. I allowed that thought to fade as the man-cart spun down the road into a section consisting of odd little streets. Native Town, Mr. Fawkes called it, with its little shops and hanging blue curtains out front inscribed with amusing English translations to beckon the shopper inside. I couldn't deny the energy and expectancy in the air sent a strange thrill through me I couldn't put into words. Similar to what I'd experienced when I first saw London, but different somehow. There I was a girl from a cloistered farmhouse in the Pennsylvania woods, thrust into a hedonist British society. Here I was a member of the glorious, elegant world of wealth and privilege who found herself in a kaleidoscope of an Oriental fantasy. A rising curiosity grew in me, a lust to try something new, a lust that would tempt me to risk everything no matter what the consequences…for one man.

"The International Hotel on the Bund isn't completed yet, Lady Carlton," Mr. Fawkes said, answering my question. "You'll only be here a short while before taking the railway to Tokio."

"I hope you will accompany us to Tokio?" I asked him, not shading my words with a subtle innuendo. "In case my luggage is lost again?"

He smiled, then nodded. "Most definitely, your ladyship."

I returned his smile. I knew then I had found a friend.

7

The Bluff, Yokohama

I wrote down my thoughts today while heavy raindrops beat down on the curved roof, a new hunger coming to my soul. Loneliness. I watched the days flow past and the sun setting, housebound as I was within these four walls, so I set pen to paper and began to write. Meanderings, short notes, nothing of an erotic nature as I have written in this memoir, for then I had not tasted the sweetest fruit thick with a man's juices. Instead, I pondered writing a travel journal. I came upon the idea from the missionary woman I conversed with aboard ship. The gentle creature smelling of lavender water told me she kept copious notes about her journey, everything from her favorite meal of baked mutton pies, green string beans and custard pudding to the suffering Chinese woman in steerage she gave comfort to when the woman's child arrived stillborn during the voyage. I do not have her dutiful memory nor her courage, so I wrote about my adventures in a breezy, careful manner, hoping to capture my impressions and regale the reader with humorous and interesting escapades of my visit when I first arrived on the Bluff. Notes that served me well when I sat down to write this memoir.

My first day in Japan included trekking up a steep hill road to the Bluff, what the natives call Root Bank Mountain. I may not have been so eager to agree to Mr. Fawkes's invitation to take up residence here had I known our mode of travel. I balked at riding in a crude imitation of a palanquin (a contraption resembling a shallow basket with a high back slung from a pole and carried on the shoulders of two natives). It required its occupant to sit on their feet with their knees doubled under them while they rocked back and forth. I elected to ride on horseback, taking the time to let the animal get to know me before mounting him.

I followed our native guide up the mountain with Mr. Fawkes trailing behind us, grumbling that only a Yankee woman would insist on such a breach of female conduct (I imagine he rather enjoyed the view of my rump bouncing up and down). My trunk and portmanteau followed us on packhorses led by coolies pulling them along with long cords. I can't tell you how exhilarating it felt to be astride a mount again, the air crisp and cool, the feel of the reins in my hand, the hard flanks of my horse rubbing against my inner thighs and stimulating me with a throbbing and burning against my clitoris with every beat of my heart and causing me to shudder in a very unladylike manner. Do you think Mr. Fawkes noticed? And if he did, did he turn his eyes away? We shall never know, dear lady reader.

Along the way, the Englishman pointed out the sights to me, including the race course, the various consulates and the foreign cemetery, including the graves of the brave souls buried there who had their heads cut off by rebellious samurai ravishing the area and slashing telegraph lines. (Had James put him up to frightening me with such wild tales? I wondered.)

What induced the natives to such vile tactics? I begged to ask him, questioning the logic of my journey if at any moment I could be attacked by samurai. Mr. Fawkes smiled, assuring me I had nothing to fear. British soldiers had been posted on the hill to protect foreigners, he said, but there was no need for that since the mikado's government had reduced the status of the samurai and removed their power. An occasional disgruntled samurai might cause a ruckus, he continued, but what outsiders didn't understand was that these brave warriors had followed a code of loyalty and obedience for centuries and were defending their way of life.

As we continued our journey, I couldn't forget his words. Something in his voice, in the way he said it, stayed with me. A deep respect for these men and the "way of the warrior," as Mr. Fawkes explained it. Strange how his words caught in my mind and hung there unseen, only to reappear again at the oddest moments months later in the samurai village.

I believe it was then I began to see Japan differently. The reverberation his words set off in my mind was like the roll of the drum one hears at the native fertility festivals, where giant phallic symbols feed the human need to procreate. Its primitive rhythm set the tone for what you are about to read in these pages, its repetitive musical pattern impossible to erase from your mind, as Shintaro is impossible to erase from mine.

When we arrived at the Bluff residence assigned to me for my short stay in Yokohama, a charming native woman called Fusae met us at the entrance, kneeling, her forehead to the mat, bowing and mumbling words I could not decipher. Mr. Fawkes indicated I should say nothing, then motioned for me to remove my shoes and leave them in the tiny foyer. He clapped his hands and a young maid appeared from nowhere. Her name was Yuko. She bowed many times before helping me into a pair of thin slippers, then Mr. Fawkes.

"After you, Lady Carlton," he said, taking my hand and assisting me up the small steps to a polished platform. I followed him down the hall to an airy receiving room furnished with a low black lacquer table, a vase with a single white lily placed in a recessed alcove and two large black silk ottomans. I put down my reticule and removed my gloves, my eyes lingering on the cushion. The idea of resting my sore buttocks upon that lovely silk was irresistible.

Too stubborn to ask for help, my Irish pride and my bustle got the better of me when I sat down and slid off the cushion and onto the matting, my legs flying up into the air, my layers of petticoats and skirts covering my face. I was a sight to behold sprawled out on the floor, laughing, with poor Mr. Fawkes trying to pull me up without grabbing the wrong part of my anatomy. Yuko joined in and together they pulled me to my feet, all three of us laughing. Before I could thank her, the girl hid her face with numerous bows, her forehead to the floor. When I asked Mr. Fawkes why, he said it was customary for a servant to put herself in that humble position to show respect. Fortunately, Fusae found a collapsible stool, providing me with the means to sit with my dignity *and* bustle intact. I am pleased to report I enjoyed the rest of the afternoon drinking foaming green tea and eating cakes, the stool allowing me to save face as well as my saddle-weary arse.

That first night on the Bluff in Yokohama was cold but strangely quiet, the grass-crickets showing their respect by silencing their chirping and incessant cries at an early hour. I shooed the maid out of my room after she helped me un-

pack, grateful the previous occupant was a pampered Englishman who preferred sleeping in a four-poster than on the
floor. I snuggled under the silk maroon futon spread out on
the bed, wearing nothing but my thin muslin chemise, its
sensuous touch as smooth and subtle as a man's hands caressing my breasts, belly and thighs. Daring? Yes. I may as well
have been nude since a lady's chemise is regarded by many as
provocative as it's worn next to her skin.

Soon after I closed my eyes, the silence gave way to what
I thought was heavy breathing, as if someone had slipped into
my room unannounced, his presence arousing but dreamlike.
Clutching the silk up to my chin, I waited, listening intently.
The breathing stopped. Shivering, I listened again. Nothing.

Exhausted, I fell back to sleep, but I woke up more than
once, convinced a man was in my room, standing at the foot
of my bed, watching me. His powerful presence overwhelming my senses with a strange desire that heated my groin, made
my nipples hard. *A samurai*. Tall, powerfully built, a warrior
come to strip the filmy chemise from my body, his need as
wanton as mine. In the chilly darkness his hands became his
eyes, tracing a delicate pattern over the fullness of my breasts
then down over my flat belly to the gentle rise of my mound,
parting my legs and winding his fingers through the silkiness
of my pubic hair before teasing my lower lips with playful
touching. He eased them apart and explored the moist pink
folds with the fleshy pads of his fingers until I felt a warm
wetness gathering, then trickling down the insides of my
thighs. Before I could say, *do,* anything, he slid two fingers
inside me and probed me with a surety that made me tremble,
then cry out when he found the tiny bud never before pleasured by a man's touch. He rubbed it vigorously over and over
until an erotic sensation surged within me, my muscles con-

tracting and sending me into a heady spiral of ecstasy, giving me the release I needed, I craved—

I sat up. Awake. Panting, bathed in sweat, my body writhing in pleasurable contractions, my emotions soaring into a fantasy of my own creation. Was it a ghost? Perhaps. Yet his image was so real to me I could smell the muskiness of his scent lingering upon my chemise wet with perspiration. I reasoned my mind had acted upon everything I'd seen, heard, touched since arriving in Japan. The excitement on the pier, the trek up the mountain, the wild stories about samurai. No wonder I retreated into a dream.

Yet a truth revealed itself to me that night, dear lady reader, one that would dictate my outrageous behavior in the weeks to come, for I no longer found satisfaction in the particular delight a dildo afforded me. I hungered for more.

I needed a man and needed him badly.

The next morning I awakened to discover those wonderful roaming fingers were neither human nor ghostly. Insects crawled around my futon, vile little creatures with squiggly legs and ugly, round bodies. A cry of horror escaped from my lips, bringing Yuko scurrying to my room, bowing. She quickly remedied the situation by sprinkling what she called *sho-no* over my bedding, a powdered camphor.

Taking a bath proved to be a more difficult chore, with the maid insisting *she* wash *me* with a small white cloth before I could enter the round cedar tub with steaming hot water. I shook my head no. Neither of us would relent, so we compromised. I allowed her to wash my back and arms with soapy water from a small bucket while I sat on a low stool. As I sat astride the stool with a hole in the middle, I imagined the maid washing the previous occupant, a staid Englishman. I tried to put my foot through the hole, but the maid giggled and motioned it was for the man's genitals to hang down through.

I must add I insisted on wearing my cotton chemise both *in* and *out* of the tub, much to the maid's dismay. I have to smile at my modesty since later I would strip nude without shame. Don't be so prissy. Cover these pages with your fan if you're squeamish, dear lady reader, for what I'm about to reveal to you may be disturbing. Aboard ship, I overheard a fellow passenger telling a shipmate he was anxious to visit a Tokio public bathhouse where men and women bathed *together*. (Eavesdropping is a habit of mine; though not necessarily an Irish trait, we're better at it than most.) *Tiled establishments with wooden vats heating up the water to extraordinary hot temperatures,* he said, *with nude women washing themselves outside the tub in full view of the men.*

"Sorry to spoil your fun, old chap," I remember his shipmate saying, laughing. "But the Tokio baths have since installed a railing between the men and woman, shielding the other sex from view."

Shocking? At the time I thought so, as well, dear lady reader, but that would change, eager as I was to shed my brand of innocence, eyes open, ears peaked. In the hot summer months, I would stand nude under a crashing waterfall with my samurai, our bodies touching, keeping me breathless, my nerves bristling with anticipation, his hands searching for my breasts, pinching my nipples before parting my legs and sliding his cock into me. Not an easy feat, I assure you, but it happened, as you shall see in a later chapter.

When I finished my bath, I faced a new challenge: who was going to lace up my corset? Most likely when you find yourself away from home, you have but to ring the bell to secure a competent ladies' maid. I was not as fortunate. A lady's toilette, as you know, is a never-ending barrage of buttons, fluffy petticoats and cruel lacing to attain a wonderfully cinched waist. I can publicly state I have never found wearing a corset to my liking. Think about it: your ribs crushed and hurting, the corset ribbons pretty and soft yet pulled so tightly you can't get your breath. And if you dare to allow your emotions to well up inside you, you can't regain your composure, making you act like the overwrought heroine in a very bad play.

I would soon discard this confining mode of dress when I ran through fields of tall flowers wearing nothing but a thin cotton kimono tied with a sash around my waist, my breasts and limbs free from constraint. I see you shaking your head, having heard the exaggerated stories told by male explorers about native women in hot, tropical lands who go about bare bosomed, and how their breasts hang down, shapeless. I assure you, after living in the samurai village for nearly two years, my breasts remain firm, my nipples pointy. I shall add that the constant stimulation of my breasts by strong male hands no doubt help them retain their shape.

But at this moment I needed help lacing up, and neither the native housekeeper nor the maid could assist me in the task. I tried to demonstrate to them how to pull the long, long ribbons through the buttonholes and hook them around the steel clasps, but they were more interested in snapping my garters adorned with perfect satin bows. Embarrassed, I sent them away and threw myself across the four-poster. I couldn't stop the tears from welling up. It wasn't lacing up the corset that generated such melancholy in me. It was the enervating effect of finding oneself alone and frustrated, deprived of masculine company and inhabiting a world without their stimulating pleasures. You know what I mean, dear lady reader. His smell when you crush his shirt against your face, the timbre of his voice calling you, the sudden squeeze of your bottom by his eager hand. I imagine you're familiar with that state of mind that comes over you when your husband is called away to his country estates or abroad. You suffer from a coldness in your soul for want of a man to hold you, touch you, caress your shoulders and wind the loose strands of your pinned-up hair around his fingers, his lips brushing the nape of your neck and sending a rushing fever down, down through your lower body to your hard bud burning with such heat you can't stop yourself. You move against him, pressing into his groin, moaning, not resisting when he pulls your leg up around his waist to give him better access into you. Waiting, aching to feel his cock buried inside you, the moment of feeling him inside you so quick, so forceful you cry out in surprise, your voice guttural, your need primal. You close your eyes and let him take you, the sheer pleasure of his cock thrusting into you making you shiver when he pushes himself in deeper still…

Yes, fan yourself, if you must. 'Tis true I have a sassy mouth and a tendency to say what others are merely thinking. No doubt you told Lady —— that when she caught you reading my memoir at your dressmaker's, telling her you picked up this book to learn more about Japan, being that everything Japanese from porcelain to silks to lacquerware is fashionable in Mayfair drawing rooms, and *not* to be sexually stimulated. I warned you.

Pacing up and down in my bedroom, my arms aching from trying to pull my lacings, I realized that since I was determined to live a separate life from James, I had to do the lacing myself. (As much as I respected Mr. Fawkes, asking him to perform a husband's duties was out of the question.) After several tries, I learned to do a decent job of it by reaching behind me and tying the long lacings to a slender bedpost, then walking away, one step at a time, to pull them taut, then untying them and wrapping them around my waist before they slackened too much. Not perfect, but satisfactory.

By the way, don't you *dare* tell Miss Tuttle at the school for young ladies about my corset indiscretion. It will make her wet her pantaloons.

I settled into a daily routine on the Bluff quite unlike anything I was familiar with in London. Yuko rose at dawn, opened the wooden shutters and heated the water for washing, giggling as she did so. Soon after, I sat down to breakfast, which consisted of cooked rice, miso soup (a native specialty, sour but good), roasted fish and tea. At first, I used the silver utensils provided, though with practice I found success maneuvering the unsplit pair of wooden chopsticks sitting next to my plate at each meal.

After breakfast, I tied myself to the bedpost and pulled my corset lacing tight, then dressed and waited for visitors to call on me. After days of putting myself through this exhausting regimen with no visitors (I blamed it on the rain, but I discovered James had spread the word that his wife was "sickly" from the sea voyage and couldn't receive visitors. The scoundrel), I abandoned western dress and began wearing nothing but a robe over my chemise. A silk kimono as bright as a daffodil with white flowers embroidered on it and trimmed at the bottom with a thick padding. I abandoned my corset (yes, I know, one scandal after another, but bear with me, please) and allowed the native housekeeper to wrap a wide obi, or sash, around my waist then show me how to use the wide sleeves hanging down to the floor as pockets. I twirled around in circles as Fusae wrapped the yards of silk around my waist, pretending a lover embraced me, but it was no substitute for a man's arms.

Wearing my kimono, I was at peace each morning as I sat on the veranda drinking tea and writing, absorbed in the act of what I called "pasting pictures onto the page." Words took on the job of color, shape and line, giving life to the visions I had seen, smelled, touched, as the cold, misty days continued with a late-winter rain making the road icy. I put off my trip to the settlement since I didn't wish to venture down the mountain alone until the rain stopped. I had received a post from Mr. Fawkes informing me he would be in Tokio for the next week, setting up meetings for James with railway officials and stockbrokers as well as finding a house for us to live in. I was on my own, so I continued my travel writing, hoping to charm the reader with my picturesque descriptions of the well-kept gardens on the Bluff with tall, lush flowers towering over bunches of moon-faced blossoms and the graceful ferns with willowy tails surrounding the trim houses spread out along floral-decked lanes.

Watch your step as you climb up long flights of crumbling stone steps, I wrote, *your head bending to admire the overhanging vines of blooms saturated with the overpowering smell of Oriental spice.*

I explained how the reader would be delighted and surprised by how many foreign residences were nestled up here together like dollhouses, each one bearing a house number out of sequence since they were numerated by their building date. I was Number 23 Lady. I must admit, I became attached to my little bungalow with its embroidered panels of silk stretched on the doors and the bamboo blinds on the windows threaded with colored beads. They sparkled like iridescent raindrops whenever I opened or closed them. Stretched embroidered silk covered the ceiling, while an eight-sided lantern enveloped in painted silk gauze hung from the center, casting a warm, soothing light over the main receiving room.

I wore only light slippers in the house since the floor was covered with straw matting, but I was fortunate the previous occupant preferred western furniture such as tables and what my mother called the *commodities of conversation:* chairs. I was grateful for this small luxury since I hadn't yet perfected the Oriental art of sitting on my legs for long periods of time without them falling asleep.

I was surprised to find a gleaming white marble washstand clearly installed for western comfort and concealed by a half-open screen painted with birds and flowers, but I shall leave it to your imagination as to the particulars of the necessary place (a hole in the ground). Poking around behind the screen this morning after my ablutions, I discovered an excellent guidebook by a Mr. G. W. Rathbone left there by the previous occupant. It was filled with information about the Bluff as well as a map of Yokohama, which would serve me well today. The rain had stopped and the road was clear. I was determined to go down to the settlement and check on my husband's financial activities as I'd promised my father. To do so, I needed the use of the pony and carriage Mr. Fawkes had left at my disposal. I wish you could have seen me trotting around the room and slapping my buttocks in front of the housekeeper and the maid. It was Yuko who understood what I needed and rushed down the road to bring the carriage with the native groom to my bungalow.

And since it is in my nature to find amusement in an uncomfortable situation, I shall remind you that as much as I hated wearing the damn corset, I had no choice but to put it on if I was going to go into town to pay a visit to the bank manager.

I laced up.

I shall not bore you with more than the necessary details of my meeting with the German bank manager except to say he puffed on his big cigar incessantly and looked at me as if he couldn't believe what he was seeing: a tall American woman dressed in Paris fashion, replete with bustle and train, claiming to a member of the British peerage *and* insisting on examining her husband's business accounts. Such an act was unheard of in this part of the world where the financial freedom of a lady traveling with her husband was confined to carrying a chit-book, a written record of her trivial purchases made on credit, items usually found in the fine curio and silk shops.

He demanded I fill out and sign a request form and present my letter of credit along with my signature book, the first page engraved and bearing my signature, for his perusal. I did so with a smile, knowing he wished to check the authenticity of my signature as proclaimed by the signed names of the London bankers appearing on the next line (I must note that an addendum affirmed my father as the securer of the monies drawn on a noted U.S. bank). Grumbling, he handed it back to me, then motioned for me to follow him.

Under his watchful eye, he escorted me to a private room in the rear of the building away from curious customers who, I suspected, would question why he permitted a woman to look over the accounts. With a confident smile I shut the door, thereby clipping off the burning tip of his cigar. I stomped out the flickering ashes with the toe of my boot then waited until his footsteps faded away before I sat down at the well-used mahogany desk and opened the plain brown leather tome embossed with a round gold seal. I checked each entry, the precise handwriting of the bank clerk noting every debt with James's large but erratic signature next to each item, his very long loop in the letter *J* unmistakable. I looked for expenses such as lumber for building wooden bridges, horses and oxen for transportation. And bigger items such as small tank engines and corridor carriages. I found none. Instead I noted large amounts paid to his hotel far beyond the cost of his accommodations, clubs and other establishments, as well as substantial monies paid to Lord Penmore and other European gentlemen whom I surmised had *nothing* to do with the railway business.

Snapping the large bound book shut, I marched back into the bank manager's office, demanding an explanation.

"Who is this Sir —— and this Mr. ——?" I wanted to know, asserting myself. I was angry and had no wish to be swept aside with a gentle pat on the hand like a titled lady who had signed more chits than she could afford for the month.

"Why do you ask, Lady Carlton?" said the bank manager, narrowing his eyes.

"I see no connotation next to their names proclaiming this is a business expense for the building of the railway from Ōzaka to Kōbé." My father's investment included completing the twenty-two mile stretch of railway joining these two cities. I pointed out various entries in the account book to the bank manager, among them one with the dubious distinction of having the same name as the local racecourse. "I have no doubt these are gambling debts, Mr. ——," I continued, addressing the bank manager by name, "*not* legitimate business expenses."

"I assure you, Lady Carlton, you are mistaken. His lordship has provided the bank with invoices that leave no question as to the legitimacy of these expenditures." He bristled and bellowed but wouldn't look at me. *The liar.* I wouldn't underestimate James's bribing him to fake his accounts.

"I don't believe you. You see, I *know* my husband," I said without hesitation, glaring at him resolutely, my stance not budging. "I shall have to insist you do not pay any more monies to these men from this account."

"Under whose authority, your ladyship?" asked the bank manager, blowing smoke in my face, the unpleasant scent of a pungent spice making me cough.

"I represent the interests of Thomas O'Roarke of New York," I said, waving away the wisps of smoke with my gloved hand. "The gentleman whose name appears next to the bankers." I indicated my father's signature with my gloved forefinger smudged with ink. "I'm his daughter and I have the authorization to stop any more payments from his lordship's account." I laid down the letter from De Pinna Notaries in London giving me such authority.

"Mein Gott…" began the German, his eyes widening in disbelief as he read it, followed by a guffaw of laughter and a distinct sneer in my direction. He refused to honor my request.

It was unheard of, unfashionable and quite alarming to have a woman making such a ridiculous request in his establishment, he said, cutting off the tip of a second cigar before he finished the first one. *Would I please leave immediately?*

Embarrassment doesn't begin to express the emotions racing through me. Anger, frustration, disappointment. Why is it that men refuse to see us as intelligent creatures with the ability to think and reason? We *are* more than delicate rose-buds, I wanted to tell him, pink and moist quivering little clitorises trying to survive in a male-dominated society. Yet we are relegated to either acting like perfect ladies or match girls (*prostitutes,* to you ladies unaware of the deceptive practice of street girls selling matches to gentlemen in hopes of procuring an extra guinea for the service of lighting *their* cigars). All because we crave respect for our talents and our minds, that doesn't diminish our ability to exude delicacy and refinement in the drawing room *or* the bedroom.

I must admit I allowed my gift of talk to get the better of me, acting more like an Irish rebel aching for a political fight than an aristocratic lady out for an afternoon promenade. I told the bank manager women would someday have the same rights as men, including the right to vote (women in the U.S. territory of Wyoming already enjoy this right, dear lady reader. Can Britain be far behind?). He sputtered and fumed, yelling at me in German and spewing live ashes from his cigar onto the floor as I made my exit. By the holy saints, I had no need of a translation to know I wasn't welcome for a return visit.

Popping up my parasol, I started walking up Main Street, my head spinning, my plan unraveling, map in hand, not knowing where I was going, but determined not to give up. Since the bank manager wouldn't explain the questionable entries, I had no recourse left.

I would demand an explanation from his lordship.

But where to find him?

I was tempted to go back and ask the bank manager where I could find the nearest brothel, no doubt where James spent his days and nights when he wasn't gambling. I imagined the German would have choked on his cigar. I would have to wait until Mr. Fawkes returned from Tokio to ask his assistance in dealing with my husband's reckless spending.

I kept walking, feeling strangely liberated after my confrontation with the bank manager and restless to become part of this strange new world around me. I reveled in having no social boundaries here (I didn't count the rebuff by the bank manager since I intended to remedy that in due time), no rules as dictated by the upper class, no fears. I believed nothing could stand in my way of enjoying this new adventure, not even James. I felt confident, flirty.

With my bustle swaying behind me, I livened my step, sweeping by large buildings, residences, stores, offices, the telegraph office and a clock tower. I strolled along the Bund, the street facing the sea, and noted heavy construction of a luxurious new hotel. I joined the already bustling traffic of British, American, French, Dutch, a few Danes and Norwegians, and numerous Chinese going about their business. I reveled in their curious stares (a western woman alone was an unusual sight in Yokohama), but I spoke to no one, though I was tempted. I wouldn't be scrutinized here as I would be in London for speaking to a man I didn't know. A fierce wind blew between my legs, rustling my skirts, teasing me. I continued walking, the soft cotton of my drawers rubbing between my legs and setting off a feverish rhythm tapping in my soul, a desire to break free of my solitude. I yearned to move my body to a forbidden beat, gyrating my hips against the nude flanks of a man I'd yet to meet. A vibrant breeze from the harbor hit my nostrils, the salty smell of the sea arousing my need. I dared to seed my mind with a provocative question: *James had his women, why couldn't I take a lover?*

This decidedly pleasant thought hung on the edge of my mind as I wandered up and down the main street in Native Town, detaching myself from the London world of heated indiscretions and whetted whispers. I delighted in the idea, my pulse racing at the thought of taking a man to my bed, but knowing if anyone found out and the gossip found its way back to London… Yes, dear lady reader, I suspected then I would face your wrath, your scurrilous remarks and perhaps your envy.

I put that thought aside, for the intensity to annihilate my loneliness was too great to be ignored. This delirious thought hummed within me, growing louder as I crossed the street and skirted out of the way of a wayward jinrikisha with its noisy passenger yelling at the driver, before entering a curio shop. I wandered around the shop, my eye dazzled by numerous items, including swords, daggers, spears inlaid with mother-of-pearl, bows and arrows, picture books of flowers and birds and shiny Mandarin coats.

I picked up a square silk embroidery studded with intertwining threads in indigo blue, burnt gold, crushed rubies, then removed my glove so I could run my fingers over the rippling surface of this perfect piece of silk. I wanted to feel its sensuousness stimulating the ends of my fingertips and radiating down to my pussy, my longing for a man inside me reaching such a passion I didn't hold back a flirty tilt of my head nor deny my Irish tongue a naughty turn of phrase when I encountered a certain tall, charming gentleman.

The delightful young clerk from the steamer.

Mr. Edward Mallory.

8

"I would like to buy *silk embroideries,*" I said to the shop owner, a slight man, shoulders hunched, unkempt black hair hiding his eyes, his neck outstretched as if he spent hours peeking around corners watching his customers while he rubbed his crotch. Something he did without shame when I entered his shop. I pretended not to notice his unseemly actions since Mr. Rathbone's guidebook recommended this open-fronted shop as having first-class curios (the author noted to the traveler that fabric purchases were rolled on a stick and covered with the ubiquitous coarse yellow cotton cloth found in every shop).

I wanted to buy old brocades, I told the shop owner again, indicating the lovely square I held in my hand, cut from a ceremonial coat from days long ago. He bowed numerous times, shaking his head as if he understood me, but he made no move to show me his wares.

"*Silk,*" I repeated.

"Allow me to help you, Lady Carlton."

I turned, then smiled when I saw the young ship's clerk tip his hat toward me. Mr. Edward Mallory. Tall, broad chest, good solid features, his face clean shaven without the abundant whiskers favored by so many westerners. He looked so gallant, like a gentleman strolling in Regent's Park, not a ship's clerk. Why hadn't I noticed that about him before?

I tapped the tip of my parasol on the floor, my impatience driving a steady beat that rivaled the beating of my heart. *Or was it because I hadn't decided to take a lover before?*

"Mr. Mallory, what *are* you doing here?" I extended my hand and he bowed over it, but he didn't follow the European practice of kissing my hand. The late-afternoon shadow cut deep angles into his face, giving him a strong, intelligent look.

"I was looking for you, your ladyship." His eyes danced over me in a lovely waltz, noting my cinched-in waist and making me grateful I had struggled with the four-poster to lace up my corset.

"You flatter me, sir," I said, rearranging my black felt hat at a saucy angle. "How did you find me?"

"I saw you come out of the bank," he said, picking up an ivory carving and pretending to study it. I saw him watching me out of the corner of his eye. My nipples tightened. "When I tried to approach you, a wayward jinrikisha cut me off."

I smiled, remembering the *kuruma* holding a gentleman passenger bellowing for the driver to go faster. The jinrikisha had raced down the street at a good clip, the nearly nude coolie panting, his chest heaving, his copper-skinned back wet with sweat. The nakedness of these natives no longer shocked me. Was that *also* a factor in my deliverance, my determination to release myself from my staid promise to remain alone?

"What can I do for you, Mr. Mallory?" My voice was teasing, light, pouting. I was behaving as if I'd stepped through a mirror into a different world, but at the same time aware, detached, in control. To evoke the response I wanted from him, I swished my skirts around in a provocative manner, tilting my head just so, lowering my eyes. I saw myself as a temptress creating a mood of mellow sunshine, creamy and smooth, and sinfully rich. Yes, I flirted with him, posing as I did like a play actress, but what of it? No one was privy to my sensual pantomime but Mr. Mallory—and now you. No scheming dowager whispering about me behind my back or snooty baroness squinting to see if I was wearing too much rice powder. Just the handsome ship's clerk and me. 'Tis a fine memory I have of a fine gentleman.

Mr. Mallory put down the ivory carving with all the nervousness of a man with something on his mind, but not knowing how to say it. "I heard you mention you wanted to buy silk embroideries."

I cocked my head. "Yes, but the shop owner doesn't speak English."

He smiled. "You needn't worry, Lady Carlton, you shall have your wish." Sensing he had no idea what I *really* wanted, I remained silent, my newfound liberty to seek my own pleasure teetering on the edge of a precipice. All I needed was a smattering of courage to jump off. I listened intently as he said a few words in Japanese to the shop owner, who nodded and disappeared to the back of the store.

"I'm impressed, Mr. Mallory, how well you speak the native language." I paused, staring at him, then before I could stop myself I said, "I imagine you're quite proficient in *many* things." There, I'd done it, opened my mouth and out popped a sensual innuendo I had no right to utter. Poor Mr. Mallory.

His handsome face flushed, startled as he was by my audacious remark. He cleared his throat several times, but I didn't hold that against him. On the contrary, his candid reaction made him more attractive to me.

"I've made this voyage several times, your ladyship, and spent many days ashore." He stuffed his hands into his pockets, no doubt to hide his sweaty palms. "I've learned enough of the native language to get what I need—"

"And what *do* you need, Mr. Mallory?" I said in a husky voice, biting down hard on my lower lip like a girl from the ramparts in search of a dandy to rub her clit with a gold coin. Yes, *clit*. An abbreviated word of what Hippocrates called the "little pillar" and one which brings an interesting thought to mind as I write this memoir. I was acting a certain way with Mr. Mallory and I am *writing* a certain way, all according to rules men set down. It seems to me when we women pen erotic novels using words *men* created, that often leaves us unhappily searching for words, descriptions and phrases that evoke the sexual experience *the way we women feel it,* not how men expect us to act. Vulgar, sassy. So I've made up my own word. *Clit*. Short and to the point. Don't be offended by my remark, dear lady reader. If I stray from expressions familiar to you, it's because I delight in finding new ways to titillate you with the language of pleasure. *And* myself.

"Lady Carlton," Mr. Mallory began, "I—I'd like to ask you if you could, I mean…"

I closed my eyes, pulse racing, trying to catch my breath, at the same time lamenting the presence of a particularly hard stay in my corset poking me in the ribs. I ignored it. I was certain Mr. Mallory was going to ask me to join him for tea at a small restaurant along the Bund. Charming, quiet, intimate. I imagined a passionate, sensual scene, time suspended in the native setting, the rhythm of two lonely people finding each other in play. It was temptation as I had dreamed it. We'd sit close, very close, sipping sweet, pale yellow tea, our knees touching, fingers entwining under the table, hearts pounding, then he'd ask me to go back to his hotel room with him. I'd sneak upstairs, wait until the corridor was clear, then he'd open the door and I'd rush into his arms, his hands roaming down the small of my back and resting on the rise of my buttocks (yes, I skipped him undressing me—petticoats, corset, stockings, chemise—so eager am I to get to the amorous part of my imagined encounter). He'd whisper in my ear how much he wanted to make love to me, his hands teasing my backside with gentle stroking, his fingers inching closer and closer to—

A cool breeze blowing in my face startled me, daring to invade my daydream, settling over me like the wings of birds flapping in my face with an insistent hum buzzing in my ears. I opened my eyes to see the shop owner unrolling bolts and bolts of silk, the gloriously light material swirling in the air around me like columns of red, blue and green smoke. Beautiful, rich silk with a tropical scent of aromatic oils wafting in the air. Next, the shop owner brought out layer after layer of old silk brocades emitting a gentle odor, incense mixed with dried flowers, I would guess, as if the silk embroideries lay buried in an old trunk for years, the moist atmosphere capturing its spiritual aroma in the fibers and not allowing it to fade.

The thickened cloth meshed with gold threads and sprinkled with designs of pine, plum and peach enchanted me, my heart pounding as my fingers slid over the shimmering fibers as liquid as the rolling sea. Waves of color lulling me into an ebullient state of mind. I wanted to lie naked in the arms of the ship's clerk, his fingers persisting in teasing the delightful little hole in my behind I had discovered once upon a dildo, the puckered aperture nestled there and the secret place I've yet to speak of (I didn't tell you, dear lady reader, because I wasn't sure how you'd react. I believe we've turned a different page, you and I, so I'm not holding back).

Eager to continue my flirtation with Mr. Mallory, I chose several old embroideries and three bolts of silk for purchase. I asked the shop owner how much and he held up five fingers. Mr. Mallory haggled with him as the man stared at me over his abacus and moved the frame of sliding buttons, calculating my bill. I reached for the local currency I carried in my drawstring, but Mr. Mallory shook his head then said something to the shop owner in the native language. He shook *his* head and answered back. This went on for a few minutes until the shop owner held up two fingers.

Smiling, I paid him and waited for him to wrap my purchases. "What did you say to him?" I asked Mr. Mallory.

He laughed. "I told him a great lady wanted to buy his wares and he should be ashamed of himself for trying to cheat you."

"You *are* a wonder, Mr. Mallory." I continued dropping hint after hint, alluding to my romantic interest in him, and still he acted the perfect gentleman. My skin crawled, as if tiny silkworms had escaped from the beautiful brocades and found their way into my drawers. *I had to do something.* I couldn't wait for *him* to make the first move. "You must drop by for tea," I said casually, though inside I quivered as I withdrew my visiting card from my beaded reticule and handed it to him. "I'm staying on the Bluff at Number 23." I lowered my eyes. "I'm home afternoons."

"Will his lordship also be there?" he asked eagerly. I didn't answer him. My mouth was parched, my mind distracted. Not exactly the answer I'd hoped for from a would-be lover.

I attempted a smile. "No. He's staying at a hotel on the Bund." I experienced a curious rush of hope as I said, "I'm all alone."

He looked disappointed, which did nothing for my ego, fragile as it was and me making a fool out of myself like a hussy raising up her petticoats to show off her trim ankles when she stepped over a rain puddle.

"I'm glad I could be of service, milady." He tipped his hat again, then turned to leave the shop.

I panicked. He was going away without inviting me to tea. "Mr. Mallory, you indicated you wanted to—to ask me something?"

He turned, thinking a moment, then, "I don't mean to be a bother, your ladyship—"

"We're both Americans, Mr. Mallory. Call me Katie," I insisted with a fluidity for breaking protocol that no doubt surprised him.

He drew in his breath, then let it out. He also took his hands out of his pockets. They were indeed sweaty, I noticed, but for a different reason than what had crossed my mind. He said bluntly, "I need a job."

"*A job?*" I asked, surprised. "What about your position with the Pacific Mail?"

"I've left their employ. I had a position lined up here in Yokohama as a clerk with the railway, but the job fell through because of an error in the paperwork at the hiring office." He glanced at me briefly. "I don't have much money left and I—"

"You want me to ask my husband if he can help you find employment," I finished the sentence for him, my face sullen, as a great disappointment rushed through me and I struggled to maintain a proper demeanor.

"Yes. You were so understanding aboard ship, not like the other first-class passengers with their snobbish attitude and barking orders. I thought you might be able to introduce me to Lord Carlton."

"I see." I crushed a silk remnant in my palm, marring its beauty, then wrapped a loose thread around my finger until it hurt. My pride hurt more. "How can my husband help you?"

"Word is that his lordship is working with the mikado's government on completing the railway line from Ōzaka to Kōbé."

"Yes, that's true—"

"I'm aching to be a part of this exciting new venture, Lady Carlton. If I could just get a chance to show what I can do, I know there's opportunity here for a man willing to work hard and get his hands dirty."

"Seems I've heard those words before, Mr. Mallory," I said aloud, thinking about my father and knowing he was once young and ambitious like this likable fellow. I put down the piece of silk, letting go of both the fabric and my fancy of taking this gentleman as my lover. How could I not do as he asked? "I'll be happy to help you—"

"Help in what manner, my dear wife?" said a man's voice behind me. Hard, cutting, the dominant tone making me stiffen. "Or shouldn't I ask?"

James.

I didn't have to turn around to know his lordship was spying on me.

"May I present Mr. Edward Mallory?" I said, not losing a step. I wasn't going to let my husband get the better of me.

"It's a pleasure to meet you, Lord Carlton," Mr. Mallory said, extending his hand.

James ignored his goodwill gesture. "Haven't I seen you somewhere, Mallory? At the cricket club? Or was it the rifle range? I'm considered a rather good shot with the pistol," he said, glaring. I took in a deep breath, wondering if he had seen the American aboard ship. I wouldn't put it past my husband to accuse me of having a shipboard romance. I had to do something. I couldn't subject Mr. Mallory to his impudent line of questioning.

"Mr. Mallory, I mean, Edward is an American and a friend of my family," I said quickly, keeping my distance *and* my virtue intact.

"Who just happens to be in a silk shop in Yokohama," James said, smirking. "You amaze me, my dear wife, with your brazenness. If Lord Penmore hadn't seen you rushing down the street with Mallory following you I may have believed your story."

"My intentions toward Lady Carlton are honorable, your lordship, and I take issue with your cheap insinuations," Mr. Mallory said, clenching his fists, his calm demeanor taking a stance I never expected from a ship's clerk.

My husband took my hand and brushed it with his lips. A sign of possession. "It seems you have a protector, my dear wife. I never would have expected it of you." James stood up straighter, his handsome face twisted into a snarl. He didn't wear his jealousy well. "You surprise me."

"Appearances are often deceiving, my dear husband, as we have both discovered." My emotions still hurt from his treatment of me in London. "I assure you, Mr. Mallory and I are merely old friends, nothing more. When you so rudely interrupted our conversation, I was trying to convince him to take up employment with you." I smiled at the American, who understood my ploy and nodded. "He's looking for a position."

Mr. Mallory continued, "Her ladyship said you're involved in the building of the railway."

James laughed. "What are your qualifications, Mr. Mallory, besides your *friendship* with my wife?"

Mr. Mallory explained how he was a telegraph clerk and also had accounting experience.

"He has other talents, as well—" I began.

"I don't doubt it," James said, sizing up his competition.

"Yes," I said with an innocence I enjoyed flaunting in front of him. "He speaks the native language fluently."

"You expect me to believe that?" My husband grabbed my arm and held it tight. "I'm not a fool."

Mr. Mallory pulled out a handkerchief from his pocket and wiped his hands. I could see his mouth tightening, his senses sharpening, as if he was biding his time before going into action. I warned him with my eyes not to come to my aid. I knew that was exactly what James wanted, any excuse to tear him down and show him that *he* was in control.

I pulled away from my husband when the shop owner handed me my silk embroideries wrapped up in yellow cloth, giving Mr. Mallory the opportunity to complete the transaction with the shop owner in Japanese. James listened, clearly impressed. I have no idea how proficient the American's language skills were, but I imagine that wasn't as important to his lordship as keeping Mr. Mallory out of my bed.

"Come around to my club at three tomorrow afternoon," James said, writing down the information on his visiting card and handing it to Mr. Mallory. "I'll speak to the head manager about putting you on."

"Thank you, James," I said, meaning it. A tenseness in my belly subsided, but I had no idea then how my husband's obsessive jealousy would force my hand in the months to come.

"My man will find a place for him in Ōzaka," my husband continued after Mr. Mallory had left, getting in one final barb toward me. "Where he'll be far away from you."

"You don't relent, do you, James?" I said. I began to see then my husband had no redeeming qualities, a hurt inside him so deep I didn't believe I could ever plumb it.

"I told you once, my dear wife, you belong to me. You'll never escape me. *Never.*"

The Irish have a saying that when the air is sweet with the smell of lacy apple blossoms and the green grass dotted with shiny buttercups, somewhere a storm is brewing, ready to darken the greens and golds with clouds and rain.

I was in for a drenching downpour, but I didn't see it coming. I was living in my own enchanted emerald land, shedding the cloak of a mere mortal and allowing my soul to become part of it, its beauty and strangely spiritual hold descending upon me. I went about my business over the next few days, noting the arrival of spring with a lightness to my step I had previously not enjoyed, learning local phrases (with the help of my tourists' guide), riding down the road into Native Town, though I avoided the bank manager, deeming it wise to wait until Mr. Fawkes returned from Tokio to again take up my request to have full access to my husband's accounts. I explored the silk and curio shops, amazed at the old swords and daggers and strange-looking spears inlaid with mother-of-pearl sold for a pittance since they were considered no longer useful.

Remembering Mr. Fawkes's words about the strict code

of the samurai, I picked up a sword and noted its heaviness as well as its sharpness. It lay in my hand, molding to my palm as if it were alive and refused to be tossed away. "The living sword of the samurai whispers many secrets," I would hear Shintaro say when he placed the sword in my hand, his fingers entwined over mine, "if one has the courage to listen." I did listen, though I admit, while I was fascinated by its beauty and strength, I was also fearful of its power.

I smile as I write this memoir, remembering how the shop owner went into a tirade, proclaiming in broken English I must not touch the swords, so fearful was he of losing face if I hurt myself. *Whoever heard of a foreign lady with a sword?* (I not only learned how to use the sword, dear lady reader, but wielded it against assassins at the side of my samurai.) He insisted I would be better off purchasing classic scroll pictures or ivory buttons or decorated rice bowls.

I allowed him to select several curios for me, but I wouldn't relent on buying a dagger. I told the shop owner it was a present for my husband, but the truth was I bought it for protection, hoping I would never need it. I didn't trust James, but my female logic insisted I had less to fear from him if we remained apart. Something he acquiesced to with little prodding from me. I reminded him I could at any time send word back to my father about his infidelity and he would be cut off from additional funds. I have to admire his brazen attitude toward me. He didn't believe I had the courage nor the will to disengage my marital status *nor* the funds due him. He insisted he had fulfilled all that was required of him and I had no reason to complain about our arrangement. *I had gotten what I wanted, hadn't I?* he chided me, sneering. I didn't try to explain to him my need for love or companionship, something he couldn't give me. He wouldn't understand, though I still didn't know what had driven him to his madness. Each day I looked upon our relationship as if I were afloat upon a great ocean heading toward the horizon, an ever-changing demarcation line I could never hope to reach.

Content to be on my own, I took long walks in the late afternoon on the Bluff, strolling through dusky gardens with paths and stone lanterns warmed by the deepening sunset, a unique shimmer upon them glowing like tiny sparks among gray ashes. Unfortunately, it wasn't the season for the delicate maple trees with their seven-pointed red leaves, but that didn't stop me from wishing I'd find an eight-lobed maple leaf, thought to be as lucky to the natives as a four-leaf shamrock is to the Irish.

At night, I set my mind to learn how to sit native style on my calves and heels on a square of green silk round the fire pit built into the floor. Wearing my kimono and drinking tea and eating sweetmeats, I'd imagine what it would be like to share my experiences in Yokohama with a lover. I wasn't thinking of Mr. Mallory, dear lady reader. A fine gentleman he is with stalwart ideals and I'd not change that about him. I am pleased to say that within a fortnight of our meeting in the silk shop, he sent me a formal thank-you note for helping him secure a position in Ōzaka as a clerk with the railway.

No, my heart reached out to find someone unknown to me. I longed for an overpowering love to parch my thirst, soothe my brow and stroke my ardor with his indescribable strength.

A maudlin homesickness seeped through the layers of my silken kimono and made me yearn for the times when I was a girl back home in our white frame house surrounded by woods, Da and Mother and my little sister, Elva, gathered around the wood fire on cold nights, eating cream cakes and listening to my father tell tall stories about what it was like back in Ireland when he was a young man during the potato famine some thirty years ago. The small market towns, the bogs, the deep hunger that lived in his bones. How he met my mother after trekking miles and miles through a wide green valley to find food at a landowner's manor house, only to be turned away—and how he rescued a pretty, young girl from the hands of the laird of the house, the devil himself. He married his Ida and together they came to America to build a new life. Such a grand tale it was, God bless him, told with all the melancholy and angst and picturesque squalor as only an Irishman can tell it. It oft brought tears to my eyes, but more so tonight as I write, an ingrained want for the comfort of those times taking hold of me and in doing so, showing me a truth that lay hidden under the folds of memories covering my soul. Yes, I'm writing my memoir about Japan, but I believe the spirit of these two lands is linked by their similar traditions of family and ghosts, greenery and rain, gods and rebellion. It was the latter I identified with the most, this rising up from oppression and fighting for the very blood of your soul to find the truth, no matter how painful. What truths did I seek, dear lady reader? An answer comes quickly to mind. I yearned to shed that part of me that hovered in the shadows, waiting to experience life, so hungry was I for a physical love, my body and imagination aroused.

I had been sitting so long, my mind infused with thoughts deep and fine, pining for the old times, wishing for the new, my legs cramped. When I got to my feet, I noticed a wetness between my legs staining the kimono. A big spot it was, angular and smelling sweet like the plucked dew from the petals of a pink rose. I scraped the skin on my knuckles raw trying to wash it out, but I could not. I lit another oil lamp and held the kimono up to the light. By the holy sainted sisters, the sight of it made me gasp. I swear to you the stain was shaped like an eight-lobed maple leaf. Smiling and humming an Irish ditty to myself, I hung the kimono over the standing screen to dry, then went to bed and fell into a dreamless sleep until—

I was awakened around 5:00 a.m. by a loud boom, a terrifying noise like the sound of artillery then a violent shaking as the bungalow lurched from side to side, nearly tossing me onto the floor. Groggy with sleep, I was dreaming I was aboard ship, the timbers creaking, the sea swelling with a great intensity, but I was soon wide-awake with the realization of what was happening.

Earthquake.

I jumped up out of bed and tried to grab onto the bedpost, my senses reeling with the feeling of dizziness akin to seasickness. I heard the oil lamp rattling on the small black lacquer table, and tiny porcelain items on the vanity crashing to the floor. The china clock on my nightstand stopped. Darkness invaded the room with the barest of a murky gray dawn seeping in through a broken wooden slat on the window, making it difficult to get my bearings before another shaking slammed me against the wall and knocked the breath out of me.

Hugging the wall, my fingers traced a long, winding crack that ran from floor to ceiling. Before I could move, another shock hit, then another, the constant shaking making it impossible for me to stand up. I flattened my body onto the floor and crawled in the dark until I found the door. I tried to push down the lever, but it was jammed tight from the shaking and wouldn't open. Trying to catch my breath, I pounded on the door with my fists, ripping the silk covering with my nails, wishing it was a sliding oiled-paper door instead of the strong European style, when I heard shuffling feet and excited voices echoing in the hall. The housekeeper and maid were calling my name. I yelled back to them, but a ringing of bells drowned out my voice and crushed any semblance of what to do next out of my head. *Fire bells.* When the ringing stopped, I called out for help in what little of the native language I knew, shaking, trembling, knowing that if another tremor shook, the brick chimney could come crashing down through the roof, crushing me.

I listened, but heard nothing. Where was Fusae, Yuko? Were they hurt? Or…no, I couldn't think that—wouldn't. I crawled on my hands and knees, my cotton chemise tearing, until my fingers found the outline of the smooth standing screen, which had collapsed onto the floor. Shivering and half-naked, I felt around until the rush of silk filled my palm. *My kimono.* I grabbed the robe and dared to stand up, hoping the shaking had stopped, then made my way over to the window, tripping on the long kimono under my feet. I was afraid of stepping on broken glass from the shattered window, but I *had* to get out of here. I banged on the wooden slats covering the window frame, managing to smash through a broken one. I gave out a loud moan when I realized I couldn't open the shutters. Since the bungalow was built European-style, it wasn't equipped like native wooden houses with small escape doors to slip out through during an earthquake. What was I going to do? I'd never experienced such a feeling of helplessness, knowing that if I did get out of the house and run, I could be hit by falling tiles and killed. Or what if there was a tidal wave sweeping across the port city with an unstoppable force?

The bungalow started shaking again. I crouched on the floor under the folded screen with my arms covering the back of my neck. Long rolling motions followed by short jolts with low rumbling noises seemingly underneath me. The natives believed earthquakes were a fearsome dragon uncoiling his tail in defiance of the gods. But it was no mythical creature that shook the bungalow so hard the wall crumbled, splattering me with debris and making it impossible for me to get out. I lay under the folded screen for what seemed like hours, saying Hail Marys and praying God hadn't abandoned me, all the while defying the gods and swearing no damn moving and shaking of the earth was going to get the better of Katie O'Roarke.

But it wasn't the gods I had to fear.

It was my husband.

"You're alone," was all James said when he broke down the door and found me covered by debris, hiding under the fallen screen and choking on the air filled with dust. I should have known he would come looking for me. His lordship had wasted no time in making his way up to the Bluff as soon as the road was clear, bringing two coolies with him. It didn't take the natives long to remove the crumbling plaster and broken glass covering the screen and keeping me prisoner.

Shaken but not hurt, I let James help me to my feet. He would have been here sooner, he said, but a fire had broken out in Native Town, clogging the area with babbling natives trying to save the wooden structures, the walls with rotted timbers split open by the quake. Chaos reigned. Frightened children crying, many separated from their parents. Small animals cowering under rocks and fallen tree branches. Frantic firemen going from house to house, searching for survivors buried under the timbers. But that didn't stop James from barging through the pall of billowing black smoke and burning embers to get to me. I had no doubt it was merely to protect his financial interests with little thought to my personal well-being.

The irony of my dear husband coming to my rescue didn't prevent me from speaking my mind.

"You were hoping to find me with a lover?" I asked, my sassy mouth returning after nearly being buried alive. A shudder went through me. I ignored it.

"If you *did* have a man here," he said, smirking, "he's a damn coward, leaving you alone to die."

"I expect you didn't have similar thoughts in your mind?" I couldn't resist asking him. "That would have been so convenient for you."

"Why would I wish to see my wife perish in this strange land when she has so much to offer me?" He picked me up in his arms before I could protest and carried me outside the bungalow, the coolies smiling and bowing before James shooed them away.

I beat my fists against his chest, trying to ignore the smell of brandy clinging to his fine broadcloth coat. He was drunk. Dangerous, unsteady. "Take your hands *off* me, James."

"I have to make certain you're not injured." He put me down but stood so close to me, our shoulders touching, I was filled with an irrational fear when he ran his hands up and down my arms, my breasts, midriff, hips, all encased in silk. I had reason to be afraid. With the skill of a man who knew the pleasure of women's flesh, his hands roamed freely over my body, pushing my chemise up above my thighs. "Your skin is so soft, so pure—"

"I told you to leave me alone." I pulled away from him so

quickly the loosely stitched kimono ripped at the seam. "Go, *now.* What if the servants come back—"

"They won't," he said crisply.

"What? They weren't hurt, dear Mother Mary...*no.*" I put my hand to my mouth, sending upward a silent prayer for them, hoping the two had found safety and were simply too afraid to return.

He looked me in the eyes, amused with what he perceived as weakness. "So my dear wife has feelings after all. I never would have believed it."

"Why do you torment me so, James?" I asked, trying to see his face in the pale light. "You have what you want. Money, women."

"I want you to come to me willingly." He shivered, whether it was from the emotion welling up inside him or his inebriated state, I couldn't tell. He intoned the words in that appealing voice of his I knew so well, but without the sarcasm, the shadings of his upper-class sheltered life gone, replaced by the haunting need of someone very vulnerable. Wanting, withdrawn.

In that moment I almost felt sorry for my husband, the pain in his eyes replacing what I often saw as a man who lived a narrow life, the low, throaty sound of his voice sputtering like a wounded animal's. But he was like a fox caught in the trap. Cunning and cruel. The memory of our wedding night washed away any sentiment clinging to the edges of my heart.

"I will never come to you, James," I said, determined not to be taken in by his sudden performance of spiritual courage for my benefit, acting like a jilted husband. "Any man who needs to whip and flog women to stimulate him doesn't know how to make love to a woman."

I didn't realize then how close I was to discovering his well-kept secret when he slapped me across the face, startling me. I put my hand to my burning cheek, but I refused to cry.

"Don't you ever say that to me again," he yelled. *"Ever."*

I was grateful we were alone. I was shaken but unhurt, a few scrapes and bruises, but I could still defend myself.

"Get out of here and leave me alone," I demanded, my fists along with my Irish dander rising. "Or I swear I will throw you down the hill myself."

"This business between us isn't over yet," James stated flatly. "I always get what I want." Then he turned on his heel and left me standing in the debris as clouds of dry dust filled my eyes, the irritation making them wet. For it couldn't be tears burning my eyes, could it?

The sting of his hand on my cheek stayed with me over the next few days, his threatening words more ominous than ever. He was planning something, but what? I didn't have time to reflect on it. I thanked every saint I could think of when Fusae and Yuko returned, laughing and crying when they saw me (I've discovered the natives tend to laugh in any situation where they are uncomfortable, even in a time of crisis). The two women had raced down the mountain road, down broken steps, facing danger from falling evergreens breaking and toppling onto the road to find his lordship and bring help. Together we salvaged what we could from the house, packed my bags and off I went to stay at a small hotel in the settlement. That's where Mr. Fawkes found me, his grand presence blustering and upset when he sat down with me for tea in the small hotel dining room.

"I feel responsible for what happened, your ladyship," he said, sipping his tea clouded with a light milk. Fortunately, the seaport of Yokohama had suffered little damage except on the Bluff, where a few foreign residences like mine that had been built quickly and without a strong foundation had been hit with the most force. When I asked him if the natives suffered many losses, Mr. Fawkes explained how they keep their valuables in a fireproof warehouse known as a godown, which is covered with mud plaster. "I should have had you on your way to Tokio before the earthquake struck."

"It wasn't your fault," I said, laughing, "unless you possess a dragon's tail."

"You wear your American humor well, Lady Carlton," he answered, wiping his face with a paper tissue. "I would have returned sooner, but urgent business with a lady kept me away."

"And what is her name?" I teased him.

"I will tell you when the time is right," he said, smiling and looking very sure of himself. "Until then I have good news."

"Yes?" I asked, curious.

"We leave for Tokio in the morning."

9

The *clickety-clack* of the train steaming down the tracks from Yokohama to Tokio brought tears to my eyes as I sank down in a plush maroon seat in the first-class English-built carriage, thinking as I was about my da and how excited he would have been to see how the natives had embraced the iron horse. The eighteen-mile double track ran smooth and fast for the hour-long trip and I could see my father inspecting every detail, whistling as he did so, tinkering with every wire and screw, figuring how to make the ride smoother, the engine burn fuel more efficiently. He loved to talk to the men who worked the tracks, loaded the mail, drove the big engines. Pulling on his suspenders like a proud rooster, he never let anyone forget he had started at the bottom and worked his way up and so could the next man.

The train trip passed pleasantly, the scenery outside the window taking an interesting turn when I saw bare-breasted native women wading in knee-deep water, gathering rice.

When I pointed this out to Mr. Fawkes, he never looked up from his newspaper, instead commenting about the sun playing tricks on my eyes. No doubt he had never met a western woman who dared speak her mind.

I didn't see a conductor during the entire trip (passengers show their tickets *after* they leave the train at their destination). When we arrived at Shinbashi station in what is now called Tokio—only foreigners call it Yedo, according to Mr. Fawkes—I had a slight mishap when my bustle caught in the turnstile in the stone terminal. After delicately extricating my silk behind, he wiped his face with thin papers he called "tissues" then tossed them away in a receptacle (I was surprised to learn the natives have used these disposable items for hundreds of years) and collected my luggage. It wasn't until then I set my resolve in gear and broached the subject of my husband's philandering. (James had seen Mr. Fawkes and me off at the railway station, reminding me he'd be coming to Tokio later in the week after he concluded his business with Lord Penmore. No doubt he meant the spring racing season, but I retained my ladylike posture and never mentioned my trip to the bank. Why tip my hand?)

I admit I embellished my meeting with the bank manager, adding a flourish about how he personally escorted me out of his establishment with his boot, which made Mr. Fawkes laugh, his rotund belly bouncing up and down like apple jelly as we got into the waiting *kuruma*. (Hundreds of jinrikishas and horse-drawn carts waited for the horde of third-class native passengers clamoring out of the train in their three-inch wooden clogs.) I believed James chose to do business with a German bank to hide his tracks, I told him, but I assured the Englishman he wouldn't get away with it.

"And what does your ladyship intend to do about his underhandedness?" he wanted to know as we rode through the streets of Tokio, my eyes taking in what was a changing city, the curio shops filled with bangles and silks, scrap and rag dealers, struggling to stay alive among the places catering to westerners. Milk parlors, barbershops and the new Uyeno Park.

"I can't get back the monies his lordship has already lost through gambling," I said when we reached the little house with the latticed front on the narrow street I would call home—a one-story dwelling with a garden and a gray tile roof. "But I *can* prevent him from losing more." I overcame any fear of overstepping my position and laid my gloved hand on his forearm. Not in an intimate manner, but in friendship. "With your help, Mr. Fawkes."

His forearm tightened, but his voice remained steady. "How can I be of service, Lady Carlton?"

I explained to him how I wanted him to post a letter to my father for me on the next steamer back to the U.S., changing the details on the letter of credit so James needed my signature as a cosigner to approve his expenditures on any bank in Japan.

"I'm convinced something bigger than gambling debts are at stake, Mr. Fawkes," I said honestly. "What it is, I don't know."

"I'd say hundreds of miles of railway track, your ladyship, and the new businesses generated along the way," said Mr. Fawkes without a trace of humor. "The natives have embraced the railroad like a new god of commerce. I'd venture to say in twenty years, they will have built more railway lines than anyone in London dreamed possible. They're an imitative lot, these Japanese, and your husband and his friends see an opportunity to make a fortune by importing raw materials into this country at a rapid rate."

I grabbed the Englishman and hugged him, making the older man smile. "Mr. Fawkes, you're a saint. My dear husband isn't *losing* the money by gambling. He's transferring the funds to Lord Penmore to invest for him and cheating my father out of the profits. The bastard."

"Your ladyship—"

"I married an English lord, Mr. Fawkes, but I cut my teeth on a Pennsylvania farm, the daughter of a hardworking Irishman and I'll be damned, but I'll *not* let him get away with it."

Full of fire and bluster I was that day, vowing to stop James from swindling my father. I had no idea then what unique set of events would make that possible, nor could I have known what surprise Mr. Fawkes had in store for me. *He had news,* he said, about the mysterious woman he mentioned in Yokohama.

"Is she pretty?" I wanted to know, prying. I couldn't help myself since curiosity is one Irish trait we never seem to find depleted and is as natural to us as believing in holy stones and spirits.

"Yes," he said coyly.

"What is her name?" I asked.

This time he laughed heartily. "Haruko."

"Are you certain she wishes to meet me?" I found it odd he wanted to introduce me to a native woman. From what I understood about the culture, men didn't mix business with pleasure.

He nodded. "It's a royal decree, Lady Carlton, from Haruko, the empress of Japan."

The empress. I couldn't believe my ears. I was about to enter a world others only dreamed about, talked about, fantasized. And you, dear lady reader, shall accompany me.

★ ★ ★

The day I, Katie O'Roarke, met the empress of Japan, was also the day this Irish lass collided outside the palace walls with the most difficult, egotistical, pragmatic man I'd ever laid eyes upon.

Shintaro.

Since that moment I've been shadowed by his haunting presence, this mysterious and philosophical master of my fate, a man who possessed my soul when he whispered erotic poetry in my ear while his hands traveled up and down my nude body pleasuring me. I once laid my trembling fingers upon the sword hanging from his belt and, by the holy beads of the sisters, I swear the white heat emitting from its blade burned my flesh. I paid dearly for my forward indiscretion when he tied my hands behind my back with damp hemp, then encircled the silken rope around my breasts before drawing it taut over my belly and down between my legs. Its twisted fibers cut into my glistening pink folds and rubbed against my innocent clitoris, swollen and hard, bringing me such intense pleasure I spot my drawers now with a fresh stain as I write…

Be patient, dear lady reader, for 'tis true I often get lost in the rich, erotic telling of my story and seek to regain the discipline to pay attention to my craft as a memoirist and not dwell on my sexual adventures. I do not use a metaphor on the page to describe his well-formed cock. I speak instead of the steel weapon that defined him, as it did all samurai, an embodiment of his spirit and a means to avenge an insult or cut down an enemy. I could set down many examples about his skill as a swordsman, but I shall tell you one I witnessed with my own eyes. It was a time, when to check the temper of his blade, I stood a chopstick on end and Shintaro severed it in two as it fell. You find that too timid? If I may be allowed a second indulgence, I shall repeat a story I heard but did not witness that further illustrates his unsurpassed swordsmanship. I must advise you, if your constitution is of a delicate nature, this may be difficult to read. No, it is not a sexual passage, so if you wish to skip it, please do so.

I shall proceed.

According to an informed source you will meet later in my story, a feared enemy of the samurai clan tried to assassinate Shintaro. My samurai saw through his disguise and lay in wait for him to pass behind the compound. When he did so, he raised his sword and, with speed and accuracy, decapitated the swine so adroitly his head did not fall from his shoulders until he turned the corner. Amazing, but true, but everything about Shintaro was not of the ordinary. My samurai was a tall man, well above the average height of natives and westerners, and possessed a strength known to few men. I state without embarrassment that I enjoyed looking at him nude, his presence filling my soul as it did my eyes, tracing my finger along the hard ridges of his stomach, the bulging muscles formed on his upper arms, his strong thighs, the wide breadth of his cock.

I must wipe the perspiration from my face since I can no longer contain myself, my longing to relive that day when the scent of this man stamped itself in the primal part of my brain. When I needed a protector, he was there to shield me from the devil's doing. I also saw a vulnerable side of him that shut out the combative world around him to reflect on the beauty of a single blossom, a part of him he was forced to suppress as a samurai, so he built walls around himself. Still, he let me into his dark yet passionate world. Erotic, mysterious, a carnal, earthly paradise of emotions and smells and pleasures so acute the only way I can soothe this unending ache in my heart for him is to continue with the scene as I remember it.

I'll never forget scurrying up the stone walkway toward the Imperial Palace with the loyal Mr. Fawkes behind me, my small red hat held in place by a luxuriously soft black satin ribbon tied in a big bow under my chin, my waist cinched, my long train picking up small pebbles in its red velvet folds, my heart racing. I shan't make you wait any longer to meet the man who pleasured my body with such delights I quiver now at this writing, reliving that pagan flaunting of his desire for me that blew like a wild wind from the cold gray sea and into the warmth of my waiting arms.

Shintaro.

A man with the force of an angry god raced through the great gate leading to the pavilion on the grounds of the Imperial Palace, the lacquered scabbard of his long sword poking my bustle when his massive frame brushed by me with all the force of a tempest whirling in a riot of color. Vibrant blue, uncanny red, burnished gold. I'd never seen a man wearing such striking colors before, their intensity magnified by his tall stature and the aroused, demanding look in his dark, forbidding eyes alerting anyone who got in his way to beware, that he plied his trade as samurai somewhere between good and evil.

"Who do you think you are?" I yelled at the man, gathering up my skirts and facing him, chin up, shoulders back with all the fire of a martyred saint in me. "Not looking where you're going, like a chicken hawk in search of his prey."

He grunted loudly, his forehead beaded with sweat, his hand on his sword, but it remained sheathed, the startled look in his eyes so gripping I had no time to pull back, react. I've no doubt in a different time, different place, he would have drawn his sword and I'd have lost my head, since a bared blade claimed the right to draw blood. He yelled words in the native language not found in my guidebook nor did I care. I stared at him openly, my anger turning into something I dared not put into words then but I shall now. *Desire, heat.* A conscious burn in my pussy as I focused all my energy on him and all my senses—ears, eyes, smell, touch—became inflamed like the bold red of a setting sun as I yearned to show him an independence far beyond what the females he took to his futon exhibited. I *wanted* him to touch me, rip my Paris silk trappings from my body with the tip of his blade until I stood naked before him, quivering with need for him…

Instead, this giant of a man breathed heavily, his eyes never leaving mine, holding back something I didn't understand then, a pain he didn't share with me.

Mr. Fawkes did his best to temper the situation, wiping his forehead with a tissue and panting as he struggled to catch up to me, the long walk up to the gate difficult for him, bowing and calling out in the native tongue when he was but a few feet from this bellowing samurai.

The samurai grunted again then barely nodded, his lack of a low bow no doubt indicating his superior status to me, a woman. I mimicked his gesture, making his eyes spew fire at me then turned my back on him. Not a wise move. I started through the gate, shaken by this encounter with the barbarian warrior yet also thrilled by the majesty of his manly presence. The sheer sexuality of his stance, the intensity of his stare stripped me naked. Tremors of a delicious nature I'd never experienced ran through me, imagining as I did what he would see, taste, if I bared myself to him and he dared to brush his mouth against my pussy lips, the moist pink folds pouting at the intrusion but wanting more—

I stopped, a sharp pull making me lunge backward and nearly lose my balance. I dropped my parasol and it clattered down on the hard ground behind me. I turned to see this man I would know as Shintaro laughing, his hand firmly grabbing the end of my train. He held on to it so tight I couldn't move. Now I was *his* prey firmly caught in his snare. I pulled and pulled but my train wouldn't budge, though I could hear the silk ripping.

"Release me at once," I yelled, hands on my hips, then I yelled an Irish expletive that made Mr. Fawkes sputter something in Japanese before I could continue my tirade, fanning himself with his hat and praying under his breath. The samurai laughed, grinning as if he enjoyed watching me helpless, in his power. I couldn't allow him to get away with his game, though I couldn't deny a humming in me that made me feel connected to him in a strange way in spite of him making a fool out of me.

Using all my strength, I pulled harder to show him I wouldn't give in to him, but it was he who let go, as if giving me permission to proceed on my mission. Picking up my parasol, I raced through the black wooden gate with Mr. Fawkes close behind, the sound of the samurai's raucous laughter following me, taunting me. *How dare he.*

It was in that moment war was declared between us.

"Who *was* that man?" I begged Mr. Fawkes to tell me as we hurried through the royal gardens to the tiny summerhouse, past towering bamboo groves, my eye catching glimpses of pine, rhododendrons and azaleas alongside rippling brooks and grassy mounds.

"Most likely an unhappy samurai from the old provinces, your ladyship," he said, perspiring and wiping his brow, "since many of them who defeated the shogun's forces came to Tokio to take part in the new government."

"He doesn't act like a government official." I'd kept my curiosity at bay as we waited for over an hour in the audience chamber to see the empress, sipping tea, then we were instructed she awaited us in the gardens.

Mr. Fawkes smiled, then said, "These fellows are warriors, Lady Carlton, and used to getting their own way."

"Someone should teach him how to act in front of a lady," was all I said, making an attempt to reel in my temper in front of Mr. Fawkes.

"A noble samurai leader is not to be trifled with," he answered brusquely. "I fear trouble is brewing within the mikado's government and the warrior clans will suffer."

Again I detected a note of sadness as well as respect in his voice, intriguing me. I asked, "Aren't they the aristocratic class?"

"Not anymore. Their yearly stipends have been cut and they've lost their privileged status. Many are leaving Tokio and returning home, what with the Frenchies setting up an army of conscripts comprising peasants and reducing the samurai to foot soldiers."

I frowned. A sudden moodiness entered my heart, knowing I may never see the samurai again. He'd struck a nerve in me as well as a physical response, what some may crudely refer to as a poke in the cunt hole (admit it, dear lady reader, you'd like to acknowledge you felt the same, wouldn't you?), but I attempted to put him out of my mind for the rest of the afternoon. After all, I was about to be presented to the empress of Japan and 'tis quite a story I have to tell you, flattered I was to be among the first of the wives from the British Legation to meet Her Majesty. I imagine that no matter how much your clit throbs with excitement now that you've met Shintaro, you are breathless, waiting to hear about my encounter with this fascinating female ruler, not more than two years older than I. A woman seen by a scant few of her people and so cloistered was her life, she traveled behind gauze-screened windows in a lacquered palanquin.

I, on the other hand, seemed to have walked onto the stage of a new era when all that was about to change. Behind the tall, towering bamboo groves I entered another world as if the players in the scene about to unfold awakened from a slumber of hundreds of years. I shall not disappoint you, dear lady reader, so I suggest you brew a cup of tea spiced with orange peel and ginger to put you in an Oriental mood and join me as I introduce you to Haruko, the empress of Japan.

The entire conversation between us was conducted in both English and Japanese with the formidable Mr. Fawkes translating our comments (the empress had requested this informality as opposed to having a court minister officiate) as quickly as we could utter the words in our native tongues. Instead of receiving me in the audience hall as her husband preferred, the empress and I walked through the gardens, the smell of pine giving off a fresh scent and the buzzing of insects a delightful background to our ears. We discussed the coming spring and the prescient opening of the cherry blossoms, descriptions of which you have no doubt heard in London drawing rooms and are well-known to you, so I shall not ply you with more.

We spoke about the recent earthquake, the building of the railway, how much she enjoyed the taste of beef for the first time (the mikado himself had deemed it introduced at court), then she remarked on my costume. I explained to the empress how quickly fashion changed in London, indicating my bustle with a gesture of my hand since Mr. Fawkes had warned me not to turn my back and to bow lower if she bowed. A slight breeze nuzzled my behind as I swayed back and forth and showed the empress how I learned to walk at Miss Brown's School for Young Ladies, making her laugh and clap her hands. I deigned to keep the conversation light and not lapse into the Irish trait of turning every comment into a story, especially since Mr. Fawkes bade me not to ask about family life since the empress had no children of her own, a subject I was happy not to pursue, considering my own longing to have a child. Fortunately, Her Majesty's fascination with western fashion encompassed much of our discussion. She was openly intrigued by my numerous petticoats and long train. Swishing my train around, I must confess, dear lady reader, I fought to keep a burning in my pussy from sparking at the thought of the handsome samurai who had dared to grab my dress. I sensed a bond between us, as if we both embraced the power of the moment and wondered where it would have led had destiny placed us in different surroundings.

Then the talk took a different turn. A most interesting one. To facilitate your enjoyment, I shall recall the scene entirely in English.

With a few keen Irish observations to liven the discussion.

"Does Your Majesty enjoy reading books?" I dared to ask, wondering what kind of literature was available to this charming young woman wearing ceremonial dress, diminutive and as delicate as an antique piece of lace spun with silk, her charm and intelligence woven together in a pleasing pattern.

"I have read the translation of several Dutch books from long ago," she answered easily, "as well as books by Englishmen on self-reliance and the rights of citizens." She explained that since the change of government everyone was free to read what they pleased, including the entertaining exploits of Ihara Saikaku.

"What stories has he written?" I asked, interested. I was in for a surprise, one with a briny taste that primed my sensual needs.

"Saikaku writes about merchants and their exploits with women," said the empress. I noted her proud, royal head never moved as she spoke. Such discipline impressed me. "Whether they be concubines in cages, courtesans or geisha."

"I have read about the geisha and find their lifestyle most alluring," I stated with surety, thinking about Lord Penmore's letters. Mr. Fawkes never lost his place as he translated my comment, but he looked at me as if I were a ball of yarn unwinding. I smiled at him and continued, "I await the time native scholars translate Saikaku's works into my language so I can learn more about geisha."

And the sexual mores of this land, I finished silently, my need to know influenced by the dark sin of my indiscretion with the handsome, brooding samurai, speaking to him as I did as an equal and not acting as a woman of my station would, swooning and having a case of the vapors.

"I shall have the famed novelist's works translated for you, Lady Carlton, as well as the stories about double-petaled blossoms," she said without fluttering an eyelash in her lucent white face, never giving away her emotions.

"I would enjoy that, Your Majesty," I answered, then without a hint of embarrassment I asked Mr. Fawkes to explain "double-petaled." My dear friend paused, then entreated me to use my imagination and regard the phrase not as an English mannerism, but strictly Oriental, since it involved the domestic situation of one's wife and one's mistress living under the same roof.

I looked at the young women standing patiently around the gardens, their pale faces placid and serene. Something in their purported elegance suggested these were not ordinary ladies-in-waiting. A gesture, a tilt of the head, a sneer. Instinct told me these were not virgins blessed with the purity of holy water, their presence subtle yet intriguing me. In this beautiful floating world, the mikado kept numerous concubines within the palace walls with the dubious title of ladies-in-waiting for his pleasure, not unlike my dear husband in his London domicile with his saucy maids with the red-streaked bottoms.

The empress bowed slightly, I bowed lower. When I glanced up, a knowing look passed between us. I understood the meaning of her words so evident in her upturned eyes, a letting down of her royal veil that surprised me. *We share a common bond,* my smile said, one I discovered that would prove itself valuable in the days to come…

All in all, I had quite an amazing day. A lovely afternoon with the empress of Japan discussing bustles and risqué literature, and a thrilling encounter with the most exciting man I'd ever seen.

And where was my husband, James, while all this was happening to me? As my dear da would say, dear lady reader, I didn't give a damn.

10

Nearly halfway through my story and I've been thinking about how I can achieve the mastery of writing a memoir. What to include, what to leave out as I attempt to create in your mind a vivid impression of what I experienced living in Tokio. Not merely as a globe-trotter, but as a western woman adapting to the native lifestyle, thinking as they do, acting as they do. I want to move events along in a fashion neither too fast nor too slow so you can understand and accept the passage of time without lulling you into boredom. (Similar to playing a game of whist at Lady ———'s on Tuesday afternoons or, dare I say, in your own bedroom.) Or pulling you along from one erotic scene to another at such an alarming speed you feel like you're unraveling, your tight lacing coming undone. Fear not, dear lady reader, 'tis *I* who am exposing myself in this memoir, creating an inner crisis within me, wondering how my work is going to be accepted. Will it be ridiculed, rejected, loved, or worst of all, ignored? 'Tis the risk I take for wishing to share my adventure with you, or if I may be honest, it is my underlying hope you will put aside your Occidental prejudices and see my life with Shintaro not as an inherently amoral, decadent affair, but for the beauteous thing it was. My intent in this tome is to allow you to travel across the seas with me to Japan and take you away from the foul smells of London, the saffron-colored fog that masks discretions and mayhem, the hurtful whispers behind fluttering fans. I believe 'tis my function as a memoirist to draw you into my grand world of samurai and rebellion and allow you to feel the riveting pulse of hard-core emotions as I have lived them.

If only you could bathe nude as I did in cold streams, scatter flowers in rich green fields, then lie on a silk futon covered with autumnal crimson leaves at the peak of their glory with my samurai, his hard cock inside you, thrusting, *thrusting* until you could stand no more. All the while pursuing these pleasures without the clouds of doubt following you, naught but a heady incense to guide you, and you would see him and his world as I do.

But I believe you're not ready yet for such pleasures. You, who look upon sex with your aristocratic nose up in the air, have become an instrument of prudery (I've no doubt you take to your bed during your "poorly time," using the queen's favorite term for menses to give it the sound of a royal decree), further adding to the illusion that we women are invalids and not sexual creatures. No, we shall continue our journey as I have, taking steps to slowly dissolve your resistance against accepting me *and* my samurai.

I imagine you have asked yourself what I expect to gain from writing this memoir. Be assured, I am not writing my story to fill my coffers (I do hope it will provide a sizable sum for my solicitor, Mr. Brown, who has well earned his fee), for I have made my decision to return to Japan and finish my life in the samurai village. Money is not important there. Family, pride, loyalty, discipline are. Living such a life demands much of me, but there I feel inspired, moved to see the beauty of nature, bend with the strength of the north wind, renew my soul with the rain.

Fear not, I have promised you an erotic tome and I shall not fail to deliver. Before we enter the scandalous floating world with its impermanence and promise of "spring for sale" whatever the season, I shall continue my recollections of daily life in Tokio, blending events together to keep you interested and omitting certain things you may find mundane. I assure you, I shall not omit anything sexual in nature. On the contrary, I find the more I write about my samurai and our amorous adventure, the easier 'tis for me to express my sensual self, let go of my shyness, prejudices, inhibitions and fears. I pray I engage your senses with my storytelling, dear lady reader, but I don't look to you for compliments, for I have learned from my samurai that the greatest compliment is given by the eyes. They tell so much more than words. Subtle, poetic, suggestive. If only Shintaro were here as I write to lay his hand upon my bare breast, twist my nipple between his thumb and forefinger, then gently suck on it.

If only…

I disliked Tokio. After spending pleasant days on the Bluff in Yokohama taking long walks among the pretty English gardens, the peace and solitude creating a special place in my soul and, when the wind was stilled, I missed the smell of roasting tea in the air. The urban smells and sights of Tokio were so varied, the old with the new, and fused together so tightly they hung over the city like a bland landscape without shape or color. It would take me many months to unravel it and allow the nuances of what I was seeing to take on the shape and form of that which was so uniquely Japanese. The arranging of flowers, house and garden design, the taking of tea (later in my story, I shall invite you to a most sensual and erotic tea ceremony in the samurai village with my samurai— *don't peek* or you'll spoil the surprise).

I would like to show you *why* my perception of Tokio changed, what delights I found, so I invite you to take a walk with me. We'll start at Asakusa Temple to see the gardens filled with goldfish and silverfish. And the old woman selling beans and toys and paper flowers. Hungry? Try a corncob cooked in steam from a sweet-corn merchant, then we'll finish with a glass of shaved ice sprinkled with sugar as we make our way through the narrow streets to the neighborhood where I live. Through the tall wooden gate, we enter my house with a heavily tiled roof and built around a small courtyard and filled with odd passages and doors that might and do lead anywhere. (Did you notice the man following us? A westerner, short, ill-fitting dark clothes, face covered by a low-brim hat. I'm certain my husband has me followed everywhere since the incident with Mr. Mallory at the silk shop, though James is rarely at home, spending his time with Lord Penmore, *where* I never ask.)

Dusk falls around us as I slide the paper door closed, my fingertips delighting in its silky texture, shutting out the coolness that is like a warning of the colder night to come. Softly, tenderly, the approaching dusk sweeps away the exquisite orange and yellow and red the departing sun has left behind like the swath of color on a kimono. When the sun goes down, the pink and gray sky gives way to twilight shadows and the incessant music of grasshoppers and other insects buzzing around my garden. 'Tis a place for solitude. I often sit there, thinking. More often I find myself thinking about the samurai I met at the Imperial Palace, sinners both of us, possessed of the desire to know each other in an intimate way should we meet by chance. I imagine we'd behave as impassioned lovers do in Kabuki theatre, thrashing about in love play. In my version we shed our layers of kimono and lay naked under the moonlight, touching each other everywhere, breasts, chest, belly, hips, until he slides his cock into me with no one but the gods shaking their heads as we indulge in the sweetest taboo.

I found Mr. Fawkes to be an excellent guide, showing me the sights in Tokio scattered across the city from our central starting point at Nihonbashi, including the tombs of the forty-seven *ronin*—eighteenth-century samurai who avenged their master's death then committed ritual suicide—an evening watching the innovative actor Danjuro, at the theatre, as well as visiting the various pavilions of the Citadel where the shoguns lived.

I remember quite vividly the day we saw a woman with her red underslip showing under her kimono, her gigantic sash tied in front, her black-lacquered, foot-high clogs zigzagging down the street in a bizarre pattern, a young girl holding a parasol over the woman's head with a male servant following them.

A geisha?

No, she was not, dear lady reader. Even I was fooled.

"Who was that woman wearing the vibrant, succulent colors?" I asked Mr. Fawkes later that afternoon while we strolled through the palace gardens with two ladies-in-waiting pointing out the blooms in season to us. Plum, pear, delicate and budlike. "The natives I've seen on the street all dress in dreary mauve or muted browns or grays."

"If I may be so bold as to speak, Lady Carlton…" he began, his eyes searching mine for approval.

"Yes?"

"The women of the pleasure quarters adorn themselves in these silks."

"She was a geisha," I said with a knowing smile.

"No, she's a…what you would call a courtesan." He cleared his throat and continued with: "The geisha entertains the customer with song and dance and repartee before the courtesan makes an appearance."

"Where *are* these pleasure quarters?" I wanted to know, my breath coming faster, wondering if it was the place I'd read about in Lord Penmore's letters. I ignored his serious expression, delighted with the idea of seeing firsthand this charming decadence of silk and eroticism.

"Yoshiwara," he said.

"I must go there."

"You *are* joking with me, Lady Carlton."

"No. I want to see these women." I wouldn't back down, so intrigued was I by these *femmes du monde* who extolled their womanly appeal in a floating world, flitting from one man to another in their embroidered silk kimonos. *Were they more myth than reality?* I wondered, these courtesans who commanded their own destiny, taking full responsibility for their place in society without losing their femininity. I was also curious about the geisha, who inhabited that world on a different plane. I wondered if a westerner like myself could become a geisha.

Imagine the story she could tell, I thought, pulling stray blond hairs off my forehead, laughing at such a notion. Who would believe a story about a *blonde* geisha? Not an easy task, the telling of such a tale left to a far better writer than I.

"The British Legation doesn't look kindly at English ladies visiting the pleasure quarters," Mr. Fawkes said, hoping that would end the conversation. "It can be dangerous, considering that samurai—"

"Samurai?" I asked, but I dared not pursue the subject and let Mr. Fawkes know what was on my mind. A provocative, naughty thought simmered in my head.

I changed the subject and enjoyed viewing the blossoms, though with my limited knowledge of the native language, I couldn't follow the lively banter of the ladies-in-waiting, frustrating me. *If there's one thing that upsets the natural order of an Irishwoman's brain,* my da always said, *it's not to be minding somebody else's business.*

Which meant over the coming months I worked hard learning phrases, nouns and verbs and how to count. Having grown up in a household where the spoken word fell from an Irish tongue, I spoke with an accent that oft got the better of me when I tried to pronounce the native words. I found my language skills improving when, at the empress's request, I began instructing the ladies in the mikado's court in the intricacies of western dress, including close-fitting bodices, full skirts and white gloves. Although I found their slender, tubular look to be elegant (I imagined what it would be like to wear a silken kimono and be unwrapped by my samurai, layer by layer), the empress was openly curious about the rows and rows of lace trimming my flounces and petticoats. I was delighted when she suggested sponsoring a school to make the beautiful fabric. I knew she longed to have a red satin petticoat and white velvet gown set with off-the-shoulder cap sleeves and dotted with pearls like the one I'd brought with me from Paris. Since no dressmaker could touch a royal personage, I suggested the wife of the premier, who was similar in size, be fitted in her place. This idea charmed the empress, who secretly had such a gown made, but to my knowledge she has yet to wear it in public.

My work schedule with the empress changed when in May 1873, a fire erupted in the women's quarters in the Imperial Palace, completely destroying the old castle and forcing the royal family to relocate to the castle of the empress dowager on the high ground in Akasaka. The trek by *kuruma* was not only inconvenient for my visits, but also for the officials who had to travel a greater distance to conduct affairs of state. (Fortunately for me, James had left Tokio on a surveying trip with Lord Penmore, compiling detailed renderings of the rivers, mountains and roads on the outskirts of the city. No doubt to further their railroad scheme to import raw materials into the country.)

In my favor, I discovered the empress showed more interest in having me visit her in her temporary quarters, though I wasn't sure whether it was to display to the British Legation that the mikado's government was committed to keeping open communication during a difficult time or a genuine show of friendship. I later learned the approachable behavior of the empress extended beyond politics and included the warm heart of one woman reaching out to another.

As she promised, the empress took it upon herself to have several passages of Ihara Saikaku's demimonde fiction translated for me. I found his renderings of life in the pleasure quarters written nearly two hundred years ago more elegant and sophisticated than the lewd tales I'd read in Lord Penmore's library. Saikaku's physical descriptions of the women in the licensed quarters made them seem fascinating and worldly, their charms expressed in great detail, from the shape of their necks, mouths and brows, down to whether or not a single mole could be found on their bodies. I was completely intrigued.

I enjoyed a great rapport with the empress and although some members of the British Legation did not approve of my female intrusion into the workings of the mikado's government, I believed there was little they could do about it. Unlike the Englishwomen sent to Japan to teach sewing and ordinary household duties to native women (their passage and board paid for by the British government), I believed they had no authority over my comings and goings. I feared that although they stated publicly they wished to elevate the position of women in Japan, their intent was to limit their rights as they had done to the female population of Queen Victoria's realm.

And what hypocrisy. I often caught hushed whisperings bantered about at the palace from stodgy old men in their black stovepipes about the "whore problem," meaning Yoshi-wara, where seeking pleasure was as natural to the natives as assuaging hunger. These pompous men insisted they wanted to curtail such goings-on, yet I gathered from eavesdropping on the intimate details of their conversation ("I say, old man, I nearly choked on my cigar when the twit arched her back and her kimono fell open and revealed her breasts." Or, "The damn girl wouldn't even look at me when I fucked her."), they were well acquainted with the women of the licensed quarters. That only made me more determined to see for myself the extent of such pleasures offered there.

Not an easy task, considering James's man followed me everywhere, except into the empress's apartments. It became a cat-and-mouse game, with me tipping my parasol to him every morning when I left for the palace, though he pretended not to see me. I brought up the matter to my husband when he returned from his surveying trip and moved out of our house and took up residence with Lord Penmore. He laughed and attributed my suspicions to my female curiosity and assured me I was free to do as I wished as long as I did not sully his reputation. *His* reputation? I admit I rumbled inside, pushing, posturing to fight back, so angry was I at his impertinence, but I stood firm, as if my feet were encased in sod and mud, and kept my mouth shut. I dared not do anything but comply with his wishes since he had adhered to his end of the bargain, meeting me at the bank to report his business goings-on regarding the railway and showing me the books as I had requested (Da sent me an addendum to his letter of credit as I'd requested, so James needed my signature as a cosigner to approve his expenditures).

I wasn't fooled. I knew he was using the funds he had pilfered from my father in Yokohama to finance his own interests, but I also knew he was up against the vexing native trait of indecision. Months went by and James became more and more frustrated by the lack of action on his plans. According to Mr. Fawkes, who discreetly inquired about the situation via an old friend seated on the mikado's council, foreign loans were no longer trusted by the government, which, for the moment, fit perfectly into my plan. Expansion of the railway line from Tokio to Kobé had been halted because of talk about a possible samurai uprising, leaving my dear husband no choice but to go along with my father's instructions to purchase supplies for the Ōzaka–Kobé railway line, due to open in late spring 1874.

I made certain he did, involving myself in the railway business and raising eyebrows at the bank *and* at court. What is important for *you* to know, dear lady reader, is that I was under great duress to make certain my father's investment in Japan did not lead to his financial ruin. Da had invested heavily in the building of the new Northern Pacific Railroad, which suffered from overspeculation. When the bank financing the railroad failed, a panic followed. While I was sipping tea and eating sweetmeats with the empress or buying silks or going to the Kabuki theatre with Mr. Fawkes, the U.S. stock market rallied then fell into a downward spiral so devastating that by the fall of 1873, thousands of businesses were ruined, unemployment rose and, as I write this memoir, the country has not yet regained any sense of normalcy.

Indeed, I worried over the fortunes of one Thomas O'Roarke and my adored mother, but I knew they were strong Irish and would rebuild whatever they lost. My da is a wise, crafty soul with the vision of Saint Patrick dancing in those steel-blue eyes. Knowing how the devil himself can trick you with his pot o' gold, he pulled his money out of the stock market before it was too late, then sold the New York brownstone and moved back home before regrouping his company with a smaller workforce. But he didn't forget the fine men who put their heart and grit into laying the tracks and running the trains.

If I may read to you from a letter he wrote to me:

Me dear Katie, this is your da talking, hoping you're having a grand time over there, but I must speak of the hardships we're facing here… [he mentions the unemployment and breadlines]. *Aye, I wish you could have seen your mother down at the station the day we had to let the workers go, handing out every single pair of shoes she owns, 'cepting the ones on her feet, to the wives and mothers and daughters of my men. So proud I was of my Ida. She's good girl, Katie, like you. I miss you, daughter, but I know you're taking care of your old man's business investment and I thank the holy saints for your courage and determination to see us through during these troubles. Da.*

I was lonely for him and my mother and my little sister, Elva, but how could I not stay in Japan? And if I may bare my soul to you, dear lady reader, I *wanted* to stay…because of Shintaro. Every time I went to the palace I would look for him, hoping to see him again, this swaggering samurai rebel exuding such dashing energy I gathered up my skirts and followed him, glimpsing his flowing bronze- and gold-colored kimono disappearing behind sliding doors in the palace. Breathless, I stopped, envisioning his chiseled muscles underneath his kimono set with gleaming crests resting like the soft glow of moonlight on his shoulders and broad back. I saw him again and again, convincing myself he possessed both strength and sensitivity and engaged in wild, careening sexual escapades with beautiful courtesans. It was a young girl's fancy and ne'er but an innocent view of what was a complex man and his paramours, a hidden side of him I'm not yet ready to speak of, but I promise you I shall be bold in all I reveal later in my tale.

I can ne'er forget the time he caught me behind the camellia hedges along the esplanade in the palace park, admiring the sculpture of a man made of white chrysanthemums and carrying on a conversation with him, so romantic was I, so naive, and pining for a lover. Beautiful to look at, his floral scent rich and heady, his petaled robes as sumptuous as those of the emperor, his flower heart was mine for the taking. Even when I discovered my samurai watching me admiring the sculpture, Shintaro never spoke, his face a mask of solitary darkness as if he struggled to let go and give voice to his desire to speak to me, reach out to me, touch me, but his way of the warrior prevented him, so unflinching was he. I shall never forget his eyes. He did so much with those eyes, making me forget he was so damn physically handsome, so explosively charismatic in everything he did, yet I would also discover he possessed great intelligence and enormous sensitivity to the world around him. He loved his people and was especially drawn to the children, taking great care to make certain their rice bowls were full and they received instruction in fencing with bamboo swords—and bamboo spears for the girls.

I digress, but we've covered a lot of territory, you and I, since that day I first saw Shintaro at the Imperial Palace in the summer of 1873. I shall now continue my story on a night of nights in the spring of the following year in the jaded brothels of the pleasure quarters in Yoshiwara for an evening of pleasure no Occidental woman before me has known.

If you will remember, dear lady reader, ladies were discouraged from visiting the licensed quarters. Knowing my Irish fancy for daring, no doubt you've already guessed how I found my way into this erotic environment, creating a dark alter ego who lived in the shadows and embraced all that she found in her rebellion against society. Lust, hot carnal passions. And sex.

And if you haven't, the surprise will set your clit atwitter.

1
1

Her eyes shone dark and luminous from the black-and-white photo hung on the outside of the Yoshiwara brothel, whispering to me in that lovely way Oriental women have of inviting you in, begging you not to resist, then lowering their eyes so you *can't* say no.

Disguised as a young English gentleman, I'd been standing outside the brothel on Nako-no-chō Street, a handbill clutched in my fist, trying to get up the courage to go inside this twilight world and involve my libido in the vices offered there. I make no excuse for my conviction to come here, establishing it first in your mind, then shifting to a different reality in upcoming pages where I shall exploit my brazenness to produce a profound sexual disturbance within you. I shall set such unease upon you, dear lady reader, that you will feel your thighs sticking together, but you won't be able to stop reading, not even to change your damp drawers as you experience with me the sweet ecstasy of what it was like to

lose my virginity within the impassioned walls of these pleasure quarters.

I have your attention, do I not? I'm pleased. I shall fight
to hold on to this cavalier attitude, possessed as I am to explore
the sexual depths of the native culture with you, and bring
you *and* your callused ideas about respectability with me to
this place where I found a timely refuge from my lonely existence with—

Shintaro. Yes, he fucked me. Again I use the vulgar word,
for love was not in his heart that first time nor was it in mine.
I *could* paint our first coupling with the romantic trappings
of wistful sighs and deep kisses, but I'm being honest with
you, dear lady reader, the reality being that it was raw and lust-
ful, two people both deeply hurt, trying to find a way to ease
their pain through sex. *Oh, but what sex.* I feel my heart racing
as I recall the exquisite tremors and burning fever of that
night. Be patient, for I shall reveal to you the intimacy and
legendary debauches of a society ever in heat, where such
pleasures are neither morally nor socially condemned.

Come. The Green Houses of Yoshiwara await us.

I'd taken a *kuruma* to the Great Gate of the licensed
quarters, pausing under the swaying willow tree at the
entrance before wandering through its portal. Since the arrival
of foreigners in Tokio, the rules have relaxed somewhat, and
bearers with handbills bragging about the quality of the food,
bedding and women are common around the entrance. I
prayed the exchange of money along with the execution of
a proper bow would gain me entrance to a teahouse. I had
no fear about my safety since swords and daggers are forbidden within the walls of Yoshiwara (I'd left my dagger at home,
hidden among my intimate garments).

I pulled down the wide-brimmed, slouch hat covering my

hair and shielding my eyes, then entered the foyer of the teahouse, praying no one would look too closely at me. James had fortuitously left behind enough pieces of his wardrobe for me to fashion an outfit, though his frock coat and trousers hung loosely on me. My black riding boots completed my ensemble. Contrary to what you may believe, disguising oneself to gain entrance to the pleasure quarters is not unusual. Monks often hide their faces under large baskets made of straw since they are forbidden from entering Yoshiwara under the pain of death. They hunt not for female flesh, but for the young male actors known to frequent the brothels. (I find this idea intriguing since such activities are whispered about in London social circles, where 'tis rumored certain gentlemen officers indulge in such sport with *other* gentlemen.)

Sexual commerce between men and women occupied my thoughts on this night, but the concierge ignored me, welcoming native men, smiling and offering them tea. I brooded over being treated as if I were invisible, but I also watched. I shall make creative use of those observations and add to this memoir what I've since learned about life in Yoshiwara to increase your enjoyment of the scene. For I imagine you've never pointed your dainty toe inside such an establishment in the Haymarket, though I *swore* I'd seen you enjoying yourself at the Surrey Theatre south of the Thames. In no way do I belittle your lack of knowledge of such entertainment. Women of the British upper class live for their own amusement and I merely point out that such debauchery exists both in England and Japan. Ah, but *vive la différence.* In London a gentleman in search of a willing pussy may procure a guidebook peppered with such language as "…the madam is recently in receipt of creamy French pastry. She insists they are fresh and expensive and nothing in her bakery stays long enough to go stale…" In Yoshiwara a customer chooses a girl from a photograph, expressing his needs and desires to the *mamasan,* then enjoys being pampered by the maids, who undress him and serve him lavish food and drink until the chosen courtesan appears. But what if his purse matches the braggarts who troll the alleys of Drury Lane in London? Then he chooses a girl on display in a latticed cage smoking on her long bamboo pipe and indifferent to his stare when her kimono slips off her shoulder and she displays a bare breast as he passes by.

After an hour, frustrated, I left.

I trekked down the long street with shops and teahouses on either side and a flower garden down the middle complete with bubbling fountains and stone lanterns. I couldn't take my eyes off the lifelike wax figures of a man and woman plucking flowers in the garden, their silent gestures evoking the feeling that time had stopped here. I continued walking, the smell of incense slipping under my nose in the guise of filmy gray clouds, its ancient allure guiding me from one teahouse to the next, while the twang of the samisen filled my ears.

Then I saw him. *Shintaro.* Moving quickly from one teahouse to another. Dressed all in white. White silk kimono, white leather divided trousers, white belt tied around his waist, shiny black hair tied in a topknot, trimmed dark beard emphasizing his square jaw. He had an aura about him, a nobility, and I swear his bare feet wearing wooden clogs didn't touch the road paved with men's broken dreams. *Not his.* I had no doubt *any* woman would untie her obi for him, including me.

I followed him into the brothel.

His striking voice drew me to him, its magnetism usurping every piercing sound of the samisen, the thin wailing of the bamboo flute, the restless sighs coming from behind closed paper doors. I followed his voice past red columns entwined with golden dragons, over the matted floor, eyeing the dark blue and green brocade on the walls, looking upward at the ceiling of mauve and violet casting cool, dark shadows everywhere.

I encountered a male servant who bade me remove my boots, then motioned for me to slip through a sliding paper door into an antechamber lit by candlelight. There I found Shintaro, sipping tea and playing with the bare breast of a beautiful girl wearing a loose pale peach kimono. He twisted her nipple, making her squeal, then pulled up her kimono, exposing her shorn pussy and inserting two fingers into her. A show of defiance that he, a samurai, chose a girl *after* he had inspected her. You may think him arrogant and forceful, but I saw his tenderness, his discipline under the most dire circumstances, his loyalty to his clan. Unbroken, unflinching.

Never taking my eyes off him, I lowered my voice, sputtering what I hoped were the proper words in the native language, indicating I also wished to buy her services. I had no idea what I was going to do with her once I paid for the privilege of her company when it was *him* I wanted.

He laughed, then said something to the girl that made her giggle. She bowed and indicated I should also inspect her. *Me?* Hesitating, I leaned closer and I could smell her sweat, like rose oil and straw, and a sweet fragrance I couldn't identify. Strange, but her body tempted me in a way I hadn't imagined, an expansion of my narrow world flowering.

I pulled my hat down lower as if to give me courage, then I began to tease her naked breasts, stroking and pinching her small hard nipples, her flesh warm and soft in my hands, knowing Shintaro was watching me. *That,* dear lady reader, made me squeeze my legs together and groan with need. I continued, touching *her* and watching *him,* fascinated with the deep contrast between this samurai and what I could see in the low-lit room, as if everything but him consisted of moody brushstrokes splashed against the glaring white of his kimono. He was more than flesh and blood, a mysterious coming together of muscle and form so physically perfect, I *had* to keep looking at him.

I caught him staring at me, his eyes searching mine, questioning me. Did he see through my disguise? Then he said something to the girl. She lay down on the white silken futon and spread her legs so I could see every inner crevice and crease of her pussy, the folds glistening with moistness, a sweet-smelling scent similar to my own overwhelming me, its familiar fragrance setting off a different response in me. I wanted to see what I *couldn't* see when I inserted the dildo inside me. So curious was I, I sat down upon my knees and inserted my fingers into her, probing her until I felt a hard bud, shaped like a tiny acorn it was, throbbing and wet. I stoked her clit gently at first, than harder, *harder* until she twitched against my fingers, moaning over and over…I kept my fingers inside her, delight shivering through me to be privy to such a sight, her clit hard like a sainted stone it was, and me gawking at the very thing that gave *me* so much pleasure quivering before my eyes. I gasped so loudly when her pussy gripped my fingers in a sudden spasm it was almost a cry, my lips trembling, my shoulders shaking. Shintaro put his strong hands firmly on my arms, holding me, speaking to me, telling me to slow down, then he said something I didn't understand nor did I care, the warmth of his breath on my bare neck sending a shudder of excitement through me, his tenderness of touch bringing a mistiness to my eyes. I had waited so long for this moment…so long I became lost in his touch, dreaming of more…I had but to linger a moment and he absorbed me completely.

When he spoke, the parameters of the scene shifted, taking on an improvisational, even spontaneous, spirit. As if he welcomed my presence as a gift from the gods and he wasn't going to turn his back on them. I *should* have run from the brothel, but that's not how it was with Shintaro. I can look back now and understand the restlessness about him, the wildness that claimed us both that night, for I came to Yoshiwara *looking* for him and if I've shocked you, so I have. I'd heard fragments of conversation at court that samurai had been meeting secretly at brothels in the pleasure quarters. A plan formed in my mind as fertile as a field of blooming shamrocks when earlier this evening I dressed in men's clothes then slipped out of the house when it was dark and I was certain the man James had following me had left his post.

Whatever the consequences, I cared not. My need for my samurai was ruled by my intense hunger for him, my fantasies, my dreams. Only one man could tame that hunger and satisfy the bedeviled itch in my pussy.

Shintaro.

Two maids removed his clothes while the courtesan changed her kimono and called for a young geisha to play the samisen. Simouyé. I recall her with great clarity because of her sophistication for one so young, her back straight, her bearing elegant and refined. Shintaro smiled at her and a twinge of jealousy coursed through me as if he knew her intimately. I found out later I was wrong, since geisha do not sleep with their customers.

Standing between the two maids, Shintaro seemed impossibly tall and suggestive less of a man than of a mythical breed of warrior. Jagged scars studded his nude torso, the pigment of time healing them, giving them the distinction of a lighter tone in certain places on his chest, his thighs, as if each cut from the sword inscribed an element of his character on his warrior's body. And his cock. Broad, hard, wicked. The way he stood, hands on his hips, feet spread apart, I could see how proud he was to show off both his scars and his magnificent cock. How could I resist him when he spoke to me? Refuse the young maids intent to peel off my disguise, giggling, hiding their mouths with their hands, bowing? Each word from his lips was a swirl of curling resonance smothering my resistance with the promise of what I wanted, needed.

Him.

The moment the maid pulled off my hat and my blond hair tumbled down my back in long waves, I detected a prevailing sense of both alienation and freedom, anger and passion. Shintaro grabbed his cock, startled, grunting, muttering words so quickly I couldn't grasp them. He'd never seen my hair loose, its golden color heightened I imagine by the riotous lighting coming from the burning candles and oil lamps behind me. His reaction frightened me, impassioned me, left me aching to understand what he was saying, *Why was he acting like this?* As if he didn't know me until he saw my hair. I would have my answer later at the samurai village, but for now this mood I felt down to my bones was less palpable than the apprehension surging through me. A spicy incense smoldering in a bronze andon overwhelmed me, its fragrance sweetly pungent like sex, while the soulful notes from the samisen filled my ears and small white hands with translucent nails plucked at my coat, vest, untying my black cravat, unhooking the braces holding up my trousers, unbuttoning my shirt…the palms of their hands soft, curious, removing my clothes, touching me, until I stood nude under the dim light. I felt no embarrassment, only desire. I didn't resist when the maid removed a warm, moist cloth from a closed woven basket and washed me as if creating a unique harmony between my body and Shintaro's as the other maid washed his chest, loins and cock with gentle strokes. I wished *I* were the cloth, pressing against him, licking the salt from his skin, wrapping my lips around his cock, my belly growing tight and hot. I moaned deep in my throat when the maid drew the coarse fibers over my hard nipples, taunting me, then lower, the warm cloth moving over my buttocks, in my anal hole and through my legs and into my pussy.

I looked into Shintaro's eyes, approving, wanting, and my skin burned, then in the next instant I shivered, the promise of a red silk kimono offered to me to cover my nakedness heightening my desire for this insanity to continue. I questioned if my samurai would show toward me an extension of his reverence for the traditional rituals of Yoshiwara, yet knowing his warrior status dictated he lived life by his own code. I wondered what naughty games he played…

Bowing, the maids slipped flowing red silk kimonos over us, but left them untied so we could gaze upon each other's nude polished bodies, our hunger for each other so ripe, our desire so strong, the tension between us was maddening. I wasn't afraid. I could do nothing but surrender to him.

What happened next, dear lady reader, is one of the best-kept secrets in Yoshiwara, a tale never told until now, the players in this drama following the native tradition of denying or ignoring anything uncomfortable or unpleasant, but I shall personalize the event as it unfolded. I swear 'tis true: on this evening, this powerful samurai, that rare man with the resolve to do anything to uphold his moral code, a man with the courage to do battle with the corrupt officials at the Imperial Court, ordered the gorgeous courtesan to leave—along with her two maids, the geisha and male servant—and not to return until morning.

We were alone.

The night I'd been dreaming of began.

We drank sake in small porcelain cups, me filling his cup, then him filling mine, both of us interacting in a rich, sensuous and cerebral ritual that was but a prelude to what happened next. I pray you will forgive me for the lack of words between us—we barely spoke, our need for each other so evident in our eyes. Intense longing swelled within me, but we didn't kiss, since such playfulness was considered the tool of the courtesan. I sipped the warm rice wine, relaxing as he stroked me with a rare degree of concentration and sensitivity to my needs, taking time to play with my nipples, a moment so sensuous I thought I could never put a cup to my lips again without his fingers pinching my brown buds. Rolling his thumbs over my hard peaks then pulling on them, making me squirm, and manipulating them with the same care I would later discover he showed toward testing the sharpness of his blade.

I remained still when he massaged my earlobes then my breasts with an oil I recognized as jasmine, its lightness and delicate fragrance luring my senses with a promise yet to come. He rubbed it between my legs and around my throbbing pussy lips, delighting in teasing me, then he poured oil into my cupped palm, indicating I should drip oil on the head of his cock. I nodded then carefully rubbed it on the sensitive underside, then he pulled me closer, whispering to me. I followed where his eyes told me to go on his broad chest, his thighs, his cock, our bodies heating up as we teased each other, emitting sweat scented with a veiled fragrance.

The air dragged heavy with our body heat, his mood softening, mine becoming feverish. Throats parched, I poured more sake for him and he brought it to his lips, watching me. He drank greedily, the wine drizzling down the sides of his mouth, then he eyed me across the cup, waiting for me to drink the wine he poured for me. Teasing, wanting, I, too, drank quickly, eager to see what would happen next, when he surprised me by snapping open a large gold fan. Playful, laughing, fanning himself as samurai do in a society where the art of being cool is genderless. I leaned in closer, offering my breasts for his touch. His eyes widened, then he rubbed my nipples with the fan, stinging them in a pleasant manner. I threw my head back, moaning, enjoying the sensation, wanting more. Giddy from the effects of the sake, I grabbed his fan and danced around him, slapping it across my buttocks, then rippling it over my pussy and teasing him mercilessly until he could bear no more. Speaking to me in a firm tone, he bade me lie down upon the silky white futon while he placed a pillow covered with shimmering gold silk under my head, its coolness soothing my flaming cheeks.

The real pleasure came when he parted my thighs and leaned over me, taking his time to observe me with a quality about him that transcended warrior and Occidental, but with a poetic sensitivity of the man himself. I jumped when he pulled on the light-colored hair on my pubic mound as if he were tugging on the strings of a lute, grinning at finding them so fine and silky yet wiry. I smiled back, then a daring idea came to me, inspired by a song I'd read about in the native works translated for me. Without shyness, I plucked three hairs from my pussy and presented them to him as a souvenir.

He laughed and I felt privileged to see a rare glimpse of emotion when his eyes softened, then he took my pubic hairs and wrapped them in a piece of red silk before sliding his fingers into me. It sets my teeth on edge as I write, thinking about his fingers probing me and though he found me tight, his touch intimate, he didn't stop, but kept going, exploring without trepidation my burning clit, rubbing it back and forth, bending both his need and my desire to fulfill the passion etched on his face. I sighed when his fingers skimmed down lower to that piece of skin where pleasure rises to such heights I cannot explain it and probed at the tightness of my anus twitching and begging for penetration. I'd discovered this exquisite joy on my own, but it couldn't compare to the intense erotic feelings it inspired in me when Shintaro used his tongue around my inner rim, then inserted his finger lubricated with a sweet-smelling oil into my anal hole. I experienced such intense sensations I buried my face into the silk futon, panting and gasping for breath. Be mindful, dear lady reader, that whatever words I write, whatever soft, sensual phrases I use, I cannot teach you the mysteries of the Orient if you do not let go of your aristocratic attitudes and insert your finger, a hairpin, a dildo, *anything* inside you to arouse you beyond words.

I existed only for this moment and what he gave me to drink heightened the feeling when he attempted to ease his way into me, my body resisting, but I was hot and wet. I raised up my hips to give him easier access to me, to thrust his cock into me. I kept repeating *dōzo*…please…him crouching between my legs…me panting, sweating…him grunting furiously and grabbing at my thighs…me pounding the futon with my fists when he slid his cock deep into me, my body raw and hurting when he broke through my virginal wall, but

I didn't want him to stop. I had waited so long for this moment, this tearing of flesh to unite flesh, my body convulsing with utter pleasure, ignoring the pain as much as I could, hot tears stinging my eyes, but I couldn't look at him. *I couldn't.* What thoughts he had he closely guarded, as was his way. He showed me a deference I would not have expected, his voice reassuring as he slid his hands up over my rib cage and turned his attention back to my nipples, his touch meant to reassure me, his fingers twisting and teasing the engorged tips to stimulate me, to ease my journey. I placed my hands over his, holding them tight, letting him know I didn't want him to stop. Deep inside my pussy began to contract, sucking his cock into me as wave after wave of pleasure claimed me, driving away the pain. It was only then I could look into his dark, brooding eyes. I saw a tenderness I never expected, for the meaning was clear without the barrier of words. What I saw was the promise of enchanted days and nights to come.

It was an aphrodisiac I could not resist.

A heaviness, a languor, held me captive to the warmth of silk where I lay. I felt myself floating, my senses numb, no feeling in my limbs when he picked me up and wrapped me, then my clothes, in the bedding of the courtesan, his eyes taking in the stains of blood upon the silk, but he showed no emotion. Then he carried me outside and down the long street past the Great Gate, past the willow tree, not stopping to speak to anyone. Were I in England with a roguish lover, an artist perhaps, I imagined he would paint me so that all who looked upon his creation would know he was in love with me. But I was not in London and he was not an artist but a samurai. No one would ever know of our indiscretion since it was the way of this land to feign indifference to anything outside the circle of obligation.

My secret was safe.

Before he left me, Shintaro found a covered *kuruma* and made certain I was safely inside and speeding away from curious eyes. Huddled in the sumptuous bedding, an aching in my groin both pained and pleasured me for I was a virgin no more. Yet I harbored no illusion about what had happened in the brothel with my samurai. I was not of his world and in the days to follow, I came to think of myself as an exquisitely fashioned paper flower added to an imperfect chrysanthemum bush in the palace garden to heighten its symmetry. A blossom that lived in his magical realm yet would wither, not from incessant rains or a hot sun, but from a lack of nurturing. *When would I feel his arms around me again?* I was certain he wanted me as much as I hungered for him. I admit my imagination of what could be between us allowed me to trace our footsteps among the gods who inspired my dream of seeing him again.

But it remained that, dear lady reader, a dream.

I awakened each morning, thinking: *will I see him today?* Then I would dress, go to the palace even if I didn't have an audience with the empress, walk through the gardens. *Nothing.* I dared to go back to Yoshiwara, though not disguised as a man, but when the cherry blossoms carried their fleeting hope on the breeze through the licensed quarters, a time when families and children frolicked, and courtesans showed off their sumptuous kimonos.

But I couldn't find Shintaro. He had disappeared.

James's man continued to follow me and my husband's visits became less and less frequent, which I barely noticed. I was bathed in frustration, fear, worry. *What if I should become pregnant?* Such thoughts brought warm tears to my eyes as soft as a baby's skin, but I feared a child born of our union would be taken from me. I didn't know whether to sigh or cry when my monthlies came, but still my heart ached for my samurai. Pray, I had to tell *someone.* I chose the only person I could trust.

Mr. Fawkes.

"Your act does not surprise me, Lady Carlton, only your frankness," he told me when we were walking through the palace garden after taking tea with Her Majesty.

"You must find out what happened to him, Mr. Fawkes," I pleaded with him. "Or I shall go mad."

He took my hand and held it, something he'd never done before. "Shintaro is a great warrior and a man who has the courage to follow his own beliefs. Such thoughts don't bode well with many in the mikado's government who see him as a threat to their progress, considering his great influence with the emperor. He is nothing more than a rebel in their eyes."

"What are you saying, Mr. Fawkes?"

"I fear trouble is brewing for him since he refused to obey the mikado's law of forced conscription. His enemies at court will use that as an excuse to raise arms against him." He spoke of the royal decree requiring all native men to serve time in the army. "To escape the law, rumor has it Shintaro has gone into hiding."

"Hiding?" I asked, surprised. "*Where,* Mr. Fawkes, tell me, *please.*"

I could see the hesitation in his eyes, knowing if anyone found out, the price he'd pay for telling me.

"I can't," he said, shaking his head. "Even if you find him, no outsider is welcome there."

"He'll see me, I know he will. You *must* tell me where he is."

He looked away from me as if making up his mind. Finally, he said, "Recent reports indicate he has taken refuge in the mountains behind the treaty port of Kobé."

"Then I shall go there."

"No, your ladyship, you're not of Shintaro's world," he said sternly. "You must give up this insane scheme to find him."

"I can't, Mr. Fawkes. I—I must see him again."

"You don't understand the way of the warrior. What you experienced that night in the pleasure quarters was nothing to him but—" He stopped, hesitant to say what was on his mind.

"Sex, Mr. Fawkes?" I said, arching an eyebrow. "Perhaps, but I have to find out for myself."

"I know these samurai, Lady Carlton. They're strong and noble and follow a course of chivalry we in the West don't understand. Like many of his class, Shintaro doesn't want to relinquish his samurai beliefs."

"Would you, Mr. Fawkes?" I dared to ask him.

"The way of the warrior is not about blind obedience, milady, but about responsibility." His face turned serious. "Are you ready to accept what comes if you leave your husband?"

"All I know is Shintaro has taught me what it means to be a woman. I *have* to find him."

"And then?"

"That's up to Shintaro, Mr. Fawkes, is it not?"

"Pack your bags, my dear wife," James insisted, his eyes avoiding mine. "We're leaving for London on the next steamer out of Yokohama."

"I'm not going with you," I said firmly.

"You *dare* to disobey your husband?"

"Ours is not a marriage in the true sense of the word, James. You have your women, I have my work at the Imperial Court. I can't allow you to dissuade me from that," I said, careful not to give myself away.

"I cannot believe I'm hearing my wife speak these words. You, who hated this pagan land, don't wish to leave?"

"I have to keep watch over my father's investment in the new railway line." I remained silent about his pilfering. "Da's instructed me to go to Ōzaka and report on the opening of the railway line to Kobé."

It was a lie, but I needed an excuse to leave Tokio. I was determined to see Shintaro and warn him that he was in danger. And I shall be so bold as to add that I also wanted his cock in me. I'm not ashamed of my feelings, call them base if you must, my thoughts those of a sinner possessed, the fire inside me burning day and night, so intense were my feelings for him I would claw my way to him if I must.

"Isn't that where your friend Mallory is?" my husband asked coyly.

I ignored his innuendo. "I'm not going back to London with you, James."

"Then neither am I returning, my dear wife," he said, holding my arm so tightly it hurt.

"What do you mean?" I asked, afraid of his answer.

"I'm going with you to Ōzaka," he sneered. "I couldn't let anything to happen to you, could I?"

1
2

Life in Kobé with James became insufferable. He followed me everywhere and afforded me no privacy dressing—staring at the swell of my breasts spilling over my corset or my bare legs when I rolled up my stockings—and constantly hounded me about ruining his life.

Your life, what about mine? I yelled back at him, reminding him I gave up my social position in London to come to Japan. A position he bestowed upon me by marrying me when no one else would, he was quick to add, then belittled my work with the British Legation, implying certain members had induced him to get me out of Tokio for embarrassing Her Majesty's government.

I panicked. *Had someone recognized me at Yoshiwara?*

I experienced a conflict between the joy of that night with Shintaro and the fear of discovery, but fortunately for me *and* for you, dear lady reader, it was not the case, since then there'd be no memoir to scandalize you. It was my meddling in the railway business that was my undoing, with certain members of the British Legation (no doubt Lord Penmore was among them) feeding on me with pleasure like leeches. To them, I was tarnished finery, seeing how I was Irish-American. *And* a woman. To keep me from delving too far into their questionable business tactics, they convinced James to secure passage for us on a steamer back to San Francisco. When James discovered I'd made plans to go to Ōzaka, he saw a way out that wouldn't arouse my suspicions about their dirty dealings and jeopardize his own financial gains. As long as I was out of Tokio, he convinced the legation, I wouldn't cause them any more trouble.

Such fools they be to think Katie O'Roarke would not prevail. That's the Irish in me, fighters that we are, looking for a row when there are rough seas to be sailed. And so they were with James and me after we left Tokio. We made the trip to Kobé first then Ōzaka on the *Oregonian,* with me spending the three-day trip alone in our cabin, nausea hitting me continuously as the ship hit rough currents and choppy seas, and my dear husband off to steerage class to enjoy the charms of the singsong girls on their way to the brothels.

After a brief sojourn in the commercial city of Ōzaka, we boarded the train as honored guests for the inaugural run of the railway line to Kobé to show cooperation between the mikado's government and the British Legation (the irony of it did not escape me). We traveled the twenty-two miles mostly over flat land, crossing rivers and streams, the journey but a footnote in history books. For me it was a step closer to Shintaro. I could barely contain myself so certain was I that I would find him and nothing destroyed that, nothing could.

★ ★ ★

For the sake of appearances, James and I lived as man and wife in a western-style house in Kobé decorated in Oriental simplicity and cozy comfort. That was as far as our living arrangements extended, but I had lost my freedom. James was always at my side, insisting I translate for him in my halting Japanese with native shopkeepers and dockworkers. I believe it was an excuse for him to keep watch over me while he helped conduct business for Lord Penmore, who was financing a private railway line from Kobé to Kioto. (Was he behind the ousting of Shintaro from the mikado's court? I've often wondered.) My dear husband assured me he was merely assisting his old friend, busying himself with the plans, working with the British engineers and inspecting the machinery when it arrived from England. *And* drinking and whoring at the town bordello run by an enterprising madam of questionable European background who insisted her girls wear flesh-colored stockings.

Why do I mention this? To set your tongues wagging with erotic gossip? No, dear lady reader, merely to explain to you my state of mind so you understand why I ran away, why I left my husband. There was no other way. The insufferable days under James's thumb were maddening, two sinners we were, possessed of disdain for each other. My husband tried to break my spirit with taunts and degradation, while I lost myself in reading the translated works of the native writers I'd brought with me, existing in their floating world of silk and fragrance, lost in smoky incense and wistful sighs. I yearned for those wonderful days in Tokio with Mr. Fawkes escorting me around the city, accompanying me to the palace…my conversations with the empress…and most of all, my sightings of Shintaro. I had acted like a schoolgirl when

I saw him, flirty and romantic, shy but daring, but those days were gone. Frustrated, deflowered, my spirit stifled, my heart lonely, I longed to lift my mood to that special place I had known with him when I slid open the silken paper door to his sensuous world and my life began behind that screen.

I had matured since that night in the pleasure quarters, though the paralyzing conflict I faced regarding my marital infidelity blocked me since I didn't know how I was going to resolve it. I wouldn't rest until I found Shintaro and damn everything else. It never occurred to me he would turn me away, not want to see me. My strength at that time was my unfaltering, physical need for him, his hands sliding everywhere over my body, my being not caught up in romantic illusions, for how could I, an Occidental woman, ever hope to know his love? I possessed such hunger for this man, ached for him, for his cock, I was like a blessed candle, its yellow-blue flame burning without shame. No woman can understand that feeling until she's experienced the trembling inside her, the throbbing anguish that never goes away until he touches her again and a seething overcomes her as if she's turned to liquid lead.

I thought I would die if I didn't see him again.

Weeks passed and my opportunity for exploration of the surrounding hillsides was blocked not only by James's constant attention to my person, but by the social duties of my being Lady Carlton. I found it ironic that the one thing I desired above all else back in London had become a stifling means to keep me from searching for Shintaro and the samurai village. While James was occupied with business, I was expected to do what foreign wives do. Sit with the other women on the balcony, drinking tea and watching the foreign ships laying at anchor and the sampans with their broad white sails bustling in the harbor. Then I'd wander around the curio shops on the main shopping street, buying up the local specialty of basket weaving and asking the secondhand-shop keepers if they'd found any more "old blues" (porcelain dishes trimmed with blue designs hundreds of years old). I also strolled along the sandy shore with my parasol shading my face *and* my thoughts. The air was clear and dry here, the sand white, but it was toward the mountains my eye wandered, wondering, Where, *where* was Shintaro?

I began to believe my ability to find him had reached an impasse, when a member of the entourage from the mikado's government assigned to us indicated he had visited England and "knew what foreigners needed." I suspected the gleam in his eye meant something more than servants and a house, most likely the opportunity for James to spread open the silken kimono of a local girl chosen for him. I was pleasantly surprised when the official brought round a horse, a fine breed she was, brown with a white spot on her forehead and as spirited as a derby winner. James balked, saying he had no desire to ride four-legged animals. I told him we must accept the gift or the man would lose face. He laughed, then told me to do as I wished with the animal. *The horse must be exercised,* I said, a plan forming in my mind as clear as the twinkle in a fae's eye, *so his lordship would have no objection to me riding him in the hills behind the settlement?* So eager was he to take his leave with Lord Penmore visiting from Tokio, he adjusted the brim on his hat and bade me not to concern him any further with such unimportant matters.

Watching the two men in close conversation as they walked down the road toward town, I realized I no longer noticed my husband's slight limp, as if the depth of his mental cruelty surpassed anything my eyes could see. Like the reality of a gray, misty morning. It hid nature's flaws, but they were still there. Did that make him more dangerous to me? I didn't know. Would I ever be able to read his true thoughts, make conversation with the man I thought I'd married, keep pace with his debauched needs? *Could any woman?*

I found an English bridle and an old saddle in a strange curio shop in an alley off Motomachi Street. No sign, nothing but an ancient sword hanging over its entrance. The old swordsmith filled my teacup and unrolled embroideries to show me, our conversation consisting of my halting Japanese and what little English he knew. When I noticed armor, banners and swords stashed in the corner, I discreetly asked him what he knew about a samurai village. He became strangely silent. *I had to find Shintaro,* I told him, but he ignored me.

I continued to visit his shop, hoping he would help me. I dared not make public inquiries. Everyone knew everyone else in the small foreign settlement built on less then a mile of sand against the abrupt green hill-walls. Home to several hundred westerners, the houses in Kobé were spread out along a long strand extending down to the water's edge, their unique position exposing them to the winter sun and the summer winds.

The hills behind us beckoned to me every morning after breakfast, a low-lying pink mist of early dawn hovering over them and daring me to enter a mysterious realm whose fragile existence I began to believe existed only in my mind, a transience that slipped a little more into the mist each day. But I wouldn't give up. I pulled on my slim black-and-gold tweed riding skirt, slipped into my boots and donned my tight-fitting black velvet jacket and gloves, pulled my hair back with a black ribbon and out I went into the day.

Over the hills I cantered, behind a thatched-roof teahouse perched on top of a hill, past a shrine guarded by a red wooden gate, down narrow dirt footpaths, crisscrossing a creek, looking for Shintaro. I searched for him with a rawness, an insistence that he was real, the village was real, desperation and passion dominating my motivation. I may not have admitted it to myself then but I do now: I wanted to get away from James before his dark, shadowy games turned into something ugly and violent. I was in a state of nakedness in my pursuit, not in the physical sense, but my emotional core was so fragile I swear it was held together by frayed silken threads. James's constant questioning contributed to my panicked state. He was convinced I'd had an affair with Mr. Mallory, though his accusations were unfounded. I had only spoken to the American to exchange pleasantries during our stay in Ōzaka. That mattered not to my husband. Whatever I did was wrong, whomever I spoke to was cause for scandal.

When I asked him to explain *his* whereabouts, he told me to ask no questions, but I knew he went to the brothel with Lord Penmore. He always seemed pleased with himself when he returned, drunk but satiated, which meant he didn't try to kiss the back of my neck or slide his hand up my petticoats. I was grateful for the respite from his husbandly advances. I couldn't let another man touch me, not after I had experienced the strong hands of Shintaro, his smoldering touch upon my bare skin with his lips, his thrusting into me with his cock. I didn't know then about his…no, 'tis too soon to pull you from the dreamlike state you're in since that night with Shintaro, for I would only intrigue you more, make your heart flutter, your voice crack with questions, not understand-

ing this land with its intricacies and innuendos in the ways of
the flesh, how pleasures can exist side by side yet be so distant,
how lips can taste the sweetness of more than one blossom…

And so it became a pattern, James's accusations, his glee at
discovering our investment in the railway was making money
(I had received news from Mr. Fawkes that wealthy native
merchants were becoming stockholders), and his philandering and drunkenness.

I've no doubt it would have continued had James not made
the mistake of taking a riding crop to an unwilling bare
bottom in the local brothel.

I was in high spirits on this fine morning, swearing it was
one of those days when the sun could coax the wild irises up
from the earth with nothing but a smile. I ignored the dark
clouds at my back and visited the curio shop, again asking the
old swordsmith for help, telling him I feared trouble was
brewing for Shintaro.

Showing no expression, the swordsmith refilled my teacup,
then opened tiny compartments in a small lacquered chest and
pulled out what I believe were dried pine and withered
orange blossom. Wrapping the fragile items in a silk banner,
he handed them to me, smiled then bowed. I thanked him
and left, eager to be on my way, but excited. I was certain
this was his indirect manner of telling me what I wanted to
know. I remembered riding through a grove of pines high in
the thickly wooded mountains about an hour's ride from the
settlement, a place where I swore I'd smelled the scent of
orange blossoms but found none.

I rode out there again this morning, galloping away from
the settlement. I urged the young mare up the vibrant green
hillside, my face perspiring, my arm aching from pulling on

the reins, my arse bobbing up and down, my boots slick with horse sweat. I *must* be close. The scent of orange blossoms was so strong here in the grassy hills covered with pine where the ridge dropped abruptly. A steep escarpment led down into a deep-cut valley, dense foliage and weathered rocks hiding whatever was below from my view.

I looked upward to get my bearings. The noon sun yawned, as if bored with my futile exploits, then feisty dark clouds covered her face, sending the day into a familiar grayness. Their bellies bulbous with rain, the clouds descended, drawing nearer and nearer until horse and rider were enveloped in a thick fog, forcing me to turn back. I was *so* close, but I feared what would happen if my horse lost her footing.

Showers came fast without warning, raindrops splattering my face, my back, yet a fever burned within me. It was the fever of consuming desire to find my samurai, burning so intensely inside me I pulled hard on the reins, ready to keep searching. Only the voice of reason I somehow still possessed made me return home, my clothes drenched, my hard nipples pointing through my wet black velvet jacket. For that indiscretion, I would pay dearly.

"Where have you been, my dear wife?" I heard James bellow in a slurred voice when I came through the front door, my clothes wet and heavy, my spirits sinking.

"I've been out riding—" I began, wondering what had happened to the native groom assigned to me. I couldn't leave the mare standing outside in the rain.

"Get over here," he ordered. "I'm lonely."

"I have to see to my horse—"

"Isn't your husband more important?" His eyes searched out my hard nipples pointing through my wet jacket.

"Please, James, the mare needs me."

"I need you more," he said, the hunger in his voice disturbing me. I stiffened as he reached for me, his hand closing over my arm. His grip tightened, making me grimace, but I refused to let him see that he hurt me. I turned away when he tried to kiss me, the smell of cheap brandy on his breath nearly suffocating me.

"You're drunk again."

"And you're beautiful." He ripped open my jacket and fumbled under my damp chemise until he found my breasts, laughing at my futile attempts to stop him. "More beautiful than those native cunts with their insidious bowing and skinny arses."

"You're hurting me, James, let me go."

"That's what *she* said, the bitch, when I bound her to the posts then laid my crop upon her nude buttocks. I can still hear her wailing and shrieking like a streetwalker as I trailed the leather across her spine, taunting her with more licks to come. I brought the crop down harder, then *harder,* until the angry red welts crisscrossed her bare arse with marks, *my* mark. Lord Carlton. I'm the son of the duke of Braystone...how dare she spit at me...the *whore!*"

I tried to cover my breasts as he poured himself another brandy, ranting on about the Chinaman who'd sold him phony liquor, the bottle badly corked without a seal, how he'd see him hang for trying to cheat a lord of the realm. I was more concerned with this frenetic mélange of threats and blows upon my person after months of his tendency toward detachment. Why now? He was dangerous. I had to protect myself.

I raced to my bedroom, opening the cedar chest, pulling out my intimate garments, searching everywhere for—

"Looking for this, my dear wife?"

I stiffened, hearing James behind me. Slowly I turned and saw him holding up my dagger and toying with its sharp point.

"I found it when I was looking for letters from Mallory."

"Give it back to me, James. It's mine."

"No." His eyes narrowed. "Who gave it to you?"

"No one. I bought it in a curio shop in Yokohama."

"You're lying. You intended to kill me."

"You're insane. It's true I hate what you've done to me, to our marriage, but I'm not a fool."

"There's something different about you," he said, running the point of the dagger along my rib cage, snagging the ripped velvet. "A private glow of satisfaction in your eyes." He grabbed my crotch through my wet clothes and squeezed it, hard. I grimaced. "As if you've been fucked, your pussy tightening around a man's cock, your heart pumping while he thrust into you."

"You—you don't know what you're talking about."

"I know that look. Womanly and sensuous, no longer chaste and innocent, but knowing. Who is he, Katie? *Who is he?*"

"I swear there's *no one*." *Lie, lie.* By the holy saints, I felt my face redden like a harlot caught with her knickers down with the local vicar. What *could* I do? Tell him I'd given myself to a samurai, a man far better than he?

"I've noticed how you draw back when I try to touch you, how you sneer and laugh at me. Like the girls at Madame Dumonde's in Paris, *laughing* because I couldn't fuck them because *he* was there, watching, waiting, the switch in his hand. Not even when he struck my naked buttocks with the rod could I get hard enough to fuck the girl in the fancy whorehouse."

"*Who,* James? Who was watching you?" I begged him. His eyes took on the look of a man much younger as he relived a painful time in his life. I couldn't believe this was my husband looking so compellingly vulnerable, a man's whose dark side cast shadows over our marriage from the beginning and now doused what small glimmer of light we may have had forever.

"My father...the *bastard*."

The words rushed out of him, how his father, the duke, had beat him for years, taking the strap to him, as had so many of his professors while making him recite irregular Greek verbs. The duke subscribed to the notion that flagellation promoted the release of male secretions, an ungodly one at that, but the upper class believed that surviving a whipping at school brought with it a certain cachet and membership in the exclusive Eton Block Club. (Ask his lordship, dear lady reader, if he survived Eton without a whipping and I dare say he did not.)

When James was sixteen, the duke insisted the boy accompany him to a Paris brothel, where James was so humiliated by the older man's flailing actions with the switch, he fled out into the night, his eyes blinded by tears, where he was run down by a carriage, his leg caught under the wheel.

He survived, but with a limp.

The duke never spoke of the incident and James never forgave him. He took out his revenge by squandering his fortune and spending his time in whorehouses, whipping the buttocks of pretty girls to get back at the prostitutes who had mocked him, shaming them first before he fucked them. But tonight he had gone too far in the brothel, taking a riding crop to a singsong girl, scarring her so badly the madam cursed him for soiling her goods and banned him from her establishment, then had him escorted home.

Where he waited for me, his dear wife, so he could finish his sordid game.

★ ★ ★

Blinded by inconsolable rage, James struck me across the face, cutting my lip. I tasted blood, but I wouldn't allow him to berate me. I realized I was up against a man of such single-mindedness that nothing could vanquish his anger toward me. We had both come to this union as damaged souls, him more than I, at the core of his tirade the issues of trust and betrayal. I can't deny I was guilty by giving myself to another man. I have not the time nor inclination to explore the moral issues I faced then. Judge me if you must, dear lady reader, but had James not driven me to it? It was no excuse, I see that now, but you can understand what an irredeemable man I had married.

I had to get out, go anywhere, it didn't matter. He'd kill me if I didn't.

"I'm leaving you, James," I said, grabbing my reticule to pack some clothes, personal items. "Our marriage is over."

"So you can go to him?"

"There's no one, I *swear.*"

"You're *mine* and I demand you show me some respect."

I had no time to react when he pushed me and I staggered across the room, dropping the valise. I had misjudged him, so fierce was his desire to possess me. With a swiftness I wouldn't have believed, he ripped my skirt, my petticoats, then grabbed me by my hair, pulling off the black ribbon, and yanked my head back so far I thought he'd break my neck.

"Let me go, James, *you're mad!*" I screamed, my arms flailing about as I nearly lost my balance. I tried to pull away, disgust and loathing for him making my stomach churn. He laughed at my helplessness, my eyes disbelieving, my breasts rising as I struggled with him, pain radiating across my back until I couldn't stand it and I collapsed onto the floor. James stood for a moment, legs spread apart, looking down at me with a strange surge of excitement on his face as I lay there, choking, then he was on top of me, grabbing at my breasts and waving the dagger around in circles.

"Don't force me to disfigure your beautiful body, my dear wife, for I shall if you resist. Spread your legs so I can fuck you." He got to his feet and fumbled with the buttons on his breeches, releasing his cock, holding it with one hand and brandishing the dagger in the other.

"I shall *never* submit to you, James."

"You will do as I command, whore, *or I will cut you*."

Fearful for my life, I pulled up my torn skirt, my petticoats, my hand shaking as I opened the slit in my drawers. His eyes widened when he saw my naked pussy, pink and moist, but I had no intention of allowing him to fuck me. I had to act now. As he leaned down over me, I brought my knee up in a swift kick to his groin, making him yell out in pain. He sliced through my silken drawers with the dagger and cut my thigh as he toppled onto the floor, mumbling. A slithery red stain drizzled down my leg like a trail of fire, burning hot. *Forget the pain*. Before he could stop me, I ripped the lacy ruffle hanging off my petticoat and wrapped it around my leg, then I ran out of the house and slammed the door behind me. I found my horse still standing in the rain, snorting, shivering. James must have released the groom, planning for us to be alone. I tried to calm her, knowing it was madness to take the mare out in a storm like this, but I couldn't stay here. I would not, *could not* allow my husband to plunder my soul as well as my body with his debauchery. I pulled myself up onto the saddle, dragging my bleeding leg over the mare's flanks, and took off into the mountains behind the settlement.

I was in full revolt against my husband, my womanly emotions sickened by his belligerence and humiliation of my person, my spirit. Yet I could not forget his words, knowing as he did I had given myself to another man. I knew the echo of my torment would never leave me. Yet I didn't turn back.

I must find Shintaro.

I rode for hours, the horse's hooves thundering over the terrain through bamboo thickets, the tension building inside me, the mare never letting up though I could tell she was chafing at the bit, yearning to run free. We slogged up the grassy hillside, me reining her in around tight curves then opening up when we came to the summit, the wind in our ears, my hair whipping at my face, the mare's breath strong and rhythmic, giving me hope. *We wouldn't fail in our mission.* We splashed through a stream, a fallen tree limb lay in our path, the horse taking the jump low and easy, then pounding over the ridge, a cloud of fog obscuring my view, a bluish-gray mist threatening me from all sides.

I headed for the pine groves, the driving rain stinging my face, throat, arms, until horse and rider found ourselves near the end of the cliff, nothing but a tortuous hillpath leading down into the steep valley below. The mare whinnied in alarm, veering sideways and tossing me onto the sticky brambles. I cried out as I landed, the needles pricking my bare skin, my legs shaking, wobbling so hard I couldn't stand up. I dragged myself under the lee of an overhanging rock to rest, a rich darkness beckoning me to go farther into the natural cave, but I couldn't. Bleeding, exhausted, my clothes soaked with rain and creek water, I lay on my back, panting, gasping for air. I must stay awake…couldn't…it was no use. I closed my eyes, the scent of orange blossoms filling my nostrils, knowing Shintaro must be near, that thought bringing me so much pleasure it was a sin.

I awoke to find a young samurai leaning over me, his hand touching my face, my throat, the swell of my breasts. The sight of him took my breath away. He was not simply a man, but the most beautiful young man I'd ever seen, the light streaming under the rock turning the sweat on his bare arm muscles into a delicate oil that dramatized its sensual contours. I brushed my fingers against the side of his face, smooth, so smooth I imagined he wasn't real, but he was. Top knot pulled back, divided trousers, shoulder armor covering his left arm and forearm, leaving his chest bare, two sheathed swords at his waist. I leaned closer, infusing my senses with his beauty so that I could savor this moment, so sweet yet intense, a shiver rattling my bones with an ancient curse when I looked deeper into his eyes. What I saw there frightened me. *Desire.* Formed by the urgency of our youth, two young buds newly blossomed.

I believe at that moment I stood at a crossroads, my fate decided upon whether or not I went forward or backward. I wouldn't know until later where the strange feelings I had for the young samurai would take me. For now, I uttered the words that proclaimed my destiny, words that would wash away the taste of fear in my mouth.

"Take me to Shintaro."

1
3

Time for self-confession, dear lady reader, while my body heals during its restful abandonment, the emotional wounds mending along with the flesh, each like silken threads entwining in a pattern old yet new, for nothing is ever the same. Scars heal, but they are reminders of deeds done that cannot be undone.

Bless me, Father, for I have sinned… I fucked a man not my husband… I ran away from his lordship…and I'm not going back.

Shameless? Yes, but having come this far with me on my journey, we have reached a place in the road, which will determine where we go from here, you and I. You can accept my decision to ally with my samurai and experience all that I did with him and not judge me. Or we part ways here and I shall not judge you for your unwillingness to go further into the story with me. For what I shall reveal henceforth will indeed make your pussy tingle with such a rare pleasure no Occidental woman can read it without experiencing an erotic reaction that will leave you questioning your own sexual pursuits. Be forewarned. The remainder of my story is not for puritanical souls and faint aristocrats whose sex lives are cloaked in secrecy, rarely discussed or ignored completely.

I understand that by writing this memoir *I* am bound to put forth the truth of what happened to me, while allowing myself the freedom of a writer to entertain you. Consequently, I am careful of the words I use, wishing to express myself in English while also being true to the interpretation of the Japanese language as I understood it. Be mindful, my proficiency in the native tongue was more than enough to make myself understood and I attained another level during my stay in the samurai village. Yet 'tis not my intent to place myself in a position to divine every nuance of the native culture and engage you in historical repartee, but instead to make you understand what a magnificent creature was Shintaro, a man with the power and sensuality to engage my soul and torment my body with such pleasures I would have died for him had our places been reversed.

Now that we've settled our discussion and you are still with me, I shan't keep you in suspense about what happened to me the day I found myself in the arms of the handsome young samurai. Akira. A young man whom I discovered adopted a chivalrous way of speaking around me to match the knightly purity of his flowing robes when he bade me learn the way of the warrior, hoping to bring me under its potent spell *and* his. I don't deny he saved my life. He found my lacy ruffle stained with blood and curiosity led him to find me under the lee of the rock where, for two days, I lay in the limbo world I'd been warned about by the good sisters. A place between heaven and hell where wandering souls gather to account for their sins. Or if you are Irish, to cajole and plead before your betters to be allowed to return to earth.

When it was my turn, I stated I was but an insignificant mortal, but I was from good strong stock and possessed of an avid curiosity for how this tale would end and would not disappoint should I be given leave to return. Whatever I said must have caught the imagination of the Grand Being Himself, for I found myself on the back of a black stallion with Akira's strong arms holding me, the warmth of his body allowing me to give out an exclamation of joy at being so close to him. I must admit that a distinct throbbing in my pussy disturbed me, for how could I feel these sensations when it was Shintaro I dreamed of holding me, his hot breath burning the back of my neck, his strong arms wrapping my soul in bliss?

Was I a wanton female with no morals after all?

I rejected this thinking, knowing I was hurt, tired, cold tremors making me shake, fever making me burn, lost as I was between two worlds, for the path we followed led down into the hidden valley to the fabled home of the samurai. The day was clear, bright, the lingering scent of fresh rain driving away the smell of sweaty horseflesh under me, but it was the scenery I shall never efface from my mind. An enchanted land it was, as if the seasons all blended together here in this one spot and showered the rich earth with the glory of the blessed deities.

Down the steep path we rode, shielded on either side by tall bamboo, deep-set corrugations filled with mud indicating it was well worn, my eyes straining to push through the haze of my weakened state to see between the wooded precipices to a rolling green plain made nearly invisible by deep indigo shadows made all the more forbidding by the wooded mountain range protecting them. The farther we went, the more the mud and sharp smell of pine gave way to the odiferous laughter of orange groves, their scent overwhelming me. Clusters of pink and white magnolias dotted the hills alive with juice-filled blueberries, shiny granite rocks and gnarled trees as the horse carried its riders over the hidden path, ankle-deep in bright yellow daisies. I did not see all this then, lapsing in and out of consciousness. I recall it now with the perception of one who has become part of this land, a broad-brimmed, straw-hatted woman in a kimono at work in the fields, her face and neck covered by an attached scarf.

A samurai woman.

I remember closing my eyes and resting my head against the young warrior's shoulder as we passed under the ancient tall wooden gate marking the entrance to the village, a remnant of a long-ago settlement. I swore I heard Shintaro stop him with a command of surprise mixed with arrogance, then he spoke to him in a gentle manner without the coarse and brutish grunts I had come to expect from him. A chill riding on a gust of wind seized me, made me tremble, gripping me with an urgency to see his face, to touch him, but I couldn't open my eyes, speak. Everything fell out of focus when a foul odor I couldn't identify hit my nostrils, making my head spin.

Then the moment was gone, like a vague dream I couldn't hold on to, and I swear by the blessed lives of the saints I cried when I felt Shintaro lift me into his arms and carry me. *I swear.* I clung to him as a fierce pain raced up my leg, as if the sharp blade of his sword slashed through my flesh.

For days I lay huddled inside a warm futon with the rushing wind outside rattling the wooden shutters, lightning ripping through a crack in the slats, followed by the rumble of distant thunder. Soft hands tended to my leg, angry and red it was, the jagged wound wrought by the dagger oozing with blood and pus. It was the rancid smell of infection that had jolted my senses when Shintaro sliced off the blood-soaked petticoat sticking to my leg wound, his deftness with a sword cutting away the material without touching my flesh. I like to believe he stroked my cheek with his hand and brushed his lips with mine, as I would teach him to do, but such was not the way of the warrior. Curt, strong, disciplined, he ordered me separated from everyone except a woman to tend to me.

Nami.

So quiet and composed, reserved yet assured. Nami wore the same beautiful kimono I had seen on other native women, whether they be geisha or courtesan, but I noticed something vastly different about her in this society where dramatic shades of femininity existed. Most notable was the way she carried herself. Head aloft, graceful yet strong body, determined. Loyal, committed to the way of the warrior, she always carried a dirk in her obi. Yet she was curious and bright-eyed, insisting I didn't need my armor (my corset), scrubbing the straw matting clean twice a day and lingering with me over fragrant-smelling tea to discuss the succulence of summer foliage.

'Tis her smile I see before me now as I recall my first days in the village, as if she could sweeten every cup of tea with that smile. Gentle feelings wash over me, such tenderness I feel in my heart for her and still I chastise myself for altering her fate, a fate disrupted by my coming to the village.

I must continue or I shall bring a melancholy mood to these pages and Nami would not wish that, for her spirit was one of godliness, her actions those of a saint, though you would call her a sinner, for the religious altar where she prays is different than yours. I ask that you who don your bonnet and gloves and listen to sermons on Sundays accept the fact that good women exist who do not believe in the same moral code as you do. Nami is such a woman and I would come to know her strengths that made her as close to perfection as it exists.

Our extraordinary friendship strengthened during my stay in the single-story wooden structure set off by itself at the far end of the village (I noticed a guard posted outside day and night), a place where a samurai woman retired during her menses. *Or the birthing of a child,* Nami said, her sad face making me inquire further. *Yes,* she admitted, she had a child, but her baby died in its first year and the gods had deemed she could bear no more children. I told her about my emptiness and she nodded, saying we must be brave, *like two red beans trying to hide in a bowl of plump white rice.*

On a different note, I found this females-only place had a spiritual effect upon me, an opportunity to reconvene with my inner self and to contemplate what it meant to be a woman. A sexual creature, yes, but when Nami taught me the native art of arranging flowers, I also learned about harmony, balance, stability. My favorite arrangement was combining pine with rose, signifying eternal youth with long life. I ask you, what woman could wish for more?

Imagine such a place in busy Mayfair, dear lady reader, where you could go and not have to bind your midsection into the formidable trappings of a corset when your monthly pains came, where you could forgo the use of rice powder and allow your skin to breathe, where you could wash your hair and let it hang loosely around your shoulders, the scent of rose and jasmine filling your nostrils instead of the tar and charcoal permeating the air of the London streets. Imagine…

After Nami stanched my wound, she bound it with clean strips of heavy cotton but nothing could stop the hours, the days of suffering that followed. How can I describe it? I daresay

you may be familiar with my turmoil if you have survived infection induced from childbed fever, those of you who insist
on having your babies in a lying-in ward in a fancy hospital. I
suffered similar agony from the dagger wound, the continual
fainting sickness, burning skin, parched mouth and delirium.
Fortunate you were to have a physician there to prescribe opium
and calomel to soothe your pain, but I was more fortunate to
have clean hands washed and scrubbed to attend me. A practice
more British physicians should acquire instead of spreading the
putrid residue left upon their dirty fingers from examining one
pussy then another and damn their impertinence not to do so.

Forgive me for going off like a sinner begging for prayers,
but I feel so strongly about the simple ways of avoiding disease
I learned in the samurai village. I promise I shall restrain
myself and dispense with my secular preaching and work to
lighten your mood as mine was in spite of my pain. I shall
instead dwell upon a less annoying ailment: *fleurs-blanches,* or
white flowers, as the sticky-sweet liquid from your pussy is
called when you're caught reading erotic novels like mine.
Don't check your drawers now. You have but to open your legs
and sniff to know if you're afflicted. Yes, I'm laughing with
a naughtiness you've not expected in this chapter, writing with
a light touch as wholly unpredictable as my Irish tongue, but
the gods were with me during that time and the infection did
not spread. When after several days I could sit up, move my
leg, take a few steps, my words were always the same: *where
was Shintaro?*

Nami would say nothing until this morning.

"He will not come."

"Why? We are not strangers—" I stopped. How could I
tell her we had been lovers?

"He is angry with Akira for bringing you to our village."

"I *begged* the young samurai to bring me here."

"Shintaro says Akira must take you back to Kobé…to your husband."

"No, I can't go… *He will kill me!*"

"I—I do not understand," she said, helping me to my feet to find my footing in a drama where the power of my samurai's personality, his unyielding will to force me to return to James, haunted me, tore at my soul.

"It was my husband who did this to me." I pointed to my bandaged thigh, the wound healing, but not the memory of that day. "If Shintaro forces me to return, my death will be on his hands."

Survival is instinctual, gut-clenching and problematic to the human psyche. It knows nothing else when its very existence is threatened. You lie, cheat, steal, claw at the fibers of your existence with the belief that if you hold on long enough, your defiance of the inevitable will somehow see you through. I wanted more than to survive. I wanted Shintaro.

And I would do *anything* to have him.

When Nami told me this morning I was well enough to move to other quarters, hope surged through me. Shintaro would never visit me here in this place of female containment, making me believe my plea to stay had moved the warrior with curiosity, disbelief or both. He intended to see me and deal with what he considered an unpleasant situation. *I* found it to be most pleasant since I harbored dreams of Shintaro holding me, our bodies locked together, him moving in and out of me in slow and rhythmic thrusts, then wrapping my leg around his thigh as he bent down to take my nipple between his teeth…

I felt confident for having kept to my conviction and not

allowing myself to be dominated or victimized first by my husband and now the samurai leader. I wore the scar on my leg with pride, for I had survived, but that didn't stop my heart from racing, so excited was I to see the samurai village, to see Shintaro. Nami helped me dress in an indigo cotton kimono, wide daisy-colored sash, earth-toned ankle-high stockings and wooden clogs. Pleased with her handiwork, she presented me with a hand mirror so I could see my image. There I saw the face of a young woman looking back at me, the nakedness of her desire, hunger and confidence in herself making me smile.

The mirror is a woman's soul, Nami said, *as the sword is the living soul of the samurai.* I turned it over and inscribed on the back of the handle was a leaf from a sacred tree, *a pledge,* she said, that the owner would be faithful to the man in her thoughts when she looked into the mirror. I didn't have to tell her that man was Shintaro. *She knew.*

I sensed a bonding with her, dear lady reader, though I would not know why until later. I must remind you, what happened in these pages was spoken in the native language, not fluent on my part, and I remain certain I have missed innuendos, so I have filled in the speeches to make them more complete for you. I have also eliminated the honorifics such as *-san* to allow you to integrate into these pages, not as an observer who finds these mannerisms strange, but as one who is part of the samurai life.

Come with me as I walk through the village, the children sailing paper boats in rain puddles, the women in their wide, straw hats washing their rice pots in the streams and pretending not to stare, the samurai practicing battle moves with swords and spears.

But on that morning, it was my encounter with Akira that remains the most vivid in my mind.

★ ★ ★

"You are well, Lady Carlton," I heard a voice say, then I turned to see Akira coming out of the shadows as if he waited there for me to pass. Word of my identity had spread.

"Yes. I don't know how to thank you for saving my life." I bowed, but not before I saw him grab the bulge in his divided trousers. I gasped, felt my blood heat with an uncomfortable urge. I couldn't help myself, but I imagined him naked and aroused, his warrior body smooth and muscular. My pubic muscles tightened and I lowered my eyes, but not before I saw Nami hide her mouth, giggling. I dared not let her see my reaction. I could hide nothing from her. I would soon learn the way of the warrior exceeded my expectations in many ways.

"I am duty bound to guard you, my lady, and shall do so with my life." He bowed, his strength and discipline intriguing me as much as the way his body moved with the litheness of a mythical warrior, all his instincts tuned in to hunting his prey.

Me.

"I would never ask that of any man," I said honestly.

"I am prepared to give…whatever you ask of me," Akira said.

With another bow, he was gone, his physical presence as disturbing to my senses as a rare essence from an exotic blossom. But the lingering thought in my mind disturbed me more. This young man, as handsome as a royal prince, wanted me, and God help me, I couldn't stop the stirring in my pussy.

Bless me, Father, for I have sinned…

I became settled in my new quarters, a ten-mat room in a big house with a main pillar so big in girth I couldn't get my arms around it. My room included a small attendant's area and was located not far from an earth-floored kitchen, along with a necessary place in the corner of the veranda with a big pot underneath so I could attend to my ablutions *inside* without having to go out in the rain. Or face the guard stationed outside.

On this day, Nami fidgeted with making everything clean and orderly, insisting on preparing ginger tea then washing me with the careful touch only another woman understands. Her fingers long and slender, nails translucent, she splashed soapy water over my breasts, stroked my hips, embraced my buttocks and washed the area between my thighs, her silence at seeing my blondish pubic hairs saying more to me than words, then bade me soak up to my chin in a rice-wine bath to smooth and soften my skin. Afterward she applied sesame oil to my hair to make it shine, then dressed me in a vibrant blue silk kimono and deep pink obi, pulling the sash around my waist tighter than my corset, and white ankle-length stockings upon my feet since I was to have a visitor.

Shintaro.

Shintaro in his world was another man. A ruler, all powerful, dominating. And a poet. His first words to me were not of rebuke, curiosity or desire, but poetry. The purity of the first snow, summer's calm slumber, battles with demons of the night and she-foxes, moors and mountains ever green. We sat upon square silk cushions in the main room, drinking foaming green tea and eating the sweetened red beans Nami had prepared. I have never forgotten his poems and though they may seem elusive, the more you study them the more you will comprehend what hides behind the words, as I came to understand the man behind the samurai. I have recorded my favorite poem here for you, the story of a girl who loses her samurai love:

A maiden's tear is like
a raindrop splattering
into a creek
rather should it be a drop of dew
upon a flower
yet to blossom.

The beauty of his poems still makes me wistful, longing as I do for him, but I was not prepared for his next words when Shintaro stood and turned his back to me, thinking before he spoke, then—

"Why have you disturbed the peace of our village, Lady Carlton?" he asked me in the native tongue, his tone direct, surprising me.

"I came to warn you, Shintaro, that your enemies have openly proclaimed you a rebel against His Majesty." I explained to him that if samurai did not follow the conscription law and accept the cut in their yearly stipends and other privileges, the government would move against them with muskets and rifles, leaving them with nothing but a name.

"Is that the only reason?" he insisted, turning around to face me.

"No," I said without embarrassment. "After what happened between us in Yoshiwara—"

"I regret I acted as men do in the pleasure quarters, my lady, and brought disgrace upon you."

"I am not ashamed of what I did."

Ignoring me, he said, "You must go back to your husband."

"I can't. He will kill me."

"He knows...about us?"

"No—"

"Then why do you not obey me?" he said to me in English, startling me. "Are my words not clear?"

"Yes, but—" I stopped, shocked. I daresay I was as surprised as you are, dear lady reader, to learn my samurai was a man of linguistic talent. But as is peculiar to those of his warrior status, he revealed such talents only when the battle tide turned against him. He wished to be rid of me and no one was to question his decision. Including me.

"You *must* return to your husband," he repeated.

"Why didn't you tell me you speak English?" I was angry with him, for how dare he play me for the fool, speaking English only when it pleased him.

"There are many things you do not know." His look was amused, though I did not find it so.

"How did you learn to speak my language?" I asked.

"I wish to know my enemy," he said, walking around me, studying me as if I were an imitation of a man with breasts and a pussy, deciding if I was significant enough to be worthy of an answer. I sensed here was a man capable of cold fury when crossed in battle.

"You mean certain members in the British Legation working with the council," I said simply.

"Yes. Japan must be strong both economically and militarily." He added how he used his position at the mikado's court to study English. "That will not happen if the *gaijin* colonize us and take away our freedoms, our status as samurai."

"Not all foreigners are against you, Shintaro." I lowered my eyes, why I didn't know since I was determined not to act submissive around him. "I find you…very appealing."

He laughed and tilted my face up to meet his eyes. "You are most daring in your actions, Lady Carlton, not unlike a brave samurai woman taught to display courage and fortitude should she need to defend herself."

"I envy her," I said with raw emotion coloring my voice,

"but that freedom will be lost if your enemies move against you. You will be hunted down and killed."

I was surprised to see his dark eyes brighten with the most curious expression. A half smile curved over his lips, then his voice hardened as he said, "The *gaijin* think they can defeat us by selling us old, rusting muskets and rifles from France. But they are no match for the sword of the samurai."

"They *will* come, Shintaro, with many soldiers, better arms and ammunitions. You can't stop them."

"You are not samurai, Lady Carlton. You do not understand our ways." He refused to listen to me, though I swore I saw a softening around his mouth, then it was gone. He became the stoic leader again. "You shall leave here in two days when the road has cleared."

"What about my husband, James?" I pleaded. "He swore to kill me."

"You said Lord Carlton knows nothing about me." His eyes hardened. "Do you lie?"

"No, I speak the truth."

"Then why do you fear your husband?"

"I cannot explain why, Shintaro. All I ask is you don't send me back to him."

"I believe the British to be barbarians, but they do not allow husbands to murder their women." He paused, as if weighing his words. I took that time to admire his striking figure in a green silk kimono tied with a white sash affixed with a white collar, wanting to rip it from him as he straightened, flexing his broad shoulders and the muscles of his back. "I have given my word that you will return."

"Your word?" I asked, surprised. "To whom?"

He grinned. "To myself. It is too dangerous for you to remain in our village."

"Dangerous for whom, Shintaro?" I demanded to know. "After what happened between us, how can you send me away?"

"I must. It is written that when the song of the nightingale pierces the air thick with battle, a black cloud descends upon the warrior and he knows not his enemy," he said, the deep creases of his face bronzed by the sun tightening with a controlled tension. "It is that darkness I fear."

"Shintaro is a fool, Nami," I said, not hiding the irritation in my voice as I watched her fold the blue silk kimono in the proper manner, *a gift,* she insisted. "Why doesn't he understand he's in danger?"

"Shintaro is samurai and sees everything in his world changing," she said in a calm voice, wrapping the beautiful kimono and white ankle-high stockings I came to know as *tabi* in thick handmade paper. "You are a part of that change. He cannot accept that."

"But he *must,* Nami, or your people will suffer."

"He is first a man, Lady Carlton."

"Please call me Katie," I said, bowing then laying my hand upon her arm. She nodded. We both knew tomorrow I would be sent back to a life I rebelled against and to a man I hated.

"You must be more of a woman than any woman he has known if you wish to still the song of the nightingale in his heart."

She overheard us. Instead of being angry with her, I accepted the native trait of listening through paper doors as a show of friendship.

Watching her tying the package with a red-and-white cord, a strange, desperate abandon came over me, a recklessness I couldn't control as it became clear to me what I had to do. I told Nami to unwrap the blue silk kimono.

I said, "Tell Shintaro I request that he dine with me tonight."

I grinned and she looked at me through her lovely dark eyes as if I were a curious honeybee about to sting, then she left with a low bow and twist of her mouth I've no doubt was a smile.

He became impatient with my lingering at the rice bowl, trying as I was to finish every grain, signaling to him I wished no more. Shintaro took the bowl from me with one hand and with the other he cupped my breast through the blue silk kimono, tracing perfect circles around my nipple until it hardened, then he did the same with the other, his eyes never leaving mine. I didn't move when his hand tugged at the soft material hiding my thighs from him and he let out his breath when the touch of bare skin met his fingers. I wasn't wearing the native undergarment, something I could tell pleased him by his grunt of approval. His hand was quick and urgent, his meaning clear when he slipped his fingers between my legs. I resisted and pulled back, though I felt dizzy with desire. *No, not yet.* Remembering Nami's words, I had to make him want me more than he'd wanted *any* woman.

He had come to me as a man with whom I'd shared a silken futon, an erotic coupling. Poetry. I still cannot get over the wonder of him on that night, his dark eyes brooding with mystery, a wildness about him that tantalized me, a smell of manliness that inhabited the room blending with the muskiness of the night air and clearly saying that sexual pleasure was on his mind. Not the informal meal Nami had prepared of rice and mushrooms, gingko nuts, chestnuts and plump boiled shrimp swimming in a sweet sesame sauce. He ate quickly then downed sake after sake, filling my cup then his own, breaking tradition as he was wont to do when it pleased him.

I, on the other hand, wanted more than sex, desperate as I was to brand my image upon his soul. I swayed my shoulders, pushed out my breasts, licked my lips, then drizzled the rice wine down my cleavage. I was there for his pleasure, all of me offered to him, moving in a graceful dance as though I was created to be desired by him alone. He grunted, spoke little, then pushed his hand, palm down, up my thigh, taking his time, watching my face when my buttocks contracted, then grinning at me. I heard him lamenting about the hunger of a man obsessed, his thirst satiated only when he pierced the locked door…

The sensuality between us wasn't all that we enjoyed, considering the playful delight we engaged in when in each other's company. No guilt, no sense of taboo. We were a man and a woman, not samurai and sinner. Tomorrow he intended to send me back to my husband, but tonight he was mine to conquer for I saw myself as a woman in control of her fate. 'Tis a deep sigh I hear from you, dear lady reader, as if you are beginning to understand the magic Shintaro held for me as you yourself fall under his spell. With every move he made toward me, I became more aroused until I leaned over and kissed his lips, wanting to taste him, knowing this was not something he expected.

I have scant experience in the art of kissing, seeing how this plain Irish lass was not favored with beaux, but I never dreamed anything could be so sensually beautiful as his mouth, his soft, warm lips parting against mine without nudging from me. I could not catch my breath when his tongue nuzzled and sucked at me greedily, searching for my soul he was, his breath heavy with the scent of sake and tasting of his fervor to explore me. His warrior hands that wielded two swords, strong and experienced, moved over the blue silk wrapping my body as we kissed and I clung to him with a fierceness I hadn't known the first time he held me. Then I was craving the newness of being close to him, teasing, pulling back before letting go. Now I hungered for him, wishing, praying, desiring him to strip me naked. I dare say Shintaro possessed that same hunger, his mouth pulling away, his breath hot in my ear when he whispered, "Why did you summon me here? Have the gods no mercy?"

"You wanted me that first time you saw me," I said in a husky voice, yet with a power I prayed I possessed to seduce him to my futon. "Then at Yoshiwara—"

"Dressed as either a temptress or a young man," he said without hesitation, "I cannot resist you."

I gave the duplicity of his words no more thought as he parted my thighs and inserted two fingers inside me, then slipped his other hand around to my buttocks and began probing the crack. His finger gently made its way inside the dark puckered hole, making me moan as he pleasured me with both hands, front and back. I cried out for more, still more, like the wild heathen I had perceived him to be, but it was my skin that wore the stigmata of the barbarian. Yelling, screaming with heated words, raging into a dark night like a banshee and showing no shame. It was white-hot my cunt, yes, *cunt,* for we mated like primal creatures in heat as the charcoals in the fire pit crackled and sizzled. His hands pulled the blue silk kimono from my body, striving to see my nudeness in the darkened room. I was another man's wife, but I was *his* lover. His hands were on me, rougher than the first time, all formality gone between us, his touch greedy as he fondled me, grunting but not speaking, as if words in either language could not express his feelings. I moaned, breathing in the impermanence of a subtle incense wafting toward us, an unseen pleasure tended to by a woman with a gentle smile performing her duty. I didn't see her, but I heard the subtle sliding of the paper door, then all thoughts turned to my samurai as he picked me up with a warrior's strength and carried me to the futon and positioned me for his pleasure. A soft silk pillow under my arse, my legs spread, my heels pointing toward the ceiling. I moaned when his tongue dived into me, finding my clitoris and licking it with such expertise I couldn't stand it, his mouth hot and wet, his flicking tongue bringing me to an intense orgasm. I bucked and writhed, but I denied myself the joy of succumbing to that pleasure, for I was bargaining for my life. It was *he* who must be pleasured, for I was desperate not to be driven from here when it was only here with him that I existed as a woman.

I begged him come to me, the head of his cock nudging at the slick lips of my pussy. Before I could take a breath, he thrust into me, hard, fast, his hands holding on to my buttock cheeks, finding his rhythm though he pumped into me like a man intent on splitting me in two. When he could hold back no more, I lost all sense of who I was, who he was, and met him in a forbidden place when he released his hot juices into me, consuming me with a rawness, a power that gifted me with such powerful contractions I couldn't stop crying out, screaming, as I had never experienced an orgasm so intense, fed and driven by an obsession we both possessed and could not tame.

His sweat mixed with mine as he nuzzled his face against my neck. I lay back, panting, yet sleep was unknown to me. A nagging fear still haunted me. Yes, he had fucked me, but I knew Shintaro didn't love me as I loved him, needed him, craved him. I *must* make him desire me with such passion he wouldn't let me go.

I put my hand on his cock, using the sticky semen covering the head as a means to facilitate sliding my hand up and down his shaft. Soon he was hard again, grunting with a surprised pleasure when I eased my body over his and placed his erect cock into me. I shall not profess experience in sexual positions, dear lady reader, except to say it was not instinct that taught me how to please a man in this manner, but the dubious and prolific escapades of Molly Pearlbottom. I rode my samurai hard then begged him to take me from behind, thrusting into my pussy while I posed before him on my hands and knees, my nude buttocks teasing him with a salacious wiggle. Then I took his cock into my mouth and licked it up and down with long strokes and around the head, his hands gripping my hair until I tasted him, salty yet pleasant to my tongue. Exhausted, I kept going, drifting between fear and hope, passion and contentment…

I would not know until morning if I had succeeded in my quest, my daring attempt at intrigue to win the man of my heart.

I *was* certain of one thing.

Bless me, Father, for I have sinned.

It was the last time I made confession.

14

The overwhelming scent of fresh blossoms thick with orange cleansed the air, as if the peel of the fruit tickled my nose and the smoothness of its leaves soothed my burning skin, but neither could erase the deed. I placed my fingers between my legs sticky with semen and brought them up to my nose, the smell of sex still thick and creamy, his scent mixed with mine, clinging to me before whatever little breeze found its way into my futon and dissipated it into but a memory. One that lingered then blossomed.

I had but one thought on my mind that morning when I woke up and found Shintaro gone. *Would he return and lie with me? Or would he insist I return to my husband?*

I waited, hoping to hear the wooden floor creak at the sound of his bare feet. I heard nothing. I didn't dress, preferring to remain nude, pacing up and down on the straw mat, thinking of our times together as a folding screen, each panel revealing a different scene of our erotic, tender moments when opened one at a time. *Were we at the last panel?* I refused to believe it and continued to pace, my uncertainty feeding on my bad temperament, waiting for something to happen, *anything,* but nothing did. I shan't fixate on the morning hours passing so slowly but move the story forward instead of dwelling on the illogical path of the Irish mind. I came to understand Shintaro's decision by interpreting his actions through what the natives call "belly language." 'Tis a form of communication where the meaning is most notably gained from their ability to understand each other *without* words; they use facial expressions along with the unspoken meaning derived by the length and timing between silences.

Silence.

I ran to the closed shutters and peeked through the wooden slats. *The guard was nowhere to be seen.* No children playing nearby or the sound of swordplay or women giggling as they passed. I *did* see two large brass basins filled with clean, clear water for my ablutions in the small iris garden behind my quarters. (It was considered a barbarity to have water for washing brought into the house.)

Silence. What a fool I was not to see something so clear as if Shintaro had his hand down my drawers. By not arriving early in the morn to oust my Irish arse, he was telling me I could stay in the samurai village. I cannot describe the pure joy racing through me, my nipples hardening in the cool morning air, my pussy contracting around his imaginary cock at the thought of what he meant. For to be part of a samurai clan one must be born into it, unlike British society, where an ivory-white breast or a rosy rounded bottom can elicit the eye of a dandy. Or where a fortune like mine can turn an aristocratic birthright into a commodity to be bought and sold simply by a gentleman threading the needle with a fair maiden.

And I, Katie O'Roarke, had been given leave to stay here, for how long, even the gods could not know the divining thoughts of Shintaro. You must understand, dear lady reader, allowing me to stay was but a small change on the part of the samurai, but a change it was indeed. On the other hand, an Englishman abhors change and would rather relinquish membership in his club rather than give up his routine visits to the girls at the "top of the tree" in the brothels on Queen Street. So I ask you, which society is more barbaric? England or Japan?

"Did you sleep well?"

Nami entered, bowing, clean kimono over her arm and holding a small tray, my breakfast rice steaming under the lacquer bowl cover, pickled cucumbers and a pot of hot tea. Yes, *pickled cucumbers.* 'Tis true I have not spoken of the native food since you may find it off-putting to find a pigeon's egg at the bottom of your soup bowl, but I shall remind you that British food has its own drawbacks. Were I in Mayfair I would be dining on lovely scones covered with melting butter and thick marmalade. Pleasing to the tongue and, I'll confess, often a substitute for sensual caresses (admit it, dear lady reader, haven't you indulged in gorging yourself with creamy puddings when you'd rather it was a man's cream you sucked off your fingers?) and never good for the figure. I found ingesting the native food kept my body so slim I maintained my small waist without the tugging of corset lacings. Regarding daily samurai life, I could speak about the etiquette *à la table* and bowing and the rituals, but I have decided to forgo such meanderings. Though no formal writings of samurai life exist in English, I shall not attempt to do so here since I perceive you are more interested in sexual escapades. I promise you, this chapter will have you reaching for the closest poker, be it his lordship's or otherwise.

"Where is Shintaro, Nami?" I begged to ask her, knowing her answer determined my fate.

"He has gone with Akira into Hiogo for supplies," she said, meaning the old holy city adjacent to Kobé.

I didn't give it much thought then why Nami was so well informed on the movements of the clan leader, why this young woman was always nearby when Shintaro made an appearance, the indiscreet nature of the native house allowing a whisper to be heard from one room to the next. Many households employed young women who became closely identified with the family, their loyalty unquestioned. Was Nami such a woman?

"Shintaro made love to me last night—" I began, a sudden shyness coming over me. I translate loosely my actual words, for I used the more polite term "I granted him the pillow," a phrase strange to your ears as it was to mine, but I wish to give you an example of the indirectness that makes the native language so beautiful.

Nami nodded, though I sensed something different in the young woman's manner toward me. She began folding the futon in the prescribed manner, her actions giving no indication if the smell of our desire aroused her.

"—and this morning he is gone without a word." I sipped the hot tea she poured for me, grateful for its warming effect, like the strong hands of my samurai holding me in his arms. "I pray this means he will not send me away."

"A man such as Shintaro does not shake the cherry blossom from the branch when she is fresh with his dew." She handed me a lightweight kimono hand painted with scarlet and white chrysanthemums. "Who knows if it will bear fruit?"

A deep flush burned my cheeks, her meaning bringing clarity to my innermost desire. *A child*. What consequences such a gift would bring lingered on my mind for the briefest of seconds, then they were gone. I dared not believe I would know such happiness.

I took the kimono from her but didn't put it on, preferring to linger in the nude, my passion for the simplicity of things here overwhelming anything else, a recklessness in me I couldn't let go. "I shall wash first, Nami, then eat. Will you come and sit with me? I have so much to tell you about last night, his laugh, his burning touch, his deep sense of self I find so irresistible."

"I, too, wish to share your happiness on this bright morning." She turned to me, and with a smile I will always remember, she said innocently, "I am most grateful to the gods that my husband has found pleasure with you."

Yes, dear lady reader, she said *husband*. Shintaro, the man of my heart, this strong, fearless samurai was married to this shy creature, a woman I had come to admire and whose friendship I depended upon to help me. I shall not linger too long on this revelation as the idea of coupling with another woman's husband is not an uncommon state to many of you, since the upper classes ignore adultery unless exposed. That will never happen to you. You are too careful with your indiscretions and are unlikely to suffer the consequences because you do not belong to the culpable class. But I digress, simply to point out guilt where guilt lies.

That my samurai was wedded to Nami was a surprise to me and it took me some time to adjust to it. She was human, fragile, tolerant and had shared with me how she'd lost her own child, but then I had no idea Shintaro was the father.

Nami assured me it was the way of samurai for her husband to go to the futon of another woman if she was unable to bear him more children. In a similar manner, she said, he also found physical pleasure in the company of Akira.

Akira.

A curious chill rippled over me then as it does now, my pen wobbling as the stirring of this memory excites me. How can I flesh out on paper the deep colors of that union against a black-and-white page? Kimonos red and deep purple swirling, golden muscular bodies wrestling on the ground, rolling, pushing and pulling, fighting for position. Panting and sweating, then smooth, bare chests touching, breathing fast…the air heavy with their desire. 'Tis twilight as I write this, but then the morning was bold and bright and filled with a promise that shook the sensibilities of my mind in a provocative way I have never known since.

I pulled the kimono closer around me, running my fingers over the white chrysanthemums. *The symbol of the anus.* Nami's subtle way to remind me I had competition for Shintaro and it was not the slender willow. *Woman.*

I must explain, dear lady reader, that the honored practice of male love was encouraged within the samurai class to teach young men virtue, honesty and above all, the appreciation of beauty. It was an elite discourse slowly fading away since western influence frowned upon anal intercourse within the fixed framework of the older warrior who loved, and the younger apprentice who was loved. When the event I am about to relate took place, such an act was more than a sin in the sainted green of my fathers. It was against the law in the land of the shogun. But as he was wont to do when he deemed a law unjust, Shintaro ignored it. Here in the samurai village, the erotic bond flourished in "the beautiful way," as it was called. I can bear witness to the truth of it, for love between two samurai was looked upon as simply turning to a different page in the book of love. Unlike olden days, when such love was purest when undeclared, I saw revealed to me how these two men were very much in sync with their mutual desire.

I must stop…allow you to think, remember all that has transpired in my story…Shintaro admiring me as a young man in Yoshiwara…his tenderness toward Akira in a natural way…why didn't I see it before?

Like you, dear lady reader, the notion shocked my staid sensibilities, but I was also intrigued by the idea of the two men locked together in a physical embrace. 'Tis not a flagrant sin in every culture, as I'd read in a very old tome about the training of warriors in ancient Greece. From what I understood, the relationship between the warrior and his squire involved fornicating between men where the younger submitted, though not as an equal. Such animal energy titillated me and stimulated a different sensual desire within me, wondering as I did about how I would react when aroused by the odor of *two* different men.

I anxiously awaited the return of my samurai and, at Nami's behest, I burned incense as native women do to ease the burden of waiting the return of a lover, all the while thinking: how different was Shintaro's smell over that of the younger man? Heavier, muskier? A vivid curiosity consumed me for days, contemplating which scent would draw up my desire first, imagining offering them my pussy, like the pistil of a flower tempting them with my smell. I thought of this scenario often when Shintaro returned to the village, though I said nothing about what Nami had confided to me.

As the days passed, I found him watching me but saying little. You are most likely wondering if we had a sexual encounter upon his return. We did not. The news Shintaro brought back with him angered many samurai and fueled their desire to take up arms. Reports of corruption in the mikado's government and warrior unrest in the southwest created an anxious edge and uncertainty that would later bring tragedy to the clan. But in that late summer of 1874, I found joy and sensuality in my enchanted land and you shall, too, dear lady reader. There will be plenty of time to grieve, its sorrow sacred to the heart, the farewell gesture necessary to the soul.

Curious about how Shintaro could find his own sex as intriguing as the female body, I watched him for signs when he was with Akira. The touch of an arm upon his shoulder, the private laughter they shared. I was jealous and did not hide my emotions around him. Sensing my feelings, Shintaro invited me to participate in the tea ceremony with them as a way of putting me at ease within their society, since rank and status did not exist within its framework. I found the idea fascinating, having watched them practice their battle moves with precision and dexterity. Archery and riding, wrestling and fencing.

I found the same pattern in their consumption of tea. 'Tis not the feminine ritual enjoyed by you, dear lady reader, lifting a teacup filled with sweetness from a fat sugar bowl to your lips with your gloved hand. The tea ceremony evolved in the most distinctive masculine world of samurai and imperial abbots. I was enchanted not only by the beauty of the way of tea, but also by the physical beauty of these two men engaged in an erotic sexual act that piqued my curiosity and made me yearn for their embrace. Do not be angry with me for keeping the secret of my *two* samurai from you, for I am not guilty of duplicity in my memoir. The answer has been there all the time for you to see. I have used the term "my samurai" since in the native language the same word is used for plural as well as singular. You shall forgive me, won't you?

And now for tea. Shintaro welcomed me to enjoy the pleasures of *two* men, both as a voyeur as they aroused each other, then the two of them satisfying my every desire. I found Shintaro dominant yet tender, Akira impetuous yet eager to please. This was but the first of many times I engaged in this provocative ménage…I shall recount here that event for *your* pleasure.

You are familiar with the taste of a man's cock, are you not, dear lady reader? If not, I request you do so before you continue and partake of that salty smoothness that makes your tongue tingle as you take his member into your mouth. This is the first step to understanding "tea taste," which has nothing to do with dissolving the foaming green elixir on your tongue. It involves the simplicity, muted colors and contrasts of rough and smooth. As in a man's cock. Such was how Shintaro introduced me to the art of tea, we three wearing simple silk kimonos in mauve, peach and olive, open and revealing, my nude body smooth, my skin so luminescent it was the only accessory I needed, Akira's hands spreading my legs, his fingers probing inside me, Shintaro's battle-roughened hands pinching my nipples as I lay upon the futon in my quarters. We indulged in this sensual tea ceremony in the concentrated privacy afforded us by closing sliding doors, our nude bodies bathed in a pearl light filtering through the paper panes. Here one accepts nature's flaws and in doing so finding pleasure and harmony within oneself. When you are able to accept his lordship's flaws as well as your own, I suggest you continue. Until then, I shall brew a cup of ginger tea, for I shall need to keep my focus clearly on the impassioned scene about to unfold.

I partook of the tea and sweetmeat offered to me as I observed Akira, his beautiful pectoral muscles with erect nipples on his hairless chest bronzed from the summer sun, his large muscular thighs making me ache to find myself between them, yet I perceived a certain innocence about him and wondered if he had been with a woman. He was a romantic, presenting me with a willow-leaf arrowhead and telling me I had pierced his heart. His flirtatious manner toward me intrigued me, but his allegiance to Shintaro no doubt surpassed any romantic love, since they believed love rooted in human feelings brought about distrust and was considered a dangerous emotion among samurai. No, love associated with duty courted *his* cock. I could see that clearly in Akira's way of standing against the paper door, hips outthrust, looking at his lord, all setting up unseen communication between them that vibrated with energy when he wrapped his arms around the large pillar, his kimono hiked up around his waist and revealing his tight nude buttocks gleaming in the muted light of the bronze *andon.* Tiny pricks of fire erupted on my arms, so acute was I to his sensual energy reaching across the room to me. Heated, excited, I sat upon a large silk brocade pillow, the effect heightening my unconscious response when Shintaro fed a sweetmeat dripping with honey into Akira's laughing mouth, the stickiness sliding down the side of his jaw. I pulled in my breath, waiting, when Shintaro scooped up the honey on the younger man's face and licked it off his fingers, his cock hard and erect, then grunted. He wiped his fingers with a moist cloth then covered them with a pleasant-smelling oil from a small red lacquered bowl before thrusting them into his squire's anal hole. Looking at me, his gaze never wavering, Shintaro lubricated the younger samurai's anus before he thrust his cock into the puckered opening. I must comment on the size of Shintaro's cock as I remember it, its naked crown spread above its shaft, much thicker than the younger man's cock swinging from his navel to his thigh, then the other way, in union with his lord's thrusts. An illusion? Or the hapless dream of a lonely woman, since I shall not have the opportunity to compare them when I return to Japan…but 'tis a grand time I promised you, dear lady reader, and you shall have it. I have made known to you my private pleasure of having Shintaro's cock inside me and design here to enlighten you with the wicked pleasures of these two men together and Akira's beauty as I watched them at play. I squeezed my pubic muscles together, riveted to them as I was like a sodden clover matted down with heavy dew, my concentration so complete I swore I also felt the hot pain shooting through Akira's body then the flash of sweet burning as he gasped for breath, his body yielding to Shintaro's thrusts over and over…the young warrior grinding his arse against Shintaro's groin when he pressed against him…his lord clenching his buttock muscles as he forged in and out… grunting loudly, he fucked Akira as incense burned, its heady scent mixing with the smell of sex, arousing me as much as the evocative sight of the two men engaged in coupling. Shintaro putting him in numerous positions, pulling his strong muscular legs apart to gain greater access into him, tipping his buttocks higher, then bursting into him with a surge of power that shook the wooden building like a thunder god emptying his fury into the heavens. I cried out when I saw Akira throw his head back in orgiastic ecstasy like a tortured saint in the throes of godliness, his forehead half covered with sweaty dark hair come loose from his braided top knot, his role as submissive no less powerful than that of Shintaro, his elegance in the nuance of surrender startling to watch. For no stigma was attached to his role since age rather than social position defined the act that brought him to such a blissful state. His alliance with such a high-ranking samurai as Shintaro conferred considerable status upon him as he shuddered in rapture as my samurai went deeper and deeper into his entrails.

I had scant idea then my moist pussy and dark puckered hole were next to be pleasured, not by one but *two* men, though tradition dictated only Shintaro emptied his seed into me, as he did in Akira.

They say an Irish writer commands the same fear as the priest because of the power of her words to make the soul tremble. Or titillate it, as I have done here by arousing the heat in you, dear lady reader, and satisfying your appetite for a new sexual experience. But I must not disappoint those readers who find the tea ceremony a provocative ritual and are curious about its sensuality. Here then is the tea ceremony with its power of suggestion, its meditation on the virility of life and art. It was a sanctuary where we three took solace in the tranquillity of the spirit before experiencing the pleasures of the flesh.

"The tea is the least important part of the ceremony," Shintaro said, explaining that purity of gesture, silence or spoken words were all a form of tea discipline. Tea utensils were washed and arranged, then powdered green tea prepared in a single bowl from which we all drank. Instead of asking permission to examine the tea items as ritual dictated, I requested to examine the cocks of these two samurai. Bowing slightly, they stood before me and placed their members before me on square silken pillows, and after I expressed admiration of their beauty, Shintaro continued.

"Rigorous order is observed with elegance," he said. "The only disorder sought is that of nature in her naked form." He ran his hands over my bare belly, then parted my thighs. "A living flower can be the sole ornament in the alcove," he continued, parting my pussy lips; upon finding moisture upon his finger pads, he inserted two fingers inside me, as if parting the petals of a blossom. The ceremony consisted of precise choreographed movements performed in a spirit of stillness and concentration. "Without hurry," he said, "then each guest is served tea and silently drains his cup." To demonstrate, he eased his tongue into me and nibbled on my burning bud, my excitement growing…growing until I couldn't stop myself from twisting about as if I were caught in a trap. But oh, what a lovely trap.

"You drink with gusto, my lord," I said, letting go with a loud moan, my newfound pleasure setting off an echoing in my lower body that produced glittering sensations within me, such delights making me squirm to and fro without embarrassment. The intensity of his nibbling increased when I pushed out my hips, urging him to continue with his playful game. "I pray you find me pleasing to your taste."

He laughed. "Your juices are sweet and refreshing," he said, then he continued licking my clit back and forth with long, satisfying strokes. Apparently I wiggled with too much enthusiasm. He stopped. "Hold still," he said, "I have not yet quenched my thirst."

I tried to speak, a silly thought to continue our banter, but before I could utter a word, Shintaro put his strong arms around my hips, gripping my bare arse with his hands and pulling me closer to him. I gasped loudly when he pressed the wet tip of his tongue deeper into me, making me cry out. I jerked forward with such passion that he let me go, making me wonder if our game had ended.

No, *no,* I begged inwardly.

"I shall assist you in restraining her, my lord," I heard Akira say behind me as if he answered my silent plea, his presence so close I could feel the heat of his breath on my cheeks. If I had expected him to grab my wrists, I was wrong. Akira wrapped his hands around my nude breasts and played with my nipples, pulling and tugging on the hard nubs. Pleasing contractions raced through me, sparking in parallel with the wanton desire radiating through my lower pubic region.

I could never have anticipated what happened next. Shintaro also became playful, his tongue darting between the moist folds of my lower lips, tickling my clit with short licks, then exploring the sensitive piece of skin near my anus and making my body jerk with tiny spasms. My legs trembled, my thighs quivered, but never once did he fall out of rhythm during this delicious taste of the tea ceremony designed to please his most anxious guest. Appetizers were often served, he explained—in this case, me—along with sake. Then he proceeded to demonstrate. Shintaro's provocative use of his tongue-tip reminded me of the art of making sake from rich, fertile rice, such as the polishing of the rice until it shone as lustrous as a cultured pearl. Here it was my samurai sucking and polishing my tiny kernel, then fluffing my pubic hair with his long fingers before pouring sake from a small porcelain cup into my navel until it overflowed, tickling me. I wiggled my hips, tingling all over as the tepid liquid trickled down over my pussy to the crack between my buttocks. Shintaro put his head between my thighs and lapped up the sweet rice wine from my throbbing pussy to satisfy his palate. I let out a long moan.

"You torment me, my lord, with your busy tongue," I said, breathless, "when it is your cock that I wish."

"And you shall have it," he promised, delighting in teaching me this most provocative aspect of the tea ceremony no foreign guest had deigned to experience. "But not before I present to you a gift from the gods bestowed only upon a woman."

"Is that jealousy I detect in your voice, my lord?"

He shook his head. "Only if I were not the first to pleasure you in such a manner." He continued licking me, then paused to tease me with, "I knew by your reaction the first time I tasted you that I have that honor."

"And what about Akira?" I dared to venture. "As your most trusted squire, should he not be the second man to pleasure me so?"

Shintaro threw back his head and laughed. "Such impertinence from a woman I have never experienced." He became serious again. "But never before have I taken a woman so beautiful to my futon." He nodded to Akira, who grinned widely, then he said to me, "You shall have your wish."

Before I could linger in glorious anticipation, Akira joined his master in his quest between my legs, the two of them thrusting their tongues in and out of me, taking turns nibbling on me, tasting me, making me hotter than I'd ever imagined and licking the sake off my very wet folds. And me being the brazen girl that I am, I lifted my hips higher to meet them, my excitement growing as one then the other continued their relentless probing inside me. I'm not sure which samurai triggered my passion to a breaking point with his frenzied tongue, forcing me to the brink and then headfirst over it, but I fell into a mad delirium, my clit burning with a delicious pleasure I prayed would never end. I wailed and wailed like a banshee in search of a spirit mate, so out of control was I, so deeply pulled into my samurai's exotic world of tea and taste that I had scant reason to hold on to my sanity.

I *couldn't.* I let go. Cries of ecstasy flowed from me like the silky sounds of a Heian court lady's long multicolored sleeves trailing gracefully behind her across a polished wooden floor until the last tremor faded. Exhausted, I lay back, my face shining with the sweat of my afterglow, my body giving off an aura of soft pink hues.

Afterward I slept in my samurai's arms. 'Twas a deep sleep, but even so I sensed the movement of my lord's hand stroking his erect cock. We both knew the time would come for his pleasure. And Akira's.

For now, my samurai had been content to grant me mine.

On subsequent occasions of partaking in the tea ceremony, our conversations became quite lengthy before we three engaged in sex. One night I expressed my thoughts about the woodblock prints I had seen in Yoshiwara and how I didn't understand then why the male organ was drawn so large until I had the opportunity to view *their* cocks, making them both smile. We formed a bond, we three from different paths, with Shintaro as the tea master, all his movements simple and natural, from dusting the edges of the fire pit with an eagle feather and dropping incense on the hot coals before boiling the water in the kettle. He showed us how to fold the square of purple silk and how to mix the powdered tea with the bamboo whisk before he prepared the tea. These steps were all important for our sensual way of tea…and though I have promised you an impassioned encounter, I cannot forget what we discussed, including my life in London and the farm where I grew up. I dared not imagine what my blessed parents would think about me running off to a samurai village. I wondered if I'd ever see them again, but I feared returning to my husband more. I broached the subject of family to Shintaro and he explained how, as the son of a noble samurai, he was placed in a monastery to receive his education and forged a bond with an older monk upon his parents' deaths. Akira told me how his parents, low-ranking samurai, had been forced to sell his sister, Simouyé, to a geisha house to send him to a select samurai school.

Simouyé. The geisha I had seen in Yoshiwara was the younger sister of Akira. Now I understood the knowing glances between my samurai and the girl. She had been pleased when Lord Shintaro asked her brother to ride with him and learn the way of the warrior. Yes, dear lady reader, *Lord* Shintaro, as I have written on previous pages. Because of his strong beliefs not to let go of the old traditions, he had lost his lands in what was until recently known as —— Province in a dispute with members of the council of the mikado's government and his ancestral home raided by hired spies intent on assassinating him. Many had died in the attack, including women and children. Nami had also suffered at their hands, her body ravished, her soul taken from her when they murdered her child. A son. She had kept this horror from me to spare me unhappiness, as was the native way.

We drank the tea in silence.

I pray not to disturb your harmony in this chapter with a

somber tone, merely to relate to you a truthful remembrance of my life in the samurai village that was not without its sorrowful times. But it is the path I have chosen…and this next exquisite moment is but one reason why.

They slid the silkiness from my skin until I was nude, kissing me, putting their lips on me as I had shown them (daring yet amusing to these two samurai). Shintaro in front—my breasts, belly; Akira in back—the nape of my neck, my buttocks—both samurai slithering up and down my body like two gods in search of an earthly place to plant their seed. I struggled to catch my breath, moaning and sighing, so delirious was I leaning against Shintaro, his strong arms supporting me, holding me in his embrace as Akira licked the back of my legs up to the crack in my buttocks. Then Shintaro turned me around and the younger samurai spread my thighs and began tonguing me, licking my throbbing clit with such expertise I nearly fainted. I would have, had not Shintaro cupped my breasts and slowly rubbed his thumbs and forefingers over my taut nipples, giving rise to my begging him, begging Akira to insert their cocks in me. I shivered against Shintaro's muscular body, and in a surprise gesture, he stroked my cheek with soft purple silk then wound it around my wrists and pulled my arms taut over my head, making me moan.

"You are my prisoner," he said, his other hand gently cupping my breast.

"I desire to be more than your captive," I whispered. "Teach me to be samurai."

His eyes narrowed, questioning. "The way of the warrior demands strict obedience to your lord, whatever he asks of you."

"I am yours—" I began, then before I could say anything

he gagged me with a silken tie, his lips brushing my forehead as he tied it behind my head, not too tight, just enough to make me helpless as he tied my bound wrists to a low hanging beam, my bare feet touching the matting. Listening intently to the building rhythm inside me, I relished the risk of being strained to a bursting point, my cheeks burning like fire, my pussy throbbing with anticipation at what naughty games he proposed to inflict upon his willing captive. I was not disappointed. Using the utensils from the tea ceremony, he teased my nipples with the eagle feather until they peaked, then swept it down my rib cage, my navel, my pussy, making me burn, while Akira struck my bare buttocks with the bamboo whisk over and over again…delighting me, pleasuring me into an act of surrender, allowing me to relinquish control of my body to them because I desired it, not because my husband wished to punish me.

Shintaro continued stroking the soft feather across my breasts and belly, his touch sensual, teasing. I groaned as my nipples responded, tightening as Akira's fingers slid inside me, finding then circling with a familiarity the hard ridge of my clit, while another eased into my anal hole, making me wiggle with delight and suffering with so much pleasure I believed I could bear no more. But their game wasn't over. I feigned distress, trying to pull away from them, but the way of the warrior was not to retreat but to advance as a hungry mouth closed over my breast, biting and sucking my nipple. Before I could catch my breath, another mouth started partaking of *his* pleasure, sucking noisily on my other breast. I let go with muffled cries, gasping when my samurai parted my thighs and I was caught between them, two pairs of hands having their way with me from the front and so very happily from the rear. Delirious, gasping, the scent of rose oil finding its way to my nostrils then into my bottom. I pushed out my arse, waiting for the cock of the younger samurai to embed itself into my tight dark passage, his lord following inside my cunt, a heady mixture of incense and male sweat wafting around me like a spiritual halo as both samurai moved in me, pumping, grinding, fucking me with urgency...their fever to possess me leaving me breathless...each grunting loudly, their bodies shuddering when their moment of release came and I felt their hot semen spurt deep inside me. I rolled my head back, my arms pulling hard at the silken restraints, moaning again as both men stretched me, filled me and loved me.

Silk, touch, penetration. Each time Shintaro performed the tea ceremony was a unique moment. The art of tea could never be repeated in exactly the same manner, so each time must be as meaningful as possible. I shall explain in detail: I would be on top of Shintaro, lying on silken pillows with his cock in me, Akira entering me from behind; or we'd be standing in the fields of blueberries with Akira fucking me in my anal hole and Shintaro taking him in the same manner. Or I would be lying beside the stream with yellow daisies as my futon, Shintaro's cock inside me while I sucked on Akira's as he knelt behind me. Always our bodies moving as one, thrusting, undulating, Akira plunging into me with a rhythm equaling his lord's, sending waves of pleasure through me, drawing back when Shintaro released his semen into him, then bucking and riding me with wild abandon until I collapsed, exhausted.

I shall conclude this chapter with a special moment, dear lady reader, when Akira brought me to release with his tongue on my burning clit then put his lips to mine, eager as he was to probe my mouth after I had received his lord's salty semen and also allowing me to taste my honeyed juices. It was akin to the tea ritual of tasting the bitter with the sweet. Then Shintaro kissed me with such tenderness, making me smile as if *he* tasted me on his tongue when our lips met, knowing he was sharing in the pleasure bestowed upon me by the younger samurai.

And knowing you share in my pleasure of *both* samurai is the perfect way to end this tea ceremony, is it not?

1
5

The autumn of 1874 was the time that I became, as the title of my memoir suggests, the blonde samurai. Be assured, what you will read here is not a rearrangement of scenarios of swordplay and grunting, as you may have been led to believe by my male counterparts who endeavor to explain the samurai culture in overblown tales. It is based on a code of personal honor. Loyalty, courage, self-sacrifice, frugality, rigorous physical and mental discipline and total allegiance to my lord, Shintaro. Though I relished my time in the futon with both samurai (be patient…more to come), I will also impart to you my lessons in *Bushidō*, the way of the warrior. To begin, samurai women are schooled in the use of weapons to defend themselves—as was Nami—and control the household and govern the clan when their men are away. They educate the children and defend their homes. (Samurai women have long fought alongside their men and only six years ago in Aizu Province, they defended their lord's castle against invaders when their men were away.) I daresay these are forbidden subjects in your realm, dear lady reader, allocating as you do the care and education of your offspring to others and your home to tight-lipped housekeepers.

I find great satisfaction bringing to memory my samurai training. It sharpens my mind as it did then when I took brush and ink and penned calligraphy, the art of writing native characters. I found a strength in doing so, as if each stroke of the brush helped me with each stroke of the sword. The samurai take great pride in having good chirography since their language is expressed in pictograms and considered indicative of one's character. I took great pride that as my brushstrokes became bolder, so did my strikes with the long sword. I learned to eliminate everything in my mind but that moment when I used the *naginata,* the traditional spear of a samurai woman, a long pole with a curved single-edge blade at one end.

But I imagine your interest has been most piqued by the idea of a woman using a sword, so I shall delve deeper into this curious phenomenon that no doubt has you fanning yourself with a disdainful sense of propriety. Be assured, dear lady reader, 'tis not my inclination to set myself up as a true samurai, though the publication of my memoir will have several among you eager to confute anything I write and that is your privilege. But to rip apart the valor of samurai women is *not* your right and so I hope to counsel you with my personal mission to honor them by entreating you to endure with me what they have endured.

The way of the warrior is not about the sword, Shintaro taught me, *but about the woman holding the sword, her mental strength, discipline, compassion.*

I shan't forget the first time I tried its sharp, razorlike edge on wood, then stone, the possession of the sword giving me a sense of responsibility and self-respect, as well as the loyalty and honor I carried in my heart and mind. The sword of the samurai is his soul...never would I draw my sword unless I intended to use it, but it was many months before I experienced that moment. Shintaro was the master and I his student. Hence I shall re-create for you through the voice of my narrative the steps so vital to your understanding the way of the warrior through swordplay.

You have to use your body, Shintaro said, noting my breasts high and firm pointing through the thin cotton of my kimono.

The sword is an extension of your body, he continued, sparring with me with a practice sword made of bamboo. Flexible and bendable. My sword broke in two numerous times, the pressure upon it manyfold more than what it could endure, but the end result after weeks of practice was I gained a feeling of effortlessness. It was no easy feat swinging a sword for hours, first bamboo then forged steel, my arms so sore at night I could do nothing but lie in my futon, blissfully helpless to resist when Shintaro entered me, his dark eyes seething with pleasure and need, gently lifting my legs over his shoulders, allowing him to thrust deeper into me.

After months of consistent training, I began to experience the wielding of the sword as meditation in motion. Elegant, graceful, empowering my aptitude as a samurai *and* as a woman. Wielding my sword with its whiplike motion made me feel strong and powerful and respectful of myself and my opponent.

Remember, your opponent is a better swordsman than you, a superior fighter, Shintaro said, his tall, muscular body bared to his waist, arousing me, *but,* he added, *you have the advantage of being quick, so you can outmaneuver your opponent.*

When we sparred, I no longer saw his nakedness, his chest,

arm muscles bulging, his presence representing itself to me as an oracle to be worshipped, but as my opponent, judging a safe distance to stay out of his attack range while being able to fight back.

For practice, I engaged in cutting rolled straw targets with my long sword, while also learning the art of drawing the sword, unsheathing it with speed and striking with accuracy, as well as how to disarm an opponent, how to run, jump and roll with my weapon unsheathed, and fighting from horseback.

You have learned how to fight and defend your life and now have the choice not *to fight,* Shintaro said to me, bowing to show me respect. *If you never learned the way of the warrior, you would never have that choice.*

By writing this, am I suggesting that you take up fencing or the use of firearms? That depends, dear lady reader, if you are wont to find yourself in the seedier parts of London or have ever been accosted by a pickpocket or a jealous lover. Imagine being able to defend yourself. 'Tis a noble idea, is it not?

As a samurai woman, it was expected I would be my own bodyguard and therefore I, like Nami, carried a small dirk in my obi should it be necessary to defend myself or commit *seppuku,* ritual suicide, by cutting my throat. I have decided not to expend energy nor ink to take you through the baser aspects of battlefield maneuvers since the ostensible subject of my memoir is my love affair with the inimitable samurai. Because my intention is to give you pleasure on every page, dear lady reader, I shall aspire to concentrate on the sexual overtones of my training where I also learned the way of rope with Shintaro, a master of the art.

'Tis a conflict between beauty and fear, pain and lust, an intriguing art that involves a delicate balance between the physical, mental and spiritual. Confused? You shan't be. I shall give you a lesson in this chapter as to its artistic beauty of ornate knots wound under my breasts, between my breasts, each successive coil outside the one previous, my samurai always mindful of my breathing, my comfort, my pleasure tantamount in his eyes as he pulled on the rope to stimulate my breasts.

Take pen and ink in hand, dear lady reader. No, not to practice calligraphy, but you may wish to draw on paper for yourself what I am about to show you.

Long, long rope…damp hemp…double it up…make a simple knot in the middle…your partner pulling each end over your shoulders, knot against the nape of your neck (the most erogenous part of your body)…another knot tied below your rib cage and above your navel…third knot about two hand lengths above your clitoris, another below that…then pass the rope through your legs, ignoring the moistness from your pussy wetting the rope…drawing the rope halfway up your back and tying another knot…

Did I see you put down your pen? Is that sweat dripping from your brow and perspiration from the heat rising up in you? I see you don't have the patience for the way of the rope, so I shall dispense with the intricate tying lesson. Do you wish to try self-bondage? Secure a hand, a foot? That way you shall always have a hand free for self-pleasure. I *do* wish to impart to you that getting into these sensuous knots does not impede blood flow, so I was able to wear Shintaro's erotic rope design under my kimono should I desire, a much more pleasurable bondage than wearing a corset, I can assure you.

Since my experiment in the tying of knots bored you, I shall instead delve into a more titillating aspect of this art, though I wish to remind you bondage is also a way to train the body and the mind, something I found most enjoyable when Shintaro labored for hours to turn my body into a work of art in every detail. I must also remind you that my samurai had a sense of humor and showed me woodblock prints of nude courtesans tied up in provocative positions and maintained I could not become samurai until I had tried each one of them. That was when Akira suddenly came from behind the screen where he was watching us and insisted he help since the art of tying up and transporting prisoners was a part of his training.

I most willingly allowed my samurai to use my body for practice in binding a prisoner, whether I alone was bound or Akira and I were tied together, my lower lip trembling, waiting my turn as Shintaro took the younger samurai first, grinding his hips roughly, pumping, his need feeding my hunger, making me feel more aroused. I arched my body upward, offering him the gift of my rear passage, but he denied me, taking his pleasure first with Akira, thrusting into him at a frantic pace while I watched. I groaned, jealous of these two strong, muscular bodies moving in tandem and I was restrained from participating. I moaned as his lord reached his climax, Akira straining against the rope binding him, his handsome face dripping with sweat, his chest rising and falling in a steady rhythm that didn't cease when Shintaro pulled out of him, his seed spilling onto the younger samurai's arse. Then he turned to me, panting heavily, smiling, his desire not waning. He pulled on the rope binding my breasts and turned me over, stroking the backs of my thighs, tiny shivers running up and down my legs. I groaned again when he spread my buttocks, then slid two fingers inside my pussy, feeling, exploring for my wetness. I moved against him, wanting him to feed on me from behind, rolling my head back when he spread my legs wider apart and put his tongue to my pussy lips, touching me, using his thumbs to hold me open, then sliding his tongue in and out of me, probing me, delving inside me, making my juices flow even more…lapping at my pussy lips, then pinching them together with his two fingers and sending me to the edge of madness.

I shall write no more today of my samurai and his beguiling tongue, for I heard you gossiping about me to Baroness ———, as you often do about such things as your friends' jewels (something you know more about than your own children, or so I've heard), whispering that I serve you falsehoods about my training as samurai. 'Tis true in olden days, Shintaro would never have allowed me to reside in his village and train to become samurai. But these times are different and a lord such as Shintaro not only found a place for me in his soul, but he knew I needed such skills to protect myself against the wrath of my husband, James. In years to come, I've no doubt novels will fancy the telling of such tales, never knowing that such a story *did* take place in this year of 1874.

I must therefore ask you to show respect, something I give to you in spite of your rudeness and audacity toward me at the Viscount Aubrey's soiree. Sneering, whispering about me sleeping with a man of a different race. Calling me base, vile. I shall not toss similar vulgarities at you. I mention the incident again to ask you to show compassion and respect toward everyone, even your enemies, as is the way of the samurai. Without it, you shall become embittered, restless, dispassionate in the ways of love and cast off to a solitary place of your own making, living your life with a haunted, grim demeanor. I'd not wish that on you, dear lady reader, for I believe you *can* change. 'Tis my hope when you finish reading this chapter, you take the lessons of the way of the warrior with you.

As I have.

★ ★ ★

I also embraced the wisdom Nami passed on to me, her charm and practicality guiding me through the nuances of this seductive and duty-bound culture. I found her advice fascinating ("If you wash your face with water that is too hot," she said, "wrinkles will appear," adding the importance of smoothing out wet towels hanging on the rack to also avoid face wrinkles). Humorous ("If your ears are ticklish, 'tis a sign you will soon have a lucky event"). And, I hoped, practical ("To hasten the onset of your menses, stick a needle with red thread onto the wall of the necessary place").

Worrying about the monthlies would be the grief of me as the crimson foliage made its autumnal appearance in our valley. They did not come, sending me to search for red thread among scraps of cloth and needles. I found none. Don't look at me, dear lady reader, with that hard and calculating stare as my blessed mother used to do when she caught me reading novels. I'm not ashamed of *anything* I did, but I beg your patience, for the scenes about to play out are not only of a sensitive nature, but a turning point in my life.

Nami and I spent several days bleaching then fulling newly woven cloth, pounding it with wooden mallets, dipping, wringing the heavy cotton, then spreading it out on the banks of the stream. I was at peace here in the early morning with the gurgling water and the mist glistening on the ferns and slick, mossy rocks, the fresh air intoxicating. Sleeves tied back, my blond hair covered by a white-and-blue scarf, I labored over the work with an Irish ditty upon my lips, humming a tune. By late afternoon, that peace dissipated as the grueling work took its toll on me, nausea rising within me, and I could no longer work on my knees. Feeling as if the gods willed me to slumber, I lay down by the stream on the soft grass, my back aching, so tired was I, which surprised me. I rarely felt the strain of hard work and prided myself on my endurance both with the sword and in the futon with Shintaro. And Akira. I had to smile. The young samurai often confided in me how he prayed to the gods he'd find a woman like me someday. I'd laugh and tell him then I would be jealous…yet as I said the words, I wondered how long I could remain with Shintaro as his…consort. Nami was still his wife, though divorce was not uncommon among samurai if a woman did not bear him a son that lived. Nami insisted I must take her place with Shintaro, but the lord himself had made no such request of me.

Which was why I found myself staring up at the sky wrapped in blue silk, peeking through the tall trees, rubbing my flat belly with my reddened fingers, wondering what would happen if I *was* with child.

Days later the thought continued to pervade my mind, charging my emotions because I refused to answer this bewildering question concerning my fate as Nami and I rushed about cleaning straw mats, gathering fresh blossoms for the alcove and cooking rice for rice balls with pickled plums at the center, everything we needed to do to prepare for the thanksgiving harvests. A time to view the moon, according to tradition, compose verses and drink sake. And share my futon with my samurai.

And in a moment of candor I shall admit to you that I experienced deep pangs of missing my family, wondering what they would think if they knew their girl Katie was celebrating a thanksgiving harvest similar to the spirited holiday back in America. I believed that Da and Mother believed me well and in good health, for I was of the persuasion that my dear husband James, would have avoided telling them anything that would jeopardize his financial position.

All these thoughts came to mind that day, dear lady reader, for I knew the paradisaical existence I had been living couldn't last. I saw the signs everywhere. Shintaro off for long periods of time with Akira and his samurai. Swordsmiths hammering then hand forging each blade, readying strong cutting edges. And Nami. Where her steps were usually lighter than a breeze, she seemed heavy with worry, as if she were watching a fallen blossom caught up on the fast current of a stream, knowing she couldn't stop its ebb and flow.

To assuage my fears, I nibbled constantly on cooked rice as we worked, my hunger overwhelming me day and night, yet the smell of the vinegar Nami used to pickle the plums made me retch. I caught her watching me when I sneaked off with a porcelain bowl to give my nauseous stomach a place to empty its woes, a sly smile coming over her face that she attempted to conceal but couldn't. I knew she would never say anything, hint perhaps, but never ask. She kept so many secrets behind that smile, would I ever know her true thoughts? Yet I wasn't ready to confide in her, for I had been late with the courses before and then came my flow. Would it come again this time?

"Are you writing a new verse to seduce the moon to your futon, my lord? Or me?" I asked, swaying my hips when I saw Shintaro back from the field, sitting in the garden, pen and ink in hand, his quick brushstrokes sweeping up and down the paper like a north wind. Tonight the moon would be full and perfect for viewing.

"My blonde samurai speaks boldly about the art of pleasuring a woman," he said, never looking up.

"Does that displease you?" I couldn't resist asking him, placing the white chrysanthemums I had gathered at his feet, though I continued standing.

"No."

A long silence. As if I were intruding into a world where I didn't belong.

"You write poetry, Shintaro, yet from what I've seen, you prepare for war."

"You think like a woman, not a warrior." His tone was gruff, not forgiving.

"I am a woman first, my lord, or have you forgotten?" I blurted out. Why was I speaking to him like this? We had not quarreled, but Shintaro hadn't come to my quarters since he had returned. *Why?*

"Soon the snows of winter will cover our valley, and the steep mountain path will be impassable." He waved his brush about in the air and in the blinking of an eye sent me into the depths of melancholy. "You are free to leave before then."

Was this a command disguised as a request?

"I wish to stay here with you," I insisted.

He grunted loudly, startling me. The emotion I saw on his face surprised me since he was a man who hid his feelings well. Still, no word from him as to when I would take my place in his futon. Was I to be discarded like a dull sword no longer useful?

I decided not to persist in my pursuit of an answer, though this was one time, dear lady reader, I tired of the subtleties that permeated this culture. Grumbling to myself in my own tongue about the futility of trying to understand this stubborn samurai, I returned to my quarters and found Nami removing kimonos from a cedar chest for washing. I made an effort to hide my emotions from her, but she could see I was upset.

"Lord Shintaro is a man at war with himself," she told me, running her hands over blue silk, pensive she was, as though she was looking at her own lonely soul. "You can change that."

I was struck by the sadness in her eyes and the lingering hope in her voice. "*How,* Nami? He wants me to go."

"No, he wishes you to stay, but fears he will lose you if you do."

"I don't understand."

"My lord knows the day will come when the way of the warrior will meet the same fate as the cherry blossom. A glorious death in the end." Her face was like the dewy mist, moist with tears one moment then they were gone. "He doesn't wish you to see that."

"I love him, Nami," I said with fervor in my heart. "What can I do? Help me, *please.*"

She turned and looked at me with truth in her eyes. "Stay and give him the gift you carry."

I took a breath. "How long have you known?"

"I see it in your eyes…so does Shintaro." She held out the blue kimono to me. "He fears you will return to your people and forget about everything you have learned. Including him."

I took the kimono and draped the silky blue garment around me. The scent of my desire lingered, mixed with his, making me yearn for the familiar warmth of my samurai's body, his hands finding his way beneath my kimono, his lips tantalizing the nape of my neck with his hot tongue…

"Tell him about the child tonight when the moon is full," Nami whispered in my ear, her cheek flush with mine. "And I promise you, all will be well."

★ ★ ★

With a lighter heart, I begged Nami to allow me to accompany her to her favorite spot over the hill to pick succulent beautyberries, all fat and sassy in their vibrant purple skin. I wanted to use their glorious color to brighten the festival arrangement and renew my spirit of this blessed autumn. Bursting with energy and youthful excitement, I was eager to share my news with Shintaro, to feel his strong hands rub my belly when I told him I carried his child.

Wearing large straw hats and long veils hiding our faces, we hiked up the hidden mountain trail and over the ravine to a thickly wooded area dark and dense with pine and fir and thick-leaved evergreen oak, beyond the gorge and washed in a sweep of gold and amber. It was a bold and daring thing to do since we had gone beyond where the samurai outposts could see us, but the beautyberries only grew here beyond the curved bridge crossing a stream. I danced with delight, picking berries and gathering fallen maple leaves, the colors changing as I twirled around and around, reflecting and absorbing the light from the late-afternoon orange sun. Gold then red then dark vermilion. Dusk was at hand. Nami called out to me that we must hurry back, but an unholy fatigue made my legs give way. I lay down on a bed of crimson leaves while she went on ahead, my face hot and perspiring under the heavy veil, but my eyes enchanted by the last of the setting sun's rays, the intense gold light shooting through the small openings overhead in the thick evergreen woods—

I heard a woman scream, followed by a shot.

Gunfire.

Nami.

I jumped up, tripping over my baskets filled with berries, and ran and ran, my heart pumping so hard in my chest I could barely breathe. *Who, why?* It was no secret samurai women were often harassed by imperial soldiers when they passed through inspection posts, but we were nowhere near there.

What could have happened?

Over the hill I saw three British soldiers on horseback, the officer among them shouting orders to a native soldier who had Nami in a tight grip, her hat and veil gone, her black hair unloosened and hanging down past her waist as she struggled to free herself.

"Ask her again if she's seen an Englishwoman in these mountains," said the British officer, his voice stern, unbending. The soldier restraining Nami repeated his words in the native language, tightening his hold on her arm and making her cry out, but she merely shook her head and said nothing.

They're looking for me. Why now after all these months?

I had my answer when I saw another rider approaching on horseback. *James.* Sitting tall in the saddle, his riding clothes out of place along with his pompous attitude. I cannot describe the morose feelings gutting my insides with such nausea I had to hold on to my stomach to keep from spewing its contents. I was completely unnerved at the sight of his lordship, as if something altogether intolerable and repugnant to my soul had been thrust at me and I couldn't grasp it.

"She's nothing but a peasant," James said with disdain, not giving her a second glance. His hard words aroused such deep feelings in me I had to hold myself back from acting foolishly.

"She is samurai, your lordship," said the native soldier, his hand fumbling between her breasts and drawing her dirk from her obi.

"Samurai?" James said, astonished. "Do you mean those bastards could attack us?"

"Rumors have abounded for months about the rebel samurai,

Shintaro, being holed up in these mountains, but I didn't believe it," said the British officer, an uneasiness creeping into his voice. Ever since the Richardson affair a few years ago when an Englishman was murdered by samurai, and his wife barely escaped, the British had been on edge, made more so by a recent attack on two French soldiers. The officer said, "We'll take her along as a hostage. If she's from Shintaro's clan, we'll *make* her talk."

I crept closer, sweat pouring down my neck, my back. *I couldn't let them take her.* I knew she'd die at their hands rather than reveal what she knew. I was but a few feet away, hidden in the dusk of bamboo thickets when the native soldier slackened his hold on her and tossed her dirk to the British officer.

Nami made a run for it.

"Stop her!" the officer yelled out, and the soldiers raised their rifles, firing off two shots as she disappeared into the thick woods. *Was she hit?* I clasped my hand over my mouth to keep from screaming. *No, no.* I had to do something. Fast.

Ripping off my veil and straw hat, I raced into the small clearing and stood there wild-eyed and savage before they could fire again, my blond hair blowing about my face, my stance straight and unflinching. I locked glances with my husband with an unswerving steadiness. I imagine I presented an ominous threat he'd never expected, but he didn't look away. A cruel smile turned up the corners of his mouth. I ignored him. I was samurai. I knew what I had to do.

I turned to the British officer and said in an even voice, "I am the Englishwoman you're looking for."

16

I hear you whispering, see your nose twitching, your finger wagging at me, accusing me of disappointing you with this twist in my tale. Yes, I did return to Kobé with James, yes, I resumed my position as Lady Carlton, yes, I was just as distressed as you are about leaving my samurai and dear Nami.

I would prefer to skip this next part of my story instead of wasting endless pages on James and his boorish games, but so I shall not be dutifully punished by fate, not to mention the critics, I shall raise the curtain on this act, letting your overworked libido rest, since I have no doubt that despite your protests, you *are* curious about what happened to me after I returned to the foreign settlement. Be mindful, several important events took place during this time. 'Tis that part of my memoir I shall recount next and the events that led up to that spring morn in 1875 (are you counting the months since my child was conceived?) when from my belly came a child, a curious sun peeping down at me through the thick bamboo, the scent of pine easing my birthing pain, the stream gurgling with delight at the sound of a baby's first cry as I lingered in the blessed godliness of it all.

A late-November day in 1874 and light rain. A chill in the air cut through my thickly lined kimono, keeping me indoors, along with the vicious gossip about me circulating around the foreign settlement. A frenzied mood went on in the parlors and shops, where everyone chattered on about my unexpected reappearance, like a flock of crows on new potatoes. *A wayward wife gone mad with the travails of duty in a foreign post,* was what my detractors said. Not surprising, according to the British Legation, since how else could an American woman not accustomed to the fortitude expected of the wife of an aristocrat be expected to act?

Harsh? Yes, but writing here about my own emotional state, I can pass judgment, evaluate, criticize, accept. I imagine you're asking yourself if you would have had the courage to return to the domicile of a man who hated you and wished you dead. I believe in my heart you would have, for I perceive you have aligned yourself with the samurai spirit even if you don't know it.

I learned upon my return to Kobé that James had told the local British consul I'd run off with another man, a Hungarian count of dubious reputation. When that couldn't be proven, he insisted I'd entered a Buddhist convent. When I asked James why he didn't accuse me of running off with Mr. Mallory, he admitted that Mallory had penned me a note telling me he was returning to America to propose to the young woman he had left behind. (That made me smile and assuaged my ego, knowing Mr. Mallory's affections had been otherwise engaged when I flirted with him.) James continued to insist I'd left him of my own accord, but when no sighting of my person could be substantiated by facts, rumors abounded that I'd been taken captive by samurai and was being held against my will. James maintained the story was ridiculous, but even a British lord was not looked upon too kindly if he showed no concern about the alleged compromised virtue of his wife. I've no doubt he realized he had to produce me or proof of my demise to save his own skin and *disprove* any innuendos of foul play since stories about his drunkenness and womanizing were well-known in the settlement.

It was with that goal in mind he set off that day with a British officer and two soldiers, along with a native soldier, into the hills. He knew something had happened to me when my horse returned with an empty saddle and I've no doubt he believed I had met with an unfortunate end. It was a matter of time before they found my body, or so he thought…strike that…*hoped*. I can imagine how humiliating it was for him when I returned unscathed and tight-lipped about where I'd been…and with whom.

I was correct in my assumption that James had not contacted my family, believing he would soon possess definitive information about my demise and he could play the grieving husband. *The bastard.* I feared what my da and sainted mother would think should they find out from another source about my adventures, so I posted a letter to them (I prayed Da would understand since he was a man who had spent his life in the line of political fire). I left out the impending birth of my child should James intercept the letter. I was three months pregnant, my belly slightly swollen, my breasts tender, fuller, but the unpleasantness in the morning had subsided, though

I suffered fatigue from the slightest task. I prayed my husband wouldn't notice the subtle changes in my figure before they became apparent since I intended to return to America to have my baby (Shintaro would approve since custom dictated a samurai woman return to her parental home to birth her child). In my naiveté I deemed I could take on the British aristocracy and flaunt tradition by having my child, then seek a divorce from James. Since I had already doomed myself to an afterlife of torment in the eyes of the church, I decided one more sin on my lengthy list mattered little. Without a blink of an Irish eye, I lied to my husband about my trips to the shopping street where I secretly visited the old swordsmith and asked him to pen a note to my samurai, telling him that as soon as I became a free woman I wished to return to the village. I admit my knowledge of the written native language was wanting, so I have no idea what he wrote, but he didn't seem surprised when I made my request. Later I learned Shintaro had visited his curio shop (in disguise) to inquire about me. (I was remiss not to previously mention that when I told my samurai about the shop, he smiled, the warmth and naturalness in his eyes telling me the old swordsmith was indeed a friend and former samurai and loyal to his lord, Shintaro.) When I returned in two days and asked the old swordsmith if the flowers in the hills would blossom in the spring, he nodded and said all was well. I took that to mean that Nami was safe…and my message delivered.

Explaining what happened to me at the British consul in Kobé was a more delicate matter. I described the same scenario over and over, never veering from my story that I took refuge in a Buddhist temple after I fell from my horse and how the samurai woman befriended me but I was unaware of her identity. I never mentioned her name or gave him a description during the questioning. When prodded, I refused to say any more, though I don't believe the British officer interrogating me believed me. But I was Lady Carlton and as such, wielded power in refuting anything to the contrary.

Two weeks later, I faced new challenges. I wouldn't be able to hide my condition much longer and had written to Mr. Fawkes in Tokio and asked him to inquire about a sailing date to Vancouver since the northern ports were a better destination during the winter months. I received a letter from him with a sailing schedule, which I dutifully kept from James. I feared another savage attack upon my person from him, though he made no mention of the day when he taunted me with my dagger. I doubt he had any memory of what happened, so intoxicated was he, but that didn't stop him from deciding to show his dear wife how lonely he had been without me.

"I've missed you, Katie," he said, putting his hands on my shoulders, surprising me by using my given name. I quickly tucked the letter and sailing schedule into my kimono sleeve as he tried to kiss me, his touch repulsing me. "A man gets lonely here all by himself."

"Are there no plump bottoms to tempt you, my dear husband?" I pulled away, determined to remain aloof.

"Nothing as pretty as yours," he slapped my arse, causing me to react with a start. With a subconscious gesture, I held my stomach. Though I detected no movement, I knew the baby was growing inside me, I *knew*.

"Don't *ever* touch me again," I said, straightening my shoulders. I found his company distasteful and had managed to keep away from him, but this morning he surprised me as I set about making sweet ginger tea with ginger root and honey.

"I don't care where you've been these past few months," he said, nuzzling his face in my hair. "I've allowed you to play your game, but it's over."

"I have no idea what you're talking about," I said.

"It's time you did your duty."

"Duty?"

"Yes, my father, the duke, is quite ill and eager for me to produce an heir as soon as possible."

"I want nothing to do with you," I cried out, spilling the hot tea and scalding my hand. I grabbed a linen towel and dipped it into cool water then applied it to my skin. "You're a braggart and a thief."

"No one calls me a thief."

"No? You swindled money from my father," I said, then told him I wished to have the marriage annulled. He balked at that, but I told him I could prove my accusation since I had examined the books in Yokohama and had no doubt a bank audit would show I was telling the truth. In exchange for an annulment no criminal charges would be filed against him. (I prayed Da's investment in the railway would make up for his lordship's gambling losses.) To my surprise, he agreed, most likely to be done with me so he could return to London and snare another heiress who could bear him a child. I should have seen that being distant around my husband was the wrong move, dear lady reader, as if I were hidden from him by veils, my body cloaked and unattainable seducing him more than naked flesh. A temptation he couldn't resist. I had no idea he had one final play in mind later that evening.

"Take off your clothes."

"You're mad, James, completely *mad*."

"I have decided that part of the stipulation of the annulment you desire will be that I enjoy your naked body for one evening."

"If you take me to your bed against my will, there can be no annulment." I panicked, upset at his daring move to invade my quarters when I was at my toilette, applying camellia oil and lemon juice to the reddened skin on my hand.

"Did I say anything about fucking you, my dear wife?" He smirked. "Instead, I will enjoy watching another woman touch you, her lips suckling your breasts, her tongue delving into your pussy…before I fuck *her.*"

Before I could catch my breath, a young singsong girl appeared (no doubt James had bought his way back into the graces of the local madam), wearing a pale sea-green tunic and trousers so sheer I could see her small dark nipples pointing through the silk and the dark patch covering her pussy trimmed into a perfect triangle.

"I won't do it," I cried, tossing the vial of oil at him. *"I won't!"*

"If you want an annulment, you'll do as I say." He ripped my kimono off me and tossed it aside. I wore only a thin cotton chemise underneath, accustomed as I was to no longer wearing a corset, my full breasts peeking over the low-cut lace and arousing an interest in his eyes that alarmed me.

"*Let me go,* James."

"No." He ran his hands over my breasts, warm and tender, making me cringe, then he cupped them in his hands, pulling the cotton taut to emphasize their fullness. "I may have been too hasty in agreeing to an annulment when you have so much to offer your husband."

"You will be disgraced, James, if I reveal what I know about your phony gambling losses, your title worth nothing when you're penniless."

That angered him, his eyes spewing fire. "You're treading on dangerous territory, my dear wife. It's unfortunate you returned, but I shall make the best of it." He ripped the tunic off the Chinese girl and pushed her toward me. "Touch her, Soong Li, like this." He made obscene gestures with his hands, touching my breasts, belly, pussy.

Bowing, the pretty girl put her hand on my breast then slid it down to my belly. I pushed her away, crossing my arms over my midsection, her dark eyes meeting mine, confused, then seeing how I protected my belly from her touch, she shook her head and backed away. She knew I was with child, but she said nothing. She tried to run, but her refusal to arouse me angered my husband. He hit the girl hard, making her cry out, her lip bleed.

At that moment I hated him more than ever, his abuse of defenseless girls setting off an intense, savage anger in me that couldn't be stopped. I placed my body between them to protect her when he attempted to slap her again, but this time his hand struck my cheek, knocking me off balance…there was a moment of struggle, then I went down, my head slamming against the straw mat…my body screaming with pain.

"Did you know your wife was expecting a child, Lord Carlton?" *I could hear a man's voice saying, impersonal yet curious. I was struck by fear despite the pounding in my head.*

"A child?" James. *His voice was not without bitterness as he continued,* "That's impossible."

"Milord?" *More curiosity in the man's voice.*

"My wife had a fainting spell," *I could hear him blustering, shock making him stutter.* "I had no idea she was in such a condition."

"She has suffered internal bleeding from the fall. I've given her laudanum for the pain." *If James called in a physician, he must have been worried I'd leave this earth under his roof and he'd hang for it.* "She must stay in bed or she will lose the child."

Lose the child.

I heard no more. I lay still, trying to steady my breathing, no scream from me, my throat tight, dry, as if the possibility of losing my baby was beyond my comprehension. I couldn't open my eyes, so heavy were they with me straining so hard to open them, moisture gathered at the corners, but something deep within me came back to life in a shuddering sigh. All I could think of was what he'd said. *She will lose the child.* I couldn't. *No, no no…*

"So my dear wife is a sinner like the rest of us."

James leaned over me, grabbing my arm and holding me in a tight grip, his breath heavy with the smell of brandy. "No court will grant you an annulment now. And I will *never* give you a divorce."

"Your threats mean nothing to me, James," I insisted, using the last of my strength to pull away from him.

"I demand to know how you found yourself with child."

"No matter what you do to me, I will not reveal the father of my baby."

"Do you take me for a fool?" he asked. "You were with that samurai woman when we found you."

I said nothing, refraining from revealing anything that would incriminate Nami. Watching him pacing up and down, the preoccupied expression on his face disturbing me.

"You've been with this Shintaro I've been hearing about from members of the legation," he continued. "A *samurai*. It's *his* child you're carrying, isn't it?"

"Leave me alone, James. *Please.*" I turned away from him. Suddenly the small bedroom seemed airless and stale.

"It matters not to me who fathered the little bastard," he insisted, smiling, then pouring himself another brandy. "Only that the child guarantees my future."

"What foul scheme has possessed your maniacal way of thinking?" I asked, the intensity of his smile terrifying me.

He toasted me, then drank the liqueur. "It's quite simple. You will give up the child and return to London as my wife and no assessment of adultery will be lodged against you."

He continued, saying this "unfortunate incident," as he called my absence, would be quickly forgotten if I produced an heir, a son. He made no secret that I must make myself available to his sexual urges until I *did* produce a male heir.

"And if I refuse, James?"

"I will make it known in every circle in Mayfair that you are no better than a common whore from the lowest lodging house. With your reputation ruined," he said in a business-like manner, "I shall be free to seek a new wife to beget me with an heir."

"You are humiliating and vile," I sputtered, knowing he was cruel enough to carry out his threat. But like a dog with its nose pressed up against another animal's arse, smelling, he wasn't finished.

"To guarantee my silence on the matter, I also want a sum from your father in the amount of—" He named a figure I found exorbitant, but what choice did I have? If I didn't do as he wished, I would be ruined along with my family.

A burning restlessness fueled by his demands made me want to strike back at him, but I didn't. Not for lack of courage, but because I had learned to keep my emotions hidden, to redirect my anger to a humble place, to never forget I followed the way of the warrior. Loyalty, discipline. I could not allow my family to suffer because of what I'd done. I had no choice but to give up my baby and return to my life in London as a childless woman.

James outlined his plan, though I admit my entire being floated in and out of consciousness, my mind reeling, knowing I was responsible for my baby's soul as well as my own and I could not fail. *I would travel to Ōzaka with a native woman to assist me,* he said, *where I would have my baby with a private midwife.* To assure himself the child presented him with no further difficulties, he would arrange to have the baby adopted. He went so far as to suggest I lace up to hide my condition as was common among women of the lower classes in England should the child be stillborn. I refused, not wishing to jeopardize my baby, while in my mind I retreated to a dark place behind the shadows, so fearful was I for my child's safety. I assured him I would see no one. Reluctantly he agreed, but I did not trust him. James could—no, it was a thought so terrible, so ugly I shan't write it down. I would bide my time until I made certain my baby was safe, or there would be no bargain with the devil.

I sit at the oak desk in my hotel room, reading over what I have written, wondering how I was able to endure the months of my confinement, knowing what James wished of me and what lay ahead for me in London. To pass the time, I relived the days and nights past with Shintaro, dreaming about the laughter and tears I would never know with my child. Yet as I look back, I see those days as an enchanted, beautiful time when I carried my baby within me, this long-sought dream growing and bending and feeding upon that dream. And so I entreat those of you who have borne a child to sit next to me and feel free to speak should you desire, for I fear trying to impart the emotions and feelings of childbirth are not unique to me alone. If you have not known feelings of motherhood, I also ask you to come along with me, for 'tis a journey of sisterhood where your life will be more abundant with understanding because you will have known the joys and pain of birthing a child.

It was a time of confusion, of questions. I missed my mother terribly, not having her to ask about how she felt or when she let out the waistbands of her dresses and donned loose skirts. She would have embraced the ease of the kimono and the way it outlined the curve of my expanding belly. I can hear her saying it must have been woven by fairies, so soft it was, like holding nothing in your hands. So I shall share my time of confinement with *you,* dear lady reader. A gossip, if you will, a gathering of female family and friends. I would like to take your hand if I may, for I know that with all your attempts to remain cold and aloof to me since I am not born into the peerage, we as women share a common bond concerning the expectation regarding the birthing of a child. The apprehension, uncertainty, pain, as well as the apparent danger to our persons, make the trial of having a child an integral part of that secret world we inhabit during that time, a world filled with whispers and endearing smiles, when the calmness we take for granted sipping a cup of tea is ceremoniously interrupted by an audacious kick in our bellies, a quickening, then another and another from the tiny creature inside us. So pleasing, it makes our hearts swell with contentment, yet 'tis something we cannot share with the strong man whose moment of passion gave us this joy, but only with another woman who has known the wonder of these days, fragrant and dreamlike moments that opened to us the secret garden where life begins.

★ ★ ★

I experienced bloating, but except for slight swelling, my condition did not show for several months. My figure thickened, though I tend to retain a certain thinness and believe that is why I was able to conceal my condition. I was often moody, tearful, given to fretting over my changing body, my nipples dark and sore, my belly hardening, my face spotted, my frequency visiting the necessary place, and toward the latter part of my confinement, I wondered if I should ever feel normal again. Yet I could never push aside the fact that when my time came, I must give up my baby.

Give it up? You can't, you cry out, squeezing my hand. *Fight for your child, the baby is yours and no man, not even his lordship, has the right to take it away from you.*

I knew you'd fight for me, dear lady reader, and so you will understand that although I lay in bed for weeks, spending a scant few hours a day on my feet, you will not judge me harshly for braving the wrath of my husband when I overheard the physician attending me speaking with James. *He would recommend two or three native women to assist me in preparing for my trip to Ōzaka,* he said, with James choosing the woman to travel with me for my safety. Then, as an afterthought, he mentioned the reported sightings of samurai in the settlement.

Orders from the consul were to shoot them on sight.

Shintaro. I swore I'd heard noises at night outside the western-style glass windows, stealthlike, as if the voyeur could peel back the thick walls and slide them open like a paper door to peer inside. I *knew* he'd come, but he would do nothing to jeopardize the welfare of our child. *How was I going to tell him I must remain with my husband?* He was a samurai, and I prayed he would understand the loyalty I owed to my family. I had to come up with a determined, infallible plan to keep my child safe, but what? Days thinking...until I realized I suffered from the Occidental ailment of *too much thinking*, not allowing my mind to act as I had been taught to do, to move forward with the confidence of a warrior. I recalled the grace and fluidity of Shintaro wielding his sword, the effortlessness. The beauty of his movements *Don't think, do*. And so I would. I sneaked out when my husband was off somewhere and made my way to the shop of the old sword-smith and bade him take word to Shintaro. I had a plan, dangerous, daring, but my baby's life depended on it, for I believed within my heart that James would never allow my child to live.

When I was but a fortnight from my due time, I started out for Ōzaka aboard the train with my black cloth traveling bag in hand, the quiet native woman hired to accompany me nervously clutching her ticket. Her dark eyes cast downward, praying my husband wouldn't look too closely at her.

Nami.

When the native women had arrived at our house for his lordship to choose my traveling companion, I took it upon myself to assume the lead. I reminded James that I spoke the native language, so he put up no protest when I interviewed the women and chose Nami, telling him she was best suited to assist me. I carried off my part with great aplomb, hoping my scheme would work. James had seen Nami but once before in the woods, her long hair loose and her posture in clear defiance of him. Here she remained placid and compliant. Submissive. I thank the holy saints he never questioned my choice.

Nami played her part well, acting the perfect servant, straightening my chest drawers without being asked, brewing hot tea at the proper times and showing the deepest respect by dropping to the floor and touching her forehead to the straw mat when James or I entered the room. By Nami keeping her head bowed low whenever my husband was present, as was the native custom, he never suspected anything was amiss. I felt rather clever at having accomplished the ruse by arranging with Shintaro to have her arrive with the other native women. I held back my joy at seeing her, using the most formal language when I spoke to her, but noted her smile when she gave me a bleached-white cotton obi to tie around my protruding belly, *a native tradition to help ensure an easy delivery,* she said. So eager was James to return to London, he gave no further thought to the comings and goings of a lowly servant. *I was not only to submit to him after the birth of my baby to produce an heir,* he said, *but cajole my father into drawing up a new letter of credit.* I had no choice but to do as he wished. Da had written to me that the U.S. was in an economic depression with no end in sight. I didn't wish to add to his mounting troubles with a scandal.

I admit, dear lady reader, it was daring and exciting to race down the aisle in the railway car after James saw us safely aboard, the two of us heading toward the rear exit. Pushing my way though the narrow corridor, hot and perspiring, I panicked when I felt the sudden rush of wetness between my legs. I sniffed it and a shiver went through me. It had the smell of bleach, not urine. *My bag of waters had broken.* My step faltered when the locomotive jerked forward, a hiss of steam pouring out the engine, the whistle sharp and shrill in my ears, startling me as if announcing my deceitful deed. I ignored it and got off the train without mishap with Nami behind me. By the time my husband received word I had not arrived in Ōzaka, we'd be safe in the samurai village. Only after I looked into my baby's eyes and held its tiny body, soft and warm, in my arms, would I return to James and fulfill my duty.

First we must complete our escape.

It was too dangerous for my samurai to move around the foreign settlement, so Akira disguised himself as a jinriki-man. Bowl-shaped straw hat upon his head, chest bare, wearing a loincloth and straw sandals, he waited for us outside the train terminal alongside the *kuruma* procured by the old sword-smith. He bowed, then nodded in approval when he saw my thin navy serge jacket barely covering my large belly. He picked me up into his strong arms and lifted me into the vehicle, his touch sending a different kind of thrill through me, comforting, tender. I will never forget that moment.

Akira lifted up the shafts, got into them and tilted his body backward, then we raced out of the settlement and up into the hills, Nami and I laughing and crying and clinging to each other. All that mattered was that Shintaro waited for us with horses atop the hill near the small sanctuary. I was alive again, and happy and free.

The hills behind the foreign settlement. Hidden in the bamboo thickets where I first lost my way, breathing in the fragrance of the orange blossoms which had guided me here, petal-soft rain cooling the fever in me brought on by my reckless escape, exhausted and nearly faint, I fell into the arms of my samurai.

Shintaro.

"I thought I'd never see you again," I whispered, his strong arms holding me, his fingers loosening my hair then burying his face in it, breathing in my scent.

"I prayed to the gods you would be safe—" he stroked my

belly, hard and round, as if he could feel the life stirring within me "—and the child."

"*Our* child, Shintaro," I said, looking up at him, his dark eyes worried and curious, a kind of wild flickering in its depths then it was gone. I closed my fingers over his, clenching my teeth as another pain ripped through me. "Hold me...*please.*"

He pulled me closer to him as the pains kept coming, closer and closer together, setting off a new fear in me. The child was not yet due but the pains had been regular, intense, a dull, heavy pain in my back and my loins before abating, stopping, then coming again. *I was in labor.* Why now? Here in the woods? How long before the baby came? What if I couldn't birth the child? And my baby...would I find the courage to endure—for no romance of illusion this—the strength to survive long enough to hear its first cry?

I rested my cheek against my samurai's shoulder, as if overcome with a great weariness, exhaustion setting in. But it was no time to surrender to my weary self when my child was stirring inside me, begging to burst out, stubborn and persistent, determined to find its way with a freshness of spirit that exhilarated me. I was in a state of grace in this setting of nature, wild and free, surrounded by large cedars smudging the landscape with subtle black strokes, tall bamboo bending with the wind, bushes dripping with white flowers sown by the seeds of the gods. I tensed when a breath of wind blew over me, making me shiver. Dusk loomed low like a shy creature of the night watching me, its breathy mist hovering over me. The rain had stopped, but darkness would soon cover us, making it too dangerous to brave the treacherous footpath down into the hidden village below or back to the sanctuary. *What lay ahead of me, pray?*

I shan't forget those long hours, my pains coming closer together and leaving me no breath for a sigh, my samurai patient and watchful...wrapping his kimono jacket around me to keep me warm, his gesture making me smile. It made the pains more bearable, reminding me of the Irish tradition of a woman wearing the coat of her baby's father so he may share her pains. I no longer feared the oncoming night nor the dawn, restless as I was to bring my child out of its solitude. Shintaro built a small fire while Nami set water to boil in a round iron pot. (Had the gods told them the child was to be born in this verdant spot?) Akira stretched a canopy of green silk between the trees to enclose us, while keeping watch for intruders. 'Tis amusing to me, to observe how I, an Occidental woman, who ran from the wrath of my husband, found comfort in the arms of this samurai, the gentle woman wedded to him and the strong young warrior who loved him. Where once I may have feared being drawn too deeply into their lives, they were now significant links in a chain that bound me to this land.

You may scoff and say I have idealized the way of the warrior, but I wish for you to experience *Bushidō* as you would a drop of pure, fine oil from a flower, a perfume, if you will, so you may apply it to your life as you would scent to your skin and make it yours alone.

I lay under the silken canopy stretched between the trees to keep out the night chill, the sound of insects chirping and keeping time with my ragged breathing as if they knew their pleasant sounds helped me to stay calm. But I shall not lie; the grinding pain in my groin became unbearable, coming at intermittent times then moving to my belly. It became so severe in my back and hips I am sweating as I write, dots of perspiration blurring the words upon the linen paper as I wished then I could blur the pain. Did you entreat your physician to employ chloroform, dear lady reader, to ease the discomfort as Queen Victoria did? If not, and so as not to make you suffer the indescribable pain of labor, I shall pause here to catch my breath. Pace the carpet if you must and warm yourself with hot tea, for the sacred event of birth is something this memoirist must leave in the hands of the gods.

I breathed deep...*slow*...in then out...bore down, pushed, then pushed again harder. *Nothing.* Shintaro held me under the arms from behind while I squatted...Nami pushing upward around my anus. Sweat dripped down my face and into my ears, saltiness on my lips...water, *water*...I needed water... but the natives didn't drink water...someone put a small piece of wood into my hand...*a lucky charm from the goddess of mercy to help me through childbirth,* Nami told me...*I want water,* my tongue was so dry it felt swollen...she lay a moist cloth on my forehead...I opened my mouth and squeezed the cloth until drops of water tickled my tongue like a fairy's toe...the pain, the pain, oh dear God, the *pain.* By the sainted head of my mother, I never dreamed such pain would come...push, yes, *push*...I was *trying*...trying, I cried out in English...a man's voice, deep and demanding, cursed the gods for abandoning me...then he touched my cheek, comforting me...I squeezed my eyes shut and bore down...*pushing downward*... then again...*again* for how long I don't know...until...oh, yes, yes...I clenched my teeth and pushed the baby out...I let out a loud sigh as my samurai eased me down onto the prepared bedding...sobbing I was when I heard a baby's cry. Through the sweat dripping into my eyes, I could see Shintaro draw his short sword then cut the cord, but not too close to the baby's navel, then Akira tied it. I strained to see my baby...there, Nami had the child...so red and wrinkly... Shintaro placing hot, wet cloths on my belly...oh, *another contraction*...I moaned as the afterbirth gushed out of me...I lay back and gazed upward, the dawn lifting the shadows...a light breeze as soft as a baby's breath fanning my burning face...I saw Nami clearing the infant's mouth and nostrils before cleaning it then wrapping the child in a thick flannel kimono...*red,* the color of birth.

I looked up to see her hand the child to Shintaro, and the warmth of his smile gave to his eyes an expression of pride and wonderment before he placed the baby into my waiting arms. I couldn't stop smiling at him when he said, "The gods have blessed us with a daughter."

1
7

"I refuse to let you go."

"I find it ironic, Shintaro, that once you ordered me to leave, and now you order me to stay?"

"You have a child—"

"*We* have a child, you and I. But my baby will not be safe here if I remain." I paced up and down, frantic, trying to make him understand I didn't trust James, that he might send soldiers to find me and kill my little girl. *And* Shintaro.

Frustrated, I sat down on a square pillow next to my child asleep on the straw matting and stroked her cheek. *So innocent.* I had no choice. I must leave everything I loved to save them.

"We will go where your soldiers cannot find us," said my samurai, indicating they would break camp and travel farther west.

I nodded, understanding. "You and the baby will be safe there, but I can't keep on running. I must go back to London and be a wife to a man I hate."

"I will not give you up."

"You *must*. Nothing can change what I have to do."

"*You* have changed *me,* yet you ask me to accept that when a man finds the perfect blossom," he said, resorting to poetry to express himself since his status of samurai allowed him no other way, "it can never be his."

"I will always belong to you, Shintaro. You must believe me."

I picked up the baby and took her to my breast, her tiny mouth latching onto my nipple and suckling. A twinge of pain made me gasp, but I wanted to nurse her for as long as I could. Nami had insisted the baby suck seaweed tea dissolved in water from a little silk bag for three days. Then, on the seventh day, we visited the shrine near the small sanctuary atop the hill and, as tradition dictated, Nami, who had assisted at the child's birth and was due much respect, named her.

Reiko. Beautiful child.

"Nami will care for our daughter," I said approvingly. "She is a good woman…and she loves you, Shintaro."

"She is as gentle as the wings of a butterfly, but *you,* you are the blaze of crimson of the autumnal leaves, tongues of fire branding my soul with your touch, the smoothness of your skin, your hair like gold blossoms, all bringing me inescapable pleasure." He rested his hand on my bare bosom and stared, his face filled with passion, into mine.

"You flatter me with your words of poetry, Shintaro, but you refuse to listen to me. Why?"

"You come from a strange shore, have learned our ways, but—"

"But I am not born samurai, is that what you wish to say?" I paused, choosing my words carefully, "Or because I am *gaijin?*"

He refused to answer me. Why were men so stubborn, even samurai? Didn't he understand that by fulfilling my duty to my husband and my family, I would prove to him I had embraced their moral code?

"Is it not true *Bushidō* demands loyalty?" I continued. "And familial duty?" I put the baby over my shoulder and loosened the cords on her chemise before patting her lightly on the back. "'Tis the only way we can appease the gods for our sins and keep our daughter safe."

He grunted, understanding. We both feared for our child's safety, *he* because he believed a child belonged to the gods until the age of seven and could be taken from him at any time, and *me* because the devil himself in the form of my husband could do the same.

I cannot say we found common ground as the days passed, my Irish temper roused with a determination to keep my child safe, forgetting Shintaro was the lord and not used to such actions, especially from a woman. I have no excuse except to say I suffered from a deep melancholia after the birth of my child. I found strength by reflecting on the unruffled water of a lake not far from the village. There, as is the way of the warrior, I calmed my mind, my spirit, able to see my life clearly without putting emphasis on any one thing, and to find peace within myself.

We talked and talked and talked, Shintaro and I: when the baby woke up at nights for feeding; carrying her on my back as we walked through the village; breathing in the orange blossoms while we sat on the veranda in the late afternoons, but in the end he knew I was right. I made preparations to return to the settlement, but I shall never forget those precious days after the birth of my daughter and the traditions I hold so dear: Nami burying a pen and ink with the afterbirth to assure the child's skill with calligraphy (important for the daughter of a samurai), along with a fan so she would rise in the world (to become a geisha? I wondered); Shintaro insisting I not be separated from the others after childbirth; the celebration meal of rice colored by red beans. And when I told him about the ancient Irish tradition of placing cooked rice on the tip of his blade and feeding it to the baby (so the child wouldn't die by the sword), he found that barbaric, making us both laugh.

After childbirth, I can unequivocally say you may have been advised by your physician or midwife to remain in bed for two weeks and not to climb stairs for six weeks. Sound advice, but what about sex? Oh, don't be so prudish. That's why you purchased this book, isn't it? Yes, I realize you may not wish to have more children and, since birth control material is difficult to procure in England (try reading *The Fruits of Philosophy,* if you can get a copy), you may avoid sex. Do I hear a snicker or two? Most likely 'tis from those stalwart matrons who prefer their husband's poker find its way into a pantry maid to save them the difficulty of birthing a child once their duty is done and they produce an heir or two (a spare, if you will). But to those of you who divine the touch of your husband as a way of finding a soothing satisfaction, I have a solution I can personally recommend.

Two men.

I shall not be so indelicate as to advise you to allow the gentlemen to probe you with their fingers *or* their cocks, but to do as I did on a summer night when the already suffocating heat raised a fever in me *and* in my samurai. The smell of arousal was everywhere as the *andon* burned low, the scent of fragrant oil filling my nostrils, its slickness rubbed on nude bodies tempting me with an eroticism I could not resist. I had qualms about the mother in me eclipsing the sexual creature, so it was with real delight I welcomed my samurai's embraces. I did not revolt against my femininity, dear lady reader, but encouraged it, both sexually and maternally. And so I pass this advice along to you to encourage you not to deny yourself and his lordship mutual physical pleasure after birthing a child. So with your permission, 'tis a fond memory I shall indulge in…

Nude. I lay on my stomach, artful hands massaging my shoulders, back, buttocks, easing the fatigue in my knotted muscles, loosening my tightened ligaments, the silky futon keeping my skin cool while the samurai took their time to pleasure me, their bodies hot, their touch hotter. I breathed in the salty smell of perspiration, theirs and mine, mixing together in a provocative scent. I moaned when Shintaro placed his hand on the nape of my neck and my shoulders, caressing me with a gentleness I found so natural, so soothing it made me forget my pussy was dry and tender, my breasts full and painful, my nipples cracking.

The game quickened, the ménage in play heated, my surrender coming in short gasps when I turned over onto my back and Shintaro curved his hands under my breasts, pushing them up slightly, grunting his approval, then anointing my nipples with plum-blossom oil in a slow, deliberate manner. Sighing at his touch, I arched my back in a long euphoric stretch, lifting my belly while Akira brushed the insides of my thighs with his fingers, the smell of scented wood from his nails a pleasant stimulant. He licked me with long, long strokes, making me shiver with pleasure before running his fingers through the bristling hairs on my pussy, pulling on them just enough to stir an ache of intense arousal in me. I knew it wouldn't be long until I reached a point of release. Hands everywhere, tongues hot and wet, licking my nipples and my clit with a knowing touch, eager to please me. I could concentrate on nothing but the heat of their mouths pleasuring me, as if both samurai claimed me as their own. I dug my nails into the silk, the intensity of stimulation building, *building,* my breathing ragged in the heavy, slow-moving air until I trembled, then shuddered uncontrollably when my release came…rolling and wavelike…and seemingly never-ending.

Wrapping me in silk, hands gentle upon my breasts, my belly, my samurai bade me rest and sip the hot tea mysteriously left for me, while their sweaty bodies seethed with the hunger for raw, sexual games. Muscles gripping, hips grinding, cocks thrusting as my samurai performed for me, their nude bodies bathed in shiny sweat, wrestling, muscles flexing, cocks erect, their deep love for each other, devotion and sincere respect reflected in their actions. How Shintaro would engage the young warrior in a contest of strength to show his love; how Akira could temper his lord's anger by merely touching his kimono sleeve with his hand; both knowing their love was like a flower blossoming at dawn, only to be swept away by the cold wind at twilight.

On this night I watched Akira warm a pool of oil in his hand and rub the musky scent on his lord's hard chest, massaging its slickness into the curvature of his muscles, over his strong back down to the deep chiseled hollows on the sides of his buttocks, his massive thighs. Shintaro flexed his muscles at his expert touch, grunting when the younger samurai grabbed his cock and ran his hand up and down the length of his hard shaft, moving his body in a steady rhythm, faster, *faster,* Akira's cock rising with need, his dark soulful eyes telling his lord what he desired.

Sipping green tea, I squirmed as my pussy began twitching, so involved was I with their coupling, my other hand caressing myself as if *I* stroked my samurai. A stirring desire rekindled within me. I couldn't stop watching as Akira continued kneading every inch of his lord's body, arousing him with the heat of his hands warming his flesh, attentive to his hard abdomen, his nipples, then returning to his cock and making Shintaro buck with desire. He ordered the younger samurai to stand while he planted his cock firmly against his arse, then spread his buttocks and inserted an oiled finger inside him, stretching his hole and penetrating him, then inching inside him in slow, steady movements. He held his buttocks as he pushed forward until all of him was in the young warrior, pumping, thrusting, grinding until their ecstasy reached a rising pitch that erupted like a battle cry. I can still hear their wild shouts echoing in my head like two fierce warriors raging a tempest with such passion and savagery I couldn't stop myself from being drawn into their flame of sensuality, their lingering touch upon my body entreating me to join them in their orgasm. I slid my hand between my thighs and inserted a finger inside me, sighing with delight at finding it slippery, the dryness gone, and began rubbing my burning clit slowly, then faster as the fire inside me intensified until a glittering trail of sensations raced through me, mirroring my lord's wild excited thrusts.

It was the last time, dear lady reader, any woman, Occidental or Oriental, witnessed such a sensual, erotic scene between these two samurai. I've attempted to re-create the vividness of that night in such a way that you will never forget it but will understand that in the pursuit of their forbidden desires, they explored their maleness and found a wholeness not known to most men.

How fortunate we are to have shared in that desire.

The day of farewells. The dawn is lead-gray, misty and wistful. Air is humid. This morning, as on every morning, I suckled my baby to my breast, my nipples sore, my fatigue dissipating when her now-familiar scent filled me with warmth and love and wonder. Reiko never seemed to cry, a trait among native babies, instead gurgling and cooing, happy and content. Except today. Somehow she knew this was the last time I would hold her in my arms, kiss her plump cheeks, tousle the fine hair atop her perfectly round head, rub her belly and watch her wiggle her little toes.

My tears fall without shame, my heart breaking, remembering how Nami took Reiko from my aching arms and Shintaro helped me mount my horse. The summer rains would soon be upon us and I must return to my husband before he sent soldiers looking for me, putting them all in danger. Physically I was strong, mentally and emotionally I was determined to *stay* strong so my heart would not break. My samurai had made me a woman, a mother, bringing out my virtues, my faults, my strengths. Laughing, crying, touching, healing, pleasuring me everywhere with his tongue, his cock. I shall never forget him.

We kept silent, Shintaro, Akira and I, making our way over the hill on horseback, past the ravine, the scent of pine overwhelming my senses. I took deep breaths but I couldn't smell the orange blossoms, as if they closed their petals to show their sadness, knowing I would not return. Nothing more needed to be said…nothing could be said…it was the way of the warrior.

I need not have fretted about James wondering what happened to me. Being the sly rogue he is, James had told the physician attending me that my child was stillborn and he had me committed to an asylum in Ōzaka for puerperal insanity (the only hospital there is an abandoned temple filled with a few patients). No doubt this is where the rumor started that I had been committed to an asylum.

Greedy, sullen, ambitious, licentious. Nothing new about my husband, but what I did find surprising was his jubilance at seeing me. As if I were a restless ghost returned to him with a purse filled with gold.

"We leave for London within the month," he was quick to tell me. The physician told him I wouldn't be ready until then to make the journey. He also told James that "sexual excesses" could have a damaging effect upon me, alleviating my fear of him forcing himself upon me, at least temporarily. No one questioned his story about me being in an asylum (the foreign residents are not as sophisticated as you, dear lady reader), and I was plied with condolence cards and visits from the dutiful wives in the settlement, drinking tea and listening to their own woeful stories of losing a child. I must admit, I found their presence comforting since I was without my samurai, a fierce rushing of blood to my lower region making me moan with desire every time I caught the scent of fragrant blossoms on a breeze or crushed the silk of my futon over my breasts at night. I craved their penetrating touch: Shintaro's hot, heated breath on the back of my neck, Akira's hands parting my thighs. Their warmth, their hunger for pleasure, their expression of absolute truth in each other's embrace and in my arms. Though Shintaro had never spoken to me of love (I sensed his deep pride as a samurai prevented him from doing so), I believe I had opened his eyes to a new feeling that encompassed more than sex. And Nami, her quiet beauty so pleasant to capture in my mind, her enduring faithfulness, refinement of feeling and passionate belief in love. She understood how much I missed my baby…my throat tightening, my chest hurting every time I thought about my child…and how she wiggled her little toes when I rubbed her belly.

One thing I cannot fail to document is James's outrageous behavior in regards to my correspondence with Mr. Fawkes. I was tempted to write over this since I have drawn my husband's character in such a debauched manner, but I must show him as he is. I found several letters from my dear friend ripped open, passages underlined, words crossed out by an angry hand, dark jagged stains crinkling the tissue paper, as if the reader spilled brandy while languishing over them. I received the letter printed below two days before our scheduled departure for Yokohama. It set into motion the final act in my story. Had I not intercepted it, dear lady reader, the ending to my memoir would have been vastly different.

My dear Lady Carlton,
Life here in the mikado's court has taken on new interest since the empress's poems have been set to music. They are quite charming…on a personal note, milady, Her Majesty desires me to tell you how saddened she was to hear about the loss of your child. She wishes you well…

Guilt washed over me for having to continue with this farce and mislead both my dear friend, Mr. Fawkes, and the empress. Knowing how much the elegant ruler wished for a child of her own, I was certain she would have been so pleased to know that a child was born from the union of her loyal subject, Lord Shintaro (in spite of his enemies at court labeling him a rebel, he had never revoked his allegiance to the mikado), and this Irish lass, who so admired the empress's kindness and tenacity in encouraging the education of native women. I had no idea then whatever measure of happiness I would know originated from this fragile thread. Mr. Fawkes wrote further:

> *I must also mention that interesting gentleman we met outside the palace gate. Word at court has it that he moved his business operations away from Kobé—*

Shintaro. I began to breathe hard, the intensity of his memory sending a very real physical reaction through me, the deep feelings I had for him and our child making me weak-kneed, unsteady. I closed my eyes, willing my mind to focus, think clearly. The Englishman was telling me my samurai's enemies knew he had moved camp. I opened my eyes, continued reading.

> *I must also advise you that political unrest in the west in what was known as —— Province has made travel difficult and you should avoid taking trips to that area at all costs.*

I panicked. If Shintaro moved his camp farther west, he would be in grave danger.

*I pray this letter finds you well, Lady Carlton, and should you
need my assistance upon your return to Tokio, please call on me
at ——.*
Your faithful servant,
Seymour Fawkes

I closed the letter and slipped the thin paper between my
breasts, my pulse racing, my face perspiring. I had to warn
my samurai, but how? *The old swordsmith.* He would help me,
he *had* to, for I wouldn't leave for Yokohama without warning
Shintaro. And seeing my child. The thought of my innocent
babe in danger racked my mind with insane thoughts, tore at
the fiber of my soul, unmasking my layers of defenses in a
cold, harsh light. *How could I have left my child, my samurai?*
What I must do and what I desired struggled with each other,
thrusting me into such turmoil I couldn't bear to live if anything happened to them. I was so distraught, I gave no
thought to the whims of the face of evil in this play when I
grabbed my hat and gloves and headed for the front door, determined to walk to the shop if I must.

"Going somewhere, my dear wife?"

James. I hadn't realized his lordship was home. As long as I
appeared at the table for meals, he hadn't given much thought
to my comings and goings.

"Yes…" I began, wiping my forehead with my glove and
to hell with my sweat staining the fine leather. "I—I want to
buy some curios and embroideries to take back with me."

"You can do that in Tokio," he said in a firm voice, then
added, "I don't want you out of my sight until we leave."

I didn't try to hide the anger in my words. "Then why
don't you tie me to the bed?"

"Tempting." He looked me up and down with a conscious

pleasure. I swore I saw a glint in his eye that sent a shiver through me. "There will be time for that once we're back in London and you're ready to resume our little game."

"I agreed to be your wife, not your whore," I retorted.

"Is there any difference?" he said, laughing, then slapped me on the backside.

"You *are* a bastard, James, aren't you?" I yanked off my hat and gloves and raced upstairs to my room and slammed the door. I don't know how long I stood with my back against the wooden frame, my heart racing, my mind planning, knowing I must fulfill the intangible promise I'd made to my samurai when I took up the way of the sword. I closed my eyes and drew upon that strength to clear my mind and find order and harmony to cleanse my soul. It was a delicate balance, to become so focused when facing danger so as to see with total clarity a single leaf upon a tree, but Shintaro had taught me well. To prepare myself for what was to come, I removed the items I had brought back with me from my black cloth traveling bag and held them in my hand, touching them, deriving strength from them: a poem Shintaro had written for me on crisp parchment in his strong black calligraphy; the sharp-pointed willow-leaf arrowhead Akira gave me, telling me I had pierced his heart; the blue silk kimono from Nami, the scent of my lord's pleasure mixing with mine; the wooden charm I clutched in my hand when my baby daughter was born. And the dirk Shintaro insisted I carry with me to protect myself.

The hours passed, waiting as I was until after James retired to his rooms, since we had taken to our original arrangement regarding separate quarters. I lay in bed, listening to the sounds of the house. The tall standing clock ticking, the wind beating on glass windowpanes, loud voices passing by outside disturbing the peace of the night. They all seemed strange to me, why? Was it because I yearned for the soft chatter of the cicada, the hoot of a tired owl, the hushed whispers carried on an ancient breeze? I dared admit, though I knew danger lurked, I found a nudge to my heart most pleasant at the thought of seeing Shintaro and my baby, holding the child in my arms, leaning my head against the strong shoulder of my samurai. I had struck a tentative peace with my husband, but I had no guarantee his lordship wouldn't find a way to take what I loved most from me.

When the clock struck twelve, I undressed, tossing my corset and petticoats onto the floor, then donned a riding jacket and divided skirt and sneaked downstairs, careful not to wake the maid or cook, and slipped through the side door and exited through the back of the garden. I worked my way from house to house, heading in a zigzag direction toward the Motomachi, darting behind an old camphor tree with a fat trunk near the main street, my senses alert. I kept out of sight, a vested prayer upon my lips that the gods would grant me safe passage to the shop of the old swordsmith. A moonless night afforded me no help in finding my way nor did I expect any, for no being, celestial or human, could deter me. I was filled with a supernatural fever like a she wolf on the prowl, my spirit possessed, hungry, driven, for only in the blackness of the night would I dare to find freedom.

1
8

In the summer of 1875 I ran away from my husband for a second time. I was twenty-two. I had birthed a child. I had shared my futon simultaneously with two samurai, wielded a sword with enough dexterity to split stone and embraced the way of the warrior with such fervor no saint could have carried her knightly banner into battle better than I. Why this diatribe so close to the ending of my tale, you ask? When I began writing my memoir, I admit I was filled with the need to seek revenge against what I perceived was the pettiness and jealousy a pampered aristocrat like you, dear lady reader, thrived on to feed your boredom. I wanted to shock you, titillate you, make you hungry for sex, knowing you find little satisfaction in your marriage or your dalliances. Yes, I was also petty, wishing to make you wide-eyed and jealous with stories of my samurai, playing games with you, teasing you, attaching more importance to my adventure than need be. Flaunting my rebelliousness and expecting you to understand. For that, I am truly sorry. You are a woman of your circumstance as I am of mine. 'Tis not fair of me to judge you, as I do not wish to be judged. To some, I remain an amusing piece of drawing room gossip that will soon be forgotten. But to *you,* the woman who has followed me on this journey of self-discovery and who believes in a deep love and in a life made richer by a child you both created, I beseech you to ride with me to the end of my story and accept whatever happens. Cry if you must, but don't set the book aside. For all that I have written is as it happened with its Oriental mystery, strange beauty and raw desire. If you wish to tout it as a fairy story, so be it. If you have the courage to come with me and understand it was a far more important thing I did than merely record my story, that I made the right decision to warn Shintaro and hold my child again in my arms, then you shall have your reward. For like a faded silk embroidery that retains the scent of the Orient even when hidden between the finest French lace, my story will linger in your heart and warm your soul when you find yourself alone and without a man to hold you. I know too well the ache that eats at you, burns your skin though the nights are cold, makes you reach for something, *anything* that will bring forth the flow of your juices and the sweetest of scents to turn your gray and bitter world into a ripe, golden fruit to quench your thirst. Know that I have also suffered, but I pray I have cast the glow of my adventure with my samurai upon you and have given you a more enlightened view of my love for them.

And now to my dilemma: I need your help to finish my story. Before I go forward, dear lady reader, I must be certain you have aligned yourself with me, because I face a great difficulty to relive this part of my tale. Yes, the loss I have spoken of occurs here…but I cannot continue writing until I know

I have your support. I will not disappoint you, but if at any time you feel you must stop and linger a moment, please do, as will I. So with your permission, I shall deliver to you the most exciting chapter of my memoir. Though it be tragic in part, it shall also fill you with the most astounding ending you will *never* forget.

I cannot describe the exhilaration that filled me as I made my way up into the hills behind the foreign settlement on horseback following the old swordsmith. Smelling of tanned leather and sake, he remained quiet, never looking at me, careful to keep the side lanterns on our mounts from dimming the farther we went into the darkness. I had found my way along the alley to his shop, calling out to him in the native language, praying I wouldn't hear the slice of his sword and feel the sharpness of his blade upon my shoulder. I told him I had an urgent message for Shintaro and he must take me to him. He nodded and within minutes we were on horseback, headed away from the settlement and up into the shadows lying over the mountains, but not toward the samurai village. No, up, *up* to the summit toward the sanctuary, where not long ago we had brought Reiko on a sunlit morning when the bees buzzed their approval and the birds sang the ancient prayers that lingered here. Sheltered by lofty pines, our mounts made their way over the terrain of cascading rocks with little light to guide them, but they were creatures of habit and seemed to know the way. I prayed Shintaro had not yet set out on the journey westward where his enemies could find him. I clung to that belief, hoping it wouldn't fade away like a mythic dream into the mist.

When we reached the sanctuary, all was quiet except for the gentle chirp of crickets mixing with the bells fringing the eaves of the black tiled roof and swaying in the wind. I noted the hedge of stone votive lanterns weren't the only guards on watch. I spied Shintaro's men hidden in the shadows, waiting, watching. The old swordsmith waved his hand in greeting and they remained in place. Dismounting my horse, I raced up the copper-tipped steps to the veranda of the prayer hall, nearly tripping over the sandals and clogs placed on the lower steps, and yanked open the double wooden doors. Only later did I remember the two crossed emblems embedded on the doors symbolized thunder, reminding the souls who slept nearby of the fatal power of the gods.

"We shall break camp and travel east to the higher mountains," Shintaro bellowed, giving orders, waving his arms wildly so his kimono sleeves blew about in a tempest, "where the streams are clean and pure and the land rich for planting until this matter is settled."

"It will never be settled, Shintaro, until you make peace with the mikado." It was a delicate matter I broached with him, something oft discussed at London soirees, where the subject of politics created fodder for men in ill-fitting tails eager to make or break each other's fortunes. A minor tragedy at best. Here honor above all disciplined the samurai soul and untruths were not tolerated and viewed as cowardly.

"Why do you still not understand that we samurai are fighting for our survival." He paused, his face filled with pain, his neck rigid with corded veins. I could see his anger challenged whatever feeling he had for me. I believe he knew then it was a matter of time before the end came, but because he was concerned for his people, he had scattered his clan into these mountains, taking refuge in thatched huts, abandoned shrines and here in the sanctuary at the summit hilltop.

"Your fight is also mine, Shintaro," I cried out. "Why can't you see that?" I breathed hard, pulling in the strong scent of incense into my lungs, feeling at one here in the dim, mysterious light, the heady scent emitting from the lit joss sticks in honor of the gods. I discovered it was more difficult for me to exit this world than I had believed.

"No, you must go back to your husband as your duty demands." He cupped my chin, his eyes so filled with emotion they lay heavy on his heart and did not find their way into words. Instead, he said, "You shouldn't have come here."

I saw the hurt in his eyes, as if he had accepted he would never see me again. "I *had* to warn you, my lord," I said, explaining, "and to see you…and Reiko."

Without taking his gaze off me, he said, "Nami, bring the child." He knew that she waited for his command behind the screen in the shadowy recesses of the room. She came forth with Reiko in her arms and for a brief moment I envied her, envied their relationship molded by centuries of duty and tradition. I imagined her kneeling with her own child in her arms, alone in a serene, quiet garden, breathing in the fragrance of blossoms. She had lost that peace, but I had given her back her place with my daughter. I could not take that from her.

"The gods must have seen you riding up the mountain," Shintaro said to me, "for the child awoke and started crying." He looked at Nami with mock rebuke. "Or so I am informed."

She smiled, then bowed low. "She is hungry and misses her mother."

"I have missed her, too, Nami, but I know you have given her your heart."

I couldn't resist the urge to nurse my child, my maternal

instinct too strong to deny. My breasts were heavy with milk, liquid often seeping through my chemise and my bodice. I removed my riding jacket, my dirk, then unlaced my chemise and bared my breasts. Smiling, I tickled the baby's lips with my nipple and when she opened her mouth wide, I brought her up quickly so she could latch onto me, her tiny mouth suckling, her small perfect head showing signs of light-colored hair among the dark. I ran my fingers through the soft strands, marveling at seeing me in her, her tiny hand holding on to my finger with a strong grip. The grip of her father, Lord Shintaro. I thanked him with my eyes. He nodded, then smiled, and I could see the fondness he had for our daughter gleaming on his rugged face clearly visible in the burning light of the chandelier cast with gilded copper and encrusted bronze.

Then, a moment later, he was troubled. I ignored the warning in his eyes telling me I must be strong and bend like the bamboo, for bamboo was hollow inside. Empty. I could not have written a better description of my life without them. Leaving here would be the hardest thing I'd ever done, a fearful restlessness grabbing my heart, but I must, my duty shaped clearly in my mind.

"My lord, is it true she is here?" I heard a male voice call out behind me.

I turned to see Akira rush into the small antechamber where we sat upon threadbare brocade cushions where honorable monks had prayed for a thousand years. His handsome face beamed an intense brightness in the silvery-gray light filtering through the dark interior. I shivered, his beauty reminding me of the passion we three had shared together, his eyes like a mirror where I could see a vivid reflection of his feelings for me.

He loved me, wanted me, why couldn't Shintaro show me his feelings? What was stopping him?

"I am so pleased to see you, Akira," I called out, bowing my head. Reiko held fast to my breast and sucked harder, sending that private joy through me that I missed so much.

He bowed low in respect. "To see you again is a gift from the gods."

"Lady Carlton cannot remain here, Akira," Shintaro interrupted in a stern voice.

Indignant that he spoke for me, I said, "'Tis true, Akira, I must leave and return to London." I refused to weaken, though I was tempted to throw myself on Shintaro's mercy and plead to stay with him, with our child. I turned to my samurai. "I beg you to think about what I have said, Shintaro. Meet with the mikado and do what is best for your people and our daughter."

"I fear she speaks the truth, Lord Shintaro." Akira laid his hand upon my shoulder to show his support. "Our enemies will not give up trying to destroy us."

"I have made my decision. We are samurai and have fought long and hard for our cause. We must be treated with respect," Shintaro snapped at me. "Until then, we will make our stand. It is our destiny."

He glared at his squire, his eyes glowing in an unusual show of emotion, but it was the jealous tone in his voice that secretly pleased me. I wasn't in love with Akira, but I harbored passionate feelings for him, made more so by his courage to challenge his lord and provoke him to think in a way no one ever had.

"They have guns, cannons," I said hotly, "many will die, Shintaro, is that the way of the warrior?"

Ignoring me, he turned to Akira. "You will take her back

to the settlement, then return quickly." He became the clan leader again, his demeanor changed, his mind planning. "We must be gone from here before the night comes to visit us again."

Dawn broke with a fierceness, windy and cold high in the mountains. I nursed my child before leaving, capturing to memory how she smelled like sweet jasmine before Nami strapped her onto her back. I smiled, watching her bare toes sticking out and curling up in tiny balls as a ticklish breeze found her. I didn't pretend to myself I would ever feel whole again, only that I would never forget that somewhere in thickly wooded mountains my child would grow up under Nami's guidance, loyal to those who loved her, her samurai family, and for that I gave thanks to the gods.

With hot tea and rice warming our stomachs, we began our journey down the summit, Akira in front, me following behind, my horse keeping a steady pace. When we reached the clearing, the shimmer of summer green hit me with such intensity I blamed that for the moistness in my eyes, for samurai do not cry. I looked up ahead at Akira, his youthful smile engaging me when he turned around to ask me if I wanted to stop and rest. I wasn't tired, but I nodded. I had the feeling he wanted to talk, but we never had that chance.

I cried out when an arrow shot past me and found its mark near his left shoulder where the armor didn't protect him. I screamed, he grimaced in pain, then another arrow and another flew around us, missing me but striking his horse, the animal's knees buckling and throwing him from the saddle. Wounded, Akira got to his feet, broke off the arrow embedded in his flesh, his eyes finding me, his face in anguish at not being able to protect me.

"Take cover in the woods, my lady!" he called out, drawing both his swords from their wooden sheaths, his head swiveling from side to side, looking, waiting, challenging the attackers to show themselves.

"Who—" I cried out, then I knew. *Ninja*. Raiders and assassins whose services were bought by anyone who paid them, most likely corrupt officials in the mikado's court. They were everywhere at once, three, four, five stealth figures in black coming out of the woods armed with short bows, darts and spears springing into full length with a flick of their wrists, like night devils with sharpened claws and tails. They targeted Akira first, then me.

"Go!" he shouted. "Warn Shintaro!"

"I won't leave you," I cried, kicking my heels into my horse's flanks and jumping him over a tree trunk to reach the young samurai. I chased after a dark-garbed assassin running toward Akira, my horse rising up on its hind legs, kicking him and making him drop his sword. The assassin picked up his weapon and tried to attack my horse, but I drew my dirk from inside my jacket, aimed and threw it…yes, I killed him.

I jumped from my horse and grabbed the dead man's sword then I took off after the two assassins engaged in swordplay with Akira. Strong, stalwart, his swords slicing, hissing, the clang of steel against steel, he held them. I came up behind the assassin going after Akira, swinging the sword in an arc and bringing it down between his shoulders, slicing through his dark clothes into his flesh and drawing blood. I saw the pride in Akira's eyes, approving, his manly beauty glowing in the rising sun and pulling at something inside me I didn't understand then, but I do now.

He knew he was going to die.

I had to help him. I grabbed the reins of my horse, the

animal sweating, snorting but uninjured and, sword in hand, I mounted him quickly. I took off, but before I could reach the young warrior, more black-garbed men dropped from the trees. Ten, twenty, I couldn't count. Swinging my sword, my mind swimming with fear, my heart pounding, I couldn't concentrate, couldn't shake the terror taking control of me. Akira was surrounded, his sword flashing, the assassins on him all at once, surrounding him.

"Akira, look out!" I shouted, bringing down the sword on the neck of an assassin then running it through him.

"Leave me, my lady, go!" he shouted, his voice strong and commanding, his words cutting through the fiber of my existence. How could I abandon this honorable samurai? I turned to look at him, blood-smeared, fighting, his swords mounting a brave attack in a battle already ended. The whole scene seemed so ethereal, as if he existed someplace where I couldn't touch him. Only by sheer willpower and strength did he keep from succumbing to his wounds. I heard Akira shout a samurai battle cry, the sound of his voice so powerful, something snapped in me. *There was nothing I could do. I must save myself.* I owed it to him, to Shintaro, to my child. I turned my mount sharply around and galloped off through the woods, arrows whizzing by my head, the sound of horses in the distance.

I didn't have to look around to know Akira was dead.

As I write, I am holding the willow-leaf arrowhead Akira gave me, its sharp edges pricking my thoughts as well as my heart. If this were a romantic novel, and I dare say aristocratic ladies who have never read it will affix that label to my work, some will insist I should have allowed Akira to live. Still, I brood over his death, his strong body cut down, his courage enduring, his love for his lord without question, his love for me impassioned. His infectious smile, the dark lock of hair hanging over his right eye giving him the devilish look of a boy at play, yet his manly needs deep with desire, his firm mouth sucking on me, his cock finding its way into my dark hole, his hands clasped around my buttocks holding me tight while he thrust into me. To me, his maleness was without question and his final sacrifice was a gift I shall always treasure.

"How many assassins did you see?" Shintaro asked, pacing.

"Ten, twenty, all dressed in black with their faces covered." I paused, fighting back heavy emotion. "Akira fought bravely, his swords cutting down many men."

Shintaro looked away from me, his face disguising his feelings as was the way of the samurai, but I saw him clench his fists so tightly the bones popped, his mouth set in a hard line, his eyes so sorrowful it was as if the last blossom had been torn off the tree branch by an angry and fearsome wind. He fell silent, leaving the chirping crickets to grate on my nerves. Why hadn't I noticed them before?

He turned to me. "Did they follow you?"

"Yes, but I lost them when I crossed the stream and backtracked up the mountain."

"Good. That will give us time to prepare." He paused. "Who knew that you came here last night?"

"James."

He looked at me quizzically.

"I've no doubt my husband had a man follow me up the mountain with the old swordsmith," I said, berating myself for my mad impulse.

Shintaro nodded, understanding. "I imagine the man who followed you is in the employ of my enemies. No doubt they tricked your husband into forming an alliance with them."

I shook my head in despair. "James played right into their hands. The *fool*."

"It won't take them long to find us. We shall make our stand here rather than out in the open," he said, thinking, planning. "Go with Nami and our child to the convent near the settlement." He gave me a slight smile, his words gentle but a command nonetheless. "You will be safe there—"

"No. I'm staying here with you."

"*I forbid it!*" he yelled. "It is too dangerous. You could be killed."

"Akira sacrificed his life so I may warn you and save the others." I stopped, suddenly exhausted, but I refused to give in to my emotions, to shed tears. A passion for vengeance surged in me that I could not deny. "I'm not going to allow him to die in vain."

In the gloomy darkness, I could not make out his expression as he mulled over what I said, the beating of my heart loud in my ears. I had gained the fighting skills of a samurai, but did I have a warrior's soul? Would I ever know?

I jumped, my pulse racing when Shintaro yelled out an order to the retainer guarding him. Was I to be removed from his presence? What then? I fought back wild emotions making me tremble, my throat tighten when the samurai returned with dark clothes, two sheathed swords and a dirk. I gasped, my hand flying to my mouth. The long and short swords of the warrior.

I thanked Shintaro, bowing low in respect, tears running down my face, their salty taste wetting my lips and reminding me of the price of duty.

I changed into the dark clothes behind the screen, wrapping the heavy black jacket around me then tucking it into a pair of divided trousers. I pulled the black belt tight around my waist to keep the jacket secure, tying it in front, then affixed my trousers below the knee and at the base of my calves with ties so I could move freely and unencumbered. Bearskin boots lined with silk kept my feet warm and dry. I performed the task with a cold efficiency that helped me focus, though it wasn't easy to put aside the emotional impact that wearing these clothes had upon me, my heart pounding, my throat dry. The jacket smelled of earth and sweat and blossoms all melded together and struck a chord so deep within me, I thought the ache in my gut would never go away. Nothing hidden or obscure in what I felt. I belonged in these clothes. I took the swords and tied the cords hanging from the sheaths to my belt, then opened my jacket and placed the dagger between my breasts. I bowed to my samurai and smiled, the moisture glistening upon my cheeks. He returned my smile, then bade me to warm my soul with hot tea and still my mind to prepare for the battle to come.

"We must show them they are powerless against us," Shintaro said, his breathing heavy, as if a great weight lay upon his heart. I would know why in due time, what sacrifice he was prepared to make to save his family and his men. He finished with: "We will fight them to the death."

"If we take prisoners," I said, "we can find out who sent them."

He shook his head. "Ninja leave behind only dead men to question."

A shudder went through me as we lay in wait for them, Shintaro explaining to me how the assassins often penetrated the compound through hidden entrances, carrying roped hooks, ladders, hand spikes, and how they used surprise to cripple their target. To counter their strategy, the samurai lord stationed his men behind a concealed wall in the sanctuary as well as outside in the tall, lofty pine trees, where they could view anyone hoisting themselves up to the roof with ropes. *They would first strike from above,* he said, then when their victims tried to flee, they'd be cut down for the final kill by the raiders attacking from all sides with their star-shaped discs, knives and hooks.

"They never expected to find you and Akira intruding on their devious plans," Shintaro said. A smile lit his face, his eyes bright with admiration. "You have done well, my blonde samurai."

"The young warrior died saving me." I couldn't help the choke in my voice, my breathing heavy.

"There will be time to honor him, I promise you." He put his hand over mine, crushing my fingers with his strength, his passion, the blood rushing hot through him. He was ready for battle.

They came at midnight, a single torch burning in the sanctuary while an overhanging gilt lamp swayed in a macabre dance, the crickets silent. The raiders attacked as quietly as a night demon slipping on a black glove…flesh and bone stretching the leather until it was taut…each finger extending, flexing…then clawing at their target with deadly precision, coming at us from all sides, moving noiselessly along the matted floor.

Shintaro drew his swords and yelled out, the signal to charge them, weapons slashing through the air like blades of lightning, the sound of steel slicing through leather then flesh. Sweating but determined, I drew my sword quickly and held it overhead in a two-handed grip, its bluish-white glow making a long, jagged streak in the dark when I brought it downward and landed it cleanly on the skull of a moving black figure caught in the yellow glint from the torch. My eyes widened, aware of a horror I had never known. I jumped aside as the dead assassin fell forward, then I turned to see a ninja with sword in hand charge me, his blade aimed at my heart. I refused to panic and drew my short sword, countering his attack by dropping to my knees and knocking him off balance then thrusting my short sword into his thigh and jamming my long sword under his armpit. Somehow, I kept my mind focused on nothing but the moment. It was maddening, I couldn't breathe, choking on the fear of what I had become: a warrior destined to kill, the whispering of the sword in my ear compelling me to keep going, tearing through flesh, punishing the evil that threatened to rip apart my life. Anger enveloped me, though terrifying at first, my hand was steady upon my sword in the intense airless heat as I killed with such fanatical skill it was as if I sprang forward like a mythical female warrior, the speed of my blade no match for my assailants.

I was taking revenge for Akira's death.

I wanted blood and death to be my allies in my quest for justice and so I indulged in a bloodlust I pray ne'er to see again. Like you, dear lady reader, I've experienced treachery, betrayals and crimes against my heart, but that night a vengeful spirit possessed me, sending all my passion into my sword. *My soul.* I had to protect myself, my samurai…and my child.

Samurai here and outside were engaged in a chaotic battle with these masters of infiltration and killing who plied their trade of *ninjutsu* without remorse. Shintaro wielded his two swords with an assurance that came from his knowledge of self. *To know is to act,* he often told me, his birthright of samurai pulling his nerves taut and rigid like cold steel. His face dripping with sweat, his eyes blazing and emboldened with the fury of a wild beast, he neither panicked nor showed mercy toward the assassins, pivoting, bending, leaping, defeating several attackers without them drawing blood until I saw—

Three assassins pounced upon him. I lurched forward to help him, but I couldn't stop them from devouring him in a swirl of black and evil.

The coming of a cleansing dawn awakened the crickets and ushered out the humid darkness. I heard the whisper of the sword no more. I laid down my weapons and sank to the floor, exhausted, weary and, but for cuts and bruises, victorious. I looked around me. The matted floor ran crimson with the blood of the assassins, corpses everywhere. Samurai, some wounded, removed the bodies. I was reminded of what Shintaro had told me, how the ninja practice a way to increase their mental focus by reciting a thousand-year-old prayer and making cutting gestures in the air with their fingers to increase their perception and see into the future. On that hot summer night, I wondered if they had seen their own death. Then a more fearsome thought pierced my mind.

Where was Shintaro?

Minutes—or was it hours ago—he fought beside me, engaged in a death fury that called for supreme courage to achieve victory. I let out a loud sob. What did I care about victory without *him?* Raising my fists, I raged against the heavens with such agony I feared I'd be cursed for thousands of years to come. My heart pumping, my eyes blurred over with dirt and blood, I crawled from end to end, clawing at the straw matting until my fingers bled, looking for him, afraid of what I'd find when I did. Tears welling in my eyes,

I buried my face in my arms, choking on the scent of the straw mixing with the stench of blood seeping through the fibers, a futile emptiness overwhelming me. *No…no…it couldn't be.* Shintaro had filled me with such happiness, given me a child, shown me the way of the warrior. *I couldn't lose both my samurai. The gods were not that unjust, were they?* I couldn't move…I wanted to retreat into a deep, dark cell and grieve.

A strong hand grabbed my shoulder, the heat of his touch searing my skin. Hand on my sword, I tensed, then I looked up and saw my samurai kneeling down next to me, his eyes caressing me with something I had never seen there before.

Love.

"I have found you," was all he said, pulling me into his arms, holding me, his warm body sending a pleasant heat through me. Nothing more needed to be said, not then, not ever.

I was his.

1
9

After the night raid on the sanctuary I was back in Tokio in a simple but elegant one-story dwelling in a busy section of the capital city surrounded by a high bamboo fence. The streets outside the parklike enclosure teemed day and night with a long line of humanity going about their business, never knowing that this house with its polished raised wooden-floor foyer and sand-and-stone inner-courtyard garden lay vacant for months waiting for its owner to return. Shintaro. The servants had taken great care of the house since his departure (it was mandatory, dear lady reader, for a noble samurai to maintain a residence in Tokio), making certain everything was in its place as each sun rose and set, their obedience and loyalty to their lord without question. I was delighted to find the living quarters filled with lacquerware, ceramics, hanging scrolls, fans, all decorated by the hand of master craftsmen. I have no doubt native motifs like these will adorn carpets and wallpaper in Mayfair town houses, perhaps even milady's drawers. As it was, I was grateful to leave behind a diet of gruel consisting of tea and rice for fluffy white grains and the delicious meals prepared for us. Milk and butter and beef are now included in the native diet, though I wonder if this will be more to their detriment than not. I almost felt as if I were back in London with the hustle of the city at my door and the streets crowded with foreign carriages and soldiers and police in western-style uniforms. I had forgotten about the fetid odors, fleas and other nuisances, but I paid them no mind. This was the day Shintaro would relinquish his sword to the mikado, its blade slightly curved with a sharpened cutting edge, its hilt covered in white enamel and gold and trimmed in red silk cord. *Enough blood has been shed,* he said. It was time for the clan to follow the mandate of the emperor. I believe Akira's death was pivotal in his decision to make this gesture of peace.

Exotic yet peaceful notes on a bamboo flute, then the soft shuffle of sandaled feet bearing home the young samurai as the doors to the sanctuary burst open, the anguished groans from Shintaro at seeing him, the bright morning sun escaping through the doors as they shut and enclosed us in darkness.

This great warrior, so sensual and so devoted to his lord, sustaining life and welcoming death to save me, inhabiting a place of manly beauty where few women dared tread, a place that represented the substance of what it meant to be a samurai, brave and unflinching in the tides of battle. And when he raised his sword for the last time, he knew his deed belonged to the past, but it would protect the future. These thoughts rose in my mind as smoky-gray incense floated over the fresh lilies, orchids and chrysanthemums placed on the bare altar as ceremonial offerings to his spirit. We wore white kimono with white sashes and straw sandals on our feet, Shintaro acting as the priest since none laid claim to the abandoned sanctuary. He pointed the body north as tradition dictated, surrounding it with fruits, vegetables and tea, then clapping his hands to call upon the gods before reciting the Buddhist sutras that have guided souls to heaven for a thousand years.

Afterward we made the trek to the holy spot where the young samurai's body was turned to ash, the wind rising as I grieved, unable to let go, summoning him in my mind, letting the tears fall, wanting Akira to *be,* if only in spirit form. Holding me close to him, so close I could hear the rapid beating of his heart, Shintaro bade me dry my tears, though I could see his eyes were also moist, his soul as forlorn as mine. With a whisper in my ear that the time had come to let go, I looked upward to the heavens as my samurai freed a white dove from a small wooden cage. The bird circled overhead, widening its circle more each time until it soared upward into a straight line and became lost to our sight, its spirit free.

Returning to the sanctuary, I pressed the flowers between thin sheets of white silk in Akira's memory, knowing he would always be the handsome young samurai who said I pierced his heart. What he didn't know was that he had also pierced mine.

I let my body go limp when Shintaro picked me up in his strong arms then carried me down a stone pathway that led deeper into the woods, purple wisteria growing everywhere around us. A wonder of enchantment came over me, so different from my melancholy mood earlier. The air hot, moist, luminous, a breeze skipping through my white kimono tickled my pussy as he carried me under a bower of birch and maple branches curving overhead until we came to the lofty pines. And a waterfall. Tumbling down smooth rocky ledges half covered with shimmering wet moss, pine trees splintered with age leaned over the foaming stream at odd angles. There next to the waterfall, he put me down and untied my sash, then slid my kimono down over my shoulders, baring my breasts then my belly, slightly rounded from birthing my child, until I was nude. He grunted his approval, then drew in his breath as the spray from the cascading water dampened my body, making it glisten, my arms outstretched toward him. He shed his kimono and took my hand and together we bathed nude under the crashing waterfall, our wet bodies entwined, my nipples puckering into hard points when Shintaro splashed cold water on me, laughing, tempting me to do the same and shower him, his cock. Grabbing me, his hard erection nudging against my groin, we found a small opening behind the waterfall where we stood on a granite ledge, embracing each other, his mouth against mine, kissing me with tenderness to comfort me, for I was on an odyssey that I didn't understand to assuage my sorrow, and needed his guidance, my hands grabbing and squeezing him with joy and discovery. The hard muscles on his back tensed under my touch, my breasts crushed against his bare chest, all melancholy rushing out of me as I gave out a low moan of pleasure. The man I cared about was here with me, the man we'd both lost was looking down upon us with an approving eye. Knowing this brought something beautiful and reverent to this sensual scene being played out under the waterfall, when my samurai spread my legs and massaged the sensitive piece of skin near my anal hole to make my juices flow. A rawness caught in my throat, making me gasp when he slipped two fingers inside me, his other hand around my waist as he rubbed my clit back and forth in an exacting manner that made it burn until I begged him for release. *Soon,* he whispered, then grabbed my hand and pressed it against his cock, wanting me to feel its throbbing hardness before turning me around and sliding his finger, sticky with my natural sweetness, into the crack between my buttocks. He plunged his finger into my anal hole to lubricate it, making me cry out in surprise at the intrusion, then as the cordon of muscles began to relax, I felt him go deeper, sending a quiver of anticipation through me. Knowing I was ready, he slid his cock into my anus, slowly inching his way inside me until I took all of him. Pumping into me, water crashing around us, he found a hard, pulsating rhythm, knowing I wanted him to take me as he had taken Akira, the sensation so strong within me I swore I heard not one, two, but three voices echoing in the hollow chamber as we yelled out, calling on the gods to allow this young warrior safe passage through the vermilion gateway. Wet, wet with passion, we cleansed our souls and renewed our spirits in this carnal act of love, his cock thrusting into me over and over until we gave out a final shout of ecstasy to honor the fallen samurai.

James was determined to ruin me before he sailed for San Francisco and went on to London. He left my packed traveling bags and portmanteau behind with Mr. Fawkes, telling him to sell them and send him the funds since I had run off with my samurai lover. Dear Mr. Fawkes wisely chose to ignore his lordship, though he confided to me if he'd been a younger man he would have knocked some sense into him. That made me smile, but James's behavior did not. He went on a tirade with every British official he could find about what had happened in Kobé. I imagined him spending endless hours with a brandy in one hand and a scurrilous remark on his lips lamenting how his American wife had been bedded

by a samurai and was living in sin. I'm told he boasted that
he would never give me a divorce so as to keep me a dishon-
est woman. I must ask a favor of you, dear lady reader, if you
should encounter my imperious husband at a soiree or tea (not
at the Viscount Aubrey's, who swears Lord Carlton is *not* welcome under his roof), know this: when I left him that night
to warn Shintaro, I was determined to return with him to
London and do my duty. We Irish are a rebellious lot, but
we're honest people and ready to defend our land *and* our
honor. I owed Shintaro that and I have no regrets. Now it
was my duty to be with him again when he appeared before
the emperor. We had not spoken of afterward, though a
strange light came into his eyes when I mentioned it, but it
was my intention to return to London to ask James for a
divorce. Force his hand to release me from our agreement
once I made known to my father his cheating scheme. I
awaited an answer from my da to a letter I posted upon my
return to Tokio. I explained everything to him (leaving out
things better left unsaid to one's da) and told him about the
birth of his granddaughter. 'Tis my hope this Irishman's love
of family and truth will win out in the end and he and my
mother can accept what I hope will be my future.

With Shintaro. And little Reiko.

I was in a grand mood that morning, humming as I layered
petticoat after petticoat over my corset (laced up by the lord
himself, my samurai's strong hands squeezing my waist as he
pulled on the soft white ribbons). I had nursed Reiko earlier
and Nami was giving her a bath. I wanted her to be clean and
sparkling in her lace-trimmed, white sleeveless chemise embroidered with fancy designs (to protect her from evil spirits),
the delicate lacy pattern fringing the hem sewn by native girls

from the school founded by the empress. It was a special day for my little daughter. She was going to meet the empress. 'Tis a reminiscent and tender scene that I recall, for what woman could ask for more? I had my child and my samurai. I was so enraptured with this scenario as perfect as a midsummer dream, I didn't think to realize that the look of longing on Shintaro's face when he picked up his child in his arms told an entirely different story. One that would not have the fairy-tale ending I believed was mine.

Whatever account you may hear about my meeting with the empress, I have chosen, by the fact that I enjoyed a kind and gentle relationship with Her Majesty, to relay our conversation in a more direct manner rather than the subtleties of facial expressions and pauses so often associated with such a discourse. The outcome of events to come hinged upon this meeting, though at the time I merely followed my instincts and impulses as a new mother, aware that the empress was childless, but hoping I could share my joy with her and enlighten her life with mine.

And so I share with you the morning Empress Haruko requested the august presence, as the formal native language dictates it shall be written, of my daughter, Reiko.

Accounts of the empress's personality vary, with some globe-trotters reminding us that royal persons have their foibles. Though you may consider it scandalous, I shall never forget the empress's habit of smoking a golden pipe—three puffs, no more, no less—and being perfectly at ease while greeting members of foreign legations. On this day in the gardens of the temporary imperial residence, the empress greeted me with her usual charm and delight, for I held in my arms little

Reiko, her golden-brown hair curling over her head, her dark eyes looking everywhere before opening her mouth for a tiny yawn then it was back to sleep. I smiled and thought about how someday I would remind her that she napped when the empress took her in her arms and hugged her to her bosom. It was a grand afternoon we had, standing under a pavilion tent erected on the lawn for our visit, the billowing silk with pink and violet irises scattered on the pitched roof providing a cool refuge on this hot, sultry day. I felt so sure of myself, dressed in a sleek version of a favorite summer dress made from deep rose silk and white voile *sans* its overskirt and cumbersome bustle, so perfectly at ease was I with my role as the consort of Lord Shintaro. It mattered not to me that I was not welcome in British circles in the capital city, whose members had a complete inventory of my sins. I cared more for the fact it was an honor for the daughter of a samurai to meet the empress, since the usual age of presentation to court was sixteen.

"Your daughter is very beautiful," the empress said, rocking her in her arms. I sigh now remembering the delightful scene with pink-violet flowers falling around us like fairy dust, though the magic would soon disappear.

"'Tis an honor for me to present her to you, Your Majesty, and also Lady Nami," I said, smiling at Nami, who bowed low, but she would not cross the threshold between serving the empress and carrying on in the casual manner I affected in the presence of the young ruler.

"I have been informed you are leaving soon for England," the empress said, her eyes curious.

"Yes, but I intend to return to Japan to be with Lord Shintaro and my daughter." I didn't have to make excuses to Her Majesty for the circumstances of my child's birth, since the native language didn't possess a word for illegitimate child. Such a concept was unknown to them, since the son of a concubine had the same opportunity to inherit a title as did the offspring of a wife.

"Your child will not accompany you?" she asked, surprised.

"No, she will stay here with Lord Shintaro and Lady Nami," I said, encouraging the samurai woman to take the baby from the empress, who looked distressed at my words. I caught a flicker of worry on the young ruler's face, which disturbed me, but I didn't know why.

"I have heard you fought side by side with Lord Shintaro and defeated the raiders," she said, stroking my baby's cheek with her elegant fingers, a sigh escaping her lips. She meant the assassins who tried to destroy us, though as Shintaro predicted, he couldn't prove who had sent them.

"'Tis true, Your Majesty," I said, then started to tell her about Akira and how he had sacrificed his life to save mine, but she continued her thought with such urgency, as if it had struck a discordant note and upset the harmony between us and she wished to say it and be done with it. A most unusual gesture.

"And that you showed great courage as samurai," she said.

I bowed low, warmed by her words. "Thank you, Your Majesty."

"I fear you must be brave again, Lady Carlton," she said with a determined smile and a parting look at my little daughter. "*Very* brave."

And with that strange warning she left, our meeting concluded.

"I request that Your Majesty accept my sword and all that it commands."

At three-thirty in the afternoon on that twenty-eighth day

of July 1875, I heard Lord Shintaro utter those words in the native language to His Majesty, the emperor of Japan, the samurai kneeling before him, his forehead touching the white straw matting. Earlier I had observed my samurai walk through sliding paper doors into the audience hall, devoid of furniture save for the raised flooring holding a tentlike structure fashioned from the most vibrant persimmon-colored silk and decorated with hand-painted white chrysanthemums, the imperial flower. Wearing formal western clothes, the emperor sat in his royal chair placed inside for his comfort. I made note of the wall-to-wall backdrop behind the tent depicting graceful but imperfect trees in green and gold, their scraggly branches a riotous display of ancient lineage that I believe was meant to add an aura of wisdom around the young emperor, who was often beleaguered by his lofty position. I imagine more so on this day when his loyal samurai leader took it upon himself to end his exile.

Shintaro.

His face stern, his eyes seeing no one but the emperor.

I detected the muscle twitching at the side of his face, his mouth set in a hard line, his fingers caressing his sword for the last time with a reverence illuminated by the knowledge that its brutal power, its strength, its spirit would now find peace. *The sword is the soul of the samurai.* How well I understood that, as if it were a blessed prayer carved upon his heart. Had I not begged him to keep Akira's swords in a sacred place as a way of honoring his memory?

Raising his head from the mat, Shintaro looked up and proffered his sword to the young emperor. I shall never forget that moment, seeing my samurai responsible, determined, his dignity intact. I think that pricked the tender skin of the men who watched him, British and native, some

determined to prove he was a rebel and not worthy of a
seat on the council. They were wrong. Shintaro was a warrior *and* a gentleman, a dichotomy of contrasts indeed. It
was a day of contrasts, Shintaro in red and indigo-blue, me
in pink-and-white voile, my samurai arriving at the palace
on a white horse as would a samurai of Old Edo, me arriving in a grand traveling carriage pulled by two horses, a
perky, rose-pink veiled hat upon my head with trailing veils
dotted with white lace flowing down my back. Walking
over the wooden bridge leading to the palace with my baby
in my arms, Mr. Fawkes and Nami beside me, the memory
of that young girl with her long train colliding with the
handsome samurai outside the old palace gate came back to
me so vividly.

So filled with sexual energy and hunger she was, so different than I am now. A mother. And a woman in love.

Mr. Fawkes stood next to me in the back of the hall, re-
splendent in his swallowtail black coat, clean and pressed,
his white-gloved hands pulling out his gold watch and
checking the time. It was he who told me the hour, as if he
wished it to be done with, a gesture which disturbed me
since that was so unlike the reserved Englishman. He had
cause for nervousness, I found out, a rumor circulating
among those in the British Legation in their knee-length
black frock coats and white gloves lined up on either side
of the royal matting.

Eager to have a good look at you, he commented dryly. I
smiled widely at these gentlemen when they turned around
to stare at me. Mr. Fawkes kept the exact nature of the rumor
from me, hoping to spare me grief if it was unfounded. Still,
I wondered, did the whispered talk have anything to do with
the empress's ominous warning? I didn't speak of it, for this

was the anxious moment when my samurai acknowledged his allegiance to his emperor and the disbanding of his samurai.

The young emperor rose from his chair and emerged from the tent. A shiver went through me, though the air was heavy, the heat stifling.

Would the emperor accept his sword?

2 0

If I may be truthful and express myself in a plain style, I harbored a secret fear of the outcome of my own destiny after this meeting with the emperor. In my heart, I couldn't bear to see my samurai divorce Nami, a dutiful woman as close to me as my own kin, yet I couldn't deny I wished to remain with him. No discussion of plans for us to be together had been broached and, with the understanding that the Oriental mind approaches such matters with much deliberation, I was content to remain at my lord's side without the benefit of any formal standing in his household. Scandalous? Yes, but nothing else mattered to me. I cannot believe how naive I was, reminding me of a story the Irish tell about a fair maiden who had a fancy for living in towers where she indulged in her romantic dreams. That maiden was me, for I had been living in a dream about to end.

"I have broken the samurai code of honor by failing to protect my men from the assassin's sword," Shintaro said.

"They followed me without question, including the young warrior Akira, whose soul was entwined with mine." He lowered his head but kept his wide shoulders, his back straight. When I think about that moment, it seems I detected more than a slight pause before he said, "I am prepared to do my duty."

"Do you know what you are saying, Lord Shintaro?" The emperor stood stiffly. Was that a waver in his voice?

"Yes, Your Majesty, to apologize for my error and to prove my sincerity that no more blood will be shed…I request the right to regain my honor and commit *seppuku*."

Seppuku. I couldn't think, couldn't feel. His words tore through my mind, bringing everything I loved, needed and wanted to an end. What a fool I was! If I hadn't been so filled with my own selfish desires, I would have seen the pain my samurai faced, knowing he had but one choice that would bring peace.

Ritual suicide.

Again he proffered his sword and I could see the hesitation etched on the young emperor's face. *Would he accept it?* No one moved. I don't know how long we stood there until finally the emperor took the sword from Shintaro and bowed slightly, then he turned and went back inside the tent, leaving all who watched in stunned silence. Deafening. Not even a hushed whisper through a thin paper door could be heard.

"We must go, your ladyship," Mr. Fawkes said, taking my arm and reminding me to make three low bows before backing out the opposite door from where we came. I had never heard him speak in such sepulchral tones, sweat pouring down his ruddy cheeks, his gloved hand damp with perspiration. I felt my own desperation rise in response. The empress had tried to warn me, but I didn't listen, my mind not grasp-

ing the notion that honor came before anything, even life.
When I heard my samurai proclaim it was his duty to end his
life, I felt as if I were biting into a poisoned fruit, its spicy
pulp seducing my tongue with its vivid promise, while its repugnant aftertaste killed my soul. What occurred next was my
reaction to what I considered a senseless act, one that caused
me considerable pain and forced me to push aside my ideal-
ism, whatever the cost. I wanted Shintaro to live and I had
every intention of fighting for what I wanted.

"I have shamed the code of the warrior," said Shintaro. He
sounded angry, *very* angry. "I cannot disgrace my ancestors."

"You had nothing to do with Akira and the others being
killed," I protested. "I led the assassins to you. *I* should die,
not you."

He ignored me, his obsession with duty blinding him to
anything else. "You must take our daughter where it's safe."
He explained that his Tokio house would be confiscated because he had no son to inherit the property. "I will do what
I must to regain my honor and show loyalty to the emperor."

"What about *us,* Shintaro?" I asked him, attempting to
keep my voice from betraying the hurt seething inside me. My
ego rebelling against a code that recognized honor, but not
love.

"Us?" he said, cocking his head to one side, as if not
understanding the concept.

"Yes, *us.* You and me." We spoke in English, a samurai and
a lady standing on the enclosed wooden bridge crossing between the main palace and the royal apartments. Our heated
conversation drew the irresistible curiosity of the royal consorts scurrying back and forth across the bridge. "Do I mean
nothing to you? And what about your daughter?"

"If you are truly samurai," Shintaro said in an even voice, holding me by the shoulders, his fingers digging into my flesh, "it is your obligation to respect my wishes and not to interfere."

"I see. If I go against your wishes and try to stop you, I am not samurai. If I do nothing, you go to your death." I couldn't stop the emotion welling up in me. I breathed deeply, the air heavy with the scent of camellia oil from the coiffed hair of the royal consorts and their perfumed flowing ceremonial robes. "Either way, I have already lost you."

"It is the way of the warrior, Katie," he said, using my given name, something he'd never done before, always calling me "my lady" or by my title.

"I find no comfort in your words, Shintaro, my spirit wandering, hungry to understand why you must die, not for some vile act, but because of what you believe."

"It is an honorable death," he insisted, "a gift from the gods."

"As is our daughter, Shintaro, a gift from those same gods. Every time I look at her, I see you."

"I believed I could never love a woman," he said honestly, "that a samurai must live his life in service to his God, the emperor. Then your presence enlightened my world and I would do anything to keep you safe, even if it means my own death."

I fell silent, pressing my lips together, taking deep breaths, fighting to keep from trembling. "When?" I asked, wondering why my voice was so calm, why I was asking this insane question, because I didn't accept it, *I didn't*.

He said simply, "At dawn."

I remember him best in that moment, the late-afternoon sunlight striking his face on one side, leaving the other in the shadows, where he would soon leave me and our child. I didn't protest when he pulled me to him and lifted the veil covering my face. My anger dissipated into passion when he looked at me, his dark eyes narrowing then opening, begging me to understand. His hands went around my waist, strong and firm, his mouth soft and tender on mine. *A kiss.* The forbidden, a taboo practiced by the courtesan, a woman draped in silken mystery. I was that woman, from that first time he had made love to me in Yoshiwara to our sensual trysts as a ménage celebrating the tea ceremony.

I closed my eyes, ignoring the royal consorts flitting past us like curious hummingbirds, for all I could think of was, this was the last time I would taste the bitter with the sweet.

I paced back and forth on the covered wooden bridge long after my samurai had gone, the hour growing late, the brilliant scarlet, fawn and lavender of the royal consorts' gowns flashing in the corner of my eye. All I could think about was Shintaro. I would miss the rich tones of his voice commanding me to strip off my kimono, his dark, brooding eyes surveying my nude body then submitting his approval with a provocative grunt, his elegant gestures wielding his sword with effortlessness, the thought-provoking beauty of his poems, the erotic imaginings of his mind, his curiosity at finding my pubic hair light-colored and wiry, the heartwarming surprise at his discovery of embracing the love of a woman, seeing him nod in approval when our child nursed at my breast. I would do whatever the gods asked of me to hear him poetize again about virginal blossoms and rushing winds. He was a true samurai and for that reason he must not die.

To prove I was samurai, he had begged me not to interfere, but I didn't care if he tossed me out on my wretched Irish arse, I told Mr. Fawkes when he bade me leave with him.

I had to do something, but what? I could see the Englishman was worried about me and such a dear friend he was, breaking the news to Nami. Dear, sweet Nami. *Did she know beforehand?* I asked him. He nodded. *Of course she did,* I chastised myself for my lack of sense. *She is samurai but she never said a word. What a brave woman she is, her spirit not weighed down with the impatient longing for something she can't have.*

And I? A fever burned in me, making me a constant source of irritation to those who knew me, questioning, testing, turning clever phrases and seeking out the impermissible in a world that frowned on female independence. The world of the samurai above all. I couldn't allow Shintaro to commit an act that made no sense, an act brought about not by his own volition but by me. Was there no escape possible? Were we all vessels moved about by the whims of the gods, their passions fueled by a single act of honor or shame? I revolted against it. No one wanted him to die, including the impressionable young emperor who had looked horrified when Shintaro presented his sword to him, as if he couldn't accept losing his faithful samurai.

Looking at me, you would have thought I had gone mad and, by the blessed saints, had turned heretic. My heart racing, my cheeks flushed, I spun around on my heel, hoping it wasn't too late, beseeching the fates to smile on my lunacy as they had once before when I followed my heart, for I had an idea. It was against the odds in a culture that celebrated an appreciation of beauty for those things transitory, including life itself, and that death was glorious, but I was determined to try.

Smiling at the beautiful royal consort scurrying past me in a flurry of silk and perfume, I asked Mr. Fawkes to wait for me, then I followed her, knowing she would lead me to the one person who could help me.

★ ★ ★

"What you ask, Lady Carlton, would be most difficult…" the empress said, her words trailing off, so much left unsaid, a polite way of saying no. I *had* to convince her to help me save Shintaro.

"I come to Your Majesty not for myself, but for my child," I said, walking beside her through the long corridor lined with glass cases of gosho dolls. "Lord Shintaro's child."

"Yes, I understand, your child…"

The empress nodded, then pointed out her favorite doll in the case, a chubby-cheeked little boy riding on the back of a turtle, his tiny eyes laughing, his oyster-shell-white face smiling at us. A defining moment of innocent sweetness caught in an enchanted frolic. The dolls were given to visiting dignities as gifts when the emperor lived in Kioto, the empress explained, their name derived from the expression meaning "from the Imperial Palace."

What am I meandering about a childlike doll when my lord Shintaro was to be denied the joy of seeing his child again? Understand, I have always been intrigued with the ambiguities played out in the native culture, and never was it done with such elegance and savoir faire as on this humid summer night. A rare scene indeed, dear lady reader, and one you'll not hear about from an overbloated member of the British Legation, for no record exists of this Irish lass and the diminutive empress with her long black hair hanging loosely around her shoulders strolling about the royal apartments like two clever women planning a coup d'état. For that's what it was, this idea of releasing a samurai from performing the act of ritual suicide. I suffered bitterly that night, tormented by the fact that this entire episode was fostered by my brashness. I gave thanks to the gods the empress didn't have me tossed out on my ear when I barged into the royal apartments unannounced, begging for an audience with her.

"It was my fault the assassins raided the hiding place where Shintaro sought peace after his first child was murdered," I said, then added, "He is willing to lay down his life to protect me."

I studied the empress's face carefully, trying to discern a blink of her eye, a tremble of her lip, anything to see if I had reached her soul, if only for a moment. I continued, "He has shown himself to be a true samurai by coming here today to relinquish his sword."

"Your words have great merit, Lady Carlton."

She is smiling. *But is her smile merely to placate me?*

"Don't let him die as samurai, Your Majesty," I pleaded. "Let him live as a man who will serve his emperor well in the new Japan, his child a bridge between both our cultures."

Standing pensively, her graceful hands pushing her long shiny hair off her brow, she opened the glass case and removed the little doll riding the turtle. She held it up to the gaslight, turning it this way and that, as if trying to make up her mind about something.

"Please accept this doll as my gift, Lady Carlton." She placed the doll in my hand, then covered it with hers, her skin cool to the touch, but I knew her heart was warm.

"Thank you, Your Majesty," I said, bowing low.

She bowed slightly. "They say gosho dolls bring good luck. I pray it shall be so on this night."

The hours passed and I waited, hoping the empress would have success in requesting leniency for Shintaro from her husband. A bleeding of the heart affected my spirit and pushed me forward into this aberrant scheme, for I couldn't let my samurai sacrifice himself for what I had brought about, even in my innocence. His rebellion against the emperor had caused him great personal anguish and, perhaps, his life. I found this way of thinking so outside my mind, I nearly went mad. Mr. Fawkes tried to comfort me, never leaving my side during that long night, his admiration for my devotion to my samurai, along with my brazenness, rattling his British reserve.

"I say, Lady Carlton, you are the bravest woman I have ever known as well as the most audacious," he said, wiping his brow. "Shintaro is a fortunate man."

"'Tis I with the lucky shamrock stuck in my bonnet, Mr. Fawkes, for my samurai has not only given me my child, but restored my belief in God."

A queer thing for me to say, as evidenced by the prominent uplifting of Mr. Fawkes's brow, but it was true. My disastrous marriage to James had shaken my spiritual self into such a tither I'd lost faith in those things most important to a woman's heart. *Husband, hearth and children.* Shintaro had restored my faith in mankind. I never believed I could be so intimately united with a man as I was with him, only to be on the verge of losing it all. Yes, I had my child to nurture, but I wanted the deep, complete love of a man, too.

Mr. Fawkes and I spoke in hushed tones as we sat upon large square purple pillows in the cypress-wood drawing room near the royal apartments, our backs to a pair of black lacquered screens inlaid with white pearl chrysanthemums, a subtle breeze of incense making my nose tingle with a woodsy scent. I reminded Mr. Fawkes of the time in Yokohama when I slid off a large pillow and onto the floor and for a moment we shared a bit of mirth. Then we fell silent, each to our own thoughts, Mr. Fawkes's gold watch ticking away as he checked the hour numerous times. A royal handservant brought us hot tea and sweet bean cakes, bowing low than leaving us alone. Raising the cup to my lips, I couldn't help but notice how the room shimmered with hanging silks in bright red and blue mineral hues. I was too restless and unsettled to remember anything more as we waited for word from the empress. All I could think about was, if no word came and Shintaro committed *seppuku,* I had no recourse but to return home with my child.

A warrior is always prepared for a violent death and fears death less than you or I. A samurai such as Lord Shintaro exists in a state of mind where he does not fear death because he is trained since childhood to believe his life is not his own but in the service of others. As a boy, he is expected to endure the heat of summer and the cold of winter and is commanded to spend the night in cemeteries to familiarize him with the fearsome sensation that death evokes. ('Tis not as strange as you may believe. How often have young ruffians fled the London streets to endure a night in Abney Park Cemetery shrouded in gothic ruins and thick fog?) As a boy, a samurai learns to endure physical pain without betraying the slightest emotion. (No doubt if you ask his lordship, he will expound about his younger days in the British army under the stone-faced officer who led his troops into battle knowing he may die.) The way of the warrior is a noble pursuit, but when a samurai violates his code of honor, he must redeem himself with the act of ritual suicide, the heart of his discipline. He performs the ceremony by using a distinct blade to cut into his lower belly, considered the source of his power, his soul, making a horizontal cut from the left to the right side of his abdomen and, if his strength allows, follows this with another cut upward toward his throat, revealing the state of his soul, pure or unclean. Death is not always immediate, but this allows him to maintain command over his own destiny until the end. Once he completes the ritual cuts, he offers his neck to his assistant standing behind him, ready to behead him.

May God rest his soul…

In the course of the longest evening of my life on that hot summer night of 1875, desperately eager to see my samurai again, to grab onto some semblance of him and the little things that meant so much to me, the deep desires that made my blood run hot, I relived every moment with Shintaro: from his seductive smile when he grabbed the train of my dress at the palace gate, to the animal smell of his lust when he thought I was a young man in Yoshiwara, to the unbelievable feeling I experienced rubbing our nude bodies together under a crashing waterfall. I tingled inside, then sadness seeped through me, for I couldn't hold on to the sensuousness of my thoughts knowing how fleeting they were, like the fair pink blossoms so lovely and full of grace that linger on the bough for a short time. I couldn't cry, my heart throbbing, flesh cold, chest so tight I could no longer think. When I put my hand to my bosom, a seeping dampness wet my fingertips, making them sticky. My breasts, full and heavy with milk, felt warm to my touch, the mother instinct in me at war with the temptress, so confused was I, wanting to run away with my child, yet craving to feel my samurai's strong arms around me again…this madness, this recklessness devouring me like an insatiable lust to go to him, be with him before he drew his last breath, the waiting was killing me. *Why was I here, why wasn't I with him?* What I'd asked for was impossible, why torture myself when I could be with him, touch his lips one last time in a fated kiss? No, I couldn't stand it any longer, I told Mr. Fawkes when his timepiece struck the hour before dawn. I was leaving now before the night dissipated into a pearl grayness blessed with mist and with tears…if only to see him one last time before the knife cut his life from me and an eternal coldness claimed my heart.

Grabbing the gosho doll, I raced from the drawing room seconds before the door to the royal apartments opened and the scent of camellia oil floated in on a silken breeze—

But I was already gone.

Dawn. Dew-filled. Hazy gray. Gathering up my skirts, I jumped from the carriage and opened the gate with a trembling hand, the stillness of the garden broken by the sound of a man's heavy breathing. *Shintaro? Is he still alive? Or do the labored breaths belong to his trusted retainer? Am I too late?*

What happened next occurred in the most fleeting of moments, every second precious. The harrowing scene before me claimed every nerve fiber in my being, as if I was scourged with a searing white pain that jarred my sense of reasoning and made me scream in my head with disbelief. My chest tightened, for the longer I stared, the stronger my sense of horror became, rooting me to the spot.

There in front of a three-paneled white screen, his second kneeling behind him with his sword held high in both hands, poised for the final act, I saw Shintaro sitting in repose and naked to the waist. Rivulets of sweat ran down his face, his muscular chest, his knees and bare toes touching the thick red matting, the sleeves of his white kimono tucked under his knees to prevent him from falling backward when the deed was done, his body resting on his heels. He possessed such a potent aura that it made me stop, hold my breath, as if the dawn approached him with reverence and homage. I wished I could hold this moment forever in my heart and not let it go, but it was a sinner's prayer and the gods would not listen to me. I gasped when I saw him pick up the ritual knife wrapped in paper off the tray and unwrap it, then examine its nine and one-half inch sharp blade, his dark, brooding eyes flashing with profound fortitude and inhuman power. Then, with a final resolute look at the deadly weapon, he raised it over his head, his lips mumbling prayers, his eyes determining its lethal path when—

"*Stop!*" I cried out, dropping the gosho doll. "I beg you, Shintaro, stop!"

He clenched his teeth, his face contorted, taut, but he would not put down the knife, as if he willed himself not to. Did I see a moment of hesitation flicker in his eyes when he looked at me with such longing and I did the same? Everything we had coming to life in those few moments? Yet never did I see him falter or weaken in his resolve. With every moment that passed, my heart pounded harder. My samurai didn't flinch but I had to stop him, *had to,* before he unleashed the unyielding power that was the way of the warrior.

"*Go!*" he yelled, at the same time motioning for his retainer to lower his sword. "You are not welcome here."

"Don't send me away, Shintaro," I begged. I took a deep breath and gathered up my strength, though I was terrified of what would happen next. I said in a clear voice, "I—I cannot live without you."

"You must go, *now!*"

"No, my lord, not this time."

I grabbed the knife from his hand. So quick was my movement he was too stunned to move. Then, ripping open my bodice, I pricked my skin with the tip of the knife, the sharp pain fueling my inner fury as I moved it toward my throat, my hand shaking, ready to end my own life.

"*I forbid you!*" Shintaro cried out, pulling the knife from my hand, then wiping the trickle of blood off the swell of my breast and rubbing it onto his abdomen. "I alone am destined to join my ancestors—"

"*No…*you must let me come with you," I begged. "I love you, Shintaro. My life is over without you."

The cry of a child.

Our child.

The baby's wail broke through the painful exchange between this crazed Irish lass and this determined samurai, the sound of bare feet scurrying away, and I knew that Nami had awakened when she heard the shouting, then fled. Sobbing like a mad fool, I collapsed into Shintaro's arms, flung into a mortal despair for thinking such thoughts when such a deed would leave my child helpless and alone. I called upon God to forgive this sinner and not despise me, so despondent was I that this grand passion I had for my samurai had wrought such thoughts in my mind, depriving me of my senses. Shintaro understood my pain and held me in his arms, stroking my hair coming undone and falling around my shoulders. I gained strength from being close to him, his bare chest shimmering with sweat, his muscular body warm and hard and so alive. I couldn't bear to see him grow cold, his blood stilled, but what choice had the gods given me? That I, a woman who had come to this land disbelieving, could have opened her heart to this man and he to me, but in doing so I had challenged the sensibilities of not only my own people but his, as well. And for our love, we must now pay the ultimate price.

But no one could ever make me stop loving him…

Cradling me in his arms, his closeness making me tremble, I sensed Shintaro forgave me for my overwrought emotion and held me blameless as we clung to each other until the first ray of sunshine struck the blade of the knife he clutched in his hand. I knew then I could not stop him from carrying out his duty.

I don't know how long we held each other, gathering warmth and strength from the closeness, knowing the end was near, when I heard shouting, a man yelling out to us in both English and the native language, the unspeakable sound of joy in his voice tempered with overwhelming fear. *Who? Could it be...*

"Am I too late, milady?" I heard him cry out. "Oh, I pray I'm not too late!"

I turned to see Mr. Fawkes, dear wonderful Mr. Fawkes, racing into the garden, waving a parchment, a long sheet of official-looking paper inscribed with vertical native writing reading from right to left and signed with the imperial signature and the official privy seal.

The emperor's seal.

"Mr. Fawkes!" I cried out, my heart racing, believing, hoping, "do you have—"

"Yes, milady, *yes,*" he said, huffing and puffing and out of breath and wiping his ruddy face with tissues. "A pardon. I have here in my hand a full pardon for Lord Shintaro from the emperor. Never in the history of the Imperial Japanese Empire has such a thing happened, never. And I doubt if it ever will again."

"This can't be true," Shintaro said, grabbing the parchment and reading it. "*It can't be.* How?"

"The empress, my lord," I said, putting my hand up to his

face and pressing his cheek against mine. A gesture of affection and tenderness. "She believes in us…and in love."

I can still see the disbelief, then joy in his eyes. Feel the sensual energy in his soul that he had contained and now released, never believing he would again feel the warmth of my hand on his skin, my love drawing him into my arms as if only we two existed in the world.

And with that moment of grand storytelling, so beautiful it was, like the heavens opening and the gods embracing us, I shall end my tale of the blonde samurai.

For 'tis a perfect ending, is it not, dear lady reader?

I think so.

It seems I have not finished after all as I read through this memoir, editing, crossing out, adding favorite moments, delighting in erotic ones. I cannot stop my pen from drafting a quick aftermath of what happened to all the key players in my adventure, for I imagine you're as curious as a hatless girl from York Street wondering if the gentleman peeking up her garters will pay well for the privilege. I shall not disappoint you, for it takes a fine woman like yourself, dear lady reader, to follow along with my story and not close the book a dozen times and toss it across her boudoir. *You did? And tore out a page or two?* Did those missing pages find their way into your drawers…that will be our secret, won't it?

No matter, you're here with me now. And so we shall have a gossip as I sit here at the oak desk in my hotel room hours before my steamer leaves for Yokohama. Did I tell you Mr. Edward Mallory and his pretty young wife stopped by and invited me for tea? She's going to have a baby and they promised to name the child Kathlene after me if it's a girl. I am most flattered.

Next I shall reflect on the unbelievable journey I have taken with all its woes and triumphs, sorrows and joys. To begin, Shintaro regained his seat on the mikado's council when certain members were forced to admit they had unjustly blamed him for the "disturbances" hampering progress on the railway from Kobé to Tokio to curtail his powerful influence with the emperor. To assist him with his duties at court, Shintaro engaged Mr. Fawkes as his personal adviser in western affairs. A most amusing duo these two, the tall samurai receiving political counsel from the consummate Englishman, while Shintaro schooled Mr. Fawkes in the art of writing poetry.

Then I was most delighted when the young geisha, Simouyé, paid me a visit. For a few moments I brought Akira back to life, and told her how her brother saved me from the assassins. She was so pleased to see that we have enshrined his swords in a place of honor, and for her kind words I am grateful. I cannot continue without taking a moment to reflect on the profound love story of Shintaro and Akira, awakening in me a taste for this unusual affair in which I was privileged to be a participant, as intense as it was sexual, without rivalry, and one I shall never forget…

On to the unpleasantness in my story. James, as you know, returned to England and in spite of his arrogance (and to save his reputation), granted me a divorce and acquiesced to pay back the funds he swindled from my father as well as remove himself from Da's dealings in Japan. Before I left London, I heard whispers that he had his eye on another American heiress. I pray she has a substantial bank account *and* a sturdy bottom to please him.

And Nami. If there was ever a sainted woman who could

compare to my own sweet mother, 'tis Nami. She begged Shintaro to release her from their marriage upon my return so she might enter a Buddhist convent and serve the poor. The gods might identify me as a sinner, but I have no doubt she is one of their own.

I must add that Da and Mother were delighted with my stories about their little granddaughter and have made me promise I will have her likeness taken at a photographic studio in Tokio and send it to them. Da confided in me he never did approve of my marriage to James and he was pleased I have found a man such as Shintaro, even if he didn't understand this "samurai business," *but if the emperor pardoned him,* he said, *that's good enough for this Irishman.*

All this, dear lady reader, in the months since that delirious dawn when I swear I saw a single tear slide down the cheek of my samurai as he read the bold strokes written on the ivory-gray linen parchment. I have never been so happy.

I am looking at the letter I received from Mr. Fawkes this morning via the purser on the ship. He will meet me in Yokohama when the steamer docks and escort me to the house in Tokio I share with Shintaro and my daughter, Reiko, and Nami. Until then, I cannot quell the ache in my heart, wanting so to hold my baby close to my bosom with my samurai's arms around us. That must wait, since my Lord Shintaro has been engaged as a special emissary of the mikado's government and was called to the old western provinces to quell an uprising there. Mr. Fawkes also relates some wonderful news: Shintaro's lands have been restored to him. As soon as his work is finished, we shall retire to the country for...

Can you keep a secret?

A wedding.

And I shall wear the most sumptuous red kimono.

★ ★ ★

'Tis truly the end of my story, dear lady reader, and since I promised you an erotic tome when I began my memoir, I shall end it by trying my hand at scripting a sensual poem inspired by my Lord Shintaro the night before I left for London. A night when I lay in his arms, my pussy tingling from the touch of his hands parting my thighs and…

> *Fingering me, my lord dripped*
> *sake upon my lips*
> *and I tasted paradise.*

And now so have you.

★ ★ ★ ★ ★

ACKNOWLEDGMENTS

I have always believed Japan is a land of contrasts. Reserved, quiet and silky on the one hand. On the other, erotic, adventurous and mysterious in the sensual ways of the Far East.

It is also the land of samurai. Bold, dedicated fighters who followed the way of the warrior known as *Bushidō:* loyalty, duty, self-respect, honor. The samurai are well-known in the West and recently we have seen female samurai celebrated in pop culture. I applaud this retelling of historical fact in a modern context since samurai women were also schooled in the way of the warrior and often fought alongside their men in battle.

To my knowledge, no female *gaijin,* foreigner, has ever become samurai. The word itself is gender specific and refers to trained male warriors. The idea of a western woman entering this world may be off-putting to some, but the thought has always intrigued me. Would she have the strength and fortitude, both physical and mental, to undergo the rigorous training required to become samurai? Could she peel away the outer layer of samurai life so often portrayed in books and films as strife and rebellion and see the inner beauty and passion that it takes to become a warrior? I have tried to answer this question in *The Blonde Samurai.*

As is the way of the Japanese, this story came about as a group effort. I wish to thank my wonderful editor, Susan Swinwood, for believing in me and encouraging me to take a bold step forward and tell the story of the blonde samurai.

And thank you to my dearest friend and agent, Roberta Brown, who sparked the idea of this book with her keen sense of story and her undying faith in me.

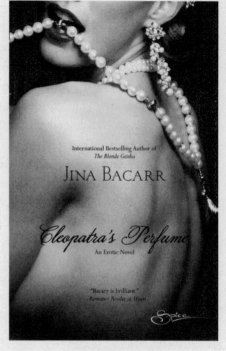

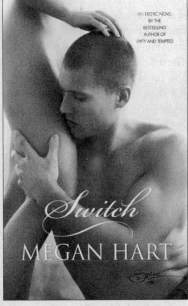

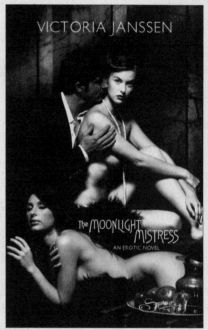